STARSITTER

D1527422

STARSITTER

A Novel

Andrea Dana

iUniverse, Inc.
New York Lincoln Shanghai

StarSitter

Copyright © 2007 by Andrea Dana

All rights reserved. No part of this book may be used or reproduced by any means, graphic, electronic, or mechanical, including photocopying, recording, taping or by any information storage retrieval system without the written permission of the publisher except in the case of brief quotations embodied in critical articles and reviews.

iUniverse books may be ordered through booksellers or by contacting:

iUniverse
2021 Pine Lake Road, Suite 100
Lincoln, NE 68512
www.iuniverse.com
1-800-Authors (1-800-288-4677)

This is a work of fiction. Name, characters, places, and incidents either are the product of the author's imagination or are used fictitiously, and any resemblance to actual persons, living or dead, business establishments, events, or locales is entirely coincidental.

ISBN: 978-0-595-43007-9 (pbk)
ISBN: 978-0-595-87348-7 (ebk)

Printed in the United States of America

For my family and friends

ACKNOWLEDGMENTS

I'd like to thank the following people for helping me bring this book to life. It's been a long haul, and your time, effort and dedication has provided me with the courage to see it through.

Joanna Track and Rebecca Eckler, for your phone calls from Hawaii convincing me to write this story.

David Trueman, for seeing the potential and putting forth so much effort.

Sherri Nefsky, Stephania Varalli, Eric Singer, JP Rasminsky, Adam Kosoy, for technical and creative support as editors and buffers.

Amy Levine, cover design.

Jordana Lieberman, cover illustration.

Todd Bennett, photographer for my author picture.

Ashley Smith, and Jordana Glassman, creative support from a younger generation.

Kristin Burke, for a memorable dinner in Tokyo, where you pointed me in a new direction, and have been a blessed guide ever since.

Hallie Lipin, Michael Gelbart, Stacey Pollock Bar-Ziv, Carly Gottlieb, Jodi Nakelsky, Corwin Hall, Elise Rudin, Lesli Kimel, Susanne Mathers, and my sister Stephanie Eisen, who were all able to coax me off that ledge, provide me with much needed practical and emotional support, laugh at all the right parts, and advise me 24/7 free of charge.

And with love and a very special thanks to Jonathan Bennett and Sam Page, for being the stars of my dreams and the heroes of my life.

CHAPTER 1

"See you next week, Grace," Scott, my personal trainer, said as he held the door open for me. I smiled at him as I limped out of Silver Rod's Gym. I was too exhausted to speak. It had been another day of torture and pain. The workout was hard, of course, but worse was the torture and pain of having to stare at Scott's muscular body for an hour and a half, twice a week, with the knowledge I may never get the workout from him that I truly desired.

I had first noticed Scott months ago during a grueling forty-five minute stint on the elliptical trainer. He had strutted over holding a clipboard in one hand and a protein bar in the other. He had deep, dark eyes and a perfect set of pearly whites. Then there were his biceps, and triceps, and well … the perfect hunk to fantasize about.

When I saw him coming, I wiped the sweat from my face and quickly pushed the arrow button to increase my speed.

"Nice pace," Scott said. That was it. I was hooked. I raced over to the front desk to sign up for a package of training sessions.

"Actually, Scott's not taking on any more clients," the receptionist said, glancing at his schedule. "How about Louise?"

She pointed to a woman with "tree trunk" legs, shouting at her client to run faster on the treadmill. No thanks! I explained that I found myself more motivated by male trainers.

"Yeah, I know. Scott's a cutie," she said, winking as she got out of her chair. "I'll see what I can do." I waited while she went to talk to Scott in the weight room. Thinking it might help, I removed the elastic band from my hair and allowed it to fall down to my shoulders. I moved closer to the window and watched as the receptionist pointed me out. Scott looked over at me and smiled. A few moments later she returned to the desk and said that Scott would be happy to fit me into his schedule.

"You're my new best friend," I said, handing her my credit card. She smiled and rang it through.

Afterward, one of the women in the change room told me that Scott and the receptionist were dating.

"Don't worry, honey," she said, seeing my disappointment. "Bitch works on commission. Everyone falls for it."

I exited the gym and after being hit by a burst of Chicago's cool November air, zipped up my jacket. I headed toward my car, praying that I hadn't gotten a parking ticket. For the second day in a row, I'd had trouble getting out of bed, and being in a rush, had forgotten to bring extra change for the meter. Fortunately, parking enforcement had been kind to me yesterday when I left my car in front of Starbucks. No such luck today. An ugly white paper flapped in the wind against my windshield.

"Fuck!" I said. Forty dollars down the drain. I grabbed the ticket and got into my car.

Driving through the smooth traffic made me feel better. Plus, I still had the rest of the day off. At my request, my boss, and brother-in-law, Jake, had granted me the day to go to a few appointments that I'd been putting off because work had been so busy lately. However, on my way to the gym this morning the receptionist from my dentist's office had called saying that Dr Rapp had a family emergency and had to cancel all appointments for the day. My sensitive gums would have to wait. At least now I was free for the afternoon to do what I pleased.

I opened the sunglasses holder above my rear view mirror and a few carpet samples came tumbling out. Shit, I'd forgotten to leave them for Jake to look over. I put them on the passenger seat and made a mental note to drop them off at his house.

Jake was the president of JD Designs, a very successful interior design company. Lately, his work had been featured in a few home décor magazines on the news stands. He was said to have a flaw-less sense of style, an impeccable appreciation of modern city liv-ing, and was quickly rising to stardom across the country.

I began working at JD Designs in an entry level position, but had moved up the totem pole rather fast when I set Jake up with my sister, Sheryl The Doctor, as she is often referred to. Jake, had summoned me to his office one morning to say he was thinking of taking one of his new apprentices under his wing, and felt I was an excellent candidate.

"I'd like to start giving you more responsibilities around here, Stacey," he had said.

"It's Grace," I answered.

"I know," he said. "I was kidding." I knew he wasn't.

He praised me for my keen sense of color coordination and vast knowledge of carpets, information he had clearly received from someone in the back of the warehouse.

"I'd be so grateful," I said, knowing that if I was the chosen one it could mean a substantial raise.

"By the way," Jake said, before letting me get back to work. "Who was that pretty girl that picked you up from work yester-day?"

"My sister, Sheryl," I said.

"Is she single?" he asked.

"She's not married," I said.

"How convenient," Jake said. "Perhaps you could play match-maker for us?"

I was afraid that if I told Jake that Sheryl had recently broken off her engagement and had sworn off men forever, I would lose my shot at being the promoted apprentice. So after a week of begging and pleading with Sheryl to give Jake a chance, she finally agreed to go out with him.

"I'm only doing this for you, Grace," she said, after my sixth day of bringing her coffee and home-baked cookies to work. "You can pimp me out for one date, and that's it."

Who would have known that was all I needed to do? One date and they were practically engaged. Four dates and they were!

Needless to say, I was the chosen apprentice and my new job came with my very own office, with a view of the water. I also got a hefty raise, allowing me to move on up—*Jeffersons* style, to a great two bedroom apartment in Lincoln Park.

It was perhaps not the most couth way to get ahead in my career, but it was definitely the easiest.

I was stopped at a red light on Cherry Street when I heard my mobile phone ringing in my gym bag. A pain shot through my arm as I reached for it; one too many chin-ups, apparently. I found my phone at the bottom of the bag and pressed 'talk.'

"Grace! Thank God you answered." It was Aunt Lana, my mother's sister. I held the phone away from my ear—she had a booming voice.

"Hi, Aunt Lana. What's up?"

"I'm desperate!" she cried. "I need you to do me a huge favor." Uh-oh. I was quite sure this would be something I would want no part of, as Aunt Lana's requests were often of that nature.

"What sort of favor?" I asked, holding the phone with my shoulder to my ear, as I made a left hand turn.

"I have a terrible cold and I'm in the waiting room of my doctor's office I needed to be at work ten minutes ago." It didn't sound like she had a "terrible" cold. "Would you mind going down to the set and filling in for me for the rest of the day?" she asked.

I stepped on the break at another red light, nearly bashing into the car in front of me. Did I mind? Of course I did. Aunt Lana currently worked on a movie set as a guardian to seventeen-year-old "rising star", Maddy Malone, who was in town filming her latest movie, *Daisy Mae*. Aunt Lana got stuck with this horrendous job when Maddy had shown up in Chicago without adult accompaniment, causing the production manager, a long time friend of Aunt Lana's, to panic. She begged my aunt to *please* come out of teaching retirement and temporarily take care of Maddy just until they found someone else, which they never did.

"Please Grace," Aunt Lana said. "I wouldn't ask you if I wasn't in a bind." If it was any other kid, I would have jumped at the chance to help out, but supposedly Maddy was a serious diva and this job had been causing Aunt Lana a high degree of stress.

A few weeks ago, Lola, a cleaning lady who had been with our family for years, died of a heart attack and Aunt Lana was late for the funeral because Maddy had sent her on an errand in downtown Chicago to pick up some Special Edition Hershey Kisses. After trips to nine convenience stores, Aunt Lana gave up.

When she called Maddy to tell her that they weren't in stock anywhere, Maddy screamed bloody murder, and verbally abused Aunt Lana until she was nearly in tears. When Aunt Lana finally arrived at the funeral home, she looked worse than poor Lola lying in her coffin. But, Aunt Lana, good soul that she is, refused to give up on Maddy. In fact it became a challenge for her to win Maddy over and try to be a positive influence in her life. I didn't think I could be quite so charitable, and this was really the last thing I wanted to do on my day off.

"I don't know, Aunt Lana," I said, "I was really looking forward to having the rest of the day to myself. I'm not too keen on spending it kissing butt to a teeny bopper." I stopped at a crosswalk as a woman walked her Golden Retriever across the street. Oh how I wanted another dog. Growing up, I had an English Springer Spaniel named Candy, whom I loved dearly, and was completely devastated when she died. My parents opted to take the ashes from the vet after she'd been cremated, and though I don't like to tell too many people this, after ten years I still keep them in an urn on top of my dresser at home. I know it's a little bit creepy, but the truth is that I haven't found the right place to scatter them yet. So for now, Candy stays with me.

"Grace," Aunt Lana said, coughing. "It's just for a couple of hours. I'll hurry back as soon as I'm done with my appointment. It won't be that bad."

"But still bad," I replied. I knew my aunt well enough to know that she would not be back on set today, no matter how long her appointment lasted.

"Hey," she said, trying to get me excited. "You'll meet some celebrities."

"Yeah? Like who?" I asked. I hadn't recalled her telling me that George Clooney or Brad Pitt were in the movie. She ignored my question, probably realizing there was no actor in *Daisy Mae* that would be enough to lure me down to the set.

"I'll pay you," she finally said. Well, now she was talking in a language I could comprehend. I knew her salary was quite substantial. "I'll pay you for the full day." I looked over at my parking ticket, which was now sitting on the floor of the passenger side, and figured that would be one problem solved. I glanced down at my grubby clothes that I had thrown on after showering at the gym. I was sure there'd be a strict dress code on set.

"I just came from working out," I said. "I'm dressed inappropriately."

"As long as you're not wearing flip-flops," she said. "I'm sure you're not at this time of the year. Don't worry because most of the crew members are sweaty and dirty too. You'll fit in just fine." I could see there was no way around this, and I knew if I was stuck, Aunt Lana would help me out. I decided to take the plunge.

"Fine, I'll go," I said.

"Oh Grace, thank you, thank you," Aunt Lana said, kissing me through the phone.

"Okay, okay," I said. "How do I get there?" I jotted down her directions to get to the set.

"Let me give you a few tips, before you go," Aunt Lana said.

"Okay."

"Wipe your feet really well before entering Maddy's trailer, and make sure her refrigerator is filled with the essentials," she said.

"Essentials?" I asked.

"Evian and Diet Coke," Aunt Lana answered. "Oh, and always tell her how good she looks, how thin she is, and how no other actress compares to her."

"Right," I said, changing my mind. "Well, I'm going to go now. Sorry I can't help you out."

"Grace, no!" she said. "Okay, forget all that. Just be really positive. She's very sensitive."

"Fine. I'll try to keep Maddy Malone happy," I said.

I hung up the phone and pulled into a gas station to turn the car around and head back toward Thirty-Fifth Street. When I got there I made a left and then a right at the next lights. I spotted the orange pylons that Aunt Lana had said would direct me towards base camp.

I pulled into "Crew Parking" where beat-up cars lined the lot—most looked as though they hadn't been washed in years. I parked my car—the company car, actually; a silver Audi A4—between a mid-size Toyota and a Ford pickup. After turning off the ignition, I grabbed my lip gloss from my purse and applied it. Next I reached behind to my gym bag again and got my deodorant. Taking a quick peak to make sure no one was around; I then swiped it back and forth under my arms. Finally I got out of the car, hoping I looked somewhat presentable for all the *celebrities* I was about to meet.

I approached base camp, which consisted of rows of trucks and trailers. Aunt Lana had told me to look for a blonde girl named Jane, who would assist me.

I found a woman sitting on the steps of one of the trailers. She was applying liquid paper to her fingernails. She was blonde.

"Hi," I said. "Are you Jane?"

"Nope," she said, without looking up. "Kacey. Make-up. Jane's over there somewhere." She pointed her liquid paper wand toward another row of trailers.

"Thanks," I said. There must be some kind of irony in a make-up artist applying liquid paper to her nails. My friends and I had done that in grade school and I couldn't imagine that it was a revived trend. At the least, I knew I hadn't read about it in *Cosmo*.

A girl who fit a better description of Jane exited one of the trailers. Her curly blonde hair was in a ponytail, pulled through the back of a Chicago Red Sox baseball cap. She saw me and waved me over. She was holding a walkie-talkie and had a headphone attached to her ear.

"Hi," I said. "I'm looking for Maddy Malone's trailer."

"Right. And you are?" she asked.

"I'm Grace Daniels. I'm here to replace my Aunt Lana until she returns from her appointment. Did she call and tell you that I was co-" Jane held her finger up and mouthed "one minute" to me.

"Copy that. Going to two," she said into her walkie-talkie. She turned back to me. "Sorry, it's so busy here today. Go ahead."

"No problem," I said, "I'm Grace Daniels. Lana sent me to assist—" Jane spoke into her walkie-talkie again.

"Does anyone have a twenty on Tom?" So far, I was entirely unimpressed with the bad-mannered crew. I watched as Jane wiped the sweat from her upper lip waiting for a response. "Great, ten more minutes for Kimberly in hair and make-up as well. Going to one. Sorry, go again?" I continued to wait, unsure if she was talking to me. I felt no need to waste my breath.

"What were you asking me?" she said again into the walkie-talkie. I noticed a director's chair outside a trailer a few yards down. The name on the back read "Kimberly Thompson." Another teen star, I assumed.

"Well?" Jane asked.

"Me?" I asked.

"Of course," she said, "Who else? You're looking for Maddy." She searched the papers on her clipboard and pulled off the cap of her pen with her teeth.

"I'm Grace Daniels." Jane nodded.

"Right, Lana's niece. She called and told me. Will you sign-in here?"

I signed along the line. Jane went on to explain that she was one of the many assistant directors on the crew, but her job specifically was to take care of the *Daisy Mae* cast while they were stationed at base camp.

"Sounds great," I lied. A proud smile formed on her face.

"Going to one," she said, pushing the button on her walkie-talkie. The last time I had seen people using walkie-talkies was on

Chips. Unfortunately, Jane was not doing it for me the way Erik Estrada had.

"Okay, let's get you to Maddy's trailer," she said. "She probably won't be too thrilled that Lana's away. She's really come to depend on her and Lana's been such a lifesaver for all of us, as you probably already know." Jane turned her head and looked me over. "I'm sure you'll be great. She'll like that you're so young."

"I'm twenty-seven," I said.

"Wow," she said. "I would have guessed younger." That seemed like a compliment, if an indirect one. Though I may look a tad more youthful than other women my age, I often didn't feel that way. I didn't have the energy that I had five years ago, and in spite of my efforts to preserve it, I felt like my body was losing its firmness. Thirty seemed to be lingering around the corner like a bad smell. I remained single after a string of bad boys had done me wrong, and like a teenager, still pining over the untouchables like Scott. According to my mother, I'm a train wreck in the man department and as soon as I stop chasing rainbows I might meet a potential husband. Just like Sheryl did.

Jane led me to Maddy's trailer, which was a huge two-level model. Surprised that she had scored such a monstrosity of a vehicle, I quickly scanned the rest of the area to see if there were others like it, but saw none.

"I didn't even know trailers with multiple levels existed," I said.

"It's a little out of the ordinary," Jane said. "Maddy's agent had it put in her contract, but it's ridiculous that a kid has ... I mean, supposedly even Susan Sarandon wouldn't demand a trailer like this and she's a huge star. It's not like Maddy's ..." Jane trailed off. I assumed she didn't want to skew my opinion of Maddy before I'd actually met her. Or maybe she thought I was a fan? Actually, I had barely heard of Maddy. I hadn't seen any of her movies, and she wasn't yet gracing any magazine covers. But Aunt Lana claimed that kids loved Maddy and that we should all keep our eyes open because Maddy would be the Hollywood "It" girl of 2007. I'll believe it when I see it.

Hanging on Maddy's door was a big sign, her character's name, "Daisy Mae," in red bubble letters with small hand-drawn pictures of happy faces all around it.

"Cute," I said.

"I made it," Jane said. "I was bored one day and made them for everyone." I smiled, remembering that Aunt Lana had told me how working on the set could get tedious, but she was able to spend a lot of time knitting scarves. Jane happened to be wearing a blue and yellow one around her neck.

"Hey, Maddy!" Jane shouted, knocking loudly on her door. We waited on the trailer steps. Silence.

"Do you think she's asleep?" I asked.

"Definitely not," Jane said, "just ignoring us." She knocked again. "Lana's niece Grace is here!" I wondered if Maddy might be observing us through one of her black tinted windows, laughing and mocking us.

"Don't take it personally," Jane whispered. "She always plays this game." I leaned against the railing and sighed. Why had I said yes to this gig? I hadn't even met Maddy and the problems were already looming.

Jane knocked a third time and the door swung open nearly hitting her in the face. There stood Maddy Malone, at approximately five foot three and a hundred and fifteen pounds. She had pale skin, rosy cheeks, and her blonde hair was pulled back in a bun. Smoke rose around her, like a scene from a movie, except this smoke wasn't from some fancy machine, but from cigarettes. Jane started coughing and Maddy laughed, her bright hazel eyes sparkling through the mist.

"They say that when you're an ex-smoker, the smell of it is even grosser. Guess there's some truth to that one, huh Jane?" Jane did not reach over and slap Maddy, like I would have. Instead, she stood there smiling and nodding her head. Maddy looked me up and down.

"I'm Maddy," she said.

"Grace Daniels," I said, extending my hand to shake hers. "Nice to meet you." She laughed.

"No need to be so formal," she said, grabbing my hand and squeezing it tightly with her clammy one. I pulled mine away.

"Looks like you two will be just fine," said Jane, eager to get away.

"Yes, we'll have a grand old time," Maddy said. Jane told Maddy she should get into her next change of clothes because they would be starting scene thirty-one.

"Whatevs," Maddy said. "Come on in, Grace. I'll show you around my digs."

I followed her inside and watched as she grabbed a cigarette off a clay ashtray sitting on the counter.

"You smoke?" she asked.

"No," I said.

"You want to start?" she asked, smiling.

"No," I answered. She put hers out in the ashtray, picked up a can of air freshener and sprayed it around.

"I'm actually trying to quit," she said. "If my life wasn't so stressful, I could probably do it cold turkey." I could only imagine how stressful life must be for Maddy Malone. In an attempt to distract myself from laughing, I looked around at the decor of the trailer. The walls were neutral taupe and the kitchenette housed stainless steel appliances. There was a small diner-style booth with magazines sprawled across it. Beyond that, was a sitting area with plush white carpeting and a big screen TV.

"This is a really nice trailer," I said. Maddy sat down at the booth and began shredding a magazine cover.

"It used to belong to Meg Ryan," she said.

"Really?" I asked.

"Well, no, but how cool would that be?" she laughed. At least Maddy had a sense of humor, though I wasn't sure it was one I shared. She eyed the pack of cigarettes sitting on the counter.

"Do you mind if I smoke another?" she asked.

"No, go ahead," I said. I didn't want to be responsible for her flubbing her lines in scenes because she hadn't smoked on my behalf.

She scurried to the counter and pulled a new one from a pack, then leaned over a lit candle.

"What kind of music do you fancy?" she asked in an English accent. "I like everything. I mean, I idolize Madonna, and Christina Aguilera has a perfect voice. But sometimes I just want to rock out to Maroon 5."

"We have similar taste," I said, watching her blow smoke rings. The only impression I had of Maddy so far was that she was a typical teenager, but a little worse.

"Nice Gucci shoes," I said, looking down to avoid smoke in my face.

"Thanks," she said. "They were a gift from my agent."

"Wow!" I said. A generous agent, I thought. The presents I usually received from JD Design's clients were gift certificates or baskets of items that I never used.

"What do you do, Grace?" Maddy asked.

"I'm an Interior Designer," I said.

"Oh my god," she said, excitedly. "Like, you decorate houses?" I nodded.

"Awesome! Do you want to decorate my house in Malibu?" she asked. My mouth dropped open.

"You own a house in Malibu?"

"Of course not," she said, "but I'm gonna buy one when I turn eighteen. I'll call you."

"Great," I said. I wouldn't hold my breath on that one.

"You've gotta see what I'm wearing for the next scene," she said with a surge of excitement. She latched on to my wrist, pulling me up the stairs and into a pink bedroom.

"Check it out," she said, pointing to an outfit lying on the rose patterned comforter of the large bed. It was a pair of Dolce and Gabanna jeans and a pink silk top.

"I picked it myself," she said, holding up the top. "I told them it was the only thing I'd wear or they'd have to use my double in the scene." She looked up at me, waiting for me to react to the expensive clothing.

"I love it," I said.

"I know! Isn't it totally stunning?" she said. "Oh, the shoes! You have to see the shoes." I watched as the long blonde strands of Maddy's hair fell out of the various clips holding it up, while she went running over to the wooden dresser standing on the opposite wall. She tossed me a Dior shoe box and I removed the cover to reveal a pair of pink patent leather stilettos with studs around the heel.

"I'm speechless," I said, handing the box back to her. "They're beautiful."

"I so know what you're saying," she said. To give the full effect of her excitement, Maddy pulled her hair out of its bun and let it bounce around in a pony tail.

"Do you get to keep the clothes you wear in your scenes?" I asked.

"Well," she whispered. "If those wardrobe wenches tell me I can't, I'll just take them anyway."

Suddenly, I had an overwhelming interest in being an actress. Free Dior? Sign me up! Maddy's cell phone started ringing. She held it up, looking at the caller ID.

"It's my mother," she said. "I don't want to speak to her." She tossed the rhinestone phone into my hands, and I stood dumbfounded for a moment.

"Tell her I'm on set," she said, reaching over to tap the talk button and pushing the phone to my ear.

"Hello?" I said.

A raspy voice attacked me with questions. Who was I? Where was her daughter? Where was Lana? What was going on there? Why hadn't anyone told her there was a different guardian today? I answered as best I could and then listened as Mrs. Malone moved on to personal ones. How old was I? What were my qualifications? What sign was I, because if I was a Gemini, it wasn't going to work. She didn't trust Geminis.

"I'm a Taurus," I said.

"Fine," she said. "Do you have children? Do you know how much of a responsibility they are?"

"I don't have any," I said, watching Maddy blowing kisses and admiring herself in the mirror and realized this could be the best form of birth control I'd ever encountered.

"Well?" Mrs. Malone asked. I realized I had tuned her out and missed her last question.

"Well what?" I said.

"Her hair," Mrs. Malone said. "How does it look?"

"Great!" I answered, wishing Maddy's battery would die.

"Just tell her to call me as soon as possible," Mrs. Malone said. I hung up and took a deep breath.

"Don't mind her," Maddy said, searching her hair for split ends. "She has anxiety problems."

"Oh, sorry," I said.

"It's okay. It's mostly because of me," she said. Somehow, that didn't surprise me. "Anyway, the bitch just wants to make sure everything runs smoothly for me, since she can't be here."

"I understand," I said.

I walked over to the dresser and picked up a photo of Maddy's family. They were all blonde. Even the dog was blonde. I held the photo up to the light to make sure my eyes weren't playing tricks on me—if that dog's fur was highlighted, I'd be calling PETA.

"Nice looking family," I said. "You have two brothers?"

"Yeah. Stevie's the oldest," Maddy said, pointing to the boy on the left. "He's twenty-one and just got a job on Wall Street. My parents think he's perfect."

"My parents feel the same way about my older sister Sheryl," I said. "She's a doctor." Maddy laughed and took a new cigarette pack out of the dresser drawer.

"Guess we have something in common," she said. I'm sure it was the only thing. She pointed to the other boy in the picture. "That's Greg. He's fourteen now. He wants to be a famous hockey player. Pipe dreams, if you ask me."

"Okay," I said. An actress talking about someone else's pipe dreams? The irony was almost too overwhelming for me.

"My mom goes to every game," she said. "Of course, it helps that Greg's coach is a major hottie." From the picture, so was Maddy's dad.

"My parents fight like crazy," she said. "Usually about me. My father tries to enforce rules and my mother tells him to stop interfering with my career. I'm sure they'll eventually get divorced. Oh well!"

When I was six years old, my parents had this horrible fight because my father had lost me at the mall. My mother screamed at him for an hour over how irresponsible he was and eventually he stormed out of the house.

"It's all your fault if they get divorced," Sheryl had said, as I hid behind my dollhouse crying. Believing that I was going to cause my parent's divorce, my response to Sheryl was definitely not "Oh well," but non stop crying until our father returned for dinner.

"So you want to know how I became an actress?" Maddy asked.

"Sure," I said. She sat down on the bed beside me and crossed her legs.

"My family's originally from Pittsburgh. Do you know where that is?" she asked.

"In America?"

"Don't make fun. This isn't geography class ya know," she said.

"Right. Carry on," I said.

"We moved to New York when I was five. My dad had inherited a bakery in Chinatown from his uncle and my mom was dying to live in the Big Apple. That's what they call New York." Maddy must have mistaken me for someone who had just landed in the country.

"This shitty stuff is supposed to stay on for hours," she said, mascara falling off her lashes as she rubbed her eyes. "Anyway," she continued. "My mother was convinced that she'd be a big Broadway star. You know, in one of those yesteryear plays, like um, what's it called, Gangs of New York, or something?"

"*West Side Story*," I said.

"Right, whatever. Well, my father's bakery was a huge success. Papa Malone's Bakery, best rogalah in the city. Do you know what rogalah is?"

"No," I said. She jumped up and grabbed a red string off the dresser.

"It's a Jewish pastry," she said. "By the way, I'm studying Kabbalah. Can you tie this on for me?" She passed me the red string, and I tied it in a knot around her wrist.

"Thanks," she said, admiring her spiritual bracelet.

"So, go on," I said.

"Huh?" she asked.

"You were talking about the bakery," I said. This girl had the shortest attention span ever.

"Right," she laughed. "Well, my mother got a part in the chorus. She's hot, right?" she asked, pointing at the photo. Maddy was practically a clone of her.

"You look a lot like her," I said.

"I know. Everyone tells me that," she beamed. "So, one afternoon I was sitting on a pail behind the counter, licking a candy Oscar the Grouch head off a cupcake. Every time I took a bite, I said 'mmm' in like a hundred different tones. Then there was like some big shot director buying some rogalach—yes that's the right pronunciation with a *ch* sound. Well when he saw my performance behind the counter, he knew I had to be in his movie, and he cast me the next day. It's called *The Window Pain*. Have you seen it?"

"Yes, you were great," I lied. It would just make things easier.

"Yeah well unfortunately becoming the next big thing took ten years," Maddy said with a laugh, "so I had to go to school with regular kids for a while. Could you imagine?"

"Ghastly," I said, "Damn peasant kids." Maddy laughed, and then coughed through the smoke.

"You're funny," she said. I glanced at my watch. Wasn't she supposed to get ready for her next scene?

"I was such a cute kid, before my thighs got so big," Maddy said, squeezing the fat she had on them. "So that's it. That's the story of my life. Ta da!" she said, doing a pirouette and bashing into the full length mirror in the corner.

"So should you change now?" I asked.

"Why?" she asked, rubbing her elbow. "You don't like me the way I am?"

"Funny," I said.

"Just joshing with ya, Grace. Good idea," she said. "Why don't you go grab yourself a drink downstairs? Unfortunately, I have no alcohol in there. My bitch publicist made sure of that."

"I'll try to manage," I said.

I found three rows of small Evian bottles in the fridge. I took one and sat down in the booth to drink it. There was a knock at the door.

"Hon, can you get that for me?" Maddy called out from upstairs. I went over to the door and unhooked the latch. I opened it to find a gorgeous guy on the other side. We both seemed equally surprised.

"Hi," we said, simultaneously.

"Where's Lana?" he asked. His voice was calm and cool.

"She's sick," I said. "I'm replacing her for the day."

"Ah the substitute babysitter," he laughed. "Well, I'm Hunter David."

"Grace Daniels," I said, shaking his hand. I stood in the doorway, gazing at him like a star struck teenager. He looked like he'd just stepped out of an Abercrombie and Fitch ad.

"I just came to return this DVD that I borrowed from Maddy the other day," he said.

"Great," I said, realizing that, wow, Hunter had even hunkier looks than Scott.

"So, do you think you could give it to her?" he asked. I looked down and saw his hand stretched out to give me the DVD.

"Oh, oops," I said, laughing. "Of course."

"Thanks," Hunter said. "Anyway, I've got to go change, but it's great to meet you, Grace, and if you need anything, my trailer's right over there." He pointed to a more modest trailer. "It's not as spectacular as 'Chez Maddy,' but I'm only number five on the call sheet." I wasn't sure what that meant.

"Okay. Thanks," I said.

"See you later, blue eyes," he said.

"I can't wait," I said, and then wanted to kick myself for sounding too eager.

I bent down pretending to tie my shoelace so I could watch Hunter walk back to his trailer. When the door closed behind him, I stood up and went back inside. Moments later, while I finished my bottle of water, Maddy bounded down the stairs all done up. She looked magnificent.

"Well?" she asked.

"You look incredible," I said. She smiled, obviously waiting for more compliments. "Really, I've never seen someone do justice to pink like you do, and wow, are those jeans ever slimming."

"I know!" Maddy said, bursting. "It's so true. I look great!" She threw her arms around me, hugging me so hard I could barely breathe. "Oh Grace, I'm so happy you were sent to me. Thank God for you." I believed her too. I think she felt as though a higher power had sent me to bless her presence.

"Grace," she said, her voice suddenly serious, "there's something I need to ask you."

"Okay," I said, a little uneasy over what the request might be. Perhaps she needed me to gnaw off a hang nail?

"Could I have your email address?" she asked.

"What?"

"I want to keep in touch," she said, passing me a broken pencil and piece of paper from the counter. "Write it down." I considered giving her wrong information, but that would be mean, and she did seem to sincerely like me. Maybe she just needed a friend in Chicago.

"Thanks," she said.

"Sure," I replied. Maddy took a few steps away from me.

"Don't get me wrong," she said, "I'm not looking to be your friend. I just like to have everyone who works for me on file."

"Of course," I said.

There was a knock on the door. I hoped it was Hunter again and was disappointed when Jane poked her head in to tell Maddy they were ready for her on set.

"Give me a few minutes," Maddy said. Jane pushed a button on her walkie-talkie saying that Maddy was "aware" and that she'd be there momentarily.

"I so don't feel like going to set," Maddy said, after Jane shut the door. That caught me off guard, as I would have thought she'd have wanted to rush out to show off her new outfit.

She threw herself down on the couch and sighed. Her D&G top was creasing, but I thought I'd better not mention it.

"What's that?" she asked, pointing to the DVD sitting on the table.

"Oh," I said handing it to her. "Your friend, Hunter, came by to return it while you were upstairs getting dressed." She threw it across the room.

"Oh!" I said, startled.

"Hunter's not my friend," she said. "He's annoying." I didn't like her calling my new boyfriend 'annoying,' but figured she didn't mean it and was just stressed about having to go to set. I tried to remember the things that Lana had told me to do to keep Maddy happy.

"Would you like some water?" I asked. She nodded. I reached into the fridge to get her a bottle. I opened it and stood there a moment, not knowing whether to pour the water into a glass or hand her the bottle. Or perhaps just pour it straight into her mouth? She took the bottle from me and sipped slowly.

"Fuck, do I ever have a mega-headache," she said, holding the Evian bottle against her forehead. Jane knocked again. Maddy took off her shoe, whipping it at Jane as she stuck her head through the door. Was she suffering an emotional disorder? It was hard to tell. I hadn't seen mood changes like this since I saw the movie *Sybil* with friends at a sleepover party when I was twelve. Jane smiled and tossed Maddy's shoe back to her.

"We really need you," she said sweetly, before exiting again. Maddy placed the shoe back on her foot. She got up and snatched her make-up bag off the counter and handed it to me.

"Hold this, 'k?" She was out the door before I could answer. I followed her to a minivan waiting outside.

As I was getting in, she screamed.

"Wait, my phone! I left it in the trailer. Grace, be a lamb and get it for me. It's in the bedroom." I was taken aback by her condescending tone but hurried back into the trailer to grab it.

"Thanks doll," she said as I climbed back into the van.

"I'm Grace," I said to Maddy's driver, an older man with gray hair and glasses.

"Al is the name, driving movie stars is my game," he said.

"You're such a cheese ball," Maddy said. She sat in the front wearing a large pair of sunglasses and puffing away on another cigarette.

"Ugh. I'm so tired, why won't they ever give me a day off?" she asked, turning up the volume on the radio. Al shouted something over the music about how she takes enough days off as is.

"Whatever!" Maddy yelled.

As we approached the set, Maddy handed her lit cigarette back to me. Guess she already forgot that I was a nonsmoker.

"I don't want the director to know I smoke. So just pretend it's yours," she said, spraying breath freshener into her mouth. Maddy ran over to Al's side of the van and gave him a high five.

"Later, homey," she said. She turned and walked through the crowd of people waiting for her, her head down as if avoiding the paparazzi. It was no secret that Maddy Malone was capable of sucking the life out of a person. I already felt a hundred years older than when I had gotten here. She was all over the map with her unpredictable behavior and short attention span.

Hunter was already on set, looking even more handsome now. He waved when he saw us approaching.

"Pretend you don't see him," Maddy said, before someone came and whooshed her away. I waved back at Hunter, but he had already turned around. I was directed to a chair by someone else wearing a walkie-talkie. Once seated, I overheard a conversation between Kacey and another woman.

"She's late every time they call for her. Yet she never seems to get in trouble for it. Who does she think she is?" Kacey asked.

"I think they're going to wrap her ahead of schedule so they can get her out of here," the other woman said.

"That will be a relief," said Kacey. "Things will move a lot quicker once she's gone. Plus, she'll miss the wrap party." They both had big grins on their faces.

Aunt Lana was right; Maddy had developed a bad reputation on set. I remember her telling me how if Maddy didn't get what she wanted, she refused to cooperate.

For instance a month back, the costume designer brought Maddy a white crew neck T-shirt for her to wear in one of the scenes, but Maddy had wanted to wear a V-neck instead, so she refused to come to set until a new T-shirt was brought to her. When the costume designer could no longer reason with her, the director and one of the producers rushed to Maddy's trailer to coax her to wear the top. After fifteen minutes of arguing, they bribed her with a gorgeous Technomarine watch. It belonged to the director and he knew she'd been eyeing it. Later that day, Maddy told Aunt Lana that she'd given the watch to one of the extras in 'background holding,' at lunchtime.

"Charity," Maddy had said, referring to the cute teenage boy she'd given it to. "Because he is not as fortunate as me."

I looked around and noticed Hunter, whose hair was being fixed by a very thin man. I caught his eye, and he winked at me. Butterflies swarmed my stomach. I desperately needed to find him online and check if he was single.

"Rolling!" the director screamed a little while later. Everyone scurried to their places. "And, ACTION!"

I watched as the scene began. A few seconds later, a cell phone's ring filled the air. It sounded like it was coming from my immediate vicinity.

"Cut!" yelled the director. All eyes were suddenly on me. I felt around Maddy's jacket and felt the vibrations coming from the pocket. Shit! Maddy looked horrified. She motioned me to answer it. I pulled out the phone and pushed 'talk.'

"Hello?" I whispered. It was Mrs. Malone. She began to babble about a pair of Kors boots that Maddy had ordered a week ago from Saks. They had arrived and were on hold for her. I explained that Maddy was on set, and that this wasn't an opportune time, but she couldn't hear me over her own voice. I was sweating heavily. Everyone stared at me, waiting for the call to end.

"By the way, Grace," Mrs. Malone said, before hanging up. "Make sure you turn off Maddy's phone when you get to set. They won't be happy if it rings while they're filming." I pushed 'end' before she uttered another word then slumped in my seat.

"Rolling!" the director yelled out, angrily. Maddy turned to me and stuck out her tongue.

After having shot the same scene seventeen times, Maddy had finally finished for the day.

"I told everyone that you were new to the movie world and had no idea that cell phones weren't allowed on set," Maddy said when we arrived back at her trailer.

"You told them you'd never seen me before in your life," I said. I'd never been so humiliated.

"I was just kidding, Grace. And, um, well, it wasn't a total lie. Before today, I had never seen you in my life," she said. She had also failed to mention to the producers the part about it being her own phone ringing.

"Don't worry, Grace," Maddy said. "The director will forget about it by tomorrow night when you see him at dinner."

"Well, I hope so," I said. I took my own phone out of my bag to check my messages and put it down when I realized what Maddy had just said.

"Maddy?" I asked, watching her pull up her jeans. She ignored me. "Maddy!"

"Yes?" she said, looking up.

"What was that about me seeing the director tomorrow night?"

"For dinner," she said. "Didn't I tell you he's taking everyone from the cast out for dinner?" I shook my head.

"Oops, must have forgotten to tell you," she said. I still didn't understand what that had to do with me. "I need a guardian there. You're cool with that, right?" She whipped off the D&G top.

"You need a guardian to go eat dinner with you?" I asked. Clearly, she was not being serious.

"Yeah," she said, "because it's work related. So, you're free, right?"

"Well, actually I—"

"Perfect," she said. "It will be so much fun. I'll email you all the details tonight."

"Maybe Lana should go with you instead," I suggested. "I mean she is your official guardian."

"I want to have fun, duh," Maddy said, "that's why I asked you."

I couldn't believe Maddy assumed I was free for dinner, and I resented her for it. Why would I want to spend my evening with her and the director of the movie, who now hated me anyway.

"I don't know if I can join you and the director for dinner," I said. "I mean, I appreciate you asking me and-"

"It's not just us," she said, interrupting. "There will be a few other cast members going. Like Hunter and—"

"Sounds great," I said, no longer feeling resentful.

"Cool!" she said, "I'm going upstairs to get my stuff. Tell Jane I'm almost ready to go back to the hotel."

I poked my head outside and called for Jane who was speaking with a few of the actresses.

"Hey, what's up?" she asked. I gave her Maddy's request and Jane called Al on her walkie-talkie. He arrived a few moments later.

"Maddy, your van is here," I called up the stairs. I heard her yelling on the phone.

"One second," she yelled back. "Mom, I'm just saying that you are my manager. I'm sure you can take a few minutes from counting my money and call someone to make sure there are *competent* people around me. Okay Mom, I've got to go, my driver's waiting." I heard her hang up. She came down with her hair back in its bun and a pair of sweatpants on.

"Everything okay?" I asked.

"Yeah," she said. "Fine. She was just annoyed about them keeping me here later than they are legally allowed to. Really, it was your job to make sure I didn't go over my limit, but it's okay, Grace. You didn't know." Maddy dashed for the door, about to leave.

"It was great meeting you," I called after her. She turned and smiled.

"Same here, Grace. Thanks for your help today. If you wouldn't mind folding my clothes upstairs before you leave, that would be great. I'll see you tomorrow night. Don't forget!" She gave me a quick hug and swung open the trailer door. I walked outside and watched as she jumped off the third step and ran to the van. Jane rushed over so Maddy could sign out before leaving.

"Say it, Jane!" Maddy said.

"What?" Jane asked.

"What I told you that you have to say everyday before I leave," Maddy said.

"I hate Chelsea Tate!" Jane said in a robotic tone.

"Oh yeah, baby!" Maddy said, laughing. Chelsea Tate was a famous teenage star, who had already exploded onto the scene. Hence, she was Maddy's arch enemy.

"Later losers!" Maddy shouted out to everyone within earshot. The wheels screeched as Al drove away. Everyone watched her leave—followed by some cheers of joy when she was out of sight. I stood with Jane, amazed and bewildered.

"There she goes," I said.

"Yes," Jane smiled. "There she goes. Hollywood's next teen queen."

CHAPTER 2

That night, I took an hour-long bath, had a glass of red wine, and popped a couple of extra-strength Advil. When I sat down at my computer, I found a short email from Maddy, filled with spelling mistakes.

> *Hi G, diner's at eight tomorow night. Come to my hotel at 7:30. I'm staying at The Drake. Adress is 140 East Walton Place.*
> *xox MM*

I wrote back:

> *Great! See you tomorrow.*
> *xox GD*

I signed out of my email account, wondering if Maddy goes to school. Then I typed in www.google.com into the address bar, and looked up Hunter David. Copious amounts of websites came up. Perfect. I learned that Hunter was twenty-five years old and used to be on the soap opera, *Western Park*. His character had gone to jail for attempted murder two years ago. Since then he had had various guest roles, on prime time television shows. *Daisy Mae* was his first feature film. I also discovered that he was the oldest of three boys and grew up in Boston. There were many dreamy pictures of him, and I saved as many as I could to my hard drive by right clicking my mouse. Finally, and most importantly, I found the raison d'etre for my search.

"Yes!" I squealed, jumping up and down in my chair. Hunter David was single, and apparently had been for a while. The only two pictures I could find with him and another girl were one at his prom, and one with his mother at a movie premiere.

As I sat deciding which picture I wanted to use as wallpaper on my screen, my phone rang. I reached over to grab the cordless.

"Hi Grace," Aunt Lana said on the other end.

Shoot, I'd forgotten to call her when I got home.

"Hey!" I said, gazing at Hunter's tilted face as he smiled at me. "I was just about to call you."

"How did it go today?" she asked.

"It went well, I think," I said.

"See," Aunt Lana said, "she's not that bad."

"Well she was bad," I said. "But everyone else was great. It was a fun experience. Maddy asked me to accompany her to a cast dinner tomorrow night. Is that okay with you?" I hoped Aunt Lana wouldn't pull out the sensitive card over this, because if there was somewhere I needed to be tomorrow night, it was at dinner with Maddy … and Hunter.

"Grace!" she shrilled, "that's marvelous. Of course it's okay by me. I'm sure you'll have a great time." I was pretty sure I would too.

The next day I was awoken by my neighbor's dog barking at ten o'clock. I yawned and sat up in bed, stretching my arms and smiling as I zoomed in on Hunter David, my screen saver.

I got out of bed and before washing up, searched my closet for something to wear to dinner. I couldn't find anything that hollered, "Love me, Hunter!" and all my "Love me, Scott!" clothes were applied to the gym only. I decided that I would need to purchase something new.

I stopped at Starbucks to get a coffee on my way to Bloomingdales. As I stood in line, my cell phone rang. It was Jake.

"Please tell me you still have the carpet samples," he said.

"I do," I assured him. "They're in the glove compartment of my car."

"You do remember I have an appointment with Teach Rogers later on today, right?" he asked.

"Of course, I remember," I said. How could I forget? Teach Rogers was a top designer from LA, who had flown in to meet with Jake. He was interested in buying into JD Designs. He had seen Jake written up in *Modern Home* magazine and contacted him soon after to talk to him about a possible merger. Teach wanted to open a division in LA. The real estate market was booming there, and the company would thrive with business. We were all very excited about the possible venture, knowing how profitable it would be.

"When will you be home?" Jake asked.

"In a couple hours," I said. "I'll call you on my way and you can meet me at my place." I hung up as I reached the entrance of Bloomingdale's.

I headed straight to trend wear on the third floor and began searching through racks of jeans.

"What do you mean it's declined?" I heard a familiar voice say. I turned and saw Maddy standing at the cash register. Her hair was in two braids and she was wearing a white button down, a pair of ripped jeans, and a big cowboy hat.

"It says 'card not approved,'" the saleslady said.

"Well try it again!" Maddy demanded.

"I did," she said. "Three times. It's not working."

"I don't have another card with me," Maddy said. The saleslady asked Maddy to move aside so she could take the next customer.

"Fuck!" Maddy yelled. "Hold on." She grasped onto the counter not letting the next customer thru.

I thought of hiding in the dressing room until she was gone, but something compelled me to take pity on her. After all, she was just a kid alone in Chicago.

"Hi Maddy," I said, walking toward her. She turned and it was obvious she didn't recognize me.

"I'm Gra-"

"Grace!" she said, finishing my sentence. "I'm so glad you're here. I'm in a total bind."

"Is there anything I can do to help?" I asked. Tears welled up in her eyes.

"Well, actually, the problem is my mother and I share my credit card and there's a daily limit on it. I guess my mother must have used it already today, and now it's not going through." I noticed she was buying a designer denim miniskirt and baby blue top, and was curious to know how much her daily limit was. I figured it was probably more than my annual salary.

"I just need to borrow three-hundred dollars and I'll pay you back tonight," she said. "Would that be okay?" She rubbed the shirt against her face as if it were a pet. Out of the corner of my eye I could see both the sales lady and the next person in line waiting for me to respond.

"Sure, no problem," I said, retrieving my card from my purse. Maddy snatched it from me.

"I'll go to the ATM on my way home and take out cash for you," she promised.

"Okay, sure," I said.

"Grace, thank God for you," Maddy said, beaming. She took the bag with her purchases off the counter and adjusted her hat.

The saleslady gave me back my card to put in my wallet. I was about to bid Maddy adieu so I could concentrate on my own shopping when she spoke again.

"Do you think I could bother you for one more small favor?" she asked.

"It depends what it is," I said.

"Do you think you could lead me out of the store so I don't get mobbed by my fans?" she asked. Her fans? The store was pretty busy and so far, anyone who had walked by us hadn't so much as flinched when they'd passed Maddy.

"Well, I guess," I said.

"Thanks."

Maddy put on a pair of oversized Chanel sunglasses and grabbed my hand.

"Okay, I'm ready," she said.

I led her down the escalators to the ground floor, where we walked by a small group of women. They looked at us oddly when Maddy put her hand up to wave. They had no idea who she was. Once outside, I tried hailing Maddy a cab. She stood against the wall and shielded herself with her bags. One pulled up to the curb and I was fortunately able to get Maddy in without any of her "fans" hounding her.

"I'll see you tonight," I said, before shutting the door.

"Right," she said. "Don't be late."

As the cab drove off, I watched as Maddy's hand extended out the cab window to ash her cigarette. Then I turned to go back into Bloomingdale's to shop.

Later, I arrived at The Drake fifteen minutes early to pick up Maddy for dinner. I was wearing a new Marc Jacobs top that I'd found on sale and a pair of straight leg jeans.

Maddy hadn't told me her room number so I went straight to the concierge desk to find out what it was.

"I'm sorry, I can't give out that information," the concierge said.

"But I'm supposed to meet her here," I said.

"Right, well I have strict orders not to allow anyone in without the code," he said.

"The code?" I asked.

"It's a one word code. If you really know her she'd have told you it," he explained. "It's to prevent stalkers."

"I'm not a stalker," I said, laughing. The concierge did not laugh.

"Let me ring her up, and see if she will accept you anyway," he said. "What is your name?" I gave him my name and then took a step back folding my arms across my chest waiting to see if I'd be "accepted."

"She has long brown hair, and blue eyes," the concierge said into the phone.

"Er … hold on I'll ask." The concierge covered the mouthpiece of the phone with his hand and summoned me over with his finger.

"Yes?" I said, moving forward.

"Miss, could you please tell me which Sesame Street character was on the cupcake she was eating when she was discovered?" Was this a joke? How was I supposed to remember that?

"Miss Piggy?" I asked. The concierge said it into the phone and then they both had a laugh.

"I know," he said, giggling, "The Muppets." I was starting to get angry, and considered leaving.

"Okay, okay," the concierge said. "I'll send her up." He hung up the phone and wiped his eyes with a handkerchief.

"Go on up," he said. "She's in the Presidential Suite."

"The Presidential Suite?" I asked.

"Yes," he said. "Fifth floor."

Once in the elevator, I pushed the button for the fifth floor. I was amazed that production was putting her up in such a fancy room.

Maddy answered the door wearing a white waffle knit robe and had her hair in rollers.

"Hi! The answer was Oscar the Grouch, dummy," she said. "Miss Piggy is from *The Muppet Show*, duh."

"I know, I know," I said.

"Come on in. I'm just going to finish getting ready," Maddy said, pulling me through the door.

"This is a beautiful suite," I said, looking around.

"It's okay. It'll do," she said, pulling out a roller. "I'm going to get dressed. By the way, you look so cute. Love your top. You got it off the sale rack at Bloomies today?" My face turned red as I looked down at my black silk top.

"No, I bought it at the beginning of the season," I said.

Maddy disappeared into her bedroom, at the end of a long corridor.

I walked around the suite, absorbing its beauty. Glass tables, taupe carpets, marble bathrooms—of which there were two. The rooms were adorned with antique pieces, beautifully designed carpets, and a stunning French crystal chandelier in the formal dining room. The living room had plush, olive-colored couches arranged in an 'L' shape with stains on them—probably caused by Maddy. Ashtrays with cigarette butts were dispersed everywhere, and there was a 52-inch plasma TV on the wall.

"Who sent you all these flowers?" I called out.

"My agent, publicist, the production company, et cetera, et cetera," she yelled from the bedroom.

"Have any of your friends or family come to visit you?" I asked. I figured that would be the reason she'd need this big place. Maddy came out of her bedroom holding a tube of lipstick.

"What was that, Grace?" she asked.

"I was wondering if you'd had a lot of people come visit while you've been in Chicago?"

"Nope, not a soul," she said. A few minutes later she was ready to go.

"You look great," I said, noticing she was wearing the top I'd lent her money for.

"Thanks," she said. "I'll pay you later 'k? We're late enough." Maddy grabbed a pack of gum from the console table and handed me her designer bag.

"Do you mind holding it for a minute?" she asked, dropping it into my arms. "Just until we get into the cab?" I nodded, and put it over my shoulder with my own.

"Thanks, doll," she said. This "doll" thing needed to stop.

The wind was blowing lightly as we exited the hotel, and I wished I'd brought a hairclip. We waited for a doorman to hail a cab. One pulled up and Maddy looked through the window, peering at the driver.

"Grace," she said. "Could you tell the doorman to get us a different one?" I looked into the cab. The driver was wearing a turban.

"Maddy," I said, not liking what I detected.

"Please, Grace," she begged, grabbing my hand tightly. So along with her other bad qualities, Maddy was also racist? Great!

"You're being ridiculous," I said, opening the door.

"Grace!" she screamed. I turned and saw tears in her eyes.

"Please," she said, touching my shoulder.

"Okay," I said. I told the driver that I forgot something upstairs and to go ahead because we'd be a while.

"Thanks, Grace," Maddy said—tears gone. "You're my hero. I hate sitting in cabs that don't have leather seats."

"Oh!" I said, happy that my assumption was wrong. I asked the doorman to hail us another cab. He whistled for one that was sitting at the corner. This one had leather seats so Maddy happily jumped in.

As we drove, Maddy gave me the lowdown about the cast members joining us for dinner.

"Well, there's Kimberly Thompson, and she's okay, but her face isn't so pretty and she has some major love handles," she said.

"Hey," I said, "those are hard to get rid of."

"Then, of course, Ali, who thinks she is God's gift. Clearly she's not. You'll see. She used to be on acne medication." I could see the driver smirking up front. I was horrified over how mean Maddy was being.

"That's sort of harsh," I said. Maddy continued.

"Renee is sweet, but God what a bad boob job. Poor girl."

"I've heard enough," I said. She kept going.

"Then there's Hunter David, who thinks he's such a heartthrob. Whatever! He has a huge crush on me," she said.

"Oh yeah?" I asked.

"I mean, it's not that I don't find him cute but he's not someone I'm supposed to hang with," she said.

"What do you mean?" I asked.

"Well, come on," she said. "He's a total B-lister."

"Huh?" I asked.

"Grace, you've been sniffing too much paint. Don't you know what an A-lister, or B-lister is?" she asked.

"A is cool, B is not cool?" I asked.

"Well, I guess, sort of. I'll put it to you this way. Marilyn Monroe, Audrey Hepburn, Humphrey Bogart, and me—A-listers," she said. Had my ears betrayed me? Or had Maddy just classified herself in the same category as Hollywood legends?

"I see," I said, humoring her. "And the B-listers?"

"Like Hunter David, and um ..." she paused. "I don't know, like Barbara Walters or someone like that."

"You think Barbara Walters is a B-Lister?" I asked. I considered making a citizens arrest.

"Wow!" she said. "Touchy, touchy. Anyway, my whole point is that Hunter's annoying. That's it."

"Fine," I said, with no strength to argue. "Point taken."

The driver pulled up in front of La Trattoria. Maddy was already out of the cab before he could utter how much we owed.

"Eight dollars," he said. I handed him a ten from my wallet.

"Keep the change," I said.

We walked in and were greeted by the hostess, who then showed us to our table where everyone was already seated.

"Fashionably late Maddy," the director said.

"Sorry, guys," Maddy answered, "Grace was a bit late getting to my hotel." I smiled uncomfortably and sat in an empty seat between Hunter and Renee. I couldn't help but notice her chest. Her boobs didn't look fake to me.

"Glad you could make it," Hunter said.

"Thanks," I said. "It's nice to see you again."

Maddy took a seat beside the director, and immediately pulled her BlackBerry out of her purse.

"Everything okay, Maddy?" the director asked after she had been text messaging for half an hour, and not contributing to any of the conversation going on around her. No one seemed impressed by her and I felt embarrassed by association. I tried to make up for her behavior by adding whatever I could to the conversation.

"My friend is having a boy crisis," Maddy said, without bothering to look up. She put her device away when the waiters brought the main course.

"Well it's about time," she said. "I'm starving." She ate two morsels of tortellini and then put her fork down.

"God, I'm so full," she said.

"You couldn't possibly be," Renee said. "You've barely made a dent."

"Renee, I'm Daisy Mae!" Maddy said, as if that should explain her anorexic behavior.

"And, you are doing an excellent job," the director said.

"Thanks," Maddy said, batting her eyes. Maddy took a tube of lip-gloss out of her purse and smacked her lips together loudly after applying it.

"I'm thinking of having a party in my room Wednesday," she said. "I know everyone's been dying to see my place."

"Dying," Kimberly said, rolling her eyes at Ali.

"I wrap Tuesday and am leaving Wednesday morning, so I won't be able to make it," said Renee.

"You don't wrap Tuesday," Maddy said. "We have a scene together on Wednesday." Renee squirmed in her seat, looking to Hunter for assistance. He shrugged his shoulders.

"It's really a beautiful room," I said, trying to avoid an argument between Maddy and Renee. "Oh and can you believe I mixed up *Sesame Street* with *The Muppet Show*?" Everyone laughed as Maddy continued the story of my daftness.

I reveled in my luck of sitting next to Hunter and everything was going so well between us. He was nice and seemed interested in everything I had to say. Hunter told me about some upcoming work he was doing, and how he was excited to be moving into a new place in Los Angeles. I told him I'd never been, but was hoping my brother-in-law would bring me with when he went out there for business.

"You should take my number," Hunter said. "And if you come to town, give me a call." I smiled from ear to ear.

Across the table, Maddy had a sour look and was shaking her head.

"Grace, I really need to go to the bathroom. Do you want to come with me?" she asked.

"No, that's okay," I said. I believed she was capable of handling that on her own.

"I really need you," Maddy urged, giving me a dirty look and motioning me to go with her.

"Alrighty then," I said.

"Listen," she said, when we were inside. "It's not really cool of you to be exchanging numbers with my friends."

"Friends?" I asked. Hadn't she specifically told me that Hunter was not her friend?

"Yes," she said. "I've had this problem before with people who work for me. They try to steal my friends."

"I'm not trying to steal your friends," I explained. "I was just being—"

"Well glad you understand," she said, cutting me off. "I'm going back to the table now. Will you just wait for a few minutes before coming back, so it doesn't look obvious that we were having a private conversation?"

"Um, ok," I said. While I waited, I jotted down my phone number and email address on a piece of paper, and stuck it in my jeans pocket.

When I returned to the table, I found Maddy in my seat, flirting with Hunter. I took her seat next to the director and reached across the table for my glass of wine. Maddy was suddenly laughing and taking great interest in everything he said. She kept trying to sneak a sip of wine from Hunter's glass and he would tell her no every time. I felt like I was having a High School fight over a guy, and wondered if it was worth it. However, when Hunter began shooting me the occasional winks when Maddy wasn't looking, I decided this was war.

After dinner we all stood outside the restaurant saying goodbye and waiting for cabs.

"It was great to meet you Grace," Renee said, giving me a quick hug. "I hope we'll meet again."

"Good luck with everything," Ali said.

"Thank you for taking such good care of Maddy for us," said the director, who had managed to warm up to me after all.

Maddy hugged Hunter so tightly it seemed he was having trouble breathing.

"Um, okay, I'll see you Monday," he said, pulling away. As he approached me to say goodbye, I stuck my hand in my pocket and pulled out the piece of paper.

"It was great to meet you," I said, holding my hand out to shake his. He smiled and took the paper out of my hand. Then he leaned over and gave me a double kiss on the cheek.

"Mine's HunterD@hotmail.com," he whispered. Easy enough to remember. I tingled all over.

"Hurry up Grace," Maddy said, already in a cab. I quickly got in and we headed back to The Drake. As we drove up to the entrance, I remembered about the money Maddy owed me.

"Could I get the three hundred dollars you owe me?" I asked, as she was about to jump out of the cab. Panic spread across her face.

"Oh right," she said. "Listen, Grace. I don't have it right now, but I could give it to Lana on Monday. Cool?" she asked.

"Well, actually, maybe you could run up and get it while I wait," I suggested.

"Thanks," she said, ignoring what I had just asked. "I promise I won't forget to give it to her. Thanks so much for coming with.

That was really fun. See you soon," She blew me a kiss and hopped out of the cab.

"Nice girl," the cab driver said.

"Yeah," I answered. "A real doll."

CHAPTER 3

By Monday morning, I was more than ready to return to work. Although my experience with Maddy had been amusing, I was glad to be in my own familiar, sane workplace.

"How was your day on set?" Michelle, the receptionist, asked, handing me my mail.

"Fun," I said. "And draining."

I went into my office, slowly drinking my coffee at my desk, while I played my voicemail messages over speaker phone.

"Hey Grace, it's Freddy Clockston. Wanted to thank you again for the fabric for our curtains. They are groovy ... Hello Grace, it's Myrna Gold. My husband loves the bedroom. Thanks so much for your advice, hon! ... Grace, it's Joanne. You're a savior; the stain came right out of the carpet like you said it would." I smiled as I hung up the phone. Then I got up and walked over to my dollhouse, my most prized possession from my childhood.

It sat under the window on a console table. It had been my mother's when she was a kid and my grandparents gave it to me when I was five. I had been obsessed with decorating it ever since.

"You should really consider a career in interior design," Landon, my High School boyfriend had once said. It was the only positive thought that came out of that relationship. I dumped him in Europe the summer after high school. We had gone on a six-week backpacking trip that included visiting eleven different countries.

"Don't go to Amsterdam," my best friend Jen warned, when I told her of our itinerary. "Spend extra time in Italy, instead." I thought she was being silly to think Landon would go astray in the Red Light District. And how could I deprive him of the one place where marijuana was legal? I even approved of him going out one night to party with some Canadian guys we met. That's how much of a cool girlfriend I was.

Why he gave Yana, a hooker in the window of a brothel, the name of the hostel we were staying at was beyond me. She showed up the next night looking for Landon. Unfortunately for him the, "But, babe, she's my Russian cousin," lie, just didn't fly with me. So it was goodbye, Landon and hello Dimitrius, my hunky, rebound fling in Greece.

In the fall, I went to Harrington College of Design right here in Chicago. I graduated at the top of my class and my first job was at JD Designs. I loved working here, but often wondered what I could do to improve my job satisfaction. Sometimes I imagined myself as part of Ty Pennington's Team on *Extreme Makeover Home Edition*, where I'd perform dramatic, life-changing renovations for those in critical need. Yes, Jake's clients were always satisfied with my work, but I was hardly bringing them to tears of joy.

"Grace," Jake said, standing in the doorway of my office. I put the miniature bed back in its place and turned my attention to him.

"Hey there," I said. "How was your meeting with Teach?"

"It was great. He's deciding between JD Designs and Total House," he said, taking a seat on my suede couch. Total House was our biggest competition, sort of like Maddy Malone versus Chelsea Tate. He ran his hand along the ketchup stain.

"You still can't get this out?" he asked.

A few weeks ago Jake had sent me to Johnny Rockets to pick up a lunch of burgers and fries. When I'd returned, I passed by two guys who were about to load the sofa on the truck, and I tripped on a leg that had fallen off of it. The ketchup-smothered fries flew off the tray and onto the couch. When Jake saw the mess, he screamed curse words that I'd never even heard of. I quickly explained that the couch was stain resistant, and then proceeded to try and wipe it clean. It spread even more. Jake spent the rest of the afternoon lying on that couch with a cold compress on his head. I had to order a new couch for our client, and we are no longer allowed to use condiments at work.

"That's great!" I said, trying to distract him. "We're sure to beat out Total House."

"God I hope so," he said. "It would be great if I could find time to go out there to convince him to choose us though."

"You should send me," I said, batting my eyes. "I'll get him to sign with us."

"I'm not having my sister-in-law seduce Teach Rogers," Jake said, laughing.

"Oh please let me, Jake, please," I said.

Just then Michelle put a phone call through from Aunt Lana.

"Saved by the bell," Jake said, leafing through a file that I had left sitting on the coffee table.

"Hi Aunt Lana," I said, hoping she was calling about the cash Maddy owed me.

"Hi honey. Maddy hasn't stopped talking about 'Lana's niece,'" she said.

"Really?" I asked. I was sure she referred to me as that because she no longer remembered my name.

"She liked you a lot," Aunt Lana said. I perked up in my chair. I hadn't been expecting a glowing report. "In fact she was mentioning that ..."

"She owes me money?" I asked, hopeful.

"Pardon?" said Aunt Lana.

"She owes me over three hundred dollars," I explained. "I bailed her out at Bloomingdale's on Saturday."

"Oh, she didn't tell me that," Aunt Lana said.

"Of course not." Jake's cell rang and I listened to him talking to one of our clients about decorating her home theater.

"Grace, are you still there?" Aunt Lana asked.

"Yes, sorry," I said. "What were you saying?"

"Maddy would like to ask you something," she said.

"Oh brother, what could she possibly need from me now?" I asked.

I waited while Aunt Lana got Maddy from the craft truck.

"We've done a few home theaters," Jake said, "I have a guy who specializes in the seating." I turned and looked at my dollhouse. I'd never even thought of putting a home theater in there. I jotted down the idea on a notepad. Finally Maddy came to the phone.

"Hey, Grace," she said, with a mouthful of food.

"Hi Maddy."

"Listen, I wanted to invite you somewhere," she said.

"Oh really? Where?" I asked, hoping it was to another dinner with Hunter.

"California," Maddy said.

"Is that a restaurant?" I asked. I hadn't heard of it. Maddy started laughing.

"It's a state," she said. "In America!" I sat down at my desk dumbfounded.

"I know where it is," I said. "Just not sure-"

"So you'll come?" she asked.

"I'll come where?" I asked.

"To LA!" she exclaimed.

"You're inviting me to go to LA with you?" I asked. Jake was off the phone and staring at me. I shrugged my shoulders at him.

"By George, I think she's got it!" Maddy screamed.

"When did you—"

"Grace, it's me," Aunt Lana said, interrupting me.

"What's she talking about?" I asked.

"Well, Mrs. Malone called an hour ago," she said.

"I'm sorry," I replied.

"She said that Maddy needs to go to L.A. for a few weeks after Christmas break to do a bunch of magazine photo shoots and a music video for one of the songs she sings in *Daisy Mae*. Oh, and also various interviews, press junkets, and well, you know, she's going to be one of the biggest teen stars this year."

"So I've heard," I said.

"Anyway, legally Maddy can't go on her own, and Maddy doesn't want her mother going with her, and—"

"She wants me to go with her?" I asked. Jake's eyes widened.

"It wouldn't cost you a thing," Aunt Lana explained.

"An all expense paid trip to LA?" I asked, sticking my tongue out at him.

"You should take it as a compliment, really," said Aunt Lana, whispering "Maddy hates everyone."

"How long is this for?" I asked.

"Three weeks," she answered.

"What?" I yelped. "I can't go for that long."

"How long?" Jake mouthed. I held up three fingers, and saw the look of horror on his face.

"Sorry Aunt Lana. As much as I'd like to live like a star for three weeks, I do have a job here," I said. "And honestly, I don't know if I could keep up with Maddy for that long." I listened as Aunt Lana explained my situation to Maddy. Maddy came back to the phone.

"I always stay at The Springs in Beverly Hills. It's five stars. I always travel first class, get picked up in limousines, and eat gourmet cuisine. And you'll be paid really well," she said. I had to admit, it sounded amazing. It would be a great way to spend three weeks, during what would probably be a harsh, cold January in Chicago. That is if Maddy wasn't going to be there with me.

"You'll totally be in your element hobnobbing with tons of stars," she said.

"That's not my element," I said, appreciating her effort.

"It will be, if you're hanging with me," she said. "I'll even introduce you to some cute guys. I think you and Adrien Grenier would make a super cute couple."

"My bags are already packed," I said, laughing.

"So is that a yes?" she asked.

"Well, I mean, I'm sure it would be fun but-"

"Great!" she said, cutting me off. "I'll let you know all the details when I have them. The phone went dead.

I hung up the phone and explained the whole situation to Jake. I knew he'd say no to three weeks off, and I'd just tell Aunt Lana later to tell Maddy I couldn't go.

"It's not a bad idea," Jake said, unexpectedly. "Actually it's perfect, Grace. You can go."

I got up and felt his head for possible signs of fever, perhaps a new and non-lethal strain of bird flu.

"Are you insane?" I asked. "You need me here."

"Yes, I do," he said. "But maybe you should be the one to convince Teach to sign with us."

"Really?" I asked. "Why?"

"I think if he sees how serious we are, then we're a sure shot in," he said.

"Maybe I could pick us up some celebrity clientele while I'm there," I said. "Afterall I will be traveling with an A-lister." Jake started laughing.

"I'll talk to Teach about meeting with you," he said.

"Okay, but I guarantee Maddy is very time consuming," I said. "I don't know how much time I'd have to meet with—" Jake walked out of my office without letting me finish.

"This is perfect," he called out. "Nice work, Grace."

After he left, I stood by my window looking toward the water and thinking about how horrible it would be to be Maddy's babysitter in LA. However, for the chance to see Hunter David again and strike up a huge deal with Teach Rogers, it could all be worth it.

CHAPTER 4

I didn't hear from Maddy until three weeks after *Daisy Mae* wrapped, when she emailed me the itinerary for our trip. I would be leaving in the middle of January and flying to New York, where I'd meet up with Maddy, and attend a party with her. Then, a day later, we would fly to L.A. I was feeling uneasy about there being no return date on the schedule, so I emailed Maddy and asked when we'd be back.

She replied:

Chill out Grace, I Promis not to keep you hostige in LA!

For the rest of the month, I spent most of my free time at the gym. I wanted to be in tip top shape when I got to LA.

"Hey, isn't that your little starlet on MTV?" Scott asked the Monday before my departure. I was jogging on the treadmill and wasn't paying attention to the TV screens that hung from the ceiling. I looked up and saw Maddy being interviewed by Trixie Marx, a VJ at MTV. Maddy looked great. Her hair was down and straightened, and she was wearing jeans and a yellow top.

"That's her," I said huffing and puffing through my fourth mile. I plugged my headphones into the socket so I could listen.

"Do you think I could get some water?" Maddy asked. A few moments later a water bottle was brought to her.

"So Maddy," Trixie said, "what was it like filming *Daisy Mae* in Chicago, the Windy—"

"Actually, I only drink Evian," Maddy said, pushing away another brand.

For someone hoping to make it as a big star, she would probably need to brush up on her professional skills.

I was leaving at the end of the week and after receiving my first class plane ticket via FedEx, I tried calling Mrs. Malone to discuss what my job duties were, but her receptionist told me she was busy, and would call me back. I still hadn't heard from her.

On my way to drop my sweaty towel in the bin, I passed Scott.

"Don't forget the little people," he said with a glowing smile. I returned the smile, but ever since meeting Hunter, I wasn't feeling Scott so much anymore. And Scott definitely noticed the lack of attention I'd been giving him.

"You know you're my favorite client," he said.

"See you in a month," I said, giving him a hug. "And thanks for helping me get in shape for the trip."

"You look great," he smiled. I looked over at his girlfriend glaring at me from behind the counter and I smiled back.

As I walked off, I felt Scott's eyes follow my new, fitter body, and it felt great. Too bad he had snoozed.

I seemed to suddenly be on everyone's mind, now that I was off to LA. Just yesterday I'd been entering my building when Mrs. Willard, the resident crabapple, had said,

"I heard you're going to Hollywood."

"Yes," I said. My landlord must have spread the news.

"You be sure and tell Ol' Blue Eyes that I send my love," Mrs. Willard said.

"Ol' Blue Eyes?" I asked. I assumed she didn't know Ol' Blue Eyes was now up in the Ol' Blue Skies.

"Yes," Mrs. Willard said. "He used to have a huge thing for me."
I smiled. That was cute of her, but was Mrs. Willard a bit delusional? She dug out an old photo from her little straw bag and handed it to me. It was a picture of a younger Mrs. Willard, arm in arm with none other than Ol' Blue Eyes.

That night, I busied myself packing for the journey, while collectively getting some phone calls in.

"I'm just looking through this month's issue of *Sixteen Magazine*," Jen said, on my fifth call to her. "Have you seen it?"

"No, I don't read magazines that have questions from readers panicking over when they'll start getting their period," I said. She started giggling. Jen subscribed to every magazine on the market.

"Well there's an interview with Hunter David," she said, "and a pretty cute picture." Just hearing his name made me smile.

I had emailed Hunter to tell him I'd be in Los Angeles, but to my disappointment hadn't heard back from him. Then again, it was silly of me to think that someone of Hunter's status would care whether I was coming to town.

"One of the questions asks what he likes in a girl and he answered that he's attracted to the girl-next-door type."

"Oh my god, that's so me," I said.

"Totally," Jen said.

"Ugh, why hasn't he emailed me back?" I asked.

"Just email him again," she said. "It's not like you have anything to lose."

"True," I said. Jen was also single. We were two of the only ones left. All our other high school friends were in serious relationships or married. Some even had kids already. We kept positive about it as we both knew that being married and having kids was not the be all to end all. Plus we were still so young as Jen always said.

"Look at Courtney Cox having a baby at forty, and she's beautiful." True at that.

"I can't believe I'm going to live in such extravagance," I said. "The hotel is stunning. Don't you think?" I had looked it up online.

"To say the least," Jen said. I heard her flipping through the magazine.

"You should really buy this magazine. It's very informative. This is stuff you'll need to know," she said.

"I guess, but—"

"Quick tip," said Jen, "nude lips are very in. Also, make sure you buy an eyelash curler before you leave on Friday."

"Okay," I said. "I will."

I lay in bed that night feeling nervous for the trip. Although this was going to be an exciting, once in a lifetime experience, I had a feeling that the journey ahead of me was bound to be filled with unexpected complications.

CHAPTER 5

"Excuse me, Miss? Would you like some Clodhoppers?"

I stared blankly at the stewardess. What in the world was she talking about? She registered my confusion. "Clodhoppers. Would you like some?" I began to sweat. I had no idea what she was offering me.

"Uh, thank you. That would be divine," I said. She rolled her eyes, tossed a pack of candy onto my tray, and offered them to the passenger across the aisle.

"Excuse me Sir, would you like some Clodhoppers?"

"No thank you, dear. I'm on Atkins. I've lost thirty pounds so far. No sense in ruining my streak with some candy." He threw me a triumphant smile.

Had I just failed my initiation into first-class seating? I examined the candy. Just a bag of milk chocolate covered graham crackers. Big deal, they were s'mores. When I was a kid, I went to summer camp for a few summers, and I had enough s'mores to last a lifetime. I put the Clodhoppers down; they weren't worth the calories.

I wondered if anyone else sitting in first class sensed that I didn't belong here.

Whatever the case, there was no one who could drag me away from the plush, luxurious seats that reclined almost as flat as a bed. I had as many pillows as I needed too, and they weren't like the flat ones in coach. These were big, fluffy marshmallows.

Hmm. Marshmallows. My thoughts wandered to chocolate. Followed by graham crackers. I soon ripped open the Clodhoppers and popped some in my mouth. Calories? Maybe I needed the energy. After all; Maddy was a handful.

The plane took off smoothly. I gazed out the window as Chicago slipped further away. It was nice to not be sitting on a wing, or at the very back, where I usually sat. It was unfortunate the flight was only an hour because I would have liked to enjoy my surroundings longer.

Once we were in the air, I reached into my carry-on and pulled out the confidentiality contract Mrs. Malone had faxed to my office yesterday. It pertained to the safety and welfare of Maddy. I called her after reading it over, to discuss some questionable clauses.

"*… while under employment, the employee will not have any plastic surgery done or go to any consultation appointments. This includes lip collagen and Botox.*"

"You see," Mrs. Malone explained, "sometimes the people that we hire get caught up in LA life. One girl we hired went and got lip injections when she was supposed to be at a very important lunch with Maddy."

"*The employee will not attempt to steal any design, fashion, or script idea from Maddy, nor will he/she go for any of the guys that Maddy is interested in.*"

"That clause was added in strictly because of you," she said. "Maddy told me if you did more with yourself you could be attractive."

"Um, thank you?" I said.

"I foresee that as being a slight problem," she said.

"I'm sure Maddy and I wouldn't be interested in the same guys," I said, trying to make light of it.

"We take this contract very seriously," Mrs. Malone explained.

"I'll try and keep my hands off Maddy's men," I said.

When I showed Jake the contract, he burst out laughing.

"There are no names on this," he had said. "Not yours, not Maddy's. None! It's the most generic and non-descript contract I've ever seen. This means nothing. It's garbage. Something Maddy's mother whipped up as an after thought. Don't worry about it." So I didn't. Plus I didn't feel much need to complain when I was thrilled to be making twelve-hundred dollars a week.

"Miss, may I take your breakfast order?" the stewardess asked. I didn't know they'd be serving breakfast on such a short flight, but was glad since the Clodhoppers hadn't curbed the hunger.

"Sure. I'd like an order of two eggs over-easy, a side of bacon extra crispy, and rye toast unbuttered," I said. She looked at me in disbelief.

"Would you like a croissant or a muffin?" she asked. I sunk a little lower in my seat.

"I'll have a croissant," I said. The stewardess nodded and checked off croissant on her memo pad, then moved on to the Atkins dieter.

"No thank you. Carbs are a big no-no," he said. He looked at me and smirked. I didn't care about his Atkins diet. It was very high in cholesterol and not good for the heart. Plus, Dr. Atkins was no longer alive. So there.

I gazed out the window. The clouds were in clusters below the airplane, drifting slowly in the wind. The sun's rays shone through them, warming the earth below. I sat back and relaxed. They should have personal manicurists, I thought, as I drifted off to sleep.

Before I knew it, I was making my way through JFK International. I exited the gate and noticed a woman, wearing dark sunglasses, holding a sign with my name written across it.

"Hi! That's me," I said, wondering if many people had come through the gates before me and read the sign. Maybe they were still lurking around the area to check out what kind of 'very important person' this Grace Daniels was. Unfortunately, they'd probably be disappointed. I didn't look like a star. I regretted not buying a new pair of rimless tinted sunglasses so that I could have pretended to be one.

"YOU'RE Miss Daniels?" she asked, looking at me up and down. Who had she been expecting? A brief wave of insecurity shot through my mind. Was it my outfit? Had I dressed inappropriately for what one would believe a guardian to be dressed as? Maybe I'd made the wrong choice when choosing my Juicy Couture velour sweat suit. Perhaps it had been idiotic to go with a monochromatic look rather than mix and match. It had been a last-minute purchase from the Old Orchard Shopping Center. I'd gone up to Highland Park to say goodbye to my family and had stopped in at one of the shops. I had to beg the saleslady to keep the place open five minutes past closing time while I grabbed all the hoodies and pants I could find in my size. When I'd arrived at my parents' house and tried them on, I felt that I had made some unconventional choices.

"Are you sure they're still in?" I had asked Jen.

"Totally," she answered. "Plus, they're on sale now." Jen and I loved a sale. We were notorious for searching through racks, bins, or wherever else we could find designer duds at half price.

"I really don't belong in Hollywood," I'd said.

"Well, don't let anyone think that!" she exclaimed.

So, I'd bought them and wore them on the plane. And now I stood in front of a woman who doubted some unknown aspect of my being, or perhaps even my identity.

"I'm not sure how this works. Do you need to see my ID?" I asked.

"Oh, no, no," she laughed. "I was just expecting someone much older than you. You look young enough to be Miss Malone's sister." I was relieved that the issue was not my velour.

We walked to the baggage claim and waited for my suitcase to come down on the conveyor. I suddenly noticed it passing me and reached for it, but missed. Would we be waiting another twenty minutes for it to come around again? Fortunately, a man a little ways down from me grabbed it.

"Thank you so much," I said, as he pushed it over.

"Sure," he said.

I rolled my bag to where the woman awaited me. She looked at her watch so I picked up the pace. I didn't want her to be late for whatever she had to do next.

"Here, allow me to take that for you," she said. "Wow! This sure is a big suitcase."

"Sorry, it's pretty heavy," I said. "I'll be here in the city overnight and then I'm flying off to L.A. with Maddy, and then ..." I trailed off when I noticed she wasn't interested in what I had to say. She walked ahead of me, bag in tow. The colored strings I'd attached to the handle flapped in the wind as the bag rolled along.

"The car should be right out here," said the woman. We stopped outside the airport exit doors. I realized this lady would not be driving me to the hotel. She was a 'transitional' woman to get me from the plane to the car.

I zipped my jacket up. I should have brought a warmer one, like my cute black bomber jacket, but I hadn't thought it went well with what I was wearing. At least I would only have to endure the cold January air of New York City for a day. Once we arrived in LA the sun would be shining and I hoped I wouldn't need to wear a jacket very often, if at all.

A large black Mercedes pulled up in front of us.

"Here you go," the woman said. She opened the door for me and I realized how rude I must have seemed that I hadn't even asked for her name. I'd been so consumed with my thoughts, and now our time was coming to an end.

"I feel terrible that I didn't catch your name," I said. She looked at me oddly.

"It's Elsa," she said. I smiled.

"It's been a pleasure working with you, Elsa," I said. She smiled back and we stood there for a moment. Suddenly, I wondered if I was supposed to tip her. I didn't know the proper etiquette involved here. I always tipped cab drivers a couple of dollars, and my hairdresser at least seven or eight. But how much was one supposed to tip the woman who holds the sign with your name and rolls your suitcase to the car outside the airport? I handed her a ten-dollar bill and prayed it would be enough.

"Oh, don't worry about it," she said. She gently pushed the money away. "Everything has been taken care of by the 'superpowers,' if you know what I mean. Thank you for the kind gesture, though."

I got into the car and she shut the door behind me.

"Have fun," she said as she stepped away. As the driver put the car into reverse, I realized I hadn't even said thank you.

I rolled down the window and screamed her name as she walked off.

"WAIT!" The driver slammed on the breaks and Elsa turned, startled.

"Is everything okay, Miss Daniels?" she asked.

"I wanted to thank you for the lovely walk to the car," I said. She looked at me strangely for a second, and then a smile lit up her face.

"It was my pleasure. You have a wonderful trip, and take care of yourself," she said. I waved and rolled up the window.

"Okay, I'm ready now," I said to the driver. "Sorry about that."

"Great," he said. "My name is James. We'll be going straight to the Jacques Hotel. Please help yourself to a bottle of water, if you so desire." He indicated cup holders that held two bottles of some very exotic looking water.

"Thank you, James," I said. Wow. I had my very own 'James the Driver.' I played out the scenarios in my head. "Home, James," I might say, or, "James, please kindly see to it that our guests' champagne glasses are filled."

It was quite amazing, really. My own personal chauffeur, James, was now whisking me off to The Jacques Hotel in New York City. *I think I'm gonna like it here.*

CHAPTER 6

Everything at The Jacques Hotel seemed to approach new heights of understated luxury. The bellboy accompanied me to the top floor, where the room I'd be sharing with Maddy was located. The elevator was mirrored and classical music played softly.

"Having a nice day?" I asked the bellboy.

"Not bad, Miss," he said.

"I like your hat," I said. He gave me a funny look and turned his head slightly askew. No one had informed me of an unwritten rule against small talk.

The elevator opened and the bellboy led me to the suite. He opened the door with a magnetic key and walked in. He sauntered straight over to draw the blinds open on the floor-to-ceiling windows that lined the room, overlooking Central Park. He gave me a few standard instructions and as he left I gave him a three dollar tip. I figured there was no way that could have already been taken care of by the 'superpowers.'

"Thank you, Miss, and I do hope you will enjoy your stay at The Jacques Hotel," he said.

"I intend to, thank you," I said. The door shut behind him and I stood in the middle of the room gazing around. Maddy really knew how to live it up. This place was gorgeous. I looked around and identified the wall colors from the Ralph Lauren Thoroughbred Collection: Chimayo Red with Cottonwood white trim. The sofas were dark brown chenille, and the rest of the wooden furniture had a dark cherry finish. A very nice look, though I would have done the walls lighter so when sunshine poured through the windows, the room would brighten. And I'd have chosen a lighter stain on the wooden furniture to create more of a contrast with the sofas. A silver Tiffany clock sat on an end table. I checked the time; it was nearly two o'clock. Maddy would be arriving soon. She was currently at the launch of a new cosmetics line at Bloomingdales.

An impressive antique brass-detailed telescope stood by the windows. I peered through, pointing it down toward the scene below and adjusting the lens. Park Avenue was filled with joggers and dog walkers. Across the street, by the park, hot dog vendors lined the sidewalks and horses and carriages traveled along the paths that wound their way through.

I pointed the telescope toward the sky. A few white clouds were gliding in the wind. They seemed to be forming into big apple-like shapes. I stepped away from the telescope and rubbed my eyes. I was beginning to hallucinate and decided I'd better find something else to occupy my time.

I continued nosing around the room. Everything was, how shall I say, fancy. Fancy furniture, fancy lamps, fancy chocolates. Hmm. A little chocolate didn't sound so bad right then. I'd already ruined my diet today with the Clodhoppers on the plane, anyway. I unwrapped the gold paper on one of the chocolates and popped it in my mouth. It melted into a creamy, smooth delight. This was certainly no Mr. Goodbar. I tossed the paper into the wire basket garbage—a very fancy one, of course.

On the shiny wooden antique desk stood the room service menu and some fine pens and sheets of handcrafted paper. I put the paper to good use and wrote my name in bubble letters. Then I sat on the sofa and stroked the chenille as if it were a cat snuggling up to me. I rested my feet on the matching ottoman and as I crossed one leg over the other, I spoke to my imaginary boyfriend, Hunter David.

"Perhaps we should vacation in France this summer, darling. Côte d'Azur, perhaps?"

"Excuse me, Miss?"

I jumped and my heart very nearly stopped. I hadn't heard the maid let herself in to the room. I'd always thought a knock on the door was supposed to come first.

"Oh, hello. I must have been talking in my sleep," I said. She wore the standard-issue maid outfit; that dictated the sexual fantasies of many men. She was holding a pile of linens in her arms.

"I was going to put some extra towels in the salle de bain, and then I'll be out of your way," she said.

While she was in the bathroom, I practiced my lady-like posture in case Oprah asked Maddy and I to dinner. When I grew bored with that I opened a large coffee table book, entitled *New York City*, carefully turning the pages to avoid smudging it with my chocolaty fingers. The maid reappeared.

"I know it's early, but I thought I would take care of the turn down service now. Would that suffice?" she asked.

"That would be great," I said. Maids at the hotels I usually stayed at put a mint on the pillow and turned on a lamp beside the bed and presto—turndown service. I wondered if she would do some extravagant origami folds with the bed sheets. Perhaps turn the pillowcases into swans?

"Have a lovely day," she said, when she returned. I breathed a sigh of relief when she exited without waiting for a gratuity. I hadn't managed tipping into my trip budget.

I darted to the bedroom to see what she'd done. Looked similar to what would be done at a less fancy hotel, except for the chocolate roses on the pillow.

A few moments later I heard chatting just outside the door. It opened and Maddy entered with another girl. She screamed when she saw me, as if surprised, and jumped up and down. Then she hugged me, very nearly squeezing the life right out of me. I hadn't envisioned my reunion with Maddy as being as exciting for her as it was.

"I'm so happy you're here. It's so awesome," she said. "I can't believe it's been a month since I saw you." It had been a month, but now it felt like we'd never parted. "This is Wendy Peltzer. Her father is the great inventor of Peltzer Software," Maddy said. The name meant nothing to me.

"It's nice to meet you," I said, shaking her hand. "Your father has produced great software."

"This room's pretty cool," Wendy said, pushing past me to explore.

"It's a-ight," Maddy said. She turned to me. "We're going to Barneys. I want to get something for the party tonight. You brought something to wear, right?"

"I brought a pair of black pa—" I began.

"Cool," Maddy said, looking elsewhere. "I'm going to change really quick because I don't want to walk out again in the same outfit." Maddy undid the buttons on her shirt and tossed it to the floor, then walked into the bedroom leaving a trail of the rest of her clothes behind her.

"Can you flick on the TV?" she asked when I reached the bedroom. I took the remote off the end table and turned the plasma television on.

"Are you so excited for LA?" she asked.

"Yeah," I said, "I'm really anxious to—"

"I won't lie to you, Grace. I'm not dying to go," Maddy said.

"Oh?" I asked.

"It's so stressful being a celebrity in Hollywood," she said. "I wish I could be a normal teenager."

"Well you could be," I said, handing her one of the chocolate roses. "I mean, if you want to give up all this, which I don't see why you'd want to."

"Nah," she said taking a bite.

Wendy stepped out of the bathroom. She had changed into a pair of too-tight Levi's and a hideous blue cashmere sweater. Maddy laughed so hard she sprayed me with chocolate.

"Gross!" I yelped, jumping back. I grabbed a tissue and started wiping off the cuff of my Juicy.

"Oh my God! I'm so sorry, Grace," Maddy said, still laughing. "I'll buy you a new one." She turned to Wendy in disbelief. "Are you really going to wear that?"

"What's wrong with it?" Wendy asked, looking in the mirror.

"Those jeans are too small," Maddy said. "You're stomach is hanging over them."

"I'm just a little bloated today," Wendy said, with a hurt look on her face.

"I don't even have anything here that will fit you," Maddy said, rummaging through her bag. "Grace, maybe you could let Wendy wear that jacket." She pointed to the jacket that I'd worn on the plane.

"Well I would, but I don't have another-"

"Ok, perfect," Maddy said, snatching up the jacket and giving it to Wendy.

"Thanks, Grace," Wendy said, putting it on.

"No, problem," I said, praying that I wouldn't freeze outside.

"Okay, let me just find a cool top to wear, and then we can go," Maddy said. She took a handful of designer tops out of her bag and threw them to the floor. Then she tried them all on trying to decide which one to wear. She sure was making a big deal of what to wear to go shopping for half an hour. Finally, she gave up and threw on a black long-sleeve shirt.

"I'll just wear this. No biggie. I don't really want people to think that I try so hard," she said.

"You look great," said Wendy excitedly. "Really Maddy, you look great in everything you wear. You totally look like Kate Hudson, just a younger version." Wendy was very impressively sucking up to Maddy and it made me happy because it enabled us to leave faster.

"I guess I sort of see it," Maddy said, trying to look at herself from behind in the full length mirror. "Ok, let's go!"

As we waited for the elevator, Maddy turned to me. "Grace, I left my sunglasses in the room. Could you just go grab them for me?" I rushed back to the room and found them on the table.

"Hurry up!" she called out, "it's here."

I jumped into the elevator as it was about to close and handed Maddy her sunglasses.

"Thanks doll," she said. "Oh can you push 'L'?"

Downstairs, in front of the hotel, a black Escalade awaited us. The driver was a handsome and clean-cut man.

"You can get in the front, Grace," Maddy said. "Wendy and I will sit in the back."

"Hi, I'm Grace," I said to the driver.

"Jay," he said. The girls whispered and giggled in the back. I began to feel tired and I knew we had a long day and night ahead of us. I shut my eyes for a moment. "You okay?" Jay asked.

"A bit sleepy," I said. "I just flew in from Chicago."

"Would you like a Red Bull?" he asked. I had tried Red Bull a few times, usually mixed with vodka.

"That would be great," I said. He took one from the armrest compartment.

"Thanks," I said. I took a few sips of the energy drink and it perked me right up.

"Get used to that," Maddy said. "We'll be living on that stuff in LA."

"You drink Red Bull?" I asked.

"I drink lots of things, Grace," Maddy said with an evil laugh.

"Why in the world do you still need a guardian?" Wendy asked. "You'll be eighteen this year."

"Well I told my parents that I'm almost eighteen and I should be able to go by myself," Maddy explained. "You know, I'd be responsible and shit, but my very sensible mother reminded me that I needed someone there to get me out of bed in the mornings and to tell me how great I look for my photo shoots and stuff."

"Oh brother," Jay whispered.

"She'll learn very quickly that she chose the wrong person to get her out of bed in the morning," I said.

"What Grace?" Maddy asked.

"Just telling Jay how we met," I said.

"So she's not really a guardian," Wendy said, continuing her conversation with Maddy. "More like an assistant." I turned and looked at Maddy. I knew I shouldn't have come on this trip not knowing exactly what my job was. She gave a slight smile.

"No, of course not," Maddy said. "But Grace will be happy to help me if I need it, right Grace?"

"I guess," I said. "I mean with in reaso-"

"Like you'll help me find something fabulous to wear tonight, right?" she asked.

"Of course," I said.

"What's tonight?" Wendy asked.

"Oh, this event I have to go to. It's only for actresses, but they said I could bring Grace with me," said Maddy.

"You promised you'd take me to the next party in New York," Wendy said, angrily. "Who's throwing it?"

"*Sixteen Magazine*," Maddy said.

"Whatever, Maddy. You always show up at those things with at least five people," Wendy said.

"So not true," Maddy said. "And I swear for this one, it's just Grace and I." Wendy turned away from Maddy and faced out the window.

"Don't be like that," Maddy said.

"Whatever," Wendy said, "have fun with your babysitter." Maddy looked shocked, and after that, the girls didn't speak to each other. I looked back and saw them fiddling with their cell phones. Surprisingly, mine began to beep, signaling that I'd received a text message. I retrieved my phone from my purse.

> *Wendy's a total cooz bag.*
> *xox Maddy*

I laughed as the car pulled to a stop in front of Barneys.

"Have fun," Jay said. "Call me when you're ready to leave." I thanked him and we headed in.

The lighting was bright inside, and after I'd downed the Red Bull, a little dizzying.

"We close in half an hour," a saleslady said. The store was starting to empty out.

"Thanks," I said. "We won't be long."

In all my years of coming to New York, both for business and pleasure, I'd never been to Barneys. I was excited to see the place where trends were born and bred.

Maddy browsed at the Diane Von Furstenberg section, searching the racks of new tops. She didn't bother looking at price tags as she began to pile the items in my arms.

A saleswoman approached me and smiled.

"Would you like me to start a room for you?" she asked.

"That would be great," I said. "They're for her." I indicated Maddy, who continued grabbing things while yelling on her cell phone at her mother.

"Mom, I already told Wendy that she can't come, so why would you be able to come?" she said.

I noticed a sale sign over the Theory sale section and inched my way over, pretending to look at the overpriced seasonal racks nearby. For some reason, I felt the need to hide my usually economical shopping behavior from Maddy.

Maddy was still on the phone. "... then call Alison and ask her," Maddy said. "But don't put me in this position."

A few moments later, she appeared next to me, holding up a low-cut black top.

"What do you think?" she asked.

"Nice. Where's the rest of it?" I smiled.

"Don't be a granny, Grace," Maddy laughed. I knew from my experience on the movie set that I'd be much better off telling her what she wanted to hear even if I had to stretch the truth thinner than some of the girls at the gym.

"I think it's cool," I said.

"No, fab is the word," she said.

"It's fab," I said.

"Where's Wendy?" she asked.

"I'm not sure," I said. I hadn't seen her disappear.

"Okay, good. Come with me to try on stuff," Maddy said. She led me to the change rooms. I waited outside the curtain. Moments later she jumped out with the first top on.

"TA DA!" she said. "What do you think? Is it too big? Do I have good cleavage? Come on Grace, you're supposed to be helping me."

The saleslady walked by.

"Wow!" she said. "Very nice."

"I love it," I said. I did actually love it; this one looked great. It was a tiny scrap of material, and somehow it fit her perfectly. She popped back in the room to try some others.

"There you guys are," Wendy said, coming into the change area. "Look what I found." She held up the same top that Maddy had just come out wearing. Maddy poked her head outside.

"I just tried it on, and I'm probably getting it," she said. "Plus, you're way too chubby for it." She went back to trying on her stuff. I saw Wendy's eyes fill with tears and I felt horrible.

"Hey," I said. "Don't listen to her. You're not chubby at all."

"That was so mean," she said, dropping the shirt to the floor. "I hope someone else is wearing it tonight." She gave me an evil smile.

"Don't look at me," I said. "I'm not wasting money on that." Wendy started laughing.

"I know," she said. "It is a piece of garbage. Thanks for trying to make me feel better, Grace," she said. "I know you understand how it feels." I wasn't entirely sure what that meant. I stood in front of the triple-paneled mirror. Did my butt look bigger than usual today? Was it the Clodhoppers?

After Maddy had changed back into her own clothes, she handed me the top she'd be buying and passed me her credit card.

"Here pay for me," Maddy said. "We'll meet you downstairs at the make-up counters," she said.

"That will be two-hundred-and-fifty-four dollars," the saleslady said. I handed her Maddy's credit card. "Is she an actress or something?" she asked.

"Yes," I said, "Maddy Malone. She's been in a few films. She just finished one called *Daisy Mae*."

"I've never heard of her," the saleslady said. "But I could tell by the way she was bossing you around that you were her assistant, so I figured she must be 'someone.'" I was offended.

"I'm actually just—" I began.

"Sorry, I didn't mean to be rude," the lady said. "Believe me, I've seen way worse."

"I'm sure," I said.

I took the escalator downstairs and found Maddy and Wendy at the Stila counter trying on some lip gloss.

"Did you get it?" Maddy asked. I held the bag up for her to take. She pushed it back at me. "You don't mind carrying it, do you doll?" she asked. "It's just so hard for me to carry everything around while talking to my fans." Yes, there were a few fans at the accessories counter, of the electric variety.

"Here, can you pay for this too, and I'll meet you outside," she said. She handed me a tube of lipstick before exiting the store with Wendy.

The saleslady at the counter began to ring in Maddy's lipstick for me. I was infuriated. Maddy was not just treating me like an assistant; she was acting like I was her slave. Her patronizing caught me so off guard that I kept missing my chance to retaliate. I thought of how I could get her back. I picked up a new shade of eye shadow that I'd been meaning to get for a while, and tested it on my hand.

"Could you add this?" I asked, showing the saleslady the shade number. The saleslady obliged.

"Thank you," I said, placing the small box in my purse and Maddy's lipstick in the bag with her new top. Great, I hadn't even been in New York for a full day and I was already a criminal. Jen would be so impressed with how well I was fitting in here.

CHAPTER 7

Maddy and I sat in the limousine on our way to the *Sixteen Magazine* party. After briefing me a dozen times on what I needed to do to assist Maddy at this event, she moved on to obsessing over how she looked.

"You swear I look amazing?" she asked.

"Swear," I answered.

"Would you say that I look more cute, or more sexy?" she asked.

"Definitely sexy," I said.

Maddy's publicist, Alison, had arranged for a make-up artist and a hairstylist to come to the hotel to get Maddy dolled up for the event. The two had worked with some huge stars and Alison explained to Maddy that she should be honored they had agreed to help her out. When we arrived at the Jacques after Barneys, they were waiting for us, and they were angry.

"Sorry we're late," Maddy said, "Grace needed to stop and visit her sick grandfather."

"Oh, sorry," said the makeup artist. "I hope he gets better"

"Thanks. It's been quite difficult," I said, wanting to punch Maddy's lights out for blaming it on me, when the reason we were late was because she decided that she didn't have any shoes to wear tonight, and made us trek all over Soho looking for a pair. In the end she decided to wear a pair she'd brought with her.

Maddy looked quite glamorous after the two women had completed their work. Her hair was curly and shiny, bouncing when she moved her head. Her eyes were made up in smoky colors and her lips were a glossy nude. She wore the black top she'd bought at Barneys, a pair of Seven jeans, and Manolo Blahnik stilettos.

On our way out of our suite, she paused to look me over.

"Grace, do you or do you not want to look hot tonight?" she asked. I'd been too busy making sure she looked hot to be overly concerned with my own appearance. Maddy ran to the bathroom and returned with an old tube of lipstick. The name of the color had been rubbed off on the bottom, but I'm sure it was called "Fuck me red."

"Go put this on. Don't worry, I'll wait for you," she said, halfway out the door. I applied the lipstick and met her at the elevator.

"Perfect," she said. "How do you feel?"

"Like a hooker." I said.

"Perfect," she said.

I sat back and absorbed the beauty of New York City at night. The lights shone into the limousine as the driver cut across Broadway. There were signs for *Rent*, *Mamma Mia!*, and *Wicked*. I wished there was enough time to catch one.

"Have you seen *Rent*?" I asked.

"What do you mean? The play?" Maddy asked. I nodded.

"Of course not. I have way better things to do then watch people living in the slums and singing about it." Of course she did.

She took her compact out of her purse and gazed at herself in the mirror. "Don't forget, this is the first time I've been really important at a red carpet event, so you can't screw up."

"I won't," I smiled.

"It's going to be overwhelming for me," she said. "So don't let me out of your sight."

"Okay," I said.

"So you understand what you're supposed to do?" she asked. Not this again.

"Yes."

"Okay, tell me one more time," she said.

"Get out of the limousine first," I said. "Then let someone know that you've arrived and bring them over to the car. Direct you to the red carpet and meet you on the other side." She nodded.

"And Grace," she said. I awaited her further instructions.

"If my mother gets drunk and loses control, please get her out of there as fast as you can," she said.

"Um, okay," I said. What a sad request. I hoped for Maddy's sake that her mother would behave.

I felt a little nervous about the event. Even though the plan was simple, I really didn't want to mess up and risk Maddy screaming at me in front of a crowd of celebrities.

The ride took longer than I'd expected. There wasn't much traffic heading into the Meat Packing District, but as we approached the club, we got stuck behind the dozens of other limousines, each waiting to deposit their celebrities.

Our limo driver finally pulled up to the red carpet, and a tuxedo-clad man opened the door for me.

"Thank you," I said, stepping out. "I have Maddy Malone in the car."

"Great," he said. "Hello, Miss Malone. Welcome to The Octopus Club." He extended his hand to help her and she stepped out.

I stood on the right side of the ropes along the red carpet. The press was also waiting there, and I watched Nikky Case, Wayne Till, and other teenage stars that I happened to recognize being escorted along it. Maddy looked fantastic as she walked, pausing for photos and questions. She had chains of great designer jewelry that Alison had snagged for her and her blonde hair glowed and shimmered under the lights along the carpet.

"Hey!" someone yelled out to me as I edged down my side of the red carpet. I turned and was stunned to see Hunter David a few steps away. I looked around to make sure he was speaking to me.

"I thought that was you, but I wasn't sure," he said, getting closer. This was not merely a figment of my sometimes very overactive imagination; Hunter David was here at The Octopus Club. He was dressed in a pair of ripped jeans and a faded vintage-style long sleeve blue shirt. I had a feeling the butterflies jumping around my stomach were going to fly out of every crevice of my body. He grabbed me and gave me a huge hug and I felt his muscles press against my body. I almost fainted.

"I emailed you back this morning to say that I'd be here too," he said. "Did you get it?" I shook my head.

"I didn't even check today," I said.

"Well we're here together now and you look amazing," he said, putting his arm around me. Maybe the red lipstick was working. Or my outfit, perhaps? I had a pair of black pants on, and my white sleeveless top showed just a hint of cleavage. My Steve Madden three-inch heels hurt my feet, but I liked to look as tall as possible.

"This is such a nice surprise," I said, stumbling on my words.

"They flew me in so that Maddy's love interest from the movie would be at the same party," Hunter said. "They thought it would be good for publicity. Not that she'll talk to me here. Too many bigger stars around."

"Yes," I laughed. "How can you compete with the kids from *Degrassi* and *High School Musical*?" Hunter laughed and asked me to wait a moment while he went to tell his publicist he was here. I watched as he approached a shorter blonde woman who was brushing something off the dress of another teen queen. He spoke with her and pointed toward me. The woman nodded her head and waved Hunter off. This had to be my reward for putting up with Maddy's abuse all day. But, I'd be her slave the way Princess Leia served Jabba the Hutt, if it meant Hunter would be mine.

"When do you leave for LA?" Hunter asked.

"Tomorrow morning."

"Cool," he said. "I'll be back there on the weekend. We'll definitely hook up." I thought I was going to burst. This was the best night of my life.

I watched as Maddy made her way to the end of the red carpet.

"Maddy, Maddy ... over here ... a smile Maddy, give us a smile," the paparazzi were still hounding her. She finally reached us.

"God, how annoying," she said, exasperated. "How did I look?"

"Great!" I said.

"I know! Have you seen my mother yet?" she asked. I shook my head.

"I'm not sure if I would know who she is," I said.

"Oh, right. You've never met. Oh, hi," she said, when she noticed Hunter. Even if she thought he wasn't an important enough star for her to hang out with, for me he was a genuinely great guy.

"Hey," he said. "How are—"

She quickly pushed her vintage Gucci purse into my stomach. "Guard it with your life. It cost me a fucking fortune," she said.

"No, why don't you just take it with—"

"It's too much for me to keep track of with everything going on, Grace. Please," she begged.

"Sure," I said, taking it.

"See you inside. I'm going to find the Olsens," she said, disappearing through the massive glass doors.

"She's a hurricane," Hunter said.

"I know," I nodded. "She does things so quickly, that I don't get a chance to respond."

"Don't worry about it," he said. "You'll catch on. Now let's go inside and get some drinks into us."

"Do you think I should drink if I'm supposed to be watching Maddy?" I asked.

"Honey," Hunter said. "The rules are different around here." He took me by the arm and escorted me inside. I could barely believe that Hunter didn't have a sexy blonde hanging off him. I wasn't sure why he was being so nice to me, but instead of wracking my brain about it, I decided to live out my Cinderella story for the evening.

Inside, the event was packed. Flashbulbs went off everywhere, and dozens of wait staff buzzed around with trays of hors d'oeuvres, each appetizer a tiny masterpiece of food design. I barely recognized any of them. As far as I could tell no pigs-in-a-blanket.

Hunter marched to the bar with me in tow and I quickly scanned the room for Maddy. I noticed her chatting with a few other girls her age, and was relieved that she was staying out of trouble. Hunter ordered a Cosmopolitan for me and a gin and tonic for himself.

"Cheers," he said, raising his glass. I was so excited that I downed my drink and was ready for another soon after. I was feeling more relaxed than I had when I'd first stepped out of the limousine. After the second drink, I decided that I should pace myself. The last thing I'd need tomorrow morning was to get on the plane entirely hung over.

I spotted Maddy across the room talking with a familiar-looking rap star. She drank from a mini-champagne bottle. She caught my eye and raised her drink to me. I smiled and raised mine.

"No drinking age at these Hollywood parties?" I asked Hunter.

"Well, that depends who you are," he said.

"If you're Maddy Malone?" I asked.

"Ah, Maddy Malone," he said. He rubbed his chin in faux deep thought. "I do believe if you are Maddy Malone there is no drinking age—anywhere."

"Great," I said. "Well, I was doing the same thing at her age. I can only hope that she's smart about it." Hunter laughed so hard, some of his drink came drizzling out of his mouth.

A blonde woman in a black bustier and leather pants approached Hunter and me.

"Uh-oh," Hunter said under his breath.

"Baby," the woman said. "Look how cute you look."

"Hi," Hunter smiled. She gave him a fondling hug, clutching her Louis purse under her arm.

"How's my handsome guy doing?" she asked.

"Great," he said. "This is Grace."

The woman processed my name in her head.

"Oh my God, Grace! It's so great to meet you." She shook my hand so hard I thought she'd pull my arm out of its socket. I was convinced she thought I was someone else. The alcohol must have been interfering with her vision.

"Are you having fun, sweetie?" she asked.

"Yes, a lovely time," I said, finally freeing my hand from her pincer-like grip.

"I really have been dying to meet you," she said. "I've heard so many great things." It dawned on me. She was none other than Maddy's mother, Mrs. Malone.

"Have you seen Maddy yet?" I asked. "She looks beautiful."

"What's that?" she asked. She appeared slightly baffled.

"Maddy," I said. "Have you seen her?"

"Oh, yes, yes. She looks lovely," she said. "Don't tell her that I've been drinking. I don't want to embarrass her."

"Mum's the word," I said.

"Literally," Hunter smiled.

"Is Mr. Malone here with you?" I asked. She laughed.

"Are you kidding me? I came here to have fun," she said. Mrs. Malone rushed off to the bar to get another drink and soon returned with a tray of seven shots.

"Drink up kids," she said. Hunter and I stared at each other, neither one of us knowing quite how to react.

"I'm okay for now. Thank you, though," I said.

"Are you kidding?" she asked. "You're taking care of Maddy for three weeks, and you're not going to drink?" I smiled. She could have been joking, but I didn't think so. Hunter took a shot and sucked it back. "That a boy," she said.

"Cheers," he said.

"You are hot!" Mrs. Malone said. Hunter smiled sheepishly.

"Oh, is that Jenny over there?" she asked, pointing. "I'll be right back." She ran to a girl who she believed to be J. Lo, though it clearly wasn't her.

"I can't believe it," I said.

"I know. The woman is a trip," Hunter said, shaking his head.

"She was coming on to you," I said.

Hunter nodded. "This is the second time I've met her," he said. "Last time she was worse."

"I can't believe it," I laughed.

"Brace yourself," Hunter said. "Here she comes again." Mrs. Malone smacked right into me, knocking Maddy's vintage Gucci out of my hands. I tried to catch it before it hit the ground, but it was too late.

"Shit," I said, picking up the wet purse. I scanned the room to see if Maddy might have seen this, but I couldn't see her.

"Is it okay?" Hunter asked. Mrs. Malone hung onto Hunter's arm.

"I don't know," I said, wiping it off with the back of my hand.

Just then, Maddy approached us, seeming quite blitzed herself. I doubted she'd notice the full extent of her mom's intoxication.

"Hi, honey," said Mrs. Malone. "Are you having a tood gime?"

"What?" Hunter, Maddy, and I asked.

"Oops," she laughed. "I meant, are you having a good time?"

Maddy looked at her mom in disgust. "How much have you had to drink?"

"Not that much," her mom said. "I finally met our girl, Grace. She's great."

"I know," Maddy said. I suddenly felt as though I wasn't currently in their presence; perhaps I had momentarily become a phantom of sorts.

"Introduce me to some of your other friends," Mrs. Malone said to Maddy. "Let them know how cool I am and how we're best friends." Maddy and her mother walked off together, arm in arm, leaving Hunter and I behind.

"There's no worse relationship than a mother and daughter that are best friends," I said. I watched as Maddy introduced her drunken mother to some other teen divas.

"A recipe for disaster," Hunter agreed.

I decided that I'd better tag along with the Malones for the rest of the evening's festivities, given that I was supposed to be working. I gave Hunter a hug goodbye and a kiss on the cheek and told him I'd see him in LA. Then I went to chase after Dumb and Dumber, realizing that, much more than anything I'd experienced back at Silver Rod's Gym, ahead of me lay what could be the most strenuous workout of my life.

CHAPTER 8

"Flight attendants, please prepare for arrival. We will be landing in ten minutes." I looked out the window at the tops of the palm trees and the blue swimming pools below us and let out a sigh of relief to have made it to LA in one piece.

After last night's soiree, getting up in the morning hadn't been easy for either one of us.

"Call and see if we can get on a later flight," Maddy had said drowsily. I looked over the schedule that was sitting on the night stand.

"According to the itinerary, you need to be in LA by this afternoon," I said.

"Fuck!" she screamed. She sat up. "I'm so tired, I'm so nauseous. My life sucks. I hate it. I just want to be normal." I was too busy rushing around the rooms, gathering all of our stuff together to pay her moans much attention.

"Thank me for making you go to bed in your travel clothes," I called from the closet. "You got an extra hour of sleep."

"Thank you, my savior" Maddy said, seeping sarcasm. "My head hurts." I got her some Advil and a glass of water.

"Here," I said. "Take these and let's get moving."

"Is this the strongest you have?" she asked.

"Yes."

"You're so mean," Maddy said. "Don't you feel bad for me at all?"

"I do," I said, putting on my most sympathetic expression. "But don't you feel even worse for me? Now put a motor on it." Really, what I had achieved this particular morning—waking up early—was quite an extraordinary personal accomplishment for me. Usually, I'd be behaving like Maddy, having a tantrum about having to face the day. However, since I was being paid to make sure she got on that flight, I had no choice but to pretend I could cope with the morning.

As our plane descended Maddy undid her seatbelt.

"Excuse me, Miss Malone," said a stewardess passing by. "Please leave your seat belt on until the plane has come to a full stop."

Maddy ignored her and continued reading the latest issue of *People*.

"Fucking Chelsea Tate," she said, ripping out a page of the magazine.

"Why do you hate her so much?" I asked. Maddy looked up at me and glared.

"Are you having a brain malfunction?" she asked.

"Huh?" I said.

"You really don't know?" Maddy asked.

"No," I said. "Honestly."

"I hate her because she won't stop ruining my life," Maddy explained. "She finds out where I'm going to be and shows up. She finds out what scripts I'm negotiating, and she goes in for the same part. Oh and get this, I said in an interview how I had pre-ordered the new Chanel bag, and the next thing I know she's wearing it at a movie premier. Dumb bitch."

"Sounds like jealousy," I said.

"You've got that right," Maddy said. "Chelsea Tate wants to be me so badly it's killing her." Actually, I had meant that the jealousy was more on Maddy's part. Chelsea Tate was the biggest and most successful young movie star since Drew Barrymore. I decided to leave that part out.

Maddy grabbed her lip salve from her bag and started applying it.

"You want to know what really sucks?" Maddy said.

"Of course," I answered.

"Well, all the bouncers in LA will recognize me and so my fake ID probably isn't going to work. And just when I finally had Larissa Pellucio's driver's license memorized perfectly."

"So what time is your curfew when you're at home?" I asked. "I'd like to set a similar one for LA." Maddy burst out laughing.

"You're kidding right?" she asked.

"Well, um, no," I said.

"Oh my God, Grace," Maddy said. "You are super cute." I realized at the party last night that Maddy would probably want to spend some time partying in LA, which was understandable considering her age. However, I just didn't want it to get out of control. Now that she told me that she would probably have trouble getting in to clubs because of the bouncers, I felt reassured.

The seatbelt signs went off and the plane came to a stop at the gate.

"You are now able to move freely about the cabin," the stewardess said.

"Grace," Maddy said. "As soon as we get off the plane, call the hotel and make sure we have the two-bedroom suite at The Springs. Even though I always stay in the same room, they sometimes give me trouble with it."

I nodded as I picked up all the magazines Maddy had thrown to the floor.

"Do you have the phone number?" I asked, trying to enjoy my last few moments in first class.

"Can't you call information and get it?" she asked.

"I could, but you must have it in your phone," I said.

"I can't exactly get to it right now," Maddy said, adjusting her earring.

"I just saw you put your phone in your pocket," I said. "Why should I pay 411, if you have it anyway?"

"Boy," Maddy said, pulling her Sidekick out. "Are you ever cheap."

"It's not about being cheap," I said. "It'll be much quicker if you get it for me while we're waiting to get off the plane." Maddy shrugged and retrieved the number. She read out the digits rapid-fire and closed her Sidekick before I'd had a chance to write it down.

"Slow down, I didn't get it," I said.

"Oh, Grace. You've gotta work quicker than that," she said. She flipped it open again and repeated the numbers even faster this time. I barely got them.

"See. You should have just called information," she laughed. "It would have been faster." I was not enjoying this childish game.

I dialed as we headed toward the baggage claim.

"Hi, this is Grace Daniels calling for Maddy Malone," I said.

"For whom?" the hotel clerk replied.

"Maddy Malone," I said louder.

"Okay," she said, with hesitation. "What can I do for you?"

"Maddy and I are our way to the hotel," I explained, "and I'd like to confirm that her usual room will be ready."

"And, which usual room would that be?" she asked.

"It's a connecting two-bedroom suite," I said.

"Hmm," she said. "Let me check that for you." A sultry, recorded voice played on the line while I waited, listing all the amenities of the hotel. The large outdoor pool and spa sounded fabulous. Hopefully I'd be able to take full advantage.

"Well?" Maddy asked.

"I'm on hold. Why don't you go watch for our bags," I said, pointing to the few that were coming around on the conveyor belt. She didn't budge. A few moments later the hotel clerk returned.

"Hello, Miss Daniels. Sorry for making you wait," she said, "but we have no record of a usual room for Miss Malone. We have you booked in the one-bedroom junior suite."

"Uh-oh," I said.

"What?" Maddy asked.

"We're booked in a one-bedroom suite," I mouthed. Maddy's face turned red with rage.

"What? No fuckin' way!" She seemed about ready to actually stamp her feet. "Tell them that I want the room that I always get. And Grace! Stop being so nice on the phone!" It was hard to believe Maddy was yelling at me when she knew I was doing all I could to accommodate her. I would have been more than happy to sleep in the lobby of The Springs let alone the luxury of a junior suite.

"Hi," I said back into the phone. "Maddy insists that she always stays in the two-bedroom suite, and she'd really appreciate if you could make that room available for us," I said. Maddy glared at me as I continued. "Maybe you could recheck your files?"

"I'll see what I can do, Miss Daniels. But I can guarantee you that I'll have the same answer for you," she said.

"Right. I'll hold," I said. I prayed the girl would come back and apologize for overlooking our reservation.

"Sorry," she said, upon her return.

"Is there any way we could be upgraded?" I asked.

"Oh for fuck's sake! Jesus Christ!" Maddy screamed. People in the airport turned and looked to see who was causing such an awful racket. Maddy violently pulled her cell phone from her purse and dialed a number.

"Sorry, Miss Daniels. There's nothing we can do until after Sunday. It's the Golden Globe Awards this weekend and the big rooms are reserved for people like Tom Cruise." I thanked her anyway, and hung up, turning my attention to Maddy, who was swearing at her agent on the other end of her phone call.

"Do you think I give a fuck, Marty? This is ridiculous. Every time I come to LA it's the same story. I want something done about it TODAY!" She slammed her phone shut.

"Maddy, don't worry. We'll work something out," I said.

"Shut up!" she yelled. "If you weren't so fuckin' courteous, maybe things would get done." Maddy stormed off. I stood in shock for a moment and could almost make out the trail of fire she left behind. Had I just been bawled out for being courteous? Was that declared a new crime? I knew five-year-olds that could have handled this situation more maturely than Maddy. I noticed the security cameras above and wondered if they had captured Maddy's tantrums. They would be very entertaining for a strung-out, caffeine-buzzed security guard at three in the morning.

For a split second I considered turning and walking back into the airport to get the next flight home, but reminded myself of the positives about this trip to offset one huge, gigantic negative.

I shook off Maddy's outburst and went to grab our bags. It wasn't hard to find them since they were the only two going round and round on the belt. I heaved them off and got ready to roll them along, but stopped short in my tracks when I realized that Maddy's bags didn't have wheels. Surprisingly, to me, Louis Vuitton had plum forgotten to put wheels on his bags. I made a mental note to myself: If I were to ever spend three thousand dollars on luggage, check for wheels. I slowly heaved and rolled our bags toward the terminal exit, where Maddy had gone off to. She was leaning against a pole under the US Air arrivals sign, smoking.

"Grace, don't drag them!" Maddy called out, when she saw me approaching. "You'll ruin the bottoms. They're vintage!" I tried lifting them a little, but they wouldn't budge. Fuck vintage, I thought.

"Do you need help?" she added as an afterthought. I shook my head 'no.'

"No, for the four more steps I need to take to reach you, I think I can manage," I said.

"Oh, okay then,'" she said, puffing away. "If you say so."

"Do you think you could possibly refrain from any more of your demonic freak outs?" I asked, calmly, when I made it over to her. She gave it a moment's thought.

"I'm sorry," Maddy said, "It's just that things don't ever go right for me. I'm just trying to lead a normal life, and shit always happens."

Maddy had a slightly warped idea of what a 'normal' life was. Someone might like to let her know that a 'normal' seventeen-year-old doesn't stay in a two-bedroom suite at The Springs, or even a one-bedroom junior. She'd be horrified to learn of some of the grungy hostels I'd stayed in while backpacking Europe.

"How about I deal with the room when we get to the hotel?" I suggested.

"Yeah all right," Maddy said, throwing her cigarette to the ground.

"Hi, are you Maddy Malone?" a woman, who was coming towards us, asked.

"Ugh, I don't feel like dealing with fans right now," Maddy mumbled, hiding behind me. I knew I'd better break it to this woman gently that this wasn't an opportune time for an autograph.

"Yes, but actually, she's really not—"

"Your driver is looking for you. He's over there," she said, pointing towards a Town Car.

"Oh, thank you," I said, feeling foolish. I handed Maddy her bag and we walked towards the car.

"Hi," the driver said. "Let me help you with those."

"Thank you," I said. Maddy was already in the car.

On our way to the hotel, Maddy instructed the driver to pull into The Hills, Rental Cars because after the hotel mix-up, she wanted to make sure that we would at least be getting the car that she wanted. The driver dropped us off at the front door. "That's okay," Maddy told him. "You don't have to wait." He looked to me for an affirmation.

"I think you better wait," I said. "Just in case something goes wrong, we don't want to get stranded. We'll just be a few minutes." The driver nodded and pulled into a parking spot.

As we approached the counter, I discerned a look of agitation on a couple of the clerks' faces at the sight of Maddy and wondered what ordeal she'd caused before.

"Hi, we're here to pick up the GMC Yukon," Maddy said to Chad, an agent behind the counter.

"Sure, and you are whom?" he asked. Maddy's mouth opened in disbelief. He must have been new to the place.

"What do you mean who am I?" she asked. She leaned closer to him to whisper. "I'm Maddy Malone."

"Okay then," he said, without so much as flinching. "Let me look that up in the computer here."

"It might be under my name," I said. "Grace Daniels. I'm the driver." Maddy stuck her tongue out at me.

"Give me a second," Chad said. He disappeared into the back returned a few moments later. "I found your reservation. We have you booked for a Mercedes C240."

"What? No way," Maddy said. "We're not taking it." Had my ears deceived me? Had Maddy just said no to Mercedes and yes to a GMC?

"Well um, this is what Piranha Films has booked for you," said Chad.

"You're wrong," Maddy said. "I have to have the Yukon. I always get the Yukon." There seemed to be many things that Maddy "always" got.

"Okay, well maybe it's a mistake, let me get the manager," he said.

Without waiting for the manager to rectify the problem, Maddy quickly grabbed her phone from her bag and called Marty. I understood exactly what the poor guy must go through with Maddy, but, because he was with one of the biggest talent agents in Hollywood and had some very distinguished clients, he must have seen great potential to have signed her on.

Once Maddy had him on the line, she walked to the window to have some privacy. Though, it didn't do much to muffle her screaming.

"You listen to me, Marty. I do every fucking thing you want me to do. You are making so much fucking money off of me, it's sick. One lousy reservation for the car I want, and they can't even get that right? It's your goddamn job to make it right. And I am not doing one magazine cover, or one interview, or anything, until I have the fucking car I want!"

She paused while Marty responded. Even at the age of 27, my mother would wash my mouth out with soap if she heard me talking to another human being like this—let alone an adult. I was flabbergasted that Maddy could get away with it.

"Okay, one second," Maddy said. She walked back towards us. "He wants to speak to you," she called out to Chad who was in another room, talking to a woman with glasses. He returned quickly and Maddy handed him the phone.

We heard a few "mm-hmms" mixed with a handful of "I sees." Finally, Chad said, "No problem then. If you could just give me your credit card number and we'll arrange for a black Yukon."

When I couldn't take it anymore, I turned to Maddy and asked the question.

"Why on God's earth would you rather have a Yukon than a Mercedes?"

"Because of OnStar, duh," she said. I stared at her stupefied. "What? You don't know what it is?" I shook my head. "You'll see. Anyway, Marty's going to put it on his credit card and get Piranha to reimburse him. Don't worry, Grace, it's not your fault." Well of course not.

"So, um, a GMC costs more to rent than a Mercedes?" I asked.

"Oh my God, Grace. Sorry to disappoint you but a Mercedes isn't the best car in the world you know," she replied. Apparently.

Chad hung up and filled out some paper work. "Now, I just need you to sign for insurance," he said to me.

"Okay, great," I said, signing on the line.

"Well here you go," he said handing me the keys to the car. Maddy tried to snatch them away.

"Uh-uh-uh," he said. "The keys go to the driver, Miss Daniels." Maddy grunted, as I took the keys out of Chad's hands.

"Fine, but can you make sure you use my name for OnStar?" Maddy asked.

"Oh, sure. I'll hook it up right away," Chad said. "The car's outside, on the left." I looked out the window and saw the black, sparkling monstrosity.

"Wow," I said.

"I know," Maddy said excitedly. "Isn't it totally pimping?" I nodded. It was hard to tell from the outside, but I speculated that the interior was filled with cutting edge high-tech gadgets and dozens of well-appointed accoutrements, and of course the mysterious OnStar. I did wonder how I'd manoeuvre the thing. I'd always had a fear of driving large SUVs, and had about three minutes to get over that phobia.

"Grace, I left my purse on the table," Maddy said from the doorway. I grabbed it for her and thanked Chad then headed out toward the car.

"Do you have your license?" I asked when I'd caught up to her.

"Basically," Maddy said.

"What does that mean?" I asked.

"It means that I can drive the car as long as there's someone else in it that has their license," she said.

"Oh, I get it," I said. "So you don't have your license."

"Whatever, Miss Goody Two Shoe," she said. "I always drive in LA."

I stopped to tell our airport driver that everything was under control and we'd follow him to the hotel.

We got into the Yukon, slid our sunglasses on and I ordered Maddy to fasten her seatbelt.

"Yes, MOTHER," she said, meaning it as an insult—which was exactly how I took it. I started the car and the engine purred like a kitten. A loud kitten.

"Grace, get ready to be blown away," Maddy said. She reached above the rearview mirror and pressed a button. The OnStar button.

"You are connecting to OnStar," a computerized voice said. Maddy opened the sunroof as we waited for instructions.

"Welcome to OnStar," a live voice said over a speaker. "This is Betty, How can I help you Miss. Malone?"

"Yes!" Maddy squealed before continuing. "Hi, can you tell me where I am right now?"

"I'd be happy to, Miss Malone," Betty said. "Right now you are driving east on Santa Monica."

"Okay," Maddy said.

"Will that be all?" Betty asked.

"No," Maddy said. "Could you run a diagnostic on my car?"

"Sure, I will make sure everything is running okay on your car. Please hold the line for one minute," said Betty.

"Okey, dokey," said Maddy. She turned to me and shook my arm. "How awesome?"

"I'm speechless," I said, still perplexed over why this was the car of choice.

"I know," she said. "It only comes in GMC cars."

"Hello Miss Malone," Betty said, now back on the line. "I've done a complete check on your car and everything is running very well."

"Thank you so much," Maddy said. "That will be all."

"Okay, you have yourself a lovely day," said Betty. Maddy pushed the button and hung up.

"That's not all it does," Maddy said. "It's a whole navigation system, and you can hook your phone into it and dial hands-free. Plus they act as information. You know as in 4-1-1? The number you were too cheap to call before?"

"Whatever," I said.

"Well?" she asked.

"Well what?"

"Well, now do you understand why I had to have this car?" she asked.

"Yes, I see it," I said. I would have much rather have had the smaller Mercedes.

As we continued driving, Maddy retrieved a CD from her purse and popped it into the stereo, cranking up the volume and nearly blasting me out of my seat.

"What is this?" I shouted over the music. She couldn't hear me and was busy bopping along to the racket. I turned down the volume.

"What is this?" I asked again.

"Nickelback," she said. She turned up the volume. I turned it down again.

"It's too loud," I said.

"It's supposed to be," Maddy laughed. She turned it back up. I knew this would be a battle I wouldn't win. I'd turn it down; she'd turn it up, and so on, ad nauseam. I hoped we'd arrive at the hotel shortly.

She took her cell phone out and began to call everyone she knew in LA, gabbing and squealing with her friends. I tried to concentrate on the roads, though it was difficult with Miss Gossip beside me.

"Like, no way. She's dating him? That's so crazy," Maddy said on the phone.

I got caught at a light and watched as our driver in front of us disappeared in the traffic. Maddy began to intersperse her phone conversations with directions for me: "Keep going straight. Turn left. Stop. Go." Aside from the palm trees and the Coffee Bean on every corner, it was difficult to get my bearings and figure out the landmarks. After a while, Maddy directed us right into The Springs, Beverly Hills.

"Welcome to The Springs," a valet said as he opened my door and helped me out. I thanked him, and as he was about to get in the car to go park it, Maddy raced to the driver's side, nearly knocking the guy over as she hopped in.

"Where do you think you're going?" I asked.

"I'm going down the street to the Coffee Bean," she said, "while you sort everything out with the room." She indicated a high-end shopping strip we'd passed on our way here.

"You're not taking the car," I said.

"What is with you?" she asked. "It's literally two blocks down the road. I've had a hard enough day without you adding more stress to it." I didn't feel like being subjected to yet another of her public tantrums. Plus, if she disappeared for a bit, it would give me time to sort things out with the room without her breathing down my neck. I gambled at the prospect of a few moments' respite.

"Fine, just this once," I said. "Don't be too long."

"I won't. Pinky swear," she said. She blew me a kiss and drove off. I stood with the bags and a suited doorman appeared by my side.

"Go on in," he said. "We'll take care of your luggage." I headed into the hotel, walking past some fountains and perfectly trimmed hedges. With Maddy out of my hair, a feeling of relief came over me.

"Welcome to The Springs," said the woman behind the front desk. "My name is Roz. How can I help you?" She had her brown hair in a bun and wore thin metal-rimmed glasses.

"Hi, I'm Grace Daniels. I'm checking in with Maddy Malone."

"Oh, right. You called before?" she asked.

"Yes," I said. "There seems to be a slight problem with our room." I hoped things would work out better in person with the room situation.

"Right," Roz said. "Well, you see the manager looked into it, and he claims that Miss Malone has stayed here twice before and both times resided in the one-bedroom junior suite, her usual room." Had Maddy made up a lie to weasel her way into a bigger room? Probably. And here I'd assumed the hotel had made the mistake.

"Would you like to speak to the manager yourself?" Roz asked.

"No, that's okay," I said. I felt it would be inappropriate to burden the hotel when Maddy wasn't being truthful. Roz began to thumb through a pile of papers. Then I had another idea.

"Actually, Roz?" I said, leaning over the counter slightly.

"Yes, Miss Daniels?" she asked.

"What happens after the awards this weekend?" I asked.

"What happens?"

"I mean if guests check out of the bigger suites, would we be able to get upgraded then?" I asked. "I mean Maddy could deal with the one-bedroom for a few days if she knew there was something to look forward to," I said.

"I see," Roz said. "I'll check that for you." I stood to the side as she walked to the back to speak with the manager. Maybe I should call Marty and warn him to have his credit card ready. I fiddled with the cord of one of the telephones sitting on the counter. I knew Maddy would be pleased if I could swing this for her.

"Excuse me, Miss?" a girl's voice said from behind me. I turned and before me stood Maddy's arch enemy, Chelsea Tate. She was just as beautiful in person. With her long, curly, sandy blonde hair, sparkling green eyes, and skin like porcelain, she was about 5'7 and her long slender legs were exposed in a pair of Daisy Duke shorts. It was easy to see why Maddy hated her so much.

"Hi," I responded. She smiled. I tried to stop staring, but it was difficult.

"Is anyone working here?" she asked.

"Yes," I said. "She just went to check something for me. She'll be right back."

"Oh okay," Chelsea responded. "No problem." She fished into her bag, pulled out an elastic and swiped her hair into a ponytail.

"Gosh the weather has been so nice in LA for January. Don't you think?" she asked.

"Actually, I'm from Chicago. So even bad LA weather is still warmer than there," I said. Chelsea laughed.

"Well that's true," she said. She held out her hand. "I'm Chelsea."

"Grace," I said, shaking it. "It's great to meet you."

"Likewise," she said. "So what brings you to LA? The Golden Globes?" I was surprised Chelsea Tate was interested in small talk with a commoner like me. Hopefully Maddy wouldn't return from her coffee run and find me consorting with the enemy.

"Yes," I said. "Well, I work for someone who is going." I prayed Chelsea wouldn't ask me who the certain someone was.

"Oh great," she said. Phew! "So who do you work for?" Fuck!

"I work for, um, Mandy Moore," I said, praying they weren't close friends.

"Oh my God!" Chelsea said. "Totally LOVE her. She's nice, right?"

"Super nice," I said. It probably wasn't a lie. I'm sure Mandy Moore was really nice, plus if you said her name quickly five times, it almost sounded like Maddy Malone.

"Sorry for making you wait, Miss Daniels," Roz said, returning with a stack of papers. "You're in luck though. After the weekend, we will have a two-bedroom suite available for you and Miss M-"

"Awesome! Thank-you," I said, cutting her off. Roz raised an eyebrow and continued.

"Right. I just need you to fill out some paperwork so you and Miss. M-" I lunged at Roz and plucked the pen from her hand before she went on.

"No problem," I said. "Here, I'll just get out of the way so you can help Chelsea." I took the papers and moved off to the side of the counter as Chelsea requested an extra key to her room for her mother.

"Do you know where Mandy's sitting?" Chelsea asked, while waiting for Roz to return with her key.

"Sitting?" I asked.

"At the awards, I mean" Chelsea said. "Which table is she at?"

"Well actually, I'm not su-"

"Oh my God, am I like a total moron?" Chelsea stammered. "Obviously she's sitting with her man."

"Oh right," I said. "Yeah, her man." I didn't even know who Mandy Moore was dating. I'd have to look it up online. Roz returned with Chelsea's key and handed it to her.

"Thanks so much," Chelsea said. "I really appreciate it." She turned to me and touched my shoulder. "It was so nice meeting you Grace."

"Same," I said.

"Listen if you need anything I'm in room 415 until Monday," she said. Let me get this straight, one of the biggest teenage stars was offering her assistance if I should need it?

"That is so sweet, Chelsea. Thank you," I said. Was it too late to quit Team Malone and join Team Tate?

"What a lovely girl," I said, watching her walk away.

"She's one of our favorites," Roz said, handing me two keys for my room. "Your bags will be brought up momentarily, Miss Daniels, if you'd like to go on up,"

"You have no idea the tantrum you have saved me from," I said.

"Regarding Miss Malone," she said with a smile. "I think I might have some idea."

CHAPTER 9

I hadn't realized the magnitude of my fatigue until I had reached our suite and sat on the couch. The ringing of the phone startled me out of a deep sleep. Reaching up to answer it, I noticed the bags had been brought up, and concluded that the bellboy saw me passed out in a semi-fetal position on the couch.

"What room are we in?" Maddy shouted when I had picked up the phone.

"909," I answered, rubbing my eyes and looking at the clock. It was five-fifteen in the afternoon. I'd slept for over an hour. I hung up and walked over to open the blinds. It was beginning to get dark. Maddy must have had a very leisurely coffee.

Our suite had one large bedroom, an en suite bathroom, and a small living room with a balcony off of it. There was another bathroom at the suite entrance.

Though I found it to be luxurious, I wondered if Maddy believed it to be on par with a Howard Johnson's.

I walked toward the door when I heard chattering voices in the hallway and a knocking at the door. I opened it to find Maddy accompanied by two friends.

"This is Katie and Nibs," Maddy said.

"Nibs?" I asked.

"Yeah baby, Nibs," he said. "Like the licorice." He put his hand up for a high five but when I tried to slap it, he pulled it away.

"Too slow," he laughed. Katie laughed with him. Yes, I supposed that classic move was always good for a laugh—if you were ten.

Katie was a petite blonde who looked no more then sixteen, and Nibs was a Hispanic boy wearing heavy navy blue eyeliner. I could only imagine where Maddy had dug these kids up from.

"They're from Burbank," Maddy said. "But don't worry, Grace. I called Nibs to come meet me at the coffee place. I didn't drive to Burbank to get them."

"Glad to hear it," I said.

"So what's with the room?" Maddy asked.

"We'll have the room you want after the weekend," I told her.

"You did well, Grace. I'm very proud of you," she said.

Maddy popped a CD into the stereo and an old Brittney Spears song played over the speakers. Nibs jumped up and down excitedly.

"I love this song!" he squealed, breaking into some provocative dance moves. Maddy and Katie joined in. I sat on the couch and watched in amusement, tapping my foot on the floor and swaying from side to side.

"Hey Grace," Maddy said during their rigorous dancing. "Can you order us some room service? We're starved!"

Food sounded good right then. I picked up the menu and looked it over. Since it was pricey, I called down and ordered the least expensive things I could find: Chicken Caesar salads and sodas. After I hung up, I picked up a magazine about Los Angeles that was sitting on the glass end table and started flipping through it. It was hard to concentrate over the loud music and I began developing a headache. It didn't help when Nibs began to chant: "Go Gracie, go Gracie, go-go, go Gracie!"

I looked up from the magazine, horrified. The girls joined him and Maddy pulled me up. She sandwiched me between her and

Nibs, and, unfortunately for yours truly, they began grinding me up and down. Not quite the Hollywood threesome I've fantasized about in the past.

"Go with it, girlfriend!" Nibs said. Maddy laughed so hard I thought she'd vomit. At least it was nice to see her in an upbeat mood after her many stresses of the day.

Katie stepped aside to light a cigarette.

"Katie, this is a non-smoking room," I said, moving away from the dance-a-thon. Katie looked past me and called out to Maddy.

"Is it okay if I smoke in here?" she asked. Maddy was busy shaking her hips, and pulling her shirt up to reveal her stomach.

"Wha-?" she said. Katie raised her cigarette and waved it around.

"Yeah, that's fine. Give me one, beyatch!"

"Maddy, I don't think that—"

"Don't worry, Grace. We can smoke in here. I always do," Maddy said, cutting me off. I looked at my watch. By this time I was just plain cranky and hungry. I thought of something that I could do that would busy myself while waiting for our food to arrive.

"I'm going to unpack," I yelled. Maddy looked up.

"Hey," she said, turning down the volume. "Do you mind unpacking some of my stuff too?" Was it in my job description? Unpacking Maddy's stuff certainly wasn't on my mental to-do list; but I wished her mother had focused more on what my duties were rather than telling me what not to do, like staying away from the men that Maddy might like.

"I guess I don't mind," I said. Anything to not have to dance. I lugged her suitcase into the bedroom and dropped it beside the king size bed. I popped open Maddy's suitcase and was stunned. She must have retained a civil engineer to help her fit all her clothes in it. A dozen pairs of jeans, twice as many tops, and shoes galore. I started hanging up her jeans and placing her folded tops in drawers.

"Grace!" Maddy cried out from the next room. "Grace, someone's at the door. I think it's the food." I answered it and a waiter pushed in a cart laden with food. He set up a table in the living room where Maddy and her friends had begun dancing again. He eyed the trio and raised his eyebrow surreptitiously to me.

"Let me sign that for you right away," I said. "No use in both of us being tortured."

He smiled and we watched Maddy perform gymnastics on the floor. After doing a few cartwheels and round-offs that ended in her bashing into the wall and leaving a footmark, she lay on the floor laughing.

"Have fun," the waiter said as he left.

Nibs sat down on the couch next to me to eat his salad.

"Hey," Nibs said. "Where you from?"

"Chicago," I said. I placed a delicious forkful in my mouth.

"That's where my boyfriend is from," Nibs said. "He's from Skokie." He slowly chewed his chicken, savoring every morsel.

"Great," I said. Maddy joined us at the table and began eating the chicken out of her salad with her fingers.

"He has a restraining order against Nibs," Maddy blurted out.

"Why?" I asked.

"Because, I broke into his house and burned his couch," Nibs said, nonchalantly.

"Restraining order makes sense then," I said, wondering if I could get one too.

"I thought he was cheating on me," Nibs explained.

"You couldn't just try talking to him about it, rather than being a pyromaniac?" I asked. He shrugged his shoulders.

"Katie!" Maddy called into the bedroom. "What are you doing in there?" Katie appeared in the doorway of the bedroom, all made up.

"A quick makeover," she said. "What do you think?"

"Whose makeup is that?" Maddy asked.

"Yours," she answered. "Grace put your cosmetic trunk on the bathroom counter," Katie said.

"You look terrible," Maddy said. "Take it off." Katie seemed taken by surprise by Maddy's reaction.

"I'm auditioning for a commercial tomorrow," Katie explained. "I wanted to practice different looks."

"YOU'RE auditioning?" Maddy asked. "When did you decide to become an actress?"

"I got an agent a few weeks ago," Katie said. "My mom's boyfriend's friend is one." Maddy had a look of repulsion on her face.

"What agency?" Maddy asked.

"Faces," Katie answered. Maddy looked at Nibs and they burst into laughter. Katie looked hurt.

"Well, you don't have to be so mean," she said. "I have to start somewhere."

"Well I'm at the point where I don't even need to audition for parts," Maddy said. "I am up to my ears with offers." I wondered if Maddy had so many offers why she wouldn't help her good friend break into the business. Or did it not work that way?

"Whatever," Katie said, slumping down in a chair by the window. A few seconds later she perked up. "So what are you wearing tonight?" She seemed to possess the talent of bouncing back easily from Maddy's abuse.

"Wear to what?" I asked. I picked up the itinerary that Maddy's publicist had faxed over to the hotel to check if there was an event planned for the evening. Nothing, just tomorrow's photo shoot for *Teen Queen Magazine* at a quarter to eleven in the morning. The two exchanged looks and then laughed.

"It's my first night back in town, duh." Maddy said. "We're going out."

"Party central!" yelled Nibs.

"Do they have many underage clubs in LA?" I asked. The laughter that erupted was not just nauseating—it was obscene.

"Oh my God! Oh my God!" cried Maddy. "I can't breathe."

"I didn't mean it to be a joke," I said.

"Just pretend it was, honey," said Nibs. "Save yourself from any more embarrassment." I had two choices: One, reach over and poke his eye out with the very sharp knife that was resting beside the remains of my chicken Caesar salad; or two, let them have their laugh and move on. I took the high road, and picked up my fork to continue eating.

"We're going to a club called Mystery," Maddy said. "You're coming."

"That's okay," I said. "You guys go have fun. I'll stay in and relax." Maddy and Katie exchanged looks.

"Actually, I meant that YOU'RE coming," Maddy said.

"As in, 'do you mind accompanying me to the bar, Grace?'" I asked.

"Right," said Maddy.

"Yes, I mind," I said. "Anyway, how will you get in?"

"I have my ways," she answered. "It won't be a problem."

"You said yourself that all the bouncers know you now that you're famous," I said. "Something about Lisa Pellu-"

"Larissa Pelluccio," Maddy said, smiling. "Good memory, Grace. I'm not worried."

"If not, we could always go bowling or something," said Katie. The three of them started laughing again.

"Hardy har har," I said. "I'm willing to bet money that you won't get in. They wouldn't be dumb enough to risk their jobs like that."

"Oh baby," Nibs said, "get ready to eat those words."

CHAPTER 10

"Maddy, wake-up. It's nine-thirty. The car will be downstairs in fifteen minutes," I said.

"What?" she said, opening her eyes a crack. When she saw me, she shut them again.

I had certainly been wrong about the bouncers at Mystery not letting Maddy and her friends into the club. Not only did they greet her with hugs and kisses, but we were escorted to a VIP table near the dance floor. A few of Maddy's friends from LA came to join us, one being Chris Lupinino, whose father was the founder and president of Lupinino Denim. Chris was a couple years older than Maddy, and all but ignored her not-so-subtle advances until she had three bottles of champagne brought to the table. That had piqued his interest. I'd felt uncomfortable watching all of them drink, but the waitresses kept serving them, and didn't ask any of them for ID. Finally, when I started to fall asleep at the table, I told Maddy I was leaving.

"No problem, Grace," Maddy said. "I'll get a ride home with Chris."

"Don't forget that you have a photo shoot in the morning," I said as I left.

I left the club and with the help of OnStar, got myself home safely. While I got ready for bed, I decided that instead of driving myself crazy I'd just accept that in Hollywood children are allowed to go to clubs and drink alcohol. I probably should have requested she be home before four-thirty in the morning. She had come banging on the door in a drunken stupor because she'd forgotten her key. She uttered a few words before passing out on the cot that I'd ordered up for myself. When I awoke in the morning she was laying next to me in the king size bed. Her make-up was all over the pillow case and she hadn't changed out of her clothes. I'd had some trouble falling back asleep with her intermittent snoring beside me. I could hardly wait to get our two-bedroom suite.

"The car is coming for us in fifteen minutes," I repeated. I smelled last night's alcohol on her and it made me nauseous. After my sixth time telling her to get out of bed, she sat up.

"I heard you!" she screamed at the top of her lungs. "I know! Fifteen minutes!"

I didn't know if this burst of anger was because she was a budding movie star or whether it had more to do with normal raging teenage hormones. Probably both. Worse was that when I turned my back, she dove back under the covers. I walked into the other room and gave her another five minutes before going back in again.

"Maddy, I gave you an extra five minutes. Time to get up now!" I said.

"LISTEN!" she bellowed. "Wake me up when the car gets here, and stop telling me how long I have. When they call you and say the car is downstairs, then I will get up." She lay back down again. I turned and ventured out to the balcony off the living room.

"Ugh," I said. She was like an animal that required her own "Please do not tap the glass" sign. Or possibly a "Beware of vicious celebrity."

I looked over the balcony and saw two little girls splashing in the swimming pool below. Being out in the warm California air energized me. The sun shone brightly, and I took a deep breath. Hearing the phone ring, I went inside to pick it up.

"Good morning, Ma'am. This is the Concierge. Your car is here," he said. I hung up, then peeked into the bedroom and decided to simply stare at Maddy until she woke up. It was an old trick my mother used to use on me when I wouldn't get up for school. It worked like a charm this time because Maddy's eyes popped open. She dragged herself out of bed and marched into the bathroom. I heard the faucet turn on and she began brushing her teeth. A few moments later, I heard the shaking of an aerosol can and she came out of the bathroom to spray on her tan.

"Is the car here yet?" she asked. Her hair was up in a scrunchy and the makeup had been removed.

"It's downstairs," I said.

"Cool. Hurry up, we don't want to be late," she said, continuing to take her time. She walked over to the closet where I'd hung up some of her clothing, and grabbed a pair of jeans from the shelf. She held them up to her and then threw them on the floor.

She looked up and saw me glaring.

"Could you take my stuff out of my Louis purse that I wore last night, and transfer everything to the Prada? The pink one," she said. I walked to the chair by the window where a few of her purses sat. I would have done just about anything by that point if it would speed up the process. After checking herself out in the full-length mirror four times, Maddy was dressed and ready.

"Are there any cans of Coke in the mini-bar?" she asked. I took the mini-bar key off the counter and opened the door to check.

"There's a couple here," I said.

"Cool, grab one for me," she said. "Take something for yourself if you want." I took a bottle of water and put it in my purse. The thought of drinking a sugary cola at this hour did not appeal to me.

"Oh Gracie, I need my sunglasses too," she called out. I found her carry-on bag from the plane and pulled out three pairs.

"Which ones?" I asked, toting all of them into the bedroom. This excess dawdling was making us even more late.

"Hmm," she said. "Let me try the pink Yves St. Laurent." She tried the huge frames on and modeled them in front of the mirror, smiling.

"Are we ready now?" I asked.

Maddy laughed. "Grace, it's so hilarious how nervous you are about being late. Don't worry, doll." Maddy's cell phone rang. She picked it up and looked at the caller ID. I watched as panic formed across her face.

"Oh fuck, it's Alison," she said. "Here, take it." She handed me the phone. "Tell her we're in the car already."

"Hello," I said to Alison Clayman, Maddy's publicist.

"Who is this? Grace?" she demanded.

"Yes. Hi Alison."

"Where are you guys? You're going to be late," she said.

"We're in the car," I said. Maddy gave me a thumbs up.

"Listen Grace, I think we need to talk about a few things that Maddy's mother might not have covered when she spoke with you," Alison said. Truthfully, I would appreciate any inside tips on wrangling Maddy that Alison might be privy to. I held the phone to my ear with my shoulder as I pushed Maddy out of the room and down the hall.

"I'd really like that," I said. Maddy pushed the button for the elevator.

"What was that bell?" Alison asked when a chime sounded as an elevator opened, going up. I felt my own panic start up. Thankfully, I was quick on my feet.

"Sorry Alison, I can't hear you. We're going under a bridge," I said, cupping my hand over the phone to muffle my voice. I hadn't seen a bridge since I'd been in LA, but there had to be one somewhere.

"I just wanted to make sure—" The elevator stopped at our floor.

"Shit, I'm losing the connection. Alison, if you can hear me, we'll talk about this later ..." I let my voice trail off and pushed 'end.'

"Nice work," Maddy said as we stepped in the elevator. "Ever think of going into acting?"

"I hate lying, Maddy. I really do," I said.

"Get used to it, you're in Hollywood now!" she laughed as she pushed the lobby button.

We pulled to a stop at Larry Pulver Studios fifteen minutes late. It would have only been ten except that Maddy had fought with our driver for five minutes, demanding that he let her smoke in the car.

"I don't see what the big deal is," she said.

"I have asthma, miss," said the driver.

"Give me a break," she replied.

He finally relented, but she had to stick her head halfway out the window, like a dog, to do it.

We were greeted by the photographer, Larry Pulver. He was a short, thin man with horn-rimmed glasses. Maddy saved us from a lecture about being late by quickly hugging him and telling him how great it was to meet him, and that she was so excited for this opportunity to be photographed by him.

"You don't understand, Larry, I worked out for an extra ten minutes this morning just so I'd look my best," she said. She then marched past him and gave a warm greeting to the rest of the staff.

"Where do I change?" she asked. Larry directed her to a room where the stylist was waiting with Maddy's clothes laid out for her.

"Grace, you can wait out here while she works with Marge," Larry said, directing me to a sofa in a lounge area. "Would you like some coffee?" he asked. Coffee sounded great. He asked his assistant to get some.

I sunk into the deep sofa. The room was filled with plants and the air conditioning was gently blowing. I felt much more relaxed now that we were finally where we were supposed to be. Larry's assistant returned with a steaming cup of coffee.

"Thank you," I said, taking a sip. I was abruptly interrupted by Maddy's shouts coming from the other room. Apparently the queen of the month didn't like her dress.

"But honey, it doesn't matter if YOU wouldn't wear it," I heard the stylist say. "It's the theme of the magazine. You see every month, on the cover of *Teen Queen Magazine*, a teen celebrity is dressed as a queen, and the main theme of each story is how this teen is living like royalty. All the girls who do the cover wear it." I waited a few moments to see if the argument would pass.

"I get it, Marge," Maddy said. "But I've never even heard of this fucking label." I couldn't imagine what Marge must have been thinking, but it was probably something along the same lines of: Was this cheeky kid raised by wolves?

"If you think I'm putting my body into this dress, you're out of your mind," Maddy said. And then she screamed for me. "Grace!"

I put my cup of coffee down and braced myself for the firestorm I would face in the dressing room. As soon as they both saw me, they spoke at the same time. Maddy was standing on top of a chair and instructed me to call her agent. Marge was grasping onto a table and asked if she could have a word with me alone.

"Get down from there," I instructed Maddy. She stepped down and sat in the middle of the floor sulking.

"Just so you know," Maddy said as I was about to step out of the room with Marge, "you work for me! So don't backstab me."

"No worries," I said, pretending to put a knife back in its holder. "Perhaps you could think of other effective ways to talk to people besides cursing them out. She's only trying to do her job." Maddy stuck her tongue out at me, and then started text messaging on her T-mobile.

We stepped into the reception area and Marge put her hand on her forehead. I could only imagine how many similar episodes she had come across with other stars in the past.

"I don't know what to do, I've never dealt with such a difficult person," she said. Okay, maybe not.

"I'm so sorry," I said.

"Could you convince her to wear it?" she asked. I thought for a moment.

"I doubt it. Is there anything else she could wear? Something up in the Gucci or Chanel league?" I asked.

"I don't know," Marge said, her voice shaking. "I'd need to be approved for it." I tried thinking of something else that would make Maddy happy.

"I think if you change the style a bit and make it like a never-been-done-before thing, where Maddy's the first one to do it." Her eyes widened. "Does that make any sense?"

"Are you serious?" she asked. I nodded. "I don't know. It would take—"

"Listen, if Maddy Malone doesn't get her way on this one, you are going to have the worst day of your life. As will I." She nodded, knowingly.

"I'll see what I can do," she said. We walked back into the room where Maddy was sitting in the hair and makeup chair reading a magazine. She looked up and glared at us.

"I think we have something you'll like better," Marge said, picking up the discarded dress.

"Good," Maddy said triumphantly. I was relieved to not have to get Marty involved in this one. The last thing I needed was to have Maddy's agent thinking I was incapable of getting Maddy into a dress. I grabbed a seat in a chair next to Maddy and we awaited Marge's return.

"All better?" I asked.

"We'll see," she said. "But I appreciate the attempt."

It was nice to receive some thanks in what was otherwise a somewhat under-appreciated position.

Fifteen minutes later, Marge returned with an Emillio Pucci dress.

"Larry called and got authorization to switch the dress," she said. She handed it to Maddy who mulled it over before stripping down and pulling it over her head.

"Awesome," Maddy said, spinning around. "The swirling colors really bring out the gold flecks in my eyes. Right Grace?"

"Most definitely," I said. Maddy stood in front of the mirror posing.

"Must be nice to have the world at your fingertips," I said, collapsing in a chair. Maddy turned and winked at me, then flashed her fingers at me before picking polish off her nails.

The rest of the day went smoother. A hairdresser and a make-up artist came in to get Maddy done up. She had her hair up in a bun with a tiara, and her make-up looked natural. Maddy was thrilled.

"Can I open one more button on the dress so I have more cleavage?" she asked Larry as he busily took her pictures.

"Sure, honey. Go ahead." Larry actually took a shining to the idea of doing something a little off-course for Maddy's *Teen Queen* issue. The issue's publication would be timed to hit newsstands just before the release of *Daisy Mae* in the summer.

Around one o'clock, Nibs and Katie showed up to the shoot. Larry had given Maddy a fifteen-minute break while he reloaded the camera and got some caffeine in him. Maddy hadn't been expecting them.

"How did you find us?" Maddy asked.

"We saw the itinerary on your coffee table yesterday," Katie said. "So, we thought we'd come by and see how it's going."

"We thought it would be fun to crash this party," Nibs said, giggling.

I didn't know if Maddy was annoyed, but I was.

"This isn't a party," I said. "Maddy's working."

"We know," Katie said. "Aren't you going to ask me how my audition went?"

"How was your audition?" I asked.

"It was really good. I think I'm going to get it," she said.

"Whatever Miss. Confident," Maddy said. "You've never been on camera in your life. I doubt you nailed it on your first try." Katie sat on the couch and folded her arms.

"You never know now do you, Miss Thang," Katie said. "Stranger things have happened."

Larry returned and Maddy looked relieved to see him.

"Okay," he said. "Ready to finish up?"

"Yes," she said. "I'm ready." We all went back into the studio. Larry's assistant stepped in to fix the lighting around Maddy and to restart the fan. Maddy's hair blew softly in the breeze and she began to strike some very seductive poses.

"Maddy, this isn't *Playboy*," Nibs laughed. Maddy did not appear entirely amused.

"Fuck off," she screamed over the loud music. Nibs and Katie continued laughing.

"Leave her alone, you two," I said.

"Alright, sorry," Katie said.

While Larry reloaded the camera again, Maddy came up to me.

"We're going for dinner with the two guys from Diamond Dreams," she said.

Maddy noticed my clueless expression. "They're rappers," she said. She turned to Nibs and Katie. "Sorry, you two can't come with."

"What?" Nibs said, upset. "But we're your best friends."

"Well, yeah, but I can't invite you everywhere. Sorry." Maddy bounced back to Larry, who was waiting for her to finish up.

"What a bitch," Katie said. "She totally did that because of what you said, Nibs."

"She has a better sense of humor than that," he said. They looked at me for an explanation.

"This is the first I've heard about it," I said. "Sorry."

"We'll just find out where they're going and meet them there," Nibs said to Katie.

"Why would you do that?" I asked. "She just told you you're not invited."

"She'll invite us once she calms down," Katie said. "I know her very well." She took out a tube of lip gloss, applied it, and smacked her lips together. Then she started playing with her hair. I couldn't decide if it was comical or creepy that Katie wanted to be like Maddy.

"You know," Larry said, after the shoot was over and Maddy went to change. "For all that fussing, I think it's going to be one of our best covers."

"I hope so," I said. "Sorry about the whole dress situation."

"That's okay," he said. "She's just lucky that I'm easy going. She sure has the art of manipulation down to a tee." I smiled. He definitely had that right.

"One day someone is going to say no to that girl," Larry continued. "I wonder if she'll be able to handle that." A tinge of fright swept through my body.

"Don't jinx me," I said. "I don't want to be here when that happens."

CHAPTER 11

"There they are! I see them," Maddy said as we pulled up to the valet parking of Soya, the trendy restaurant we'd be having dinner at. I looked out the car window and saw Diamond Dreams, the two rappers we were meeting.

According to Maddy, these were not your average boys from the 'hood' as they appeared; but the hottest rappers to hit the scene since Nelly. Diamond Dreams album "Love Daddy," had gone platinum in no time.

Maddy freaked when I wasn't up to date on the stellar gangsta rappers of this year, so when we arrived back at the hotel after the photo shoot, she called down to the gift shop—dialing the numbers on her very own—and had them send up every entertainment magazine published this week. For half an hour we'd scoured the magazines and didn't find a single photo of either of them.

"What the fuck?" Maddy had said as she rough-handled the magazines, pages ripping as she turned them. "I just don't get it. How are there no shots of them? They're like totally famous."

"Maybe they like to stay out of the limelight," I suggested. "Some people aren't into that." She looked at me like I was crazy.

"Go down to the business center and check the Internet," Maddy said. "They must have their own website."

"Why don't you let me be surprised when I meet them," I said. "I mean if they're that famous it might be refreshing for them to meet someone who isn't star-struck."

"Are you fucking kidding me?" she wailed, throwing her pink Prada against the wall.

Down to the business center I went to Google the rap stars. I found some photos of them posted on their site. They were from Detroit. Diamond Dawg was twenty-years-old and had a shaved head. Diamond Kat was eighteen and had cornrows. Good, I had some details. That was enough time spent on that pursuit.

"Hey girls!'Sup?" Diamond Dawg said as we approached. He raised his hand and Maddy and I both high-fived him. Then suddenly Maddy became ghetto.

"Yo, dudes! Wuz shakin'? Dis here's my girl Grace. She works for me. She's coo'." She hugged them and I had to internally beg myself not to laugh out loud.

"'Sup?" I asked, smiling at Maddy. She was still in full makeup from the photo shoot. We were only five minutes late to meet the rappers. I never realized that evening accessorizing took less time than daytime. No decisions needed to be made about sunglasses, and not as many electronic devices fit into evening bags.

I shook Diamond Kat's hand, my eyes fixated on his watch. It was the chunkiest, most bejeweled timepiece I'd ever seen. Its face was precisely the size of the top of a pop can and was studded with black diamonds. The rim was lined with dozens of glittering white diamonds.

"Great bling," I said.

"Thanks," he said. "It's from Jacob the Jeweler. You wanna wear it for the night?" He started loosening the strap.

"Oh, I couldn-"

"Really, take it," he said, handing it to me. I stood there unsure if it would be considered unprofessional as Maddy's guardian, to wear an item that was worth more than her whole outfit.

"She'd love to wear it," Maddy said, excitedly taking it from him and strapping it to my wrist. I remembered my fifth grade crush, Riley Jones, once let me carry around a caterpillar he'd caught at recess, and I was the envy of all the girls in my grade. This was that experience at a whole new level.

"Don't embarrass me," Maddy said as I flashed the watch in her face, following Diamond Dreams into the restaurant. Walking to our table, I noticed all eyes were drawn to us. Maybe Maddy had been right; perhaps these teenagers were indeed hot stars. Or maybe it was the watch.

The decor of Soya was exquisite—the walls adorned with beautifully painted murals of gardens and waterfalls. I felt a surge of excitement to be at the latest hot spot of celebs, but tried not to let the feeling show too much.

The hostess seated us at a table in the center of the room and handed us menus. She held out a wine list hesitantly, seemingly trying to figure out which one of our party was the 'adult.' Diamond Dawg took it from her hands.

"Thanks hon," he said. As he ordered a bottle of their finest red wine, Maddy leaned over to me and whispered,

"Don't bother looking at the menu." She pulled it from my hands.

"Huh?" I asked.

"Diamond Dawg always does the ordering," she said.

"You've been out with them before?" I asked.

"No," she said. "Someone told me." I looked over at Diamond Dawg intensely examining the menu. I hoped he would choose well.

When the waitress returned, Diamond Dawg surprisingly ordered a selection of vegetable dishes, which upset me greatly, since I had my heart set on steak.

"Vegetarians?" I asked.

"We're vegans,'" Diamond Dawg said. Even worse. Another waitress walked by with a chicken dish. My mouth watered.

"How old are you, sweety?" Diamond Kat asked me.

"She's twenty-seven," Maddy answered. "Isn't she so hot?" I was surprised Maddy would compliment me in public.

"Oh yeah?" Diamond Dawg said. "I love older women." He reached across the table for my hand and held it for a moment. I thought I heard the screams of millions of teenage girls around the country.

"When's your Birthday?" he asked.

"April twenty-sixth," I said. He spat out a mouthful of water.

"That's the same day as mine," he said.

"Really?" I asked. No wonder we had so many similarities.

"We're like kindred spirits," he said.

"Soul mates," I answered.

"You guys are Taurus, the bull. Roarrrrr," yelled Maddy. The restaurant went quiet for a moment as guests paused to stare. Did she always need to draw attention to herself in an inappropriate way? I closed my eyes and kept them shut until the din of chatter rose again.

Two waitresses arrived, balancing our dishes of food. I gazed at my plate as it was placed before me. There were a few leaves of lettuce and a half-dozen round, grayish-brown pieces of what looked like meat smothered in grains. On the side was a pile of seeds soaked in a beige sauce.

I had no idea which utensils to use, so I waited to see what the others would do. I also wondered how Maddy would deal with eating this meal. Up until now, I'd only seen her eat kid-friendly foods. She surprised me by taking the first bite, followed shortly thereafter by a second and a third. Diamond Dawg and Diamond Kat stared at her, awaiting her response.

"Yum!" she said, dabbing the corner of her mouth with her napkin.

"Delicious." She motioned for me to try it. I stuck a forkful into my mouth. It had a bitter taste and a rubbery texture, and I almost gagged.

"Interesting consistency," I said, with great enthusiasm.

"Is the mushroom too well done for you?" Diamond Dawg asked me. Mushroom? I thought it was a condom.

"No, no. This is just fine. Really, it's great," I said. Happy that Maddy and I were enjoying our food, the boys began eating. I felt like a child, wondering how many bites I'd have to devour until it was okay for me to be 'done.'

"We come here all the time," Diamond Kat said to me. "All our other friends always order the steak. But when Maddy told us how you girls were interested in testing out healthier foods, I thought you should try our favorite dishes." I glared at Maddy and she winked back.

Maddy's phone rang from inside her Christian Dior purse.

"Hi, mom. Hold on a second," she said handing it to me. Why did she always do this to me?

"Hi Mrs. Malone," I said. As usual, she yelled out her questions.

"Yes, I've straightened out everything with the room. The photo shoot went well. Maddy's hair was perfect. I won't let her pick her split ends. You're right, it is very unhealthy. We're finishing dinner and then going back to the hotel. I'll tell her. Have a good night. Goodbye." I was beginning to believe that my phone calls with Mrs. Malone were foreshadowing my future mental breakdown, if Maddy didn't cause it first.

"She wants you to call her in the morning," I said to Maddy.

"Yeah, whatevs," she said.

"Maddy, girl, you gotta respect yo' mama," said Diamond Dawg.

Had he just used the term 'yo mama' in a sentence, that was not part of a 'yo mama' joke? Was that legal?

The waitress served us milk-free green tea ice cream with a sprinkling of sesame seeds for dessert. Diamond Dawg and Diamond Kat each took a spoonful, and then broke into song. I recognized it as a rapper rendition of Eddie Murphy's 'Ice Cream' skit from his "Delirious" album of 1983, before either of them were born.

They used their spoons and bowls as drums and soon had a catchy beat going. No wonder these guys were sporting such proverbial 'bling-bling.' They probably really did make some big bucks.

Other guests looked at our table, amused. My eyes wandered to Maddy who was busy pinning on her BlackBerry and paying no attention to them. The song grew louder and soon they had the entire restaurant watching and cheering. A few of the chefs came out of the kitchen to see what was going on. When their song had finished, they received a standing ovation, and the chef shook their hands. Maddy, who must have believed the applause was for her, stood up and blew kisses to the crowd.

"Would you care for some more wine?" the waitress asked.

"No, that's fine. Just the check please," said Diamond Dawg. She smiled and left.

"Ladies, we'd be honored if you'd allow us to buy your dinner tonight," Diamond Kat said.

"Don't be silly," Maddy said. "It's my treat." I mentally calculated how much the bill would be and figured it had to total more than five hundred dollars. I was amazed that she would offer to pay. They argued back and forth a few times and then Maddy handed me her Visa Gold card. The two boys look stunned, and didn't know what to say.

"Pay Grace, we'll go get the cars," Maddy said.

"I can wait with you," Diamond Dawg said to me.

"No, she's fine, and I want to see your wheels," Maddy said, putting away her BlackBerry. I handed Maddy the valet ticket and the three of them left. I waited to pay for dinner.

"Excuse me?" A lady, with a large pink flower in her hair, had approached me. She looked familiar, but I couldn't pinpoint how I knew her. "I wanted to tell you that I noticed your table tonight, and well, this might seem silly, but you really remind me of myself when I was seventeen."

"Pardon?" I asked.

"When I was your age, I was always the responsible one too," she said. "Making sure everyone was okay, dealing with the bills at restaurants." She thought I was one of the teenagers?

"It just made me a bit nostalgic," she said. "So I thought I'd come by and let you know."

"Well, thank you," I said. It was nice to have some affirmation that I was doing a good job looking after Maddy, even if it was from someone who had nothing to do with her.

"No problem," she said. She paused before leaving. "Nice watch."

The waitress came back to my table.

"A glass of red wine," she said. "Compliments of the table over there." She indicated the table where the lady with the flower sat with her friends.

"Thank you," I said. She placed the glass in front of me and I smiled at the gesture. Then it hit me. The woman with the flower in her hair was Nathalie from *The Facts of Life*, my favorite childhood television show. I wish she had offered me to wear her flower. It would have been more exciting to me than wearing Diamond Kat's silly old watch.

CHAPTER 12

Outside Soya Maddy and the boys were sitting in a silver Lamborghini waiting for me. The roof was down and the stereo was blasting. Diamond Kat was in the driver's seat and Maddy was on Diamond Dawg's lap on the passenger side.

"Hey Grace," Maddy said. They all got out of the car to say goodbye. I handed Diamond Kat his watch back.

"It was great meeting you both," I said. Diamond Dawg leaned in to hug me.

"Mmm, same," he said, his hand tracing the outline of my bra. I felt my face turn red as I pulled back. "We'll have to get together again while you two gals are still in town," he said. He then gave Maddy the same type of hug goodbye, whispering something in her ear. She giggled, pulling away.

"What did he say?" I asked as we drove away.

"I can't tell you," she laughed, "It's way dirty. Way!" She turned up the radio's volume and hummed to the music.

On our way up Sunset Boulevard Maddy had some fun with OnStar, asking them to check our brakes, getting directions back to The Spirngs, and trying to get them to give out Charlie Sheen's phone number.

"I'm sorry Miss Malone, that number is unlisted," the woman said.

"Oh come on," said Maddy. "I know you have it. You just don't want to give it to me."

"Thank you," I said, and reached up to turn it off.

"You're no fun," Maddy said, slumping back in the seat.

"You know maybe there are emergencies that can't get through because you're harassing them," I said.

"I need Charlie Sheen's number. It's an emergency," Maddy said laughing. I didn't find it amusing at all.

"Can't you drive any faster?" Maddy asked.

"I'm going the speed limit," I said.

"I didn't realize that you're such a straight arrow," said Maddy.

"I'm not," I laughed.

"Then put a motor on it," she commanded. The light ahead of me turned yellow. I sped up and ended up going through a red.

"Fuck!" I yelled. A siren wailed and in my rear-view mirror a police car's lights were flashing. "Now look what you made me do." I pulled to a stop. Maddy turned around and saw the cop park behind us.

"Oh my God!" she said. "Wait until you see how hot this guy is."

"Maddy!" I yelled.

"Okay, don't worry. Just be calm. Don't cry!" she said.

"I'm not going to cry," I said. An officer came over to my window and Maddy was right for once, he was hot. At around six feet tall and dirty blonde hair, he would have made a better surfer than a cop.

"Good evening ladies," he said, pointing a flashlight in Maddy's face.

"Hi," I said.

"You were speeding," he said, his flashlight still on Maddy.

"I know," I said, moving into the light and putting on my most regretful facial expression.

"You went through a red light," he said.

"I know," I said.

"Have you had anything to drink tonight?" he asked. I looked at Maddy who, for once, looked nervous.

"A glass of wine," I said, immediately wishing I had said five because it would be nice to spend the night in jail, where I'd be free of her.

"She's not drunk!" Maddy blurted out.

"Oh. Really?" he asked.

"Yes," I said, and was about to explain myself when Maddy jumped in again.

"It's all my fault, Sir," she said.

"How so?" he asked. I was curious as well.

"You see, Grace here," she said, jabbing me in the stomach, "usually drives so slow. I mean, we're talking at an ant's pace. It's really just so cute, right?"

The cop was expressionless and leaned in closer through the window.

"Anyway, I swear this is the one time I told her to hurry up. I guess my timing for the light was a little off. I didn't think she would speed up, though. I mean, Grace takes care of me, and she never does what I tell her to do." What? I did just about everything she told me to do.

"This was the one time she called my bluff, and well, here we are, and well, here you are!" she said looking up at the officer with big eyes. He stared at her in disbelief, probably wondering how many glasses of wine she had rather than me.

A voice came over his walkie-talkie.

"Sorry ladies, give me one moment," he said and walked to his car.

Maddy giggled when he was out of sight.

"Oh my god, Gracie, if we get out of this one I should win an Academy Award."

"Or something like that," I said.

"Grace, that cop is hot. I think he's into you. You should go for him," she said.

"Best idea you've had all day," I said. "Did you notice how his eyes sort of sparkled? And his skin tone was so even." Maddy nodded.

"Go on," she said.

"Well, he looks like a surfer, that hunky, muscle...." I noticed her staring straight past me. "He's back in the window, right?" I asked.

"Right!" Maddy and Hot Cop said in unison. I wished I could have pushed a button and eject Maddy out of her seat, for allowing me to make a fool of myself like that.

"Anyway, ladies," he said, clearing his throat. "I need to be somewhere else right now so I've decided to overlook this mishap. Of course, there are two conditions."

"What would those be?" I asked. This was right out of a porn movie. He would probably make us get out and force us to give him head against the police car.

"First, I'd like a couple autographs for my niece and nephew from the young lady in the passenger seat," he said. Maddy squealed with excitement. She pulled a pen from her purse.

"Grace, give me some note paper from your purse" she said. I reached into my purse and ripped some paper out of my daily diary.

"What are the names of your niece and nephew?" she asked.

"Lucas and Mary," he said. She scribbled a message and signed her name, then handed them to him.

"Thanks!" said the officer, putting them in his pocket.

"Wait," Maddy said, scribbling something else and throwing it at the cop. "Here's one for the guys down at the station."

"Oh, um, thanks," he said.

"What was the second thing you wanted" Maddy asked.

"I was hoping for something from this young lady," he said as his eyes fell upon me.

"Um, sure," I said.

"How about a d——?" He was interrupted by his walkie-talkie again. "We're going to move in on him. Kyle, are you with us?" the voice said.

"Copy that," Kyle said. "Sorry, I've got to run." He took off like the Flash, jumping in his car and driving off before I could utter another word.

"Wait!" I yelled after him. "Fuck!"

"That so sucks," Maddy said. "I think he was going to ask you out, which is so weird. I mean you didn't even reapply your make-up after dinner." I looked in the rear view mirror at my bare lips.

"Maybe he liked my winning personality," I suggested. Maddy laughed.

"I'm serious," I said.

"Don't you want to get married?" she asked. "I mean you're almost thirty."

"In three years!" I stated. "Don't rush me, and did my mother tell you to talk to me about this?"

"Of course not, silly," she said, giggling. "I was just wondering why you don't have a boyfriend. I mean you're fairly decent looking."

"Two hours ago you were calling me hot," I said, fluffing my hair and fake sniffling. "Now I'm just decent?"

"You know what I mean," she said.

"I guess I haven't met the right guy," I said.

Satisfied with my answer, Maddy pulled out her BlackBerry again and started pinning her friends.

When we pulled into The Springs, her phone rang. She put down her Blackberry, and grabbed her cell from her bag.

"Hi Katie," Maddy said. "It was really fun. Where are you guys?" Maddy grabbed my arm and mouthed for me to wait a minute before handing the valet the keys.

"We're coming too. See you soon," Maddy said and hung up. She put her phone back in her Dior bag and fixed her hair in the mirror. "Mother Fucker!" she yelled, startling the valet.

"Sorry, we'll just be a minute," I said. I turned to Maddy. "What's the problem?"

"We need to go to Chris's house," she said. "Pronto!"

"Chris from last night?" I asked. Maddy brushed her hair out of her eyes and then lit a cigarette.

"Yeah," she said. "Chris from last night. He lives in the hills. Katie and Nibs are there already, and there's no way that slut is getting her hands on Chris." I assumed she meant Katie. I started the car again and begrudgingly pulled out of The Springs.

There were so many sharp twists and turns driving through the hills and the streets were lit so poorly that I thought we'd end up driving off a cliff.

"This is crazy," I said, turning into someone's garage by mistake.

"It's fun," Maddy said, squealing. I reversed out and continued doing circles around the hills. Finally we arrived at the big iron gates of the Lupinino's home.

"Wow," I said as the gates opened for us.

"See, wasn't that worth it?" she asked.

"It looks like the house from *Dynasty*, I said.

"From where?" Maddy asked. Before her time.

"Forget it," I said. I parked the car in the driveway, and we got out and proceeded to the front door. It was half opened and Maddy pushed it all the way and walked in. A little girl holding a half-finished macramé bracelet greeted us. With her long, dark, shaggy hair, and big puppy dog eyes, it was obvious she was Chris's sister.

"Hi Maddy," she said. "Look what I made." She held up the bracelet. Maddy ignored her.

"Who are you?" she asked me.

"I'm Grace," I said.

"I'm Jade. I'm seven," she said.

"Where's Chris?" Maddy asked.

"Upstairs in his room," Jade answered. Maddy handed Jade her purse.

"Jade's my MAT," Maddy explained.

"Your what?" I asked.

"My MAT," she repeated.

"Maddy's Assistant in Training," Jade said, with great enthusiasm. "She has a lot of them, but I do the best job, right Maddy?"

"Um, are there a lot of people in the MAT program?" I asked. Maddy started laughing.

"Most are under twelve, but it's good to get them while they're young," she said. "Last time I was here, Jade gave me two hundred braids when I came out of the pool so I could have wavy hair. Now that is the work of an excellent MAT."

"She should be president," I said, as I followed Maddy up the staircase.

"You can just wait for me down here," Maddy said. "I'll be down soon."

"Oh, okay," I said. I stopped climbing. I was sure bad things were probably going on up in Chris' room anyway. Things that guardians should not be a part of. Jade handed Maddy her bag at the top of the stairs and then turned to follow me back down.

"Hey, Jade, wait," Maddy said. She pulled off her false eyelashes and handed them to an eager Jade.

"I can have them?" she asked. "To keep?"

"Sure," Maddy said. "Don't throw them away. Those will be worth a lot of money one day." Maddy disappeared upstairs and Jade stood shaking with excitement staring at the eyelashes. Finally she put them in her pocket.

"Do you want to get a snack?" I asked.

"Yeah, okay," Jade said. She grabbed my hand and we walked to the kitchen. Then she took a stool that was sitting by the pantry and climbed up to reach the cupboard. She opened it, revealing at least ten different types of cookies.

"Oreos?" she asked.

"Sure," I said.

"Single-stuffed or double-stuffed?" she asked. I don't think in my life I'd ever been given that choice.

"How about one of each?" I suggested.

"Okay," Jade said. "That would be triple-stuffed." She took both bags off the shelf and handed them to me. Then she got down off the stool and went to sit at the large wooden table. I walked over with the cookies and sat down beside her.

"Can you get me some milk?" Jade asked.

"Sure," I said. I reached into the refrigerator and grabbed the carton.

"The glasses are in that cupboard," Jade said, pointing to the one beside the oven. I opened it and found very nice crystal glasses. Fancy way to drink milk, I suppose, but this is how the rich live. I poured her a glass and set it down in front of Jade, and then took a seat beside her.

"Is Maddy your best friend?" she asked.

"No," I said.

"Why not?" she asked.

"I'm her guardian," I said.

"What's a guardian?" Jade asked. Hell if I knew.

"Sort of like a babysitter," I said. Jade started giggling as she opened the first bag of cookies and took out an Oreo.

"What's so funny?" I asked.

"She's too big to have a babysitter," she said.

"Yeah, maybe," I said. She handed me an Oreo, and I separated the two ends.

"Do you tell her what time to go to bed?" she asked.

"I try," I said.

"You're so lucky you get to work with Maddy," she said, biting into her second cookie.

"Huh?"

"Yeah, when I grow up I want to work for her like you do," she said. This was too much irony overload for me. The daughter of one of the most successful denim designers in the world wanted my job working for Maddy Malone.

"Is Maddy ever bad?" Jade asked.

"You mean is she ever good?" I mumbled.

"Huh?" Jade asked.

"Sometimes," I said. "But she's usually pretty good."

"Yeah, well don't worry Grace," Jade said, putting her hand on my shoulder. "Sometimes kids are just bad. It's just because they need a hug." She continued licking the white icing off her cookie. I now believed Jade wasn't a crazed fan of Maddy's, but instead a messenger sent to me from the pearly gates to tell me how to solve the problem of Maddy. She picked up her crystal glass of milk and drank it quickly. I anxiously waited for more insight from this angel. She put the glass down and belched. Well that definitely summed it up for me.

"Excuse me," she said laughing.

A few moments later I heard the sound of footsteps from outside the kitchen.

"Oh, hi!" Chris said, appearing in the doorway. "I didn't know you were here."

"Yeah," I said.

"Grace has been watching me," Jade said. "Even though you were supposed to."

"Sorry," he said, joining us at the table. "I hope you didn't mind."

"That's okay," I said. "I didn't mind."

"Grace is a movie star babysitter," Jade said. Chris smiled.

"Yeah, I know," he said.

I heard Maddy and Katie's voices growing louder in the hallway.

"There's a bit of a problem," Chris said.

"Oh?" I asked. We listened as Maddy yelled at Katie.

"I don't give a shit what happened while I was away," Maddy said. "You knew very well that I hooked up with him last time I was here."

"He said nothing happened with you guys," Katie said, "so I assumed you wouldn't mind. Plus you've been telling me about that dude from your high school for the past month." I looked at Chris who was sitting in his seat turning red.

"It's about you?" I asked. He nodded. I could certainly understand why they were fighting over him. He seemed to have a lot going for him. Gorgeous model looks, the heir to a huge fortune, and from what I could tell, a pretty nice life up here in the hills. In fact, maybe Mrs. Malone was right that I'd like the same guys that Maddy did.

"She's lying," Chris said. "Nothing ever happened between Maddy and I."

"Oh?" I said.

"I'm not into her," he said. "She's way too possessive." Uh-oh. This was going to get messy. I tried to think of a way to coerce Maddy out of the Lupinino estate.

"Maddy, don't be mad at me," Katie said, both of them entering the kitchen.

"I don't care. Whatever," Maddy answered. Then she came over to the table and grabbed an Oreo. She took a bite and then whipped the remainder at Katie.

"Stop it!" Katie cried.

"Let's go," Maddy said. "We have to drive Katie home."

"To Burbank?" I asked. I knew Maddy didn't want to leave Katie alone with Chris, in fear of something romantic happening, but I couldn't believe she'd go to the extent of driving Katie home just to prevent it.

"Yes," she said.

"No, don't leave," Jade cried.

"Don't worry, Jade. I'll come back again," Maddy said.

"No!" Jade cried. She jumped into my arms. Maddy gave me a dirty look. Surely she wasn't going to be jealous that Jade was showing more affection toward me than her. There was no clause in the contract stating that I stay away from young children that Maddy might like.

"Made a new friend, did you?" Maddy asked.

"Yes," I said, thinking how I enjoyed hanging out with Jade more than I enjoyed hanging out with Maddy.

Chris and Jade walked us to the door and Maddy and I waited as Katie put her shoes on. I could tell she was lingering, obviously not wanting to leave Chris.

"Hurry up!" Maddy commanded, then leaned over and gave Chris a kiss on the lips. "Bye honey, talk to you later." She grabbed the keys from my hand and hurried out the door.

"Bye," I said. "Nice seeing you."

"Thank you, Grace. Much appreciated by both of us," he said putting his arm around his little sister.

"No problem," I said. Katie gave Chris a quick hug and hurried out the door in front of me.

When I got to the car, Maddy was in the driver's seat talking to OnStar. She put her hands together praying that I'd let her drive.

"Not a chance," I said.

CHAPTER 13

I woke the next day and re-read the itinerary Alison had faxed. It said that Maddy was to go to room 403 at eleven o'clock for a fitting for the *Daisy Mae* video she would be shooting next week. A stylist named Debra Glyder would be there to assist her.

"Grace, I really don't feel up to doing that today," Maddy said, when I woke her at ten-thirty. "Could you call and reschedule?"

"You want me to call Alison and tell her you don't feel like going?" I asked. Maddy shot out of bed.

"No, no," she said. "You don't need to. Okay, let me think for a second." She lay back down and put her hand against her forehead. I sat down at the end of the bed waiting to hear the master plan.

"Maybe you could just go and pick some stuff out for me," she suggested.

"Maybe YOU could just go, and not make such a big deal out of this?" I said. "Besides, I could swear you've told me many times that I have very little fashion sense."

"Very little doesn't mean none at all," Maddy said, speaking directly to the ceiling. "And are you going to take everything I say so literally? I trust your taste. Aren't you a designer or something?"

"Yes," I said. "But I decorate homes. I don't decorate teenagers."

"Whatever," she said. "If you get it done quickly, we could go hang out at the pool for the day." It sounded like a fabulous plan, but I knew she was bluffing. I knew her well enough by now to know that something would come up that would prevent us from lounging at the pool.

"Come on," she begged. This made no sense to me. She was already awake so wouldn't it be easier if she took half an hour and got it over with? Especially since she didn't have to do anything else work-related today?

"If you go, I'll let you keep all the freebies they give out," she said.

"They give out free clothes?" I asked.

"Of course," she said. "They'll take you around show you everything they have in mind for me for the shoot. Then you pick what you think I should wear, and then get a few things for yourself. They usually have pretty awesome brands." It seemed too good to be true, but Maddy would know about these things better than I would.

"Well, okay," I said. "But you have to promise you won't get mad if you don't like what I choose."

"Pinky swear," she said. Excitedly, I slipped on a pair of flip-flops and headed to the door. I couldn't wait to get my hands on some free designer duds.

"Grace, will you shut the blinds all the way before you leave?" Maddy shouted out. "Thanks!"

On my way to room 403, I started coming up with reasons why I was replacing Maddy, without making her seem like such an asshole. The only thing I could think of was to pretend she was sick.

"Sorry, I'm not sure I quite understand," Debra Glyder said, after we were introduced and I explained the situation. She was a pretty brunette wearing a pair of ripped Levis and a blue t-shirt. "She's not coming?"

"Between you and me, and these racks of clothes, she's been throwing up since six o'clock in the morning," I explained.

"Why didn't her publicist call me?" Debra asked.

"I left a message for Alison," I lied. "Maybe she didn't pick it up yet."

"Alison Clayman, not check her phone messages?" Debra laughed. "I doubt it."

"I'm not sure," I said, stumbling. "But, Maddy didn't want you to have to come back again to set everything up. That's why she sent me. She assured me that this has probably happened previously with other celebs."

"Never," said Debra. She sat down on the couch and looked around at all the racks of clothing that she had obviously worked so hard at displaying.

"I suppose we can make do," she said. Good, because I don't know what I would have done if Debra had picked up the phone and called Alison.

Debra stood and walked me around the racks. Selecting trendy designer tops and jeans for Maddy to wear was actually quite enjoyable. Debra would pull a shirt off the hanger and I'd either shake my head no or nod yes.

I tried to subtly hint at the freebies I'd be interested in, since Debra wasn't mentioning the items she'd be willing to part with.

"Gosh, I absolutely love that striped Ella Moss top, and it looks like it would fit me," I said. I awaited her response, but she ignored me and kept moving. As we advanced to discuss footwear for Maddy, my cell phone rang. It was Alison.

"Hi, Grace," she said. "Everything okay? Is Maddy picking some nice things?"

"Oh hi," I sang. "Everything's going great. We're busily getting her wardrobe picked out." Debra observed me with a quizzical look. I winked back.

"Is she behaving?" Alison asked.

"Oh yeah," I said. "Really well."

"Good, I was nervous she'd be difficult," said Alison.

"No, no, it's all good," I said.

"Okay, then. Carry on," Alison said, "Oh make sure Maddy doesn't take any clothes from the racks for her own pleasure. She has a habit of doing that at these things and then pretends they were given to her as freebies." I hung up, pissed off that Maddy had made me believe that they'd give away free clothes.

"Was that Maddy?" Debra asked. I thought of blowing her cover right then and there, but decided I'd look just as idiotic for going along with the charade.

"Yes," I said. "She was calling to see how it was going, and wanted me to apologize again."

"Is she feeling better?" Debra asked, sounding quite concerned.

"She said she her fever's gone down a little," I said, "but she's still sort of nauseous." Debra nodded her head and we picked up where we left off.

"I think there's something going around," she said pulling boxes of Converse out of a trunk.

When I returned to the hotel room half an hour later, Maddy was sitting on the edge of the bathtub wrapped in a towel and shaving her legs.

"Did they give you those?" she asked of the two boxes of Converse in my hands.

"Yes," I said. "Debra appreciated me coming in place of you," I said.

"I can't believe they gave you those," she said. "Those fuckers."

"Why?" I asked. "You're the one that told me about all the freebies they give out at these things."

"Oh Grace," Maddy said, laughing. "You're hilarious." I wasn't finding any humor in Maddy's manipulation and constant lying.

"Do you want to know what clothes I picked?" I asked.

"Nah, that's okay," she said. "Let's go down to the pool." She grabbed her bikini off the bathroom counter and went into the bedroom to change. I followed her in.

"Why don't you want to know?" I asked.

"Know what?" Maddy asked, tying her top on.

"What clothes I chose for you," I responded.

"Oh, because thinking about it gives me a migraine," she said. Really, where did this girl come from?

I put my new shoes away and got myself ready to go relax by the pool. As I searched around for my terry dress to throw over my bikini, Maddy tapped me on the shoulder. I looked up.

"What?" I asked.

"Do you have another bathing suit you could wear?" Maddy asked.

"Why?" I asked, looking at my reflection in the mirror. Did I look fat?

"Well, I mean, it's not that you don't look good in that, but um ..." she trailed off. I turned around and looked at my backside in the mirror. I worked so hard to get rid of my thighs; I couldn't believe how she was making me feel insecure about them.

"What is it?" I asked.

"I just think that as my guardian, you shouldn't show your body around like that," she said.

"Show my body around?" I questioned.

"Well, I mean it's not good for my image to have a guardian who looks all sexy and stuff," Maddy said. I realized that in fact Maddy was feeling inferior to me in a bathing suit. I was ecstatic, and because I now knew how she felt, I had no qualms about changing.

"I think I have a tankini," I said. "Would that be enough coverage or should I go buy a wetsuit?" She gave it some serious thought.

"A tankini is fine," she said. I replaced my supersexy bikini with a striped pattern tankini and then pulled the dress over my head. Satisfied with my less sexy look, Maddy went into the bathroom to finish getting ready.

"I'm going to change into a different bikini," she said. "Can you get my Gucci sunglasses and my iPod ready?" I found her iPod charging next to all her other electronics and I put them into the bag.

"Ta-da," she said, coming out of the bedroom. She was wearing a Missoni string bikini.

"Well, how do I look?" She was right, I did look better than her in a bikini, and not just because the one she was wearing was a size too small for her. There were a few rolls of baby fat hanging over the bottoms and her boobs barely fit into the triangle bikini top.

"Awesome," I said. "You look great. Oh, to be seventeen again."

Maddy laughed. "I know. My body is almost identical to Carmen Electra's. But, Grace, don't get all down on yours. Maybe you could go use the gym in the hotel or something?"

"How will I ever find the time?" I asked, smiling.

The pool wasn't too crowded. There were a few kids playing in the shallow end, with parental supervision nearby. We found two lounge chairs by the deep-end directly under the sun, and set up shop there.

"I'm going to go for a swim. You want to cool off too?" I asked, after thirty minutes of sunbathing. "You're starting burn." She looked over at her light pink shoulder and shrugged.

"I don't feel like swimming," she said, flipping through a magazine. "The chlorine ruins my hair."

I slipped into the pool and dunked my head. It felt great. I heard my cell phone ringing when I came up for air.

"Maddy," I shouted. "Can you get that for me?" I watched as she slowly put down her magazine and looked over to where it was sitting on the side table between our chairs.

"It's too far to reach." She went back to reading.

"Are you serious?" I asked. After what I had just gone through for her this morning, she couldn't even bother to do me one tiny favor. I quickly got out of the pool and rushed to get it as it rang a third time. I looked at the caller ID and didn't recognize the number.

"Hello?" I said, breathlessly.

"Hey. It's Hunter," he said. I was thankful that Maddy hadn't answered it.

"Hi, Mom" I said.

"Oh, is Maddy right there?" Hunter asked.

"Yeah, hold on, let me just move so I don't disturb Maddy," I said, walking away with the phone. Maddy smiled, pleased that she wouldn't have to listen to my conversation.

When I had more privacy, I told Hunter that we were at the pool and hoped to be there for the rest of the day, as long as Chanel didn't call with a limited edition bag for Maddy.

"Do you think you could escape her for the evening and come to a movie with my friend Todd and I?" he asked.

"Yes! I'd love to," I said, without even giving Maddy a second thought. Hunter told me where the theater was and to meet him there at a quarter to nine. I hung up the phone and happily walked back over to Maddy who was engrossed in *InStyle Magazine*. I sat in my chair wishing away the minutes so it would be a quarter to nine. Then I thought about a lie to feed her.

"Hey," I began. "I need to meet up with someone tonight who's planning on partnering up with my interior design company."

"Mm-hmm," Maddy said.

"So, can you manage without me for the night?" I asked. She didn't answer. I adjusted myself on the chair and leaned a little closer to her.

"You don't mind right?" I said louder.

"Mind what?" she asked.

"About tonight," I said.

"I'm not a baby you know," she answered. "You don't need to watch me around the clock." I wish I had that in writing.

"Okay then. Great!" I said. I leaned back into the cushioning.

"Why the hell is there a picture of Hunter David in here?" Maddy asked, ripping the page out of the magazine and scrunching it up.

"Let me see," I said. She threw it at me and I opened it. I smiled at the shot of him walking into a grocery store. I looked up and saw Maddy glaring.

"What?" I asked. "He's nice."

"Give me a break," she said. "He's so annoying. He was always following me around on the set and wanting to get together on our time off."

"What's wrong with that?" I asked.

"He was using me to raise his celeb status," she said.

"Come on," I said. "You really think he'd do tha-"

"Whatever Grace," she said. "I won't be the one to rain on your celebrity crush parade. Maybe you should marry him." Ooh, I liked that suggestion.

"Another frozen pineapple skewer, ladies?" a waiter asked, approaching us with a big silver tray. Perfect timing. I took two off the tray and offered one to Maddy. She shook her head.

"I'm surprised you don't want any pineapple," I said. "Pineapple is healthy and I know how you're trying to move toward a healthier lifestyle." She stuck up her middle finger and I started laughing again. I was getting great satisfaction at taking digs at her, but knew I shouldn't push it.

"Put sunscreen on, or that's going to hurt like crazy," I said, pointing to her burnt chest. I handed her the bottle of sunscreen and she slathered it on her body.

"Do you think she's hot?" Maddy asked, shoving the magazine in my face. It was a picture of Angelina Jolie at a charity event. She was wearing a long black strapless dress.

"Yes, of course," I answered.

"She's not so great," she said, holding the picture closer to her face.

"She's stunning," I said, "and nothing you can say will convince me otherwise."

She ripped the page out like she had done to Hunter's picture, and scrunched it into a ball.

"Here, marry her too then," Maddy said. Ooh, I liked that suggestion too. I laughed, knocking my second pineapple off the skewer, which in turn made Maddy laugh.

"Look!" Maddy said, reaching the next page. "There's a whole thing about Kabbalah."

She showed me a spread of all the movie stars—Madonna, Demi and Ashton, and Britney—now involved in it.

"I need to buy a new red string," she said. I looked at the photos. Even Paris was wearing one.

"Do you think they have a gift shop there?" Maddy asked.

"At the Kabbalah Center?"

"Yeah," she said. "Maybe they have a cool bag or something." I had previously been impressed by Maddy's interest in Kabbalah and thought it would maybe even help her in some way. However, now that I knew it was another outlet to accessorize rather than a pathway to spirituality, I thought it much less admirable.

"Do you think I should start using self-tanner to get a pre-tan before I come out in the sun?" Maddy asked. I had never known anyone who could switch topics as quickly as Maddy could. It was hurting my brain.

"Sure," I said. "Great idea."

"But will it make me too orange if I also spray tan?" she asked. I shrugged my shoulders.

"You want to go get us some food at the snack bar?" she asked.

"Yes," I said. "I'd love to. But real food. Like burgers and fries. None of that fancy nutritious stuff."

"Well, duh," she laughed.

"Okay," I said, getting up. "I'll go order." I needed a break from the sun and from Maddy's racing mouth too.

"Well, don't leave me here alone for too long," she said.

"I'm just going over there," I said, pointing. "You can watch me the whole time if it makes me feel better."

"Ugh, you're starting to get to me," she said. My mouth dropped open. "Hurry up, I'm famished!" I wrapped a towel around my waist and walked to the snack bar.

After I placed my order, I watched a little girl order a chocolate ice cream cone. She kept turning to look at her mother, who stood a little ways back. She carefully counted out her money and then handed it to the cashier.

I smiled as the cashier handed me my bill and my order. After I signed our room number I went over to the condiments stand to put ketchup and salt on the fries. Then I saw the same kid approaching Maddy. I watched as her pigtails bopped around and her ice cream dripped from the cone. I thought I better hurry up before Maddy tried recruiting another MAT.

"There you are, Grace," Maddy said upon my return. "I was just explaining to my little friend, Carly, how smoking is bad for you, and that YOU really should quit."

I was confused for a moment, but caught on when I noticed a newly lit cigarette in her left hand.

"Um, okay," I said.

"Well, here you go. Take it. I'm not holding your cigarettes for you anymore," she said, shoving it in my face. "People are going to think I'm the one that smokes. Plus it really stinks," she added with a fake cough.

"Yeah!" Carly exclaimed, imitating the cough.

"Okay," I said. "Sorry." I turned to Carly whose ice cream was now dripping down her arm.

"My daddy used to smoke," Carly said, "But he quit."

"You know what? I know it won't be easy, but I'm going to quit too," I said. I walked over to a nearby ashtray and put it out.

"Yay!" Carly said. Maddy had a look of horror on her face.

"Is that your mom calling you?" Maddy asked pointing to the chairs by the shallow end. I turned and saw the woman waving and holding up a camera.

"Yeah," Carly said.

"I think she calling you to go back," Maddy said.

"No, she wants to take a pic-"

"Yes. I can hear her calling your name," Maddy interrupted.

"Can I come back after and get an autograph?" Carly asked.

"Of course, honey. No problem," Maddy said. Carly turned and went happily back to her mom.

"Why did you put that out?" Maddy asked, "I had just lit it."

"It made sense at the time," I said. "No big deal. Light another."

"Couldn't you have just held it for one minute? Do you always have to be so righteous?" she asked angrily.

"I wasn't. It just seemed that since you were scolding me for smoking, I should probably put it out," I said.

"Whatever. What do you care? It's not your money being thrown away," she said lighting up another.

"You shouldn't smoke so much anyway," I said. She lay back, ignoring me and plugged her iPod into her ears.

"Ahhh, this is the life," she said over the music.

A few moments later, Carly and her mom walked towards us, pen and paper in Carly's hand and a camera in her mother's.

"Hi, we're back," Carly said. Maddy didn't hear them through her music.

"Hi," I said.

"My daughter said it would be okay to get an autograph from Maddy," Carly's mother said. "We were hoping for a picture too." I looked over at Maddy who still did not budge.

"Sure, can you give us one second?" I asked. Carly's mom pulled her daughter back to give us some privacy. I tapped Maddy's arm. She opened her eyes and took out an earphone.

"Carly's back for her autograph and picture," I said.

"Ugh, this is so annoying," she whispered. "Can't they see that I'm busy?"

"So you want me to tell them no?" I asked. If Maddy wanted to be famous, why was it never a good time to be approached by her fans?

"Fuck! No, I'll just do it fast now. Make sure you don't let them hang out here. I'm trying to relax," she said. I motioned Carly and her mom to come back for the photo.

"Have a great day," Maddy said after the picture had been taken. She put her sunglasses back on and lay back. Carly's mom seemed taken back by Maddy's abruptness.

"Thank you," she said and pulled Carly away from Maddy.

"Sorry," I mouthed to Carly's mother.

"It's okay," she answered. "I understand."

"Are they gone?" Maddy asked a few seconds later.

"Coast is clear," I said.

"Cool," she said. "God, I'm going to have to dye my hair or something," she said, "if I ever want to be able to lead a normal life."

"Normal?" I asked.

"Well, yeah," she explained. "So I can enjoy my teens without being bothered by fans all the time." I sat back eating my fries, wondering how she had been able to enjoy her teens so far with all her fans constantly and unforgivably swamping her in L.A.

CHAPTER 14

That evening, as I was getting ready to go out with Hunter, Maddy called me from the bathroom.

"Hey Grace, could you come here for a second?" I zipped up my jeans, turned down her music, and went to see what I was being summoned for. I found her sitting on the counter top of the bathroom, cross-legged, curling her hair.

"What time do you need to meet with your business person?" she asked. I prayed she wasn't about to put a damper in my night.

"I have to be there for eight-forty-five," I said. "Why?"

"Because," she said, holding the iron against her head. "I need you to go up the street to the pharmacy and get me a new curling iron?"

"Is that broken?" I asked.

"No," she said, showing me a limp strand of hair. "But it's making my curls way too small."

"Do you want me to braid it instead?" I asked, "Like Jade did?"

"Come on Grace, I can't walk out the door like this," she said. "My hair is in shambles." Her hair looked the same as always.

"Where are you going tonight?" I asked. "I mean, what's so important about this evening that you need bigger curls?" She looked at me in disbelief.

"Grace, it's Wednesday night," she said.

"So?"

"Are you kidding me?" she asked.

"No. What happens on Wednesday nights?" I asked.

"Wednesday is THE night to go out," she said.

"Really?" I asked. I had assumed that when you're seventeen and could get into any club you want in Hollywood, every night of the week was THE night to go out.

"So you'll go?" she asked. I didn't want to. I wanted to take the time to make myself look nice for my THE night out. She saw the unpleasant look on my face.

"Please Grace, please. You still have so much time." I looked at my watch. It was only seven o'clock. I did still have time. This was one errand that probably wouldn't take very long.

"Okay," I said. "Fine."

"Great!" Maddy said. She jumped off the counter. "I'll call the valet to bring up the car. Oh, wait!" She ran into the bedroom and found her Louis Vuitton pochette.

"Here," she said, handing me a fifty. "Take this. Keep the change." I put her money in my pocket and looked around the room for my purse. I found it thrown into the corner near the window.

As soon as I stepped out of the hotel, I was blinded by the flashes of cameras. The paparazzi was in full force. Maybe Maddy was right that Wednesday was THE night. I heard a few photographers yell "Damn!" as I got in the way of flashes and they realized I was not a money shot. I stood waiting for the car to be brought up, and wished I had brought a sweater or something, because it was chilly out. Of course the fact that I hadn't had time to dry my hair yet wasn't helping. Hopefully I'd be able to fix it before going to meet Hunter.

After what seemed like forever, the valet pulled the car around. My big black beauty, awaited me. I handed the valet guy a dollar, which may seem like a small amount, but paying that at least three times a day was starting to add up. I made a mental note to affix that to the list of expenses that I shouldn't have to pay for out of my own pocket that I would present to Mrs. Malone at the end of the trip.

I got into the car and readjusted the front seat. It annoyed me that the valet guys kept changing the seat settings just to bring the car up from the garage. Couldn't they deal with my settings for the two minutes it took to drive up the ramp? I took a deep breath and headed off to the pharmacy down the road to buy the princess her iron.

As soon as I walked into the store, I found a saleslady and asked her where I would find the curling irons. I didn't want to waste any time hunting around for them.

"Aisle seven," she said.

Aisle seven was filled with various curling irons. Maddy had not been specific about what kind of curls she wanted. She had said big curls, but how big? What size? Ringlets? Waves? Crimps?—ha-ha, crimps! I picked up the phone and called her. Time was of essence.

"Yeah?" she screamed into the phone, music blaring in the background.

"Maddy, there are five hundred curling irons here. Which one am I looking for?" I shouted. A woman walked by and put her finger up to her lips and said "shh."

"We're not in a library!" I said back rudely, and then immediately felt bad. "Sorry." The woman kept walking.

"I need a seven-and-a-half inch barrel iron. Thanks so much Gracie, gotta go! Love ya," she said and hung up without letting me ask more questions. Why did she always assume that I knew what she was saying? I began searching for seven-and-a-half size irons but couldn't find any. I came across someone stocking shelves in the shampoo aisle.

"Hi, I need a curling iron that produces seven-and-a-half inch curls," I told her.

She held two bottles of Pantene in her hands and shook her head. "Sorry, we ran out earlier today."

"Seriously? That many people bought them?" I asked.

"They were featured in Star Magazine. I think Kate Bosworth used one," she said. "You could try Adam's Pharmacy a few blocks away, but most likely they won't have them in stock either."

I decided not to attempt another store and just get Maddy an eight-inch barrel iron. She'd have to live with it. But when I reached the cashier, I had an even more brilliant idea. I would explain to Maddy that obviously everyone in LA would have seven-and-a-half-inch curls tonight in L.A., and she'd be more original with her eight inches of flowy, bouncy, beautiful hair. I paid for the iron and headed to the car. The phone rang and Maddy's number showed up on the caller ID. I let it ring a couple extra times.

"I forgot to tell you that I also need tampons," she said.

"Well, I-" I was about to tell her that I had already paid and was on my way back to the hotel.

"Super jumbo, 'k? Thanks bee-yatch!" she said, and hung up.

"You are a fucking pain in the ass!" I screamed, throwing the cell on the passenger seat. I took some deep breaths and envisioned Hunter's face in my head to calm me. Then I replayed my conversation with Maddy in my mind. Had she just asked me for super jumbo tampons? Did they come in that size? What kind of virginal seventeen-year-old wore super jumbo tampons? I got back out of the car and headed into the store again, where I found the same girl stocking the shampoo aisle.

"Tampon aisle?" I asked.

"Aisle three," she said. I walked up and down aisle three for about five minutes, stopping at every box of tampons, but I couldn't find 'super jumbo.' I decided to ask the stock girl to make sure. Otherwise, Maddy would be using plain old jumbo this month.

The girl stared at me in disbelief after I'd asked.

"Um, I don't think they make that size. I mean, is your flow THAT heavy?" Did she just ask me about my flow?

"Forget it," I grunted. I found the jumbo tampons and went to pay.

"So, will that be all?" asked the cashier.

"Actually, and these," I said, adding two packs of mint gum. I might have bad hair when I met up with Hunter, but I'd be damned if I had bad breath. I walked slowly back to the car, in case Maddy called again with a brand new request. I looked at my watch which said seven-forty-five and with only an hour left, sped up my pace.

When I got out of the elevator on the ninth floor of The Springs, I heard loud music and voices. I followed it to our room, opened the door and was immediately hit with a thick cloud of smoke. Maddy, Katie, Nibs, and a new guy with auburn, curly hair, were sitting in the living room. Katie and the new guy were smoking pot. No one noticed my entrance.

"Hello!" I shouted into the air. Maddy looked up. Her hair was washed and had been blow dried pin straight.

"What's up?" she asked, flashing a smile. She grabbed the joint from Katie's hand and passed it to me. I pushed it away.

"Your hair! It's straight," I said. I was so overwhelmed by her hair style that the illegal drugs in our hotel room didn't even faze me. Maddy looked at me as though I was crazy. Which, I thought, I may well be on my way to becoming.

"Oh, right. I know. Well it was taking you so long to get back so I decided to go straight, instead," she said. "Oh my God, then I had a major wardrobe crisis and had to change tops. This one's

Chloe. You've heard of Stella McCartney, right? Paul's daughter? She designs for Chloe." I felt my face burning, and a rage rising inside me. I thought of how I had just sacrificed my time so that Maddy could look good, and she had fully taken advantage of me. This time I couldn't hold back.

"Yes, I fucking know who designs for Chloe!" I screamed at the top of my lungs. There was complete silence except for the music which Katie immediately turned down. They all stared at me, probably waiting for me to pull out a machine gun, which if I had one I'd probably use. Maddy finally spoke.

"Okay, Grace. I believe you," she said. My mouth dropped open and all that came out was another scream.

"Ugh!" I threw the bag with the curling iron and tampons onto the couch and went into the bedroom. Behind I could hear them whispering.

"Why's she so sensitive about Chloe?" Katie asked. "Does she always react to big designer labels like that?"

"I'm not sure," Maddy said. "I'll go talk to her." I quickly moved into the bathroom. Looking in the mirror, I realized how ridiculous that episode must have seemed to them. I would be a fool to expect Maddy to understand how I felt. She's a spoiled kid with no regard for people's feelings. Who was I to think that being with her for only a few days would have changed who she is?

"So, um, are you okay?" Maddy asked, from the bathroom doorway.

"Yes, I'm fine," I said.

"Can I ask you something personal?" she said, with caution. I nodded in the mirror, all the while trying to miraculously fix my hair in the little time I had left.

"Did you know someone that died while working at the Chloe factory?" she asked.

I turned to Maddy, trying to absorb the gravity of her question. She stared back at me with a naiveté that reminded me again that she was a child. Like a lunatic I grabbed her and hugged her, laughing until tears ran down my face.

CHAPTER 15

"Dialing 310-964-3555."

"Hey, it's Grace," I said to Hunter over the speaker. "Sorry I'm late. I'll be there in fifteen minutes."

"No problem," he said. "We got you a ticket. See you soon." I hung up and followed the directions to The Grove that I had quickly jotted down from OnStar. I had to admit, I was really enjoying this feature. I was also happy to be only moments away from seeing Hunter.

Before I left, Maddy kept asking me if I was okay, and if I hated her and wanted to quit. I assured her that hate was a strong and draining emotion, similar to love, of which I felt neither toward her. As well, though I might have behaved like I would quit, I would not abandon her at this point. She then offered to do my make-up using all of her most expensive products. I agreed to it, taking advantage of the opportunity for her to serve me for once.

The Grove was an outdoor mall on Fairfax near Melrose, a very trendy, but affordable, area of L.A. It contained a lot of boutiques and restaurants, and a few bars that stayed open late. I'd read that it attracted a less "scene-seeking" crowd—those who were not so caught up in the perils of Hollywood. At least I knew I wouldn't bump into Maddy. It was beside the old Farmers Market, another popular spot, which seemed primitive compared to The Grove, but still had a certain charm.

As I pulled into the semi-circular driveway of The Grove, I spotted Hunter, calm cool and collected, sitting on a bench by the valet.

"Hey good looking," he said, as I jumped out of the Yukon. I handed the valet my keys and gave Hunter a big hug.

Hunter introduced me to Todd, who was a friend he'd made while working on the soap opera a few years ago. He was also off the charts handsome. With a sweet face, adorable puppy dog eyes, and a perfectly chiseled chin, I wondered how I would choose between the two hunks. The icing on the cake was a set of fantastic dimples that appeared when he smiled, making me almost forget my name.

"I'm, um …"

"Nice to meet you, Grace," Todd said, grabbing my hand.

"Grace," I said, a little late. I wish I had seven-and-a-half inch curls.

Hunter didn't look too shabby either. His long, straight hair shimmered as we walked to the theater and I had a strong desire to take a detour to a bar, get my hotties drunk, and take them both home with me.

"Hunter tells me you have the job of the year," Todd said.

"God forbid it lasts for a year," I said. I didn't want to be unprofessional and start blabbing away about what a nightmare Maddy was, but found it increasingly hard to refrain from it.

We approached the entrance to The Grove.

"Did you tell Maddy that you were going out with me tonight?" Hunter asked.

I shook my head and whispered conspiratorially.

"I wouldn't be here if I had," I said. "I told her I was meeting someone regarding work."

"I love it!" Hunter laughed.

I pretended to soak up the atmosphere of The Grove, though truthfully, I was finding new angles to gaze at Hunter and Todd. I wondered if Todd was single as well. I'd have to do some research.

"This is pretty cool," I said, once we were past the entrance and caught in a swarm of people. There were all sorts of kiosks set up selling new trendy items.

"Baby Crocs," I said, of the new hip shoes. "So cute."

"Hey, move it lady," someone said. A teenage boy was trying to peer past me.

"You're in my way," he said. "I can't see the fountain."

I looked to see what the view was that I was blocking. A large crowd encircled a giant water fountain. I moved closer to see what everyone was so taken by. The fountain was built of marble and gray stone. Music played from the speakers as white water shot into the air and danced. The music sounded familiar.

I poked Hunter. "Is the water moving to Donna Summer's 'Last Dance'?" Hunter and Todd laughed.

"I know," Todd said. "Isn't it crazy?"

Hunter explained that the fountain at The Grove drew people together; everyone who came here fixated on it. I tried to figure out why it was such a phenomenon. A few white lights encircled the water jets, but no complex light show accompanied the music. I didn't see any children tossing pennies in the water and making wishes. Actually, I'd never seen so many well-behaved kids in one area. Maybe if I brought Maddy here she would behave better too. I stared at the fountain longer and, before I knew it, found myself taken in by its magic. I closed my eyes and listened to the music. I sang the words in my head. The air smelled clean and fresh and I took in a few deep breaths. It was nice that these breaths weren't the usual Maddy-induced, anger-filled breaths of frustration. Hunter and Todd stood spellbound, too. I opened my eyes and peered past the fountain. There was a trolley traveling from one end of The Grove to the other. The total length of the mall seemed nearly that of a football field, but there didn't seem to be a good reason why visitors couldn't walk. I watched as The Grove's guests hopped on and off, from one store to the next.

"What's with the trolley?" I yelled into Hunter's ear. He jumped.

"Shh …" a woman in front of us said.

"Sorry," I said. Hunter and I laughed. He told me that the trolley was another odd accessory of The Grove. It traveled back and forth all day like a shuttle. I imagined the trolley announcer. "Now leaving The Gap, next stop, Bath and Bodyworks.…" I smiled at the thought of people giving their seats to the elderly on board, or people waiting for a late trolley, delayed because of an extra long line-up at Haagen-Dazs. I was getting carried away in my thoughts when a tap on the shoulder from Todd brought me back.

"Are you ready to go, babe?" he asked. I liked that he was calling me 'babe' after only ten minutes of knowing me. I checked to see if he had a fancy watch on that I could wear. It was a Swatch, but I'd still wear it, without hesitation, if he offered.

In the theater I strategically placed myself in between Hunter and Todd, and I could barely concentrate on what was happening in the movie. I remember seeing Vince Vaughn on the big screen, but was completely focused on how flawlessly Hunter ate his popcorn, not dropping a morsel on him. Then there was Todd with his natural cherry color lips wrapped around the straw of his diet coke. How I managed to refrain from jumping either one of them was beyond me.

Halfway through, I escaped to go to the washroom so I could regain my composure, and make an emergency phone call to Jen back in Chicago.

"I have boy crazy overload" I said, after dialing her from the washroom stall. I told her about Todd.

"You are so lucky," Jen said. "Do not come home without sleeping with one of them."

"What do you take me for, some sort of floozy?" I asked.

"Yes," she said. "I need to live vicariously through you. Don't disappoint me."

"I won't," I said. "From the impression I'm getting from Hunter, I think it's in the bag." Jen squealed on the other end.

I returned to my seat and concentrated on the rest of the movie, occasionally sneaking a peak of Hunter and Todd's distinguished side profiles.

By the end of the movie I had managed to calm myself and pay attention to what was going on in the flick. Even when Hunter put his arm around me and give me a slight hug, I was able to maintain a regulated body temperature. On our way out of the theater we were followed by two teenage girls.

"Hey," one of them said to Hunter when she had caught up to us. "You're one of my favorite celebs." Her bright red hair was pulled up in a high pony tail and it bopped back and forth as she spoke.

"Thanks," Hunter whispered, shifting uncomfortably from one foot to the other. I admired that he didn't relish the attention.

"I saw your last movie on DVD the other day. I loved when you rescue the humans from the apes." Todd and I both exchanged looks realizing that this fool thought Hunter was Mark Wahlberg from the *Planet of the Apes* remake.

"Yes, it was a challenging role," Hunter said, smiling. "But fun working with the um … apes."

The other girl, with stringy brown hair and chewing her gum like a cow, turned to Todd and asked.

"You were on Friends, right?"

The girls were now 0-for-2. Todd didn't look like any of the three guys from Friends.

"Right," Todd said, humoring her.

"Could I get a picture with you guys?" the first girl asked, holding up a disposable camera.

"Sure," Hunter said. "What's your name?"

"I'm Cammie, and this is Tess," she said, batting her eyes. Uh-oh, I hope these girls weren't making a move on my man. I inched in closer to Hunter so they would think I was his girlfriend.

Cammie handed her camera to Tess, then stood between Hunter and Todd. I stepped out of the way of their shot.

"No, no," Tess said. "Get in!" I hesitated for a moment.

"Oh, I didn't think tha-"

"Get in!" she commanded. I went and stood next to Hunter on the end and he put his arm around me. Tess snapped two pictures, and I wondered if it would be inappropriate to ask her to make me a copy.

"This is so exciting. I can't believe I caught three stars all at once. This never happens," Cammie said. It hadn't even dawned on me that they thought I too was of fame and fortune.

"Was it so hard to live on that island?" Cammie asked me. I stared at her for a moment not knowing how to answer that. Did she think I was on Lost?

"Well I, uh, actually. I'm not-"

"What's Jeff Probst like?" Cammie asked. Oh, Survivor.

"Oh, um he's awesome," I said. "Really nice." I wondered which season Cammie thought I was from.

"I know!" Cammie said. "And how romantic that he fell in love with a contestant?"

"Totally," I said, wondering how I'd missed out on that juicy tidbit.

"Cammie, hurry up," Tess said. "My mom's going to kill me if I'm late for curfew." They thanked us incessantly and then hurried out of the theater.

"That was classic," I said. "*Survivor* would be the last show I'd ever make it on. I'd be voted off on the plane ride over."

"Me too," Hunter said, wiping some lint off his shirt. "I hate sleeping outdoors."

"Let's go grab a drink," said Todd. "There's a great new place at the other end of The Grove."

We headed to a bar at the east end of The Grove. It was a quaint little place with a few tables, and sconces lit up on the walls. At the end of the bar an older man was sitting at a black baby grand piano, playing 'Copacabana.'

A waitress sat us at a table and handed us some drink menus. I opened it and tried to concentrate on the selection, but was too distracted by Hunter humming along to the song. When the waitress came back to take our order, I asked for a lychee martini, Hunter ordered a vodka and cranberry, and Todd a vodka and soda.

Remembering that I needed to turn the ringer back on my cell phone in case Maddy tried to call, I reached into my bag and grabbed it. Thankfully there were no missed calls. As we waited for our order, Hunter probed me for some entertaining Maddy stories.

"How did you stay so calm?" Todd asked, after I gave them the abbreviated version of what had happened earlier on this evening. I thought it better if they didn't know some of the minor details like how I fell apart in front of Maddy and her friends. I'd rather them admire me for being cool.

"You're very patient," Hunter said. "Most people would have told Maddy to go fuck herself."

"It was definitely a thought," I said. "But, my brother-in-law will kill me if I get fired without closing this deal." Hunter and Todd laughed. Just then my cell phone rang, Maddy's number coming up on my caller ID.

"Someone's ears must be burning," I said, answering it. Maddy started screaming before I had a chance to say hello.

"I've called you like five times. Where the hell have you been?" she said.

"What are you talking about?" I asked. "My phone didn't ring."

"You liar," she yelled. "I left you five messages. You're a bitch!" She hung up.

"What happened?" Hunter asked with concern. I was so flabbergasted, I could barely speak. What was that all about?

"She said she left me five messages," I said, examining my phone's message indicator. "But I don't have any. Then she called me a bitch and hung up."

"Don't worry," Hunter said. "She's clearly having some sort of teenage breakdown. I mean, five messages? At least one would have come through, right?" He reached for my hand from across the table. Enjoying the sympathy I was getting from Hunter, I considered pretending to be more upset than I really was.

"I know. I just don't understand," I said, with a worried look. Maddy called back a few moments later. I pushed 'talk.'

"Yes?" I said.

"I didn't mean to call you a bitch," she said somewhat apologetically. "I just thought you weren't answering my calls on purpose and it really hurt my feelings."

"Honestly, Maddy, I have no messages from you," I said.

"I don't get it because it was your voice on the machine," she said. "There's obviously something wrong with YOUR phone." I still didn't know why she was calling me in the first place, and the sooner I found out, the sooner I'd be able to get rid of her.

"So, is everything okay?" I asked.

"I just wanted to tell you that I'm not going to wake you to come pick me up tonight," she said. "I'll get a lift home with um, someone else."

"That's the emergency?" I asked.

"Yes," she said. "Oh, and out of curiosity, what time will you be home at?"

"Not as late as you, I'm sure," I said. "Why?"

"Okay, great! Talk to you later," Maddy said, and hung up.

"Don't even waste brain power trying to figure out Maddy Malone," Hunter said, after I explained what happened.

"How about another round of drinks?" Todd suggested. "Perhaps a double for you?"

"No, that's okay," I said. "I have to drive."

Hunter and Todd had taken a cab to The Grove, so I gave them a lift home after. Since Todd lived the closest to The Grove I let him out first and then headed toward Melrose to take Hunter home. It was a great opportunity for us to be alone together, and chance something romantic happening.

"I had a great time," I said, coming to a stop in front of Hunter's place. He lived in a beige low rise building. I liked how humble Hunter was. Such an attractive quality. "Thanks so much for inviting me out." Hunter leaned in and gave me a long kiss on the cheek.

"Anytime," he said. "We'll do this again soon. I'll call you."

"Please do," I said. I hoped that wasn't too forward, but I only had three weeks to work this.

"You okay to get home by yourself?" Hunter asked.

"Oh, yeah," I said. "I have my best friend OnStar to see me home safely." Hunter laughed and stepped out of the car.

"See you soon, gorgeous," he said. He shut the door and I waited until he was inside the front door before I started screaming.

"Gorgeous! Gorgeous? Ahhh, he called me gorgeous!"

When I got back to The Springs, I made a quick trip to the business center on the first floor of the hotel to check my email before turning in. There was one from Jake reminding me to call Teach Rogers and to also please check and clear any messages I might have on my voicemail at work, since no one else had my password to check them for me. I sent a quick note to my parents to tell them everything was going well, and then logged off.

Before climbing into the cot, I checked my phone messages at work. I had five messages. They were all from Maddy. So she really had called me five times—at work. I shook my head in disbelief.

I slipped into bed and hid my head under the covers, trying to force myself into sweet dreams before I was awoken by Maddy's loud knocking, as I was quite sure she would not have remembered to bring her own key.

CHAPTER 16

I awoke in the wee hours of the morning to the sound of the telephone ringing.

"Hello?" I said, rubbing my eyes. I looked over at the clock. It was four in the morning.

"Grace?" Maddy whimpered on the other end.

"Where are you?" I asked. It was late even for Maddy.

"Please don't be mad at me!" she cried.

"What did you do?" I asked, holding my breath.

"Well, I um, I bumped into someone," she said quietly.

"Oh," I said, relief flowing through my body. Why was she calling me to tell me that? "Who'd you bump into?" I figured it was probably one of her latest crushes, maybe Matthew McConaughey.

"No, I mean, I bumped into someone. I mean, I crashed into someone ..."

"Yes, and?" I wished she would just say what she meant instead of always beating around the bush.

"I crashed the car," she said.

"Huh? Who's car?" I asked. Maddy began to cry, begging me not to be mad at her. It wasn't exactly her fault, she said; everyone said so.

"Maddy what are you talking about?" I asked, wondering how much she had been drinking. "The car is here at the hotel. I brought it home hours ago."

"I know!" she said. "But I came and took it while you were sleeping."

"What!" I screamed, jumping out of bed.

"We came back to the hotel and then decided to go back out again, but you were sleeping and I didn't want to wake you up to give us a ride because I wanted to be considerate. So I thought we'd just take the car, and bring it back." I had so much anxiety racing through me I thought I was going to have a heart attack.

"Was anyone hurt?" I asked.

"No, we're fine," she said. "Just shook up."

"Tell me everything," I said. She started speaking slowly and giving me every detail.

"I was looking for my CD case. I wanted to listen to Madonna," she explained. "Nibs was in the front seat. He said it wasn't beside him. So I asked Katie if it was in the back. It wasn't there. I knew it was on Nibs side because that's where it always is, so I asked him again." This story was driving me insane and she wasn't getting to the point, so I lost it on her.

"I don't care about your fucking CD!" I shouted. "What happened?" This made her cry harder, but at least she actually sounded scared. She explained through her sobs that as she reached over again to Nibs' side, her Christian Dior-shoed foot managed to slip off the pedal and she rear-ended the person in front of her.

She stopped crying for a moment long enough to say,

"Can you believe that the guy in the other car that I hit, told me that his daughter was a huge fan and—"

"Maddy!" I wailed. "The car!"

"The damage isn't that bad," she said, sniffling. "Just a bit off the bumper. I made a deal with the guy that I hit so he wouldn't call the police." The mere mention of the word police made me dizzy.

"I wrote him a very generous check from my account to cover the damages," she said. "He promised to never spill the story to the tabloids. So phew!"

"Yeah, phew," I said. I couldn't imagine it would be a story that would make the front page of *People* magazine anyway. "Where are you now?" I asked.

"In West Hollywood, at a gas station," she said.

"Is the car drivable?" I asked.

"Of course, Grace," she said.

"Fine, just get yourself back here," I said.

"Okay," she said, no longer crying. "Promise me you won't tell my mother," she said.

"It's not at the top of my list of things to do," I answered.

"Good," she said, perking up. "See you soon." I placed the phone back in its cradle praying the damage on the Yukon wasn't too horrible, and most importantly that OnStar was still intact.

Two hours later I opened my eyes to the sound of Maddy banging at the door. I don't know how I'd managed to fall back asleep with her car accident on my mind. I jumped out of bed curious if I'd make it back to Chicago with at least one full night's sleep. I unlocked the door and there stood Maddy, Katie, and Nibs. Maddy immediately grabbed me and gave me a suffocating hug. Then she started crying.

"Now what?" I asked, pulling away.

"I'm having a delayed reaction to the accident," she said.

"I see." I replied.

"As the car hit, I saw my life flash before my eyes and I realized that I'm so young, Grace," she said.

"Yes, you are," I answered.

"I mean, there are so many things I want to do. So many outfits sitting in my closet that I haven't even worn yet," she said, tears forming in her eyes.

"Well, I'm sure now you'll have lots of time to—" She threw herself back at me, taking me by surprise.

"What?" I said.

"I'm too young to die!" she said. Katie and Nibs burst out laughing. I peeled her off me, and she laughed hysterically. I wasn't in the mood for this drama, and was eager to go back to bed.

"Where have you been anyway?" I asked. "It's been hours since you called."

"We went to meet Chris," Maddy said, sitting on the floor in lotus position.

"What about the car?" I asked.

"It's seen better days," Nibs said, "but still drivable." I shot him a dirty look.

"Maybe I should go look at it," I said.

"Just see it in the morning," Maddy said. "You can ask someone where you can take it to be fixed."

"Fine," I said.

"Swear to me that you won't tell anyone that I got in the accident," Maddy said.

"I won't tell," I said.

"If you have to, just say that you did it," said Maddy.

"Absolutely not!" I answered.

"You have to!" Maddy yelled.

"Why?" I asked.

"Because this is all your fault," she said.

"My fault?" I asked.

"Well, yeah," she said. "You're supposed to be watching me all the time."

"You took the car when I was sleeping!" I exclaimed. "I can't watch you while I sleep."

"Well maybe you should have stayed awake until I got home," she said. It was official, I hated her. We all sat in silence not knowing what to say. I tried to reason with myself so as not to do something I might regret, like strangle her. Instead of despising her, I should feel sorry for her. When pitying her didn't make me feel better, I remembered how great of a night I had had with Hunter and Todd. That worked, and I felt a little better. Katie went over to the entryway to put her shoes on.

"Nibs and I are going to go," she said. "It's really late." Maddy shot Katie a look to kill.

"And how will you be getting back to Burbank at this hour, you idiot?" she asked. Katie's mouth dropped open, taken aback by Maddy's tone.

"We'll take a cab," Nibs said, jumping in.

"My mom's expecting me home tonight and—" Katie said, but stopped when out of nowhere, Maddy picked up a glass ashtray and violently threw it at her.

Katie ducked and the ashtray hit the wall, smashing into a million pieces.

"Are you trying to kill me?" Katie screamed.

"Admit it!" Maddy howled, flailing her arms. "You're going back to Chris's house aren't you? That's who you were text messaging in the car."

"No, I'm not!" Katie cried. "I wasn't! I just keep getting in trouble when I hang out with you, and I don't want to get grounded again." I watched as Maddy looked around for something else to throw. I quickly went over to the desk and moved a large vase out of the way. It was heavy but I held onto it tightly. Maddy glared at me.

"Oh for fuck's sake," she said to Katie. "Fine go! Both of you leave!" No, don't, I thought. Don't leave me alone with this psycho.

In fear of someone cutting themselves on the broken glass, I walked over to the ashtray and began picking up the pieces.

"Fine!" Katie yelled. She tapped me on the shoulder and I looked up. She sweetly asked,

"Grace, could you call us a cab?"

"She doesn't fucking work for you!" screamed Maddy. "Call one yourself!" She stormed into the bedroom and slammed the door. I looked at Katie and shrugged my shoulders. It was nice to know that even though this was all my fault, Maddy had the heart to defend me from her friends.

While Nibs called down to the concierge to order a taxi, Katie phoned her mother from her cell.

"Hi, Mom," she said. "I'm just leaving Maddy's hotel." Katie's mother screamed through the phone.

"Okay, Mom, okay," Katie said after the yelling had subsided. "I'm on my way home right now." She hung up. "I'm in so much trouble. I'm going to be grounded for the rest of my life." I was happy to see a parental figure depict some discipline.

"I don't understand what her problem is," Nibs said, plopping down on the couch next to me. "I mean she knows you're with me." My guess was that was part of the problem.

"I know," she whispered, "but she thinks Maddy is so wild and a bad influence on me."

"I heard that you cow!" Maddy yelled from the bedroom. She must have had a cup against the door, because I barely even heard it. She opened the door and came prancing out in a pink tube top and a lace thong.

"Ahh," screamed Nibs.

"Get over it!" Maddy said. "Grace, could you order me some room service?"

"You're hungry?" I asked.

"Yeah, I just want a grilled cheese sandwich with fries, and a coke," she said. "I need comfort food." She looked over at Katie and Nibs, salivating at the mere mention of her order. "Don't order anything for them."

I called down to room service and gave the telephone operator the order.

"Why would it take half an hour?" Maddy asked when I told her how long it would be. "They can't be that busy at this hour."

"I don't know," I said.

"Call them back, and tell them this is really important," she said. "Tell them I have diabetes."

"Well, actually," Katie said. "My grandfather has diabetes, and if you were having a sugar attack then you wouldn't order—" I watched the anger rise from the dark pit of Maddy's heart up to the copious amount of makeup on her face.

"Okay," I said, before Maddy had a chance to blow her top. "You guys go wait downstairs for your cab." I stood up and rushed them out the door.

"Wait, my purse," Katie said from the other side of the door. Maddy whipped Katie's purse at me and I handed it to her shutting the door quickly.

"I thought we were your best friends, Maddy," Nibs yelled through the door. "That's fine, we can take a hint." Then there was silence and they were gone.

"I need new friends," Maddy said, as we waited for the food. "I think I'll get my people to track down Dawn and Jana," she said.

"As in Dawn and Jana Longo?" I asked. The Longo girls had a popular dating reality show called *Opposites Attract*. They were the hostesses of the program and they traveled around the US setting people up who had nothing in common.

"They seem like nice girls," Maddy said. "I'll get Alison to introduce us. She's like best friends with Jana." I couldn't imagine that the Longos would be interested in befriending Maddy, seeing as she was quite a bit younger.

"Cool," I said, standing up. "I'm going back to bed."

"You're going to make me eat alone?" Maddy asked.

"Yes," I said. "And I will trust you can keep yourself out of trouble until morning." Without waiting for her to answer, I returned to my cot and slipped under the covers, praying that I would be able to catch a few undisturbed hours of shut-eye before another day of Maddy's torture emerged.

CHAPTER 17

The next morning, I threw on an uncoordinated outfit and rushed downstairs to see the injured car. I was surprised to find it looking worse than I thought it would.

"Big smash, huh?" said Juan, one of the valets. He traced his hand over the chipped black paint. I nodded.

"I don't want to seem like a snitch," he continued. "But when I saw your little chiquita and her friends bring the car back last night in this condition, the paparazzi was out."

"Oh?" I said. Maddy hadn't mentioned that. Perhaps in her anguished state she didn't notice.

"Yes. I think Miss Malone and her friends really enjoyed the attention they were drawing," Juan said. After she'd begged me not to tell anyone.

"Fuck!" I said. Juan took a step back. "Pardon my French."

"That's okay," he said. "I just thought you should know since you're her babysitter." I wish people would stop calling me that.

"How much do you think it will cost to fix?" I asked.

"I'm not sure," he said. "But if you want, I can arrange to have it sent to a body shop."

"Really?" I asked.

"Sure," said Juan. "I can have someone come and pick-up the car. You'll have it back in a few days." Surely it couldn't be that simple. I was expecting to have to sit with a phone book dialing up a bunch of different places to get estimates. However, if I could just send it off and wash my hands of this situation, I'd be one happy camper.

"That sounds too good to be true," I said.

"Trust me, you can't imagine how many times a month this sort of thing happens," Juan said. I was relieved to hear that.

"Well, okay then," I said.

I went inside with Juan to fill out a few forms. Juan told me he'd call with an estimate for the car when he found out what it was. I thanked him and then headed back to the room. Now that I knew Maddy had been relishing in the attention from the paparazzi, I didn't feel such a need to protect her and had no qualms about waking her for a phone interview she had to be up for. It was an interview to accompany the *Teen Queen* cover that had been shot the other day. I found her sitting up in bed talking on the phone. The lights were still off and the curtains still drawn.

"I'm not doing that right now," she said to whomever she was speaking to. "I'll get Grace to cancel it." She hung up the phone and lay back down.

"Hey. I was just downstairs dealing with the car," I said. "And they're going to—"

"Grace, I have no time to talk about this right now," she said. "I need you to do me a favor."

"You don't even want to know what's going to happen with the car?" I asked.

"No, just let me know what the bill comes out to and I'll pay it from my chequing account. My mother doesn't see that one," she said.

"Oh," I said. I should have known by now that yesterday's problems wouldn't spill into today. "What's the favor?"

"You need to call and cancel the telephone interview," she said.

"Why?" I asked. "What's wrong?"

"I don't feel well," she said. "I need to rest." She grabbed a cigarette off the side table. "Pass me my lighter. It's on the floor beside you."

"You're going to smoke in bed?" I asked, tossing her the lighter.

"Grace," she said. "Don't badger me. This is my breakfast." She lit up and started puffing away. I was sickened.

"The itinerary says that the phone interview is only ten minutes long," I said. "It's all you have scheduled for work today. Don't you just want to get it over with?"

"Nope," she said, blowing ohs. "I'm sick." She started coughing, then started laughing.

"Is this a game to you?" I asked. Maddy put on a very serious face.

"Of course not, Grace. Why would you ask that?" she asked.

"I just don't understand why you don't want to do the interview," I said.

"Okay, I can see we're going in circles here. Just call my publicist and ask her to reschedule," Maddy said. "Really, it's no biggy." She took her phone off the end, pressed some numbers, and then passed it to me.

"It's ringing," she said.

Alison's assistant, answered, and I explained to her how Maddy was ill and unable to do the phone interview.

"Hold on. I'll transfer you to Alison," she said. "She's not going to like that." I waited a few moments for Alison to pick up the line.

"Tell Maddy it's not an option," Alison said, without saying hello.

"Well as I was explaining to your assistant. Maddy's not feel-"

"I don't care," Alison yelled. "We got Maddy this cover and the interview is a part of it. She knows that." I was at a loss for words. People sure yelled a lot in this business.

"Is she giving you a hard time?" Maddy asked. I nodded. Maddy put out her cigarette and leapt up from the bed.

"I'm fucking sick, Alison," she said, taking the phone from my hands. I heard Alison shout out profanities.

"I don't feel well," Maddy repeated. More muffled screaming.

"How quickly you're forgetting that you work for ME," she said. "And how easily you can be replaced." A calmer response from Alison came through the other end. After a few more minutes of arguing, Maddy hung up.

"Done," she said.

"You got her to cancel?" I asked.

"Yep." Maddy sat back down on the bed and turned on the television. Her ability to bully adults was strangely impressive to me. She could get away with anything.

"You're very talented," I said. Maddy smiled. In fact, I was sure her talent lay in the art of excuse making rather than onscreen.

"So what do you plan on doing today?" I asked.

"We'll need to go rent another car," she said.

"The Hills Rental Cars will never give us another car," I said.

"There are other rental car places in LA, you know," she said. She got out of bed and went to the bathroom.

"Are you going to pay for a new rental?" I asked. She picked up an aerosol can of bronzer and sprayed it on her face. Unfortunately she missed and got me instead.

"Ugh!" I coughed. She waved the rest of the vapor in the other direction.

"You don't want to pay for the rental car out of your pocket? Maybe as a gift for your favorite gal?" I shook my head. Maddy laughed.

"Don't worry," she said. "I'll pay cash for the deposit. I'm like a millionaire, you know." I watched as the millionaire plugged in her hair straightener. "So will you call the front desk and see if someone can recommend another car rental place?"

"Yes," I answered. I went back to the bedroom and called the concierge. He told me of a place called ADA Rental Agency, a small agency on a side street off of La Cienega.

Maddy and I arrived at ADA Rental Agency, by taxi, an hour later to pick out a new car.

"What should we get?" Maddy asked. "Your choice."

"Really?" I asked.

"Of course not," she said, laughing. "But I do value your opinion." I grabbed a folder off the counter filled with pictures of cars that were available to rent. I showed Maddy an advertisement for the new Honda Accord that there was a promotion on. It was eighty dollars a day. Maddy burst out laughing.

"What are you some kind of a pauper?" she asked.

"Fine, you choose," I said.

"May I help you?" an agent asked from behind the counter.

"Do you have a Mercedes SL 500 in stock?" Maddy asked.

"Don't you think that's a bit extravagant?" I asked.

"Of course not, Grace. I'm not going to get a black one. Silver is way less fancy," she said. Maybe on the planet she came from, silver was less fancy than black, but on earth it didn't make much difference. Unfortunately for Maddy, they didn't have the SL 500 in silver or black in stock. Maddy scrambled to find a second choice.

"Hmm, what about the BMW 6 Series Convertible?" she asked.

"Let me check," said the agent.

"Won't our hair get messed up in a convertible?" I asked.

"Oh my God, you are such a diva, Grace," she said. "The front seat is less windy." Well she sure put me in my place.

"You're in luck," said the agent. "We have one in …"

"We'll take it," Maddy jumped in before the color was announced.

"White," the agent finished.

"White?" Maddy asked. "Are you sure that's the only color you have?"

"Yes," he said. Maddy gave it a moment's thought and then perked up.

"We'll take it," she said. The Beamer ended up being fifty dollars less than the Yukon.

"What a bargain!" Maddy exclaimed. I filled out some papers and waited for Maddy to put down the deposit. The agent handed us a set of keys.

"Does it have OnStar?" I asked. Maddy started laughing.

"Of course not. Only in GMC cars," she said.

"Oh," I said, gravely disappointed. Maddy and I walked to the parking lot, and when I saw the car waiting for us, top down, I had to admit I was looking forward to giving it a spin.

"Please can I drive?" Maddy begged.

"Absolutely not!" I said. "One wrecked car this week is all I can handle."

"Whatevs," Maddy said. She hopped in the passenger seat and I started the engine.

She pushed the button to turn on the radio.

"Oh my God! Black Eyed Peas! I love this song!" she yelped as she blasted the volume. I turned it down a bit. Maddy turned it up again. And so began round two of this lousy game.

"What should we do now?" Maddy asked, as we drove out of the lot. "Let's make really good use of our time."

"That's a good idea," I said. "Like maybe—"

"I know," she said. "Let's go get hair extensions."

"No thanks," I said.

"You're no fun," she said. All of a sudden she perked up. "Grace, do you know that girl?" she asked, leaning towards me while I drove.

"What girl?" I asked, staring at the road ahead.

"The girl in the car beside us," she said. "She's waving at you." I looked over and saw a girl I didn't recognize waving wildly through her sunroof.

"No," I said, trying to get a better look at her face. "A groupie or something?" Maddy took her sunglasses off and unbuckled her seatbelt.

"Weird," she said, squinting her eyes. "I think she's driving a Mazda."

"Well then it's definitely no one you know," I said. "Not in that lowlife car."

"True," she said. "You sure it's not one of your friends?" I watched through the rear-view mirror as she continued to drive behind us—hand still waving madly in the air.

"Well, whoever she is, she's relentless in her chase," I said.

"This is creeping me out," Maddy said. "You better lead her off the path."

"What do you mean?" I asked. "Get off of me." I pushed her away so I could drive properly.

"Take a detour so we can shake her off," Maddy said. I stepped on the gas and drove past Doheny. The girl started honking.

"Oh my God," Maddy said. "She's such a stalker." Finally we came to a red light and she pulled up beside us again, window down.

"Maddy! Maddy!" she shouted. "It's Bridget." I watched the expression on Maddy's face change as recognition dawned on her.

"Oh my God!" Maddy squealed. "Pull over, Grace."

"What? Who is she?" I asked.

"I know her! I know her!" Maddy said.

I turned into a strip plaza after the light and stopped the car in the parking lot. Bridget drove up right beside us. Both girls go out of the cars and ran into each others arms, jumping excitedly.

"What are you doing here?" Maddy screamed.

"I just moved here a month ago," Bridget said. She was a pretty girl, sort of like a young Catherine Zeta Jones, with straight black hair and an olive complexion. She also looked a few years older than Maddy.

"Grace, this is my good friend Bridget," Maddy said. Good friend? Two minutes ago she had no recollection of who this 'stalker' might be.

"Nice to meet you," I said.

"Same," Bridget said, clinging on to Maddy's arm. They stood in the parking lot gabbing away, and I figured out from their conversation that they knew each other through a guy from a boy band that Bridget had dated. After that, I only picked up bits and pieces of the conversation because they were talking so quickly and cutting each other's sentences off.

"I was in rehab last February, but I'm clean now," Bridget said. I watched Maddy's eyes grow wide, and I was slightly taken back myself.

"Are you serious?" Maddy asked. "For what? Alcohol?"

"Coke," Bridget whispered. "My boyfriend got me into it. I was a bit of a mess," she said. "Plus he kept telling me to lose weight and then presto, I became bulimic."

"Oh my gosh, you poor thing," Maddy said. "I hope you dumped his ass."

"No, no. I love him. He's thirty-five."

"Holy shit, Bridget," Maddy said. "You should come back to the hotel and hang out with us for a bit. We can chat by the pool or something."

"I'd love to. Where are you staying?" Bridget asked.

"The Springs, of course," Maddy said.

"Cool."

"Do you want to ride with Bridget?" I asked, thinking how I'd love to have some peace and quiet for a while.

"Great idea, Grace." Maddy said. "I'll meet you at the hotel." She ran to the passenger side of Bridget's car and jumped in.

Even if Bridget was messed up, the fact that I could delight in the next ten minutes without Maddy beside me, made me appreciate her more than she would ever know.

CHAPTER 18

Bridget stayed over the rest of the day and was then persuaded by Maddy to sleep over.

"You can borrow my clothes," Maddy said. "You're not that much bigger than me. I'm sure some of my more oversized things will fit." Not exactly the most appropriate thing to say to a recovered bulimic, but I didn't want to draw attention to it since it seemed to have gone over Bridget's head. Maddy was clearly clinging to Bridget, and with things shaky between her and Katie from the night before she was probably nervous that if Bridget walked out the door she'd never see her again. I was glad to have Bridget there—it meant I didn't have to be the only one to entertain Maddy.

I ended up having a very restful sleep with no disruptions. I dreamt that Hunter and I danced the cha-cha on the television show *Dancing with the Stars*. It was magical. As we were about to receive our scores I was awoken by the phone. It was Jake.

"Hey Grace, I have Teach Rogers on conference," he said when I'd answered. Teach told me how he was looking forward to meeting with me to discuss the possible business venture, but took me off guard with a few personal questions.

"What color eyes do you have, Grace?" he asked.

"Huh?" Weren't we discussing strategic locations for office space in LA?

"I wanted to know the color of your eyes," Teach repeated.

"Blue," I said.

"What kind of blue?" he asked.

Was Teach flirting with me? Or was this some kind of test?

"Well, um …" I said, trailing off.

"You still with us, hon?" Teach asked. Jake coughed. I straightened up and took a breath.

"Sorry," I said. "I was going to say that they are blue-green, similar to the color of the same name in the Crayola-24 pack; however then it occurred to me that the color was renamed in 1990 to Cerulean. So yeah, that's the kind of blue they are. Cerulean." There was silence for a moment. Then a snicker from Teach.

"I am so looking forward to meeting you," he said.

"Wow, Grace. That was impressive," Jake said, after Teach had hung up. "Total House doesn't stand a chance."

Maddy, Bridget, and I went for lunch at a trendy restaurant off of Rodeo Drive called Daffodils. We ate outside on the terrace, surrounded by rose bushes and plenty of celebrities. I could barely concentrate on the menu with my eyes fixated on Reese and her beautiful little girl. It was a bright sunny day and Maddy was decked out in Chanel. From sunglasses to shoes, one would think she was on the 'it' list. However, her behavior proved to be as obnoxious as usual.

Maddy had ordered a Greek salad with no tomatoes and onions, and the waiter brought a Greek salad with onions. Needless to say, she caused a fuss, screaming so loud at the waiter that every conversation in the restaurant stopped and all heads turned to look at us. Maddy, who was enjoying the spotlight as usual, yelled at me to go to the kitchen and watch the chef make if for her so he wouldn't screw up again. I calmly explained to her, through my own embarrassment, that I was quite sure the chef would get it right this time.

"I know that," she said. "I just don't want spit in my food." I couldn't argue with that because if I was the chef, I'd probably do worse things to her food than spit in it. I walked to the kitchen with the waiter, earning a sympathetic look from Reese. I was introduced to the chef, Pierre, who laughed so hard when he heard the dilemma, that he knocked a jar of pickles off the counter, sending them smashing to the floor.

"Oh zee famous peoples," he said, as a busboy rushed to mop up the mess. "Zey are such char-actors. Ha-ha. Get it? Char-actors?" The waiter and I both laughed, and I realized that with all the high maintenance celebs in the city, he'd probably seen worse.

"I don't zink I've seen anyone ever be zis bad," Pierre said. I guess Maddy truly was the worst.

When I returned to the table, Maddy was text messaging while Bridget picked at her salad.

"Here you go," I said, as Maddy's salad was placed in front of her by the waiter.

"All better."

"It's about time," she said, scowling. Maddy looked over at Bridget, who had put her fork down. "You've barely eaten a thing. I thought you've recovered from your eating disorder," she said.

"Maddy," I said, thinking she could be a little more supportive. "You shouldn't say things like that."

"Well I am recovered," said Bridget. "But after all that, I'll be damned if I'm going to gain the weight back." I had to admit as demented as it seemed, she did have a point. If I had gone to that extent to lose an ample amount of weight, I wouldn't want to gain it back either.

"For someone who's not an actress, you sure have encountered a lot of hurdles," Maddy said.

"Make fun of me all you want," said Bridget. "I don't care."

"I wasn't making fun of you," Maddy said.

"Really, it's fine," said Bridget. "Forget it."

The rest of the meal was slightly uncomfortable as none of us uttered a word. Maddy and I devoured our salads, while Bridget continued to pretend to eat hers. When the bill came, Maddy handed me her credit card to pay while she went to the washroom with Bridget. I hoped Bridget wasn't going to teach her how to throw up.

"Let's spend the rest of the afternoon at the pool," Maddy suggested, once we were in the car. It was two o'clock in the afternoon and the sun was bright and shining. Not a bad idea. Turning onto Beverley, something caught Maddy's eye and she lunged at me.

"Stop the car!" she screamed, trying to grab the wheel.

"What's wrong?" I asked, screeching to a stop. A car honked and swerved around me.

"Look in the window!" Maddy said, pointing out my window.

"Okay," I said, glancing in the direction she was indicating. "What am I looking at?" I pushed her away from my face.

"At the shirts in that store," she said. "The ones with all that stuff written on them. I've got to get some. Just pull over here!" She indicated to an empty spot in front of a parking meter. Bridget was in the backseat speaking on the phone to her boyfriend the ex-drug addict.

"I love you too, Biff baby," she said. Maddy rolled her eyes. I parallel parked and turned off the ignition.

"Hey!" I yelled, as Maddy somersaulted right out of the car, 'Dukes of Hazard' style. A few bystanders who witnessed the stunt clapped as she landed on her feet. She kicked the car and startled Bridget, who was still on the phone.

"Time to go. Get off the phone!" she commanded.

"Of course I miss you baby," Bridget said, getting out of the car and following behind Maddy. When I saw a sale sign in the window of Ron Herman, I yelled after Maddy and told her I was going to go look around.

"Fine," she yelled back over her shoulder.

I locked the car doors and hurried toward the store. I'd heard of the Ron Herman store, and was excited for this opportunity to check it out.

I didn't get far because a short woman with bleached out hair and her little girl blocked me.

"Could my daughter get a picture with you?" she asked, holding up a camera.

"With me?" I asked.

"It really would mean a lot to her," she went on. "We're from out of town, and she's been dying to see a star, and when we saw you girls pull up she knew who YOU were instantly." I looked at her, perplexed.

"I'm just that sort of mother that would embarrass myself for my child's sake," she said with a sheepish laugh. "Missy watches your show all the time."

No one at home would ever believe that I'd been mistaken for a star twice, yet still didn't know which one. I did hope it was Brooke Shields or someone equally as fabulous.

"Sure," I said. "No problem."

Missy waddled over and stood beside me while her mom snapped a photo.

"Honey you blinked," said her mom. "Let me take another." I impatiently waited while her mother got another shot.

"Pookie, you've got to smile!" she said. "One more!" This was getting annoying.

"I've really got to—"

"There! Perfect," she said.

"Okay well have a great day," I said, trying to rush away. Missy grabbed my hand.

"Are all stars as nice as you are?" she asked.

"Well, um some," I said. "Hey you know who went into that t-shirt shop?"

"Who?" Missy asked.

"Maddy Malone!" I said, excitedly hoping that would get rid of them quicker.

"Who's that?" she asked. Fuck! I watched her mom take a pen and paper from her handbag. Oh no, not an autograph. She handed it to me, and I was stumped over what to sign. I quickly scribbled a totally illegible name with a few hearts and a happy face, and handed it back to her.

"Well take care," I said, rushing off before they realized I was a fraud. I didn't look back to see their reaction.

"Everything in the store is eighty percent off today," a salesgirl in skinny jeans and a strapless top said.

"Really?" I asked. That was the greatest sale I'd ever heard of.

"Yeah," she answered. "Let me know if you need any help." I was happy I had brought some spending money, and my credit card wasn't completely maxed out yet, so I flipped through racks of designer jeans and tops looking for things to purchase. A few minutes later my cell phone rang. It was Maddy.

"Where are you?" she asked.

"In Ron Herman," I said, grabbing a blue top off a hanger. "Everything is eighty percent off," I said.

"Gross!" she said, "Sales are nauseating." I pulled the blue top over my head.

"Yes," I said. "Sick."

"Hurry up and come back. We're done," she said. I quickly took the shirt to the counter and paid.

"That was fast," the saleslady said. I was sweating by the time I got back outside. Maddy and Bridget were nowhere in sight. I felt aggravated that she had made me rush.

I was waiting in the car for ten minutes before Maddy came somersaulting back through the window. There were more cheers and clapping from pedestrians.

"Don't try this at home, kids!" she said with a wave to the crowd. Bridget climbed into the backseat. She carried some bags and was no longer on the phone. "Give me the bag," Maddy said. "I want to show Grace." Bridget handed her the bag and Maddy pulled out a T-shirt. "Look what I got," she said. It was a white ribbed tank top that had the phrase, 'Blue-eyed Floozy,' across it. "It's for you."

"And I thought I hid it so well," I said. It was silly, but I suppose it was the thought that counts, though I wished she had thought of me in the Fendi store instead.

"Maddy bought me four T-shirts," Bridget said.

"That was nice of you," I said.

"Pennies from my pocket," Maddy answered, pulling out one of her own tops that read 'I'm the shit.'

On our way back to The Springs, Maddy instructed me to pull into the Coffee Bean. At this rate we would never get to the pool. I turned into the plaza and parked in the sea of Mercedes, BMWs, Land Rovers and Hummers.

Inside was crowded and I noticed a few people staring at us as we walked in; but now the question seemed to be, did they recognize Maddy, or did they recognize me?

"Three iced vanilla lattés," I told the barista behind the counter, when it was our turn in line.

"Make mine low fat," Bridget jumped in. Maddy seemed annoyed.

"You make things so complicated with your diet," she said.

"Twelve dollars," said the barista. Since neither of them reached for their wallets, I ended up paying for our drinks. Guess Maddy had used up all the "pennies from her pocket" on the shirts.

"Thanks," Bridget said.

"Ditto," said Maddy.

"Sure," I said.

When our coffees were ready we took them off the counter and headed for the door.

"I can't believe how many people use this place as their office," Maddy said. It was true, people often set up their workstation at coffee shops. They were most probably aspiring writers, as they sat with their laptops, typing away. A cute guy sitting near the door caught my eye and he winked.

"You sure attract weirdos," Maddy said.

"Actually," Bridget said. "He was winking at me."

"Whatevs," Maddy said. "You are so cocky." Bridget laughed and flipped her hair back, brushing it in my face.

"By the way," Maddy said, on our way back to the hotel. "I'm going out after my interview tonight." Interview? Had she rescheduled the *Teen Queen* one and forgotten to tell me?

"What interview?" I asked.

"For Radio LOCO tonight," she said. I had no idea what she was talking about.

"Oh that's right, you weren't in the store with us," she continued. "My mother called to tell me about it."

"What time is it at?" I asked.

"I don't remember," she said.

"Well what did she say?" I asked.

"I don't remember," said Maddy.

"You mean to tell me that you can memorize numerous pages of lines for a movie, but you can't remember what time your mother said you need to be at a radio station?" I asked. I found that hard to believe.

"That's different," she said. "It's like comparing apples to oranges."

"Clearly," I said. Hopefully Mrs. Malone had faxed the information to the hotel so I wouldn't have to call and request it from her.

"I'm not going to come with you to the station," said Bridget. "I need to go home and freshen up before we go out later. I'm exhausted."

"YOU'RE exhausted?" Maddy said, with an evil laugh. "I'm the one working my ass off."

"Well, I, um, need to check on my cat," Bridge said. She was really grasping at straws. I was getting the feeling that Bridget was regretting stalking us from her car yesterday.

"You have a cat?" Maddy asked.

"Yes, um, Puddles," Bridget answered.

"Oh," said Maddy. "Well fine then. I'll just get my best friend Katie to come with me. She's really skinny." I watched through the rearview mirror as Bridget slid down in her seat, and I felt terrible for her.

"Fuck, I think our key is broken," I said, jamming the key card into our door, when we'd arrived back at The Springs. The magnetic strip wasn't working.

"Do you have yours?" I asked. Maddy shook her head. Silly question. "I'll go downstairs and get a new one," I said.

"We'll wait here," she said. "Hurry up!"

While I was waiting in line at the front desk, my cell phone rang. It was Maddy.

"What's taking so long?" she asked.

"There's a line," I said.

"Ugh! Go to the front and tell them it's an emergency," she said. "I need to pee."

"Miss Daniels? Is there a problem?" Roz asked, when I'd weaseled my way through the line, earning dirty looks from the people ahead of me.

"Hi, sorry. My key's not working, and Maddy's waiting outside the room not feeling well," I lied.

"Oh, I see," Roz said. She took my key and scanned it through a machine behind the desk.

"It should work now," she said.

"Thanks so much. I really appreciate it," I said.

When I got back upstairs, Maddy and Bridget were sitting on the floor talking on their cell phones.

"Yes. Fine. Okay," Maddy said. She rolled her eyes at me as I tried the key in the lock.

"There we go," I said. The girls rose from the floor.

Maddy handed me her phone as she strode by me.

"Talk to her," she said. It was Mrs. Malone.

"I just wanted to make sure Maddy gave you the message about the radio station," she said.

"Yes, she told me, but couldn't remember the details," I said.

"Okay, hold on," she said. I heard her rustling around papers on the other end.

"Fuck, where did I put that paper," she said. I waited patiently while Mrs. Malone shouted out profanities trying to find the information.

"I'm going to have to call you back," she said. Then changed her mind. "Actually maybe you could just call Alison Clayman and find out the time."

"Um, okay, I'll just do that then," I said. I hung up the phone and dialed Alison to continue the wild goose chase for Maddy's call time.

"Oh, I don't know," Alison said when I asked. "I'd have to look it up."

"No problem," I said. "I'll wait."

"What?" she asked. "Oh, well, ugh, okay, hold on."

"Eight o'clock," Alison said, after five minutes of keeping me on hold.

"You mean she has to be there at eight? Or is that what time the car's coming to get us?" I asked.

"Jesus Christ, Grace!" Alison said.

"I'm sorry, I just don't know." I realized she'd put the phone down again.

"The car is coming at seven-thirty," Alison said, back on the phone. "I'll be there at seven-twenty."

"You're coming with?" I asked.

"Grace, I have no time to hold your hand right now. I'll see you later," she said. I hung up. What was her problem? I decided to go de-stress poolside.

"I'm going down to the pool," I said, poking my head into the bedroom. The girls were lying on the bed text messaging. "Do you want to join me?"

"No," Maddy said. "That's okay."

"I wouldn't mind going," said Bridget. "I could wear one of your suits."

"No, no. You stay here with me," said Maddy.

"It's so nice out, Maddy. Don't you want to—"

"No!" Maddy said, cutting her off.

"Um, okay," said Bridget. She looked at me with envy. "Have fun."

My cell phone rang as I walked past the spa. It was Hunter. My savior. It seemed like an eternity since I'd heard his voice and I knew whatever he had to say would instantly make me feel good.

"I heard Maddy was in a car accident," he said. Anything but that. "What happened?"

"How did you find out?" I asked.

"My friend at the LA Times told me. They're deciding whether it's worth running the story tomorrow," he said.

"Oh no!" I said. "I might as well go upstairs and start packing."

"You won't get fired for that," he said.

"Of course I will," I said. "I'm the irresponsible babysitter who didn't stop her from taking the car because I was asleep." Hunter laughed.

"Sorry," he said. "But that's sort of funny."

"You wouldn't believe everything that's gone on in the past two days," I said.

"Oh my God, tell me," he said. I loved that he was so interested in my life. It was a great quality in a companion. I told him everything that had happened in the past two days, including Bridget joining our adventures. As Hunter and I chatted, I found a chair by the pool and sat facing the sun.

"She refused to do a telephone interview?" Hunter said. "But those are such a joke."

"I know," I said. "And she got away with it. She gets away with everything." I flagged down a waiter carrying a fruit tray. He approached and crouched beside me, so I could reach the skewers.

"Thank you," I said, taking a blackberry and strawberry mix.

"Hey, do you want to come out tonight?" Hunter asked. I was giddy over the offer.

"Well Maddy's being interviewed at Radio LOCO," I said. "I have to go with, but I know she's going out after, so maybe I could meet up with you then?"

"Sure," he said. My call waiting beeped and it was Maddy.

"One second, honey," I said. "Oops, I mean Hunter." I clicked over.

"I need you!" she said. "Badly." She hung up.

"I've gotta go," I said when I'd clicked back to Hunter. "Crisis in room 909."

"Sounds serious" he said.

"She probably can't reach her nail polish or something," I said.

"Call me after you're done at LOCO," he said.

"I will," I said. I pushed 'end' and lay back for a minute, figuring whatever was wrong could wait for me to get a slight bronze color.

The rooms were pitch-black when I returned and I heard Maddy on the phone. Bridget was gone, after having been released by the Queen to go home and feed her pretend cat.

"I swear to God, Marty, I didn't. I don't know what you're talking about," she said. That didn't sound good.

"Gracie, is that you?" she said, hearing the door close behind me.

"Yes," I said, removing my flip-flops.

"Here," she said, throwing the phone at me, when I appeared in the doorway of the bedroom. "Shut the door on your way out." I closed the door and took the phone into the other room.

"Hi Marty," I said, grabbing a package of M&Ms from the mini-bar. M&Ms definitely tasted better when they cost four dollars a package.

"Grace, what is going on?" Marty said. "We got a call from the *LA Times* saying that Maddy was in a car accident and she barely made it out alive." I started choking on a green M&M. I put the package on the table and grabbed a bottle of water from the fridge.

"Grace? Are you there?" Marty asked.

"Yes, I'm here," I said. I didn't even know how to respond.

"Maddy claims that she has no idea what I'm talking about and that you dropped her off and picked her up from the club last night," he said. That little bugger. "Is it true?"

"Yes," I answered.

"So you got in an accident with the Yukon?" he asked.

"Marty could you hold one second? Maddy's other line is going," I said. I put him on hold and rushed into the bedroom.

"What the fuck did you tell Marty?" I yelled, startling Maddy out of bed.

"I didn't tell him anything," she said.

"Well who did you tell him got into the car accident?" I asked. "You or me?"

"I said I didn't know of any car accident," she said.

"Ugh!" I yelled, before taking the call off of hold. "Hi Marty, sorry about that." I decided to dive right into it.

"Well?" he asked.

"I got rear ended after I dropped Maddy and her friends off at the underage club," I said.

"You are a terrible liar, Grace," said Marty. I walked back out of the bedroom. I was sweating and felt like a student who had just been caught cheating on an exam.

"Listen," Marty said. "It's very nice of you to take this one for Maddy, but I know it's her fault. This has happened before."

"It has?" I asked.

"Yeah, she's been trying to drive since she was fourteen years old," Marty explained "She had an accident last year when she was here with her mother."

"Oh," I said.

"Yeah, and I knew you were lying when you said she went to an underage club," he said. "I wasn't born yesterday."

"Sorry," I said.

"It's okay," he said. "I know you've been trying hard, and if truth be told, I've never seen Maddy happier with a guardian than she is with you."

"Really?" I asked.

"Oh yeah," he said. "Usually she calls home everyday crying about something. This has really been smooth sailing for all of us." Smooth sailing for everyone but me, maybe.

"Well, thanks for the compliment," I said.

"Sure," said Marty. "So where's the Yukon now?"

"I sent it in to be fixed," I said. "One of the guys in the valet department at the hotel helped me."

"Oh, okay," he said. "I'll take care of it from here. You don't need to worry."

"Take care of it?" I asked. "You mean the bill?"

"I'll talk to her mother about paying for it," he said.

"You're going to tell her mother?" I asked. "Maybe that's not a good idea."

"Oh, she'll understand," he said. "Like I said, she's been in your shoes before."

"I guess," I said.

I had to admit I was glad Maddy's accident would be out of my hands completely. But when Maddy's phone rang again a few minutes later, and I saw it was Mrs. Malone, I knew I was doomed. I reluctantly answered after letting it ring a few times.

"Hello?" I said.

"Maddy, it's Mama! Are you okay?" she said.

"It's Grace, Mrs. Malone," I said, popping a new M&M into my mouth.

"Where's my baby? Where's my baby?"

"She's in the other room. Is everything okay?" I asked. I hoped Marty hadn't told Mrs. Malone the line about Maddy barely making it out alive.

"I just spoke to Marty and he told me about the accident," she said.

"No one was hurt," I explained. "Really it was just a—"

"Let me speak to my daughter! NOW!" she roared.

"Gladly," I said. Maddy could deal with this herself. I went in and shook her out of her fake slumber.

"Speak to your mother," I told her.

"I don't want to."

"She wants to know about the accident," I said. "She knows the truth." Maddy rolled her eyes at me and took the phone from my hands.

"Hi Mom," she said. I heard panic-stricken screaming coming through the line. Maddy held the phone away from her ear. "Would you calm down!" she shouted to her mother. Mrs. Malone was not calming down.

"It's been taken care of," she said.

The wailing continued. "I'm hanging up Mom. Right now if you don't stop yelling," Maddy said. There was silence, then Mrs. Malone spoke more softly.

"I'm listening," Maddy said. "Yes … right … okay, I know. Love you too, Mom," she said and then hung up.

"What did she say?" I asked, wondering how the conversation could have ended so normally.

"She just said that she'll pay for the car to be fixed out of the business account," Maddy said, lying back in bed.

"Oh?" I said.

"Yeah. And don't worry about it, Grace. My mom doesn't hate you or anything. She just said that she wishes you were a bit more responsible and not so selfish, considering you have my life in your hands." I walked out of the bedroom and slammed the door. Fucking bitch, were the only words that came to mind.

CHAPTER 19

"Maddy, hurry up! Alison will be here in twenty minutes," I yelled. Maddy was in the bathroom using the curling iron I'd bought her and was treating every strand of hair as if it were a brand new Louis bag. This was to be my first meeting with Alison in person and I was nervous to meet her since Maddy had painted a picture of a Queen Latifah type character in the movie *Bringing Down the House*.

"Alison's one of the biggest ball breakers of Hollywood," she said, when explaining the extent her publicist would go to for her, "Like, if I want to go see a movie on a Sunday afternoon, I just have to call Alison and she'll make a phone call and get a row of seats duct-taped off in the theater."

"I have no idea what to wear," Maddy said, when she saw me in the mirror. She was in her bra and underwear. I reached over and turned the hot iron off. She jumped off the counter and I followed her into the bedroom.

"Grace your hair looks so pretty," she said. She had been sucking up to me ever since she made that comment about her mother saying I was selfish and irresponsible.

"How do you get it wavy like that?" she asked, pulling on a pair of ripped jeans. The LA weather had made my hair so curly that I could barely get a brush through it.

"I didn't dry it," I said.

"It's not fair," Maddy said.

"Thank you," I said. It was almost like a compliment.

"Should I wear my white Dior wrap top?" she asked. "Or this?" She held up a sleeveless black top.

"I like the black one," I said. She threw the Dior top to the floor. I spent so much time tripping over Maddy's wardrobe that I practically knew everything she owned by heart.

"You really need to pick up the pace," I said.

"Okay Grace, whatever you say," she said, hurrying to finish getting dressed. "Thank you for being so concerned." Nice Maddy was starting to nauseate me.

A few minutes later there was a loud knock at the door. I got up to go answer it.

"I was just about ready to bang the door down," Alison said.

I could hardly believe this tiny woman with short blonde hair was the bully of Hollywood whom everyone feared. She hardly screamed out intimidation. She was holding a big red leather Kate Spade planner and a big Gucci purse in her right hand.

"You're Grace," she said matter-of-factly as she walked straight past me.

"Yes," I said, closing the door.

"Just checking my messages, one sec," she said, cell phone to her ear.

"Sure," I said. I sat down on the couch and waited for her to finish.

"Is she ready?" Alison asked, placing her phone into a Louis Vuitton holder on her belt.

"Just about," I said. "She's in the bedroom."

"Great. You're doing well." I felt a mild urge to punch her.

"Have you cried yet?" Alison asked.

"Pardon?"

"Has Maddy made you cry yet?" she asked. I laughed.

"Of course not," I said. "Why would I cry?"

"You've been with her for almost a week and you haven't cried?" she asked.

"Well, um, yeah," I said.

"Fine, lie to me. Be that way," she said. I remembered the other night when Maddy made me go get the curling iron.

"Well, I laughed until I cried the other night," I said. "Does that count?"

"Nope," said Alison. "I want to know if you've had a big sobbing, bawl your eyes out fit while working with Maddy."

"No," I said. "I haven't. Though sometimes I feel like I—"

"Just let me know when you do," Alison said, cutting me off. "I want to be the one you tell."

"Are you writing a book about it or something?" I asked.

"Of course not," she said.

"Well, um, has she made you cry before?" I asked. I couldn't believe we were having such a ridiculous conversation.

"Are you kidding?" she asked. "I've known her for eight years. That girl has made me cry more times than my abusive, alcoholic ex-husband did."

"Oh!" I said. That was serious.

Alison got up and barged into the bedroom, startling Maddy.

"Jesus!" Maddy yelped.

I took Maddy's black Marc Jacobs Stella bag off the coffee table and got it ready to go.

"What do you mean she's coming with?" I heard Alison say. Was she talking about me? It would be great if I didn't have to attend. Then I realized she meant Katie.

"We don't have time to wait for her. The show starts at eight," Alison said. "Sharp." For the next few minutes all I heard was shouting and I expected Alison to come back to the living room crying to show me what it was like. She didn't. Maddy entered instead.

"I'll just wait with Grace in the living room," Maddy said. She came and sat next to me on the couch. Alison stormed in after her.

"Waiting for Katie?" I asked.

"Yeah," she said. "I promised she could come." She grabbed a pack of cigarettes off the floor and threw them in my lap.

"Here, put these in my purse." Alison came in glaring at her.

"They're Grace's," Maddy said.

"Liar," Alison said.

"Katie will be here any second," Maddy said.

"We need to leave, now!" Alison barked.

"Listen to me," Maddy said, "Katie has to come. She comes from a poor and unfortunate family in Burbank. It's like I'm doing a mitzvah," she asked.

"What the fuck is that?" Alison asked.

"It means good deed," Maddy said. "That's how you say it in Kabbalah."

"Give me a light," Alison said, pulling her own pack of cigarettes out of the Gucci.

"Hypocrite," Maddy said, passing her a lighter. I could almost feel Alison's blood boiling, and I kept waiting, almost hoping, for the tears to flow.

"You know Maddy," Alison said, puffing away. "You're the one who wants this fame and fortune. Why would you screw it up like this?" Alison was very blunt. And angry. And even mean. Definitely bitter. This was going to be loads of fun. There was a knock at the door. It was Katie.

"See, problem solved," Maddy said, getting up to answer. Alison sighed loudly, her face returning to its natural pasty white color. We all grabbed our purses and headed to the door. Maddy paused for a moment.

"Grace, you should probably drive separately," Maddy said. "Katie and I are going out after."

"We don't have time," said Alison. "We're all going together." I was glad Alison said that since I didn't really feel comfortable driving to the studio not knowing where I was going. Especially since I didn't have OnStar in the Beamer.

"Please, Grace. You and Alison go in the car, and Katie and I will meet you there," Maddy said.

"No!" said Alison.

"The longer you argue it, the later we'll be," Maddy said. She went and sat back down on the couch.

"Fine!" Alison said. "Let's go." Maddy and Katie hurried out the door as I quickly called downstairs for the car to be brought up. When Maddy and Katie drove off in the limo, Alison turned to me.

"Do you know how to get there?" she asked.

"No, how would I know? I'm from Chicago," I said.

"Well how the fuck will we get there?" she asked. I would have assumed that the publicist would know how to get to the interview.

"I'll go ask someone," I said. "Just wait here for the car." I ran inside and asked for directions.

"It's in East LA," I said when I returned.

"I know THAT," Alison said. "Fuck, I better call and let them know Maddy's on her way without me."

We drove out of The Springs and headed towards Sunset Boulevard.

"Honestly, Grace, I don't know how you're holding up so well," Alison said. "I couldn't do your job. Absolutely not. It must be hell."

"It's alright," I said. "It's just temporary."

"Still," she said. "Are you not human? I don't understand how she hasn't made you cry." I shrugged my shoulders, proud of that fact. Alison's phone rang, and she reached into her bag and produced an earphone, then plugged it in.

"Alison Clayman," she sang. "Hi Rufus, honey, how are you?" Her voice was sugary. "No problem babe, I'll put in a call in to Armani first thing in the morning. See you later." She hung up smiling.

"Was that Rufus Howe?" I asked when she hung up. Rufus Howe was a rock star turned actor, and incredibly sexy.

"Yes," she said, gloating. "He's one of my clients. He's presenting at the Golden Globes."

"Awesome," I said. The part that excited me the most about going to the Golden Globes was the opportunity to swipe up all the great swag from the celebrity lounges that Maddy told me we would be going to.

Alison directed me to East LA with the instructions the concierge had provided us with. She told me all about herself, without me asking; like how she grew up in Ohio and married her high school sweetheart, not the abusive alcoholic—that was husband number two. She moved to LA three years ago, after her second divorce had been finalized. Alison had been engaged a third time recently but broke it off when she found out he was cheating on her. It always amazes me how some people can find husbands at the drop of a hat. There should be some unwritten rule that once a woman gets divorced she should get to the back of the line and let others give it a whirl.

"So what happens when we get to the station?" I asked. I anticipated Alison would go off on her whole hand-holding line rant again, but luckily she didn't. Instead she described how Garth Spitz was the most popular DJ at Radio LOCO, and Maddy was very lucky to have gotten this interview. Alison had to pull a lot of strings to get Maddy in.

"I hope she appreciates what I did. I mean, she's not exactly A-list yet," Alison explained. I nodded, but knew Alison's efforts would be overlooked.

Thankfully, when we arrived at the station, Maddy and Katie were already inside. and the interview hadn't started.

"I'm not feeling so great," Maddy said. She was sitting in a chair near an open window. "Could you ask them to cut the interview to half an hour?"

"Well you're booked for an hour," I explained. "I can't imagine they'd be able to shorten the program." She grabbed my new shirt that I'd bought at Ron Herman and pulled me closer.

"My throat is killing me," she whispered. "I'm losing my voice. I'm deathly ill."

Unless the driver had stopped at Cedar Sinai hospital and Maddy ran naked through the quarantine floor, I can't imagine how she could have caught something that fast. She had been fine up until now. I felt her head. Cool as a cucumber.

"I hope it's nothing contagious," I said.

"It is!" she exclaimed. "Totally!" She started chattering her teeth together. She was faking.

"I'll go ask Alison what we should do about it," I said.

"No!" she yelped. "Ask someone who works here." She stood up and looked around. "Like him." She pointed to an older man on the other side of the window. "He looks like a man of authority," she said. "Go! Go!" She pushed me toward the door.

"Okay," I said.

Apparently Maddy's life threatening virus had caused delusions because when I made it to the other room I discovered the man was the caretaker.

"Hi," I said. He looked up from mopping the floor and smiled.

"Hi! Did you need help?" he asked. I looked over at Maddy. Her eyes were fixated on me.

"Yes," I said. "Do you know where the ladies room is?" I waved my hand around a bit so it would look like I was carrying out Maddy's request.

"Yes," he said. "Through the door by the reception desk and to the left."

"Thank you so much," I said. I stood there for a moment longer.

"Was there something else?" he asked.

"Hmm? No, no. That's great. Thank you," I said. "Have a great evening." I came out of the room and gave Maddy the thumbs-up sign. She smiled and clapped excitedly. I knew once she was on air there was nothing she could do about it, and then figured by the time it was over she'd have forgotten this whole incident anyway. That's how well I knew her by now.

"Oh Grace, there you are," Alison said. "Is everything okay?"

"Perfect," I said. She dragged a chair over to where she was sitting.

"Here. Sit." I obeyed.

A live audience was brought in for the show. I didn't know they were going to do that. Apparently neither did Maddy because I watched as her face went pale. She grabbed a bottle of water off the table. It wasn't Evian, but she drank it anyway.

After a few minutes, Maddy began to relish in the attention. She clearly enjoyed her banter with Garth Spitz. He asked her some questions, joking with her about being the next teen queen and then wondering how many more years until she was legal. Katie sat beside her, glowing as Maddy talked about her on-air.

"Who's your friend?" Garth asked.

"This is my best friend, Katie," she said.

"I think this is going well," Alison whispered, leaning over. I nodded. Next, Garth opened the phone lines for the callers with questions for Maddy. The first was a nine-year-old Amy from Minnesota.

"Maddy Malone, the real one?" Amy asked.

"Yes, in person," Maddy answered.

"There's a lot of posers online," Amy said. "That's what my older brother says."

"Right," Garth said. "What's your question for Maddy, Amy?"

"Do you like the color pink?" Amy asked.

"Yes," Maddy answered.

"Me too!" she exclaimed. "And green, and—"

"Thank you," Garth said, cutting her off. "Our next caller is Joel from Colorado."

"Hey Maddy, I think you're pretty hot," Joel said.

"Thank you," she said, blushing slightly.

"Are you a virgin?" he asked. We could hear other boys laughing in the background. Maddy's mouth dropped.

"Oh my God," she said. "I don't discuss my personal life in public." The live audience clapped and cheered at her mature response. Of course I took that as a definite yes, she was one. Not that I had any doubts.

"Now we're going to turn to our live audience who happens to be from the St. Joseph's Choir. Ladies, who has a question for Maddy?" Garth asked. They all raised their hands excitedly. "Girl in the orange shirt," he said.

"Hi Maddy, I'm Leona, and I'm fourteen," she said. Maddy smiled and said hi.

"I was wondering now that you are a role model for young girls today, what advice would you give in reference to steering clear of social pressures?"

"Uh-oh," Alison whispered.

"Um, social pressures?" Maddy asked. She looked over at me. I quickly did a little charade to portray drinking. Then I put my finger to my nose and acted like I was snorting coke.

"Oh!" Maddy said. "Social pressures. Right. Well, Since I am in the public eye, and everyone knows me it is so important that I continue to stay away from alcohol and drugs, and even smoking." I felt a cough inching it's way into my throat. My eyes teared as I tried to suppress it. I quickly got up and ran out of the room, missing the rest of Maddy's fictitious answer, so I could let out my cough.

"Hey are you okay?" the caretaker asked.

"Yeah," I said. "I swallowed the wrong way. I couldn't hold it in." The caretaker laughed as he straightened out some posters that were hanging on the wall.

I walked back in the room just in time for the next question. I sat back down in the chair.

"Thank you Maddy, you are such a wonderful actress. I can't wait to see you win an Oscar one day," Leona said. Maddy smiled.

"We're going to take one more call. Shawn from New York is on the line." There was silence first, followed by a few whispers. Shawn cleared his throat.

"Actually this is more of a statement than a question."

"We'll welcome your comment," Garth said.

"Maddy," Shawn began, "You know the Fashion Police section at the back of *US* magazine?"

"Yes," Maddy said. "Those are hilarious."

"Yeah well, now that you're the next It girl," he continued. "You might want to hire a stylist or we'll be seeing you in there 'cuz girl you can't dress for shi-"

"Right," Garth said, cutting him off. "We're going to take a commercial break and be right back with the lovely Maddy Malone." Everyone watched as Maddy took off her headphones and threw them on the table. She ran to Alison and me, crying.

"How could you allow that to happen?" Maddy said. Alison grabbed her and pulled her into the hall. I followed.

"How am I supposed to know what people are going to say?" Alison asked.

"You could have had them fucking screening the calls," said Maddy, in hysterics.

"They can't. The point of the show is that it's live," Alison said. Katie came out and joined us in the hall.

"Maddy, come on," Katie said. "You're not that bad of a dresser."

"Shut the fuck up, you loser," Maddy screamed. "Now the whole world thinks I'm a bad dresser because you're too busy to get me a stylist."

"You're getting one," Alison said. "It's being arranged."

"Anyway," I said. "You're always well dressed. What would he know about style?" I handed Maddy a tissue and she blew her nose. She tried handing it back to Alison.

"Garbage," Alison said, pointing to a can. "Wait here, I'm going to talk with Garth." She disappeared back into the recording room.

"You okay to go back in?" I asked.

"Yeah," she said. "How much time has passed anyway? Is it half an hour yet?"

Actually it had been forty-five minutes.

"Just about," I lied. "You have another fifteen minutes."

"I'm never doing a radio interview again," Maddy said. "What a waste of time."

"Totally, did you see those weirdo choir chicks?" Katie asked, just as two of the members walked out of the recording room.

"Katie, don't be rude," Maddy said. She smiled at the girls. "Thanks for coming." They walked away whispering.

"Idiot," Maddy said.

"I didn't see them," Katie said.

"Grace is going to sit with me for the rest of the show," Maddy said.

"But-" Katie started to say.

"Don't argue with me," Maddy said. "I'm not in the mood." She grabbed my sleeve and tugged me back into the room.

The last fifteen minutes of the show were a breeze. Mainly because, thanks to Alison, the rest of the live calls were from employees at the station asking scripted questions. I didn't need to explain any of them, either. They were right up Maddy's alley. What are her favorite beauty products? Which actor/actress would she dream of working with? Basically nothing overly complicated.

As soon as the interview ended, Maddy quickly said her good-byes, grabbed Katie, and told me they'd meet us outside. Alison and I stayed a few extra minutes to thank Garth and the rest of the staff. On our way out of the building we found Maddy and Katie in the downstairs corridor ripping a poster of 50 Cent off the wall. Alison walked ahead talking on her cell phone, ignoring the felons.

"Did you ask someone if you could take that?" I asked.

"You think I need permission to take a poster?" Maddy said.

"Yes," I said.

"I'm sure they have hundreds of these. They can replace it." Maddy said, rolling it up and passing it to me.

"I'm not in charge of the stolen goods," I said, pushing it away.

"Hmph," said Maddy. She gave it to Katie.

Maddy and Katie followed me outside, where Alison was waiting with the limo driver.

"You guys want to come out with us?" Maddy asked Alison and I.

"I have to go meet another client at a movie premier," said Alison.

"Grace?" Maddy said. I had to think fast.

"I have to go back to the hotel and do some work," I said.

"Lame-O," Maddy sang out. I didn't mind her thinking that. The girls got into the limo and as it pulled onto the road, Maddy's hand reached out of the window to ash her cigarette.

"How much is she smoking?" Alison asked.

"Too much," I said.

"Fuck," Alison said.

It took Alison and I half the time to get back to The Springs then it had to get to the station. I was more familiar with the streets now. I couldn't wait to get upstairs and call Hunter. I waited with Alison while one of the valet guys went to get her car from The Springs parking lot.

"I'm so jealous that you're going to just go chill out now," Alison said.

"But your night sounds like it will be so much fun," I contested.

"It's not so much fun. The parties, the freebies—ay-yi-yi. I guess you're seeing how stressful Hollywood can be," she sighed. I could almost hear the violin playing for her. The valet pulled up with Alison's car and for some reason, I found it hard to feel sorry for a woman who drove a Lexus convertible.

CHAPTER 20

I called Hunter as soon as I got back to the room. He seemed equally excited to hear my voice as I was his.

"There's a party at a new club in West Hollywood," he said. "It should be cool. You want to go check it out?"

"Sure," I said.

"We'll come get you in forty minutes," Hunter said. I had been sort of hoping it would just be the two of us. It seemed people in LA liked to travel in packs. So, when in Rome, I suppose.

I hung up and on my way over to the closet, tripped over some of Maddy's designer tops scrunched in a ball on the floor. I picked-up a silver Armani one and held it against me before placing it on a hanger. Next I spotted a Diane Von Furstenberg and put it on the bed, smoothing out the wrinkles.

"Hmm," I said. I took off the shirt I was wearing and tried on Maddy's. It was a little small in the chest, but otherwise a fit. I modeled it in front of the mirror and thought how cute it would look with a pair of Citizens jeans. I grabbed mine from the closet and put them on.

Next I went into the bathroom and took out my small make-up bag from the drawer. I applied some black mascara, lined my lips with a neutral liner, and coated them with Maddy's pink Chanel lip-gloss. After I finished with the makeup, I slicked my hair into a ponytail and tied an elastic around it. Then I grabbed Maddy's perfume off the counter and spritzed myself.

"Perfect," I said, admiring myself in the full length mirror.

I picked up a few assorted articles of Maddy's clothing from the floor and hung them in the closet. Then nearly broke my neck tripping over one of her shoes.

"Ouch," I said, rubbing my foot. A Marc Jacobs sandal. I looked at the size on the bottom. Eight-and-a-half. Perfect. I put it on. It was a Cinderella fit. I got on my hands and knees and searched under the bed for the left shoe. I found it, but it was beyond my reach so I ran to get a hanger and pulled it out.

"Nice work, 'Single White Female,'" I said into the mirror when I was ready. "Perhaps I should dye my hair blonde and start throwing spontaneous tantrums as well." I could have, and probably should have, called Maddy to ask if I could borrow her clothes, but figured she'd just tell me I was way too fat to fit in them. Plus I was certain I'd be back from the party long before Maddy returned.

Hunter was waiting in the driveway of The Springs when I came through the front doors.

"Perfect timing," he said, when I got in the car. "We just got here." I was thrilled to see Todd in the passenger seat and shocked to see Jana Longo in the back.

"Nice to meet you," she said after Hunter introduced us.

"It's such a pleasure," I said.

Hunter pulled out of the hotel and we headed toward West Hollywood. I immediately blurted out the story about everything that happened at Radio LOCO, including Shawn, the loathsome caller.

"Wow," Todd said, "That's kind of funny."

"Maddy was very disturbed over being called a terrible dresser," I said.

"She is a terrible dresser," said Jana. I looked down at the outfit I had been so proud of putting together and sunk into the seat.

"So, what party are we going to?" I asked, as Hunter made a right onto Santa Monica.

"It's a premiere after-party," he said. "The movie is *Three Days on Venus*. Rufus Howe is in it. It's at Voo Doo, a new bar."

"Oh, no!" I exclaimed. "Rufus Howe's movie?"

"Yeah," Jana said. "He's such an asshole."

"Ugh, I'm going to see Maddy's publicist there," I said. I remembered Maddy saying that Alison and Jana were 'like best friends.'

"Who's her publicist?" Todd asked.

"I forget her name," I said.

"Isn't it that twat, Alison Clayman?" Jana asked. Oh good, Jana didn't like her.

"Oh right, that's who it is," I said.

"She's been trying to get me on her roster for years," Jana explained. "Totally ruthless and a huge pain in the ass."

"It seems like she gets what she wants, though," I said. I felt bad hearing Jana talk about Alison this way, especially since my first experience with her had turned out to be fairly pleasant.

"She's good at sleeping her way to the top," Jana laughed.

"Wow, traffic is really heavy," I said, changing the topic.

"It always is along Sunset," Hunter said. "But we should be there soon,"

We pulled up in front of Voo Doo fifteen minutes later. A valet appeared at Hunter's door to park his car. There was a red carpet in front of the bar's entrance so once out of the car. The Paparazzi was lined up waiting for their shots. I headed to the other side of the carpet, like I had done with Maddy in New York. I wondered if Jana would ask me to hold her purse.

"Hey Grace," Todd yelled. "Come back!" Fifty pairs of Paparazzi eyes fixated on me as I slowly walked back over.

"What are you doing?" Hunter asked.

"I thought I should wait for you guys over there," I said, pointing.

"Nonsense," Hunter said. "You're with me." He grabbed my hand and walked me along the carpet.

"And who's your date tonight?" a male reporter asked, during a series of questions.

"This is Grace," Hunter said. A few people scribbled my name down on a notepad.

"How long have you been dating for?" he asked.

"A few months," Hunter said, winking. It was music to my ears. Could life get any better than this? I no longer even cared if Alison happened to spot me with Hunter. In fact, I hoped she would.

We waited for Todd and Jana to reach the end of the carpet then went inside. Voo Doo was exactly what you might expect of a bar with that name. Darkly lit and decorated with a Haitian motif complete with artifacts.

"Great place," I said, making a mental note of some of the wall hangings that would look great in a client's home that I would be decorating when I went back to Chicago.

"We need drinks," Todd said. We went over to the bar where the bartenders were dressed as voodoo priests. Hunter ordered a tray of shots and we proceeded to get buzzed. He kept putting his arm around me, pulling me close and introducing me to everyone who stopped to say hello. I barely noticed all the celebs I was meeting because I was so caught up with being Hunter's date.

After a while, I excused myself to go fix my hair and makeup.

"I'll be right back," I said. Hunter released his hand from my waist and I headed for the ladies room. On my way, I witnessed Jana working the room. She impressively floated from celeb to celeb, exuding the confidence of a real it girl. No wonder Maddy wanted to befriend her.

"Jen," I whispered into the phone from the bathroom stall.

"Hi! What's wrong?" she asked.

"Nothing's wrong," I said. "But, I think this is going to be the night I have sex with Hunter David." I took the phone away from my ear as Jen screamed.

"Finished?" I asked.

"Sorry," she said, giggling. "So how do you know?" I explained all the events leading up to my premonition, including Hunter telling the reporters that we'd been dating for months.

"That's fantastic," Jen squealed.

"I know," I said.

"Honestly, Grace," she said. "I feel like you're a celebrity through osmosis."

"Oh please," I said, laughing.

"Call me tomorrow," Jen said. "Don't forget!"

"Like I'd forget," I said. I heard someone come into the bathroom and turn on the tap.

"Bye," I whispered and shut my phone. I walked out of the stall and stood face to face with Alison. This was awkward.

"Grace?" she said, as if she wasn't sure I was the same girl she'd dropped off hours ago.

"Hi," I said. The wheels in my mind began turning full speed as I tried to formulate a story as to why I was at this party.

"What are you doing here?" she asked.

"I came here last minute with a friend," I said.

"Friend?" she asked.

"I have one or two," I said.

"Oh, I'm sure," she said. "Of course. I'm just surprised to see you."

"Yeah," I said. "I guess this party is a little out of my league."

"No no," Alison said. "But you should have called me. I would have helped you get in without having to wait in line." I didn't think I should mention that I was pretty hooked up at this party.

"I didn't realize this was the party you were talking about," I said. "Or else I would have." The door to the bathroom swung open and in walked Chelsea Tate. Hello awkward situation number two. She looked stunning, wearing a mauve satin dress, with her hair up in a fancy chignon. I prayed she wouldn't remember me.

"Grace!" she exclaimed. Alison's mouth dropped. "Oh, hi Alison."

"Hi," I said.

"You know each other?" Alison asked.

"We met in the lobby at The Springs," I said.

"I see," said Alison.

"When Grace told me who she's working for I was so excited," Chelsea said. The look on Alison's face was priceless.

"Wait, what?" Alison asked. I cleared my throat.

"Yeah, when I met Chelsea in the lobby," I began. "I told her who I'm working for and she told me how much she likes her."

"Really?" Alison asked. "I mean, I don't understand. You like her?"

"I just think she's so great," said Chelsea. "Really, I'm a huge fan. She's a great role model. I think she's going to have a long career." Alison leaned back against the counter, probably about to faint. Then a huge smile formed across her. This was going very well, and as long as neither one of them mentioned who I worked for, I could be helping to make history at this moment.

"Chelsea, I am so happy to hear that," Alison said. "It's really mature of you to take this step."

"Hey, I just say it like I see it," Chelsea said. She opened her purse and pulled out a lip liner, clearly oblivious to Alison's astonishment.

"Okay, well I better go get back to Rufus," Alison said. "Nice to see you, Chelsea. You've made my night." Chelsea leaned over and gave Alison a hug.

"You take care," said Chelsea.

Alison was in such a daze that she momentarily trapped herself at the door, trying to push instead of pulling it open. I walked over and helped her.

"There you go," I said.

"Thanks," Alison answered, walking through.

"How do you know her?" Chelsea asked. "She's not Mandy's publicist, right?" I don't know, was she? I took a lucky guess.

"Um, no. Actually, I don't know her," I said. "I mean, I just met her tonight, um, right here."

"Oh," Chelsea laughed. "I didn't realize that. Poor woman, do you know who she represents?"

"No, who?" I asked. Suddenly Chelsea's beautiful skin turned red, her eyes widened, nearly bulging out of her head, and I could see her veins pulsing out of her arms. It was a look of anger, and a transformation similar to David Banner when he turns into the Incredible Hulk.

"Maddy Malone," she said. "That fucking bitch from hell." I watched her body parts resume to their normal positions. I paused for a moment, before responding in a way that anyone in my current predicament might.

"I've never heard of her," I said.

The reaction that I got from Hunter, Todd, and Jana, when I told them about my bathroom incident with Alison and Chelsea, was exactly what I had anticipated. Laughter. We were driving home from the party, Hunter and I in the front seat, Jana and Todd in the back.

"Grace," Jana said, after the laughter had subsided. "That is the greatest story I've ever heard in my life."

"You could get a job as the person who reunites celebrities with their enemies," Todd said, laughing.

"No way," I said. "Even if Alison tells Maddy how much Chelsea likes her, Maddy will still hate her."

"True," Hunter said. "Chelsea's a beautiful girl."

"Hopefully Alison is capable of taking it from here," I said. I prayed that when she let Maddy know that she saw me at the party, she wouldn't mention what I was wearing at the time.

Hunter dropped Jana off first in front of her beautiful Beverly Hills mansion. She asked if we wanted to come in, and I won't lie, I was dying to see the inside. However, I had more of a desire to fool around with Hunter David. Once Jana was gone, Todd sprawled out across the backseat.

"Too much vodka," he said. "I'm going to feel this tomorrow."

After dropping Todd of, Hunter made a beeline for my hotel. I originally thought it would be better to go back to his place because with my luck, it would be the one night Maddy returned home early. He obviously had other plans.

"I'm so glad you came out," Hunter said, pulling into the circular driveway of The Springs.

"So am I," I said. "Thank you for inviting me." He put the car in park and sat for a moment. The valet came around to take his keys.

"One minute," Hunter said to him. Did that mean in one minute Hunter would give him the keys and then he would come upstairs with me? Or did that mean he was dropping me off in one minute. Men were so hard to read.

"I really like hanging out with you, Grace" Hunter said. "You're like a breath of fresh air around here." He leaned in and kissed me on the cheek.

"The feeling's mutual," I said. I could feel my hands slightly shaking as I ran them through his thick lustrous hair.

"I wish I didn't have to be at a photo shoot so early in the morning, otherwise we could hang out longer," he said. Talk about raining on a parade.

"Oh," I said. "I understand." Really, I didn't. I mean what guy would give up a sure thing because he needed to wake up early?

"If I wasn't being featured on the cover," Hunter said. "I'd definitely come up with you and hang." I thought about it rationally. This wasn't rejection, just a rain check. It was nice to know that Hunter respected me enough to not just want to come upstairs for a quickie. Obviously we were going to hook up. It didn't have to be tonight. He was such a gentleman that he probably wanted to take me for a nice dinner, maybe a little dancing, before getting me into bed. I felt so lucky to have him.

"I'll give you a call tomorrow, babe, okay?" he said.

"I can't wait," I said. "Thanks again." I leaned in closer and planted one on Hunter's lips. He seemed surprised at my boldness, but didn't move away. Not bad for a start. I hopped out of the car and the valet rushed over to shut the door behind me.

"Did you have a good night?" Roz asked as I sailed by the front desk, on my way to the elevators.

"The best," I said.

CHAPTER 21

I had a dream that night that I was lying on the floor in the Fred Segal shoe department, and Hunter David was kissing me. First he gave me little pecks on the cheek, then moved on to longer sweeter ones against my mouth, all the while whispering sweet nothings into my ear. Due to the amount of noise in the background, it was hard to make out what he was saying but it sounded like poetry.

"Beyond my day. Beyond the way," he said. I felt his weight on top of me as I relished in his kisses. I don't know how we got in that position, and even though the store was crowded, no one seemed to be paying attention to us. I glanced down and noticed I was still wearing one of Maddy's shoes from the night before, but the heel had broken off and was lying beside me. She was going to kill me, but I didn't care because Hunter David was finally mine.

He gently lifted my chin up and we were face to face again. Then out of nowhere, he started licking my face. Weird, but kinky.

"Beyond the sea," he uttered again, in between lapping. Then his voice changed to a higher tone and he said, "Beyonce." Wait, what? I tried pushing him away for a second, but he continued licking fast and firm. I felt like I was drowning.

"Beyonce," he said again. "Beyonce."

"I'm not Beyonce. I'm Grace," I tried to say, but no words would come out. I was voiceless. I tried to scream, but it was as if

Hunter was oblivious to anything except licking my face. I was terrified.

"Beyonce! Beyonce!" I opened my eyes. My face was still being licked. Oh no, it was one of those dreams where you wake up to find out that you're dreaming about having a dream.

"Help!" I yelled. This time I had a voice. "What the—" I shot up off my pillow. There was a yelp as a small white dog went flying to the other side of the bed. I reached over and caught it before it fell off and put it down in the middle of the bed. Maddy was yelling Beyonce's name from the other room.

"You're Beyonce's dog?" I asked. The dog wagged it's tail quickly and lunged at my face again.

"That's enough kisses for today," I said, holding her back.

"Beyonce! Beyonce!" Maddy was still shouting like a lunatic from the other room. Perhaps Beyonce had snuck out while Maddy slept?

I picked up the dog and went into the other room. I found Maddy stretched out on the couch, smoking. She looked up when she saw me.

"Oh there you are," she said, jumping up. "Did Beyonce wake you?"

I looked down at the little dog in my hands. Beyonce was her name.

"Who's dog is this?" I asked.

"It's mine silly," Maddy said, puffing away.

"What did you do, rob a pet store in the middle of the night?" I asked. Maddy started laughing.

"Of course not, silly," she said. "Katie and I ended up at this benefit for Hurricane Katrina. They had all these dogs that were homeless, so I adopted one."

"Oh," I said. "That was nice of you."

"Yeah," she said, with excitement in her voice. "Plus, if you saved a dog, then they gave you a free designer carrier bag." She got off the couch and ran over to the front door to retrieve her freebie. "It's gorgeous, right?" I took it from her and looked it over.

"I had no idea Prada made pet carriers," I said.

"Here, let's see how she looks," Maddy said, taking Beyonce from me and plopping her in the bag. "Aww," Maddy cooed. "How precious is she?" She held her hand on Beyonce's head to prevent her from escaping.

"Stay, Beyonce," Maddy said. The dog finally gave up her struggle and disappeared into the bottom of the bag. "Do you love her?"

"She's adorable," I said.

"She's a maltee-poo. It's a cross between a maltese and a poodle."

"Right," I said. "Will you have time to take care of her? I mean you'll need to walk her a few times a day, be home to feed her, take her to the groomer...."

"God, Grace. You're like Debby Downer from *Saturday Night Live*," Maddy said. "Wah wah wah." I stopped talking.

"Look, I know it's a big responsibility," Maddy said, "But, I can handle it."

"Okay," I said. "I'll give you the benefit of the doubt."

"Cool," she said. "Plus, you'll help me, right?" I figured the dog would be much easier to take care of than Maddy was.

"Yeah, of course," I said. "How old is she?"

"She's one-and-a-half," Maddy said. "All the papers are over there." She pointed to some crumpled up papers on top of the television set. Beyonce jumped out of the bag and followed me over.

"She already likes you so much," Maddy said. "That's great."

"Yeah," I said, picking Beyonce up off the floor. "Did she come with a collar and leash?"

"Yeah, there by the door," Maddy said. "Actually do you think you could take her out? She probably needs to pee." For someone who said she could handle the responsibility, she wasn't off to a good start.

"Maybe you should," I began. "I mean you said—"

"I'm zonked," Maddy said, collapsing back on the couch. "After all, I was banging on the door for nearly an hour before I had to get someone from security to let me into the room."

"Huh?" I asked.

"You were obviously having some pretty sweet dreams there, Grace," Maddy laughed. "You didn't even hear me knocking." I blushed slightly. She was right about that.

"I suppose I could take her this once," I said. I went over and pried Beyonce off the Prada carrier strap that she was chewing on and brought her into the bedroom so I could throw some clothes on. When I came out Maddy was on the phone.

"Wait until you see her Bridget," Maddy said. "She is the best thing that ever happened to me." I attached the leash to Beyonce's collar, and then proceeded to walk the best thing that had ever happened to Maddy Malone.

"What the hell did you say?" Maddy shouted when I returned to the room.

"Huh? What are you talking about?" I asked. Maddy was pacing around the room, smoking.

"Tell me what you said!" Maddy said. I unhooked Beyonce's leash and she ran into the bedroom and jumped on my cot.

"What I said to whom?" I asked.

"To Chelsea Tate!" Maddy shrieked. Oh that. I'd forgotten about that. "Why does she suddenly like me?" I stood staring at

Maddy trying to think of something quick. She put out her cigarette and lit another.

"Well?" she asked.

"Well," I said. "The truth is—"

"Just tell me!" she screamed, cutting me off. Beyonce came running into the room at the sound of Maddy's voice, which in turn gave me a little more time to make up a lie.

"I'm trying to tell you," I said. "Sit down." Maddy sighed and took a seat.

"I'm listening now," she said.

"When I was checking in for us the other day, I met Chelsea at the front desk," I began. Beyonce jumped up beside Maddy and put her head in Maddy's lap. Maddy pushed her away.

"Not now, Beyonce," she said. She looked up at me. "Go on."

"So we got to talking, and Chelsea asked why I was in LA and I told her I was working for someone staying at the hotel," I said. "When I told her who I was working for, she got really excited and told me how much she loved her … um, you. Loved you." This really was the whole truth, nothing but.

"But why?" Maddy asked. "Why would she say that? I mean, she hates my guts as much as I hate hers." Beyonce was at my feet wagging her tail. I picked her up and snuggled her close for security. My own, of course.

"I guess she feels this feud has gone on long enough," I said. "Wants to make amends."

"No way," Maddy said. "She's bluffing." She already had her T-mobile in her hands and was text messaging away.

"I don't think so," I said, crossing my fingers behind my back. "She really seems to admire you. You should have heard her going on about it." Maddy looked up with the wide eyes, similar to those of the runaway bride in that infamous picture.

"Are you shitting me?" Maddy asked. "Don't shit me, Grace."

"She said it, Maddy, I swear."

"Even after I made up horrible lies about her in the media?" she asked.

"Chelsea's over it," I said.

"Even though I tripped her when she was walking down the red carpet and she tore her Versace gown?" she asked.

"Like water under the bridge," I said.

"Even though I paid someone to knock her off the boat at the Jaws ride at Universal Studios?" What?

"Barely remembers the incident," I said.

"Wow," Maddy said. "Alison thinks I should buy Chelsea a gift. Sort of like a peace offering." What a terrible idea. My plan would be foiled. Not that I had a plan. Up until now things seemed to be falling into place nicely.

"What kind of gift?" I asked.

"I don't know," Maddy said. She looked around, eyes fixated on Beyonce who was now nestled in one of Maddy's sweatshirts lying on the floor.

"You want to give her Beyonce?" I asked. I'd be afraid for Beyonce's life if Chelsea got hold of her knowing she was from Maddy.

"No, no," Maddy said. "I wouldn't give up my new dog for anything. Maybe I could just buy Chelsea her own dog?"

"Does she like dogs?" I asked.

"I don't know, Grace. It's not like I know her most intimate secrets. We've only been friends for ten hours."

"Right," I said. "I don't think you should chance your peace offering on a dog or any other pet."

"Yeah, maybe," she said. "But then what?"

"Why don't you just send her flowers or something?" I suggested.

"Because then it looks like someone told me to just send her flowers," Maddy answered.

"True," I said. The phone on the table next to Maddy rang. She looked over at it and shrugged.

"I'm not getting it," she announced. I went over and picked it up.

"Hi, this is Ginny from *Teen Queen Magazine*," the woman said. "I'm calling to interview Maddy for the cover shoot she did the other day."

"Oh hi," I said. "Sure hold on one second." I covered the phone with my hand and whispered to Maddy.

"Phone interview."

"No way," she said, shaking her head.

"You have to," I said. She held up her middle finger.

"I don't have to do anything." I uncovered the phone.

"Ginny, Maddy's just running out for ten minutes," I said. "Can you leave me your number and she'll call you right back?"

"Oh, um, sure," Ginny said. "That shouldn't be a problem."

"Thanks so much," I said. "I promise you'll hear from her soon." I hung up the phone and turned my attention to Maddy.

"I'm not going through this again with you," I explained. "It will take you ten minutes." I braced myself for Maddy's tantrum. Fortunately, she didn't throw one.

"Okay, okay," she said. "Chill out. I'll call her back. I need time to collect my thoughts. Could you get me a cold compress?"

"Huh?"

"Just, you know, wet a washcloth or something so I can put it against my forehead."

"Oh brother," I said. I went into the bathroom and soaked a washcloth for her. Beyonce was on the floor chewing on Kleenex she had pulled out of the garbage can.

"Hey, give me that," I said, yanking it out of her mouth. We'd have to go get her some toys to play with.

"Thanks Grace," Maddy said as I lay the cloth across her forehead. "Yikes, it's cold."

"Shall I start dialing for you?" I asked, picking up the phone. Maddy shook her head.

"Grace I need to ask you something," she said. This sounded serious.

"Okay," I said.

"Tell me the truth," she began. "Do you own a Chanel bag?"

"Do you even need to ask me that?" I asked.

"Well what bag do you carry to all your important business meetings?" she asked. The sudden interest in my personal accessories was a horrible attempt at procrastinating before the telephone interview.

"Well, usually that one," I said, pointing to my old Coach bag. "Anyway, call that lady."

"You should really carry something like this to an important meeting," she said, handing me a page she had torn out of a magazine. The photo was of a large black quilted Chanel bag. "It's new this season."

"You think I can afford a bag that costs hundreds of dollars?" I asked.

"You mean thousands," Maddy said, laughing.

"Whatever," I said. "Shall I pass you the phone?"

"I want to buy it for you," she said. I stopped dead in my tracks.

"What are you talking about?" I asked. "Why would you do that?"

"Well, because you do so much for me," she said. "Whenever I really need you, you're there." This was true. Was I Chanel bag worthy for it though? I stared down at the picture of the bag. I was ecstatic just holding the photo of it. I don't know if I was physically or emotionally ready to own it myself.

"That's so thoughtful of you Maddy," I said. "I don't even know what to say."

"Oh Grace, it will be my pleasure to get this bag for you," she said, smiling. "We'll go as soon as you finish the phone interview."

"Okay," I said.

"I think you know me well enough by now to know how I would answer the questions," she said.

"What?" I said, loud enough that Beyonce came running.

"Here let's practice you sounding like me," she said.

"Maddy what are you suggesting?" I asked.

"You said you'd do the interview for me," she said.

"I never said that," I said.

"Yeah, you said that you'll do the interview for me if I buy you the Chanel bag," Maddy said.

"I said no such thing. You're putting words in my mouth."

"So you don't want the bag?" she asked. How could I compromise my morals for a dumb old Chanel bag. If everything went well with Teach Rogers I could probably buy my own Chanel bag, maybe even two. It would be horrible and wrong of me to—"Okay, you drive a hard bargain. I'll throw in a pair of matching Chanel sunglasses too." She sure had a way with words.

"So you're asking me to impersonate you?" I asked. "It's completely illegal."

"You have my permission," she said. "You won't get arrested for it. You said yourself it'll just take ten minutes. Then we'll go shopping."

"Oh God!" I said, sitting down on the couch. Maddy sat up and put the cold compress on my forehead.

"Here, just collect your thoughts," she said.

Maddy sat for fifteen minutes, which was longer than the actual interview would be, teaching me to speak like her.

"Do you think I should just a hire a voice coach for you?" she asked. I knew she was serious.

"I think I'll be okay without one," I said.

Finally, when she was convinced I sounded enough like her, she started dialing. Maddy was so excited for my acting debut she could barely sit still.

"Just hand me the phone, loser," I said. "Sound like you?"

"Hell, yeah," she laughed.

Turns out Ginny was in a hurry to do the interview because she still had three other calls to make by lunchtime. Since I had promised Maddy would return her call in ten minutes, she waited instead of calling the others and getting those done first. I felt terrible.

"I'll try to answer as quickly as possible," I said, forgetting that I should have added the word like somewhere in that sentence. Ginny asked her first question.

"So how does it feel to be the it-girl of 2007?" Oh brother, I was already annoyed.

"It's like, so great," I said. "To finally be recognized for my years of hard work, is like so …" I looked at Maddy.

"Rewarding." Maddy gave me two thumbs up.

"Great," Ginny said. "Next, your favorite designer?" Ginny asked.

"Marc Jacobs," I said. That was a no brainer.

"Who's your celebrity crush?"

"George Clooney," I stated. Actually that was my own celebrity crush. "No, wait. Orlando Bloom." Maddy yawned and picked up her mobile phone. She began text messaging her friends, while I sat sweating waiting for the next question.

"Name someone who you admire," Ginny said. She stumped me. Since there wasn't anyone from Maddy's life that I found to be admirable, I didn't know who to choose. I decided to select the safest bet.

"My mother," I said. "Because she's like my best friend." Apparently that wasn't the best choice.

"How could you say that about my mother?" Maddy asked, when the interview was over and I hung up the phone. "Couldn't you say someone like Audrey Hepburn, or Nathalie Wood?"

"It didn't cross my mind," I said. "I was thinking of someone you knew personally, and is still alive."

"They live on inside of me, Grace," Maddy said. "They are who I admire and who I aspire to be like. Saying that about my mother makes me seem so—"

"Normal?" I asked.

"Yes, eww," she said.

"Well then, maybe next time you'll do your own phone interview," I said. "Now go get dressed, the Chanel counter awaits us."

CHAPTER 22

"I can't believe you're going to get her a bag and sunglasses," Bridget said on our way to Rodeo Drive.

"She said she'd only do the interview if I bought them for her," Maddy said.

"That's completely untrue," I said. "You tricked me into it." Maddy started laughing.

"Okay fine," Maddy said. "Really, Grace. I don't mind. I mean, I have millions of dollars."

"If you have millions of dollars, can I have one too?" Bridget asked.

"No! Anyway, I'm only actually getting her the bag. I mean obviously she can't accept both." I can't? Maddy continued.

"I mean it would be so greedy of her." It would?

"I don't need both," I said. "Just the bag itself is very generous." I pulled into a spot in front of the Chanel store.

"Hold onto Beyonce, Bridget," Maddy said, passing her the leash. "I need both hands free while shopping." Bridget picked up Beyonce and passed her to me.

"Here Grace," Bridget said. "I don't trust myself. I've never owned a dog." I happily took Beyonce from her because I didn't trust her either.

"I have no idea what to wear to the Golden Globes tomorrow night," Maddy said, browsing around the store.

"What do you mean you don't know what you're wearing?" Bridget asked. "Aren't you totally freaking out? I would be." Surely Maddy could come up with her own things to freak out about that she didn't need Bridget to fuel the fire.

"Well there's a pink Dior dress that would look so amazing on me," Maddy said. "It's in the window on Sunset."

"So get Grace to call the store and have them send it over to your hotel?" Bridget suggested. "I mean it's the least she could do considering you're going to buy her that purse." Wow, I was never going to live this down.

"Grace can't carry out that task, idiot," said Maddy. "Alison should be calling. She's so useless."

"I'll call her when we get out of the store and ask," I said. Anything it would take to get Maddy to the bag counter.

"You should call her now," Bridget said.

"Yeah, call her now," Maddy said.

"Okay," I said. As I was about to dial Alison's number, a deliciously gorgeous man stopped to pat Beyonce.

"Cute dog," he said. "How old?"

"Almost two," I said. Maddy suddenly appeared beside me flashing a big smile.

"I'll take my dog, Grace, while you call Alison," she said, grabbing the leash from me. She turned her attention towards the hottie.

"Isn't she just adorable?" Maddy asked.

"Yes, I was just saying to your frien-"

"You mean my assistant?" Maddy asked.

"Oh?" he said, lifting his sunglasses off his face. I could tell he didn't know who she was. I held the phone to my ear, pretending to have dialed and in one last attempt to speed up the process so I could get the bag, spoke to Alison, who wasn't really there.

"Hi Alison, this is Grace Daniels, Maddy Malone's assistant calling," I said. "Yes, I wanted to call and see if you could have some clothes sent over to Maddy's hotel room at The Springs. She'd like to choose something to wear for the Golden Globes." Maddy looked extremely pleased.

"No Beyonce, don't jump on the nice man. He's wearing Dolce & Gabanna pants." Maddy said. The man smiled.

"You really know your stuff," he said.

"Thanks," Maddy replied, batting her eyes.

"Anyway, I better get going," he said. "My wife's waiting for me in the car." Damn, I was hoping he would be Maddy's new love interest. He gave Beyonce another pat on her head and then headed out of the store.

"Asshole," Maddy said.

"He's too old for you anyway," I said.

"No Grace," Maddy said. "I need to be with an older man."

"Why?" I asked.

"Because my father is absent from my life," she answered.

"I thought you said your dad's the greatest father that ever existed," Bridget piped in.

"Well, um, he is," Maddy stammered. "But he's absent from my life." I still didn't understand.

"But he—"

"Is he here right now?" Maddy asked, her voice loud.

"No," I said.

"Well then he's absent," she said. "Here take the dog and let's go." She handed me the leash and we headed to the bag area.

I had only looked at one bag when Maddy decided this was taking too long and she wanted to go get her nails done across the street.

"Just take my card," she said, opening the zipper of her Gucci messenger bag. "Pay and then meet us at the nail place after."

Maddy explained to the woman behind the counter that I was a Chanel virgin, and to please go slowly with me. Then she grabbed Bridget who was browsing at sunglasses, and dragged her out of the store. I let out a huge sigh of relief. Now this would be enjoyable. In the end I decided on the exact one she had shown me in the picture.

"Don't let your friend tease you," she said. "When I was your age, I didn't own a Chanel either."

"Thanks for understanding," I said, smiling. I walked around the store looking at accessories while the woman disappeared into the back to wrap up the bag and swipe Maddy's card through the machine to pay.

"Well hello, Starsitter!" I turned and saw Todd standing there. He was in a faded brown leather jacket and looked as though he'd just stepped off the set of *Top Gun*.

"Hi!" I said, hugging him. He felt fabulous. "What are you doing here?" Todd squatted down and scratched Beyonce behind the ears. She moved in closer to him.

"I have to pick up a pair of sunglasses for my sister," he said. "Who's dog is this?"

"Maddy's," I said. "She adopted him from a Hurricane Katrina benefit."

"How humane of her," he said. "So where is the little starlet?"

"Across the street with a friend getting a manicure," I said. "I'm getting a bag."

"Wow, nannies sure make a lot of money these days," he said.

"No, no," I said, laughing. I told Todd the story of how I had been bribed to do her phone interview. He burst out laughing.

"That is such a joke," he said. "Who can't carry out a phone interview?"

"Well, I know now that I can," I said. "I'm just lucky she's holding up her end of the bargain."

My luck changed when the saleslady came out of the back, without a big Chanel shopper bag in her hand.

"There's a problem with Miss Malone's credit card," she said. "It's declined."

"Ugh," I said, putting my hand to my head. I hadn't even thought of that as a possibility. Todd looked at me sympathetically.

"That's so sad," he said, shaking his head. I dialed Maddy's number and her machine came on right away.

"How convenient," I said, hanging up. "I guess I'll go over to the nail place and tell her." Todd put his arm around me.

"You're upset, huh?" he asked. Actually I was devastated and embarrassed. If Todd wasn't there, Alison's dream would come true, as I probably would have cried.

"I'll be okay," I said. "I should have known better. I deserve it for being such—allowing her to bribe me like that. You probably think I'm ridiculous."

"Not at all," he said. "You're disappointed. I understand. Really." I picked Beyonce up off the floor.

"Well, I better go," I said.

"Hey," he said. "I'll see you tomorrow night at the Golden Globes after party, right?"

"Yeah, we'll be there," I said.

"I look forward to seeing you there," Todd said.

"We'll have a drink together for sure," I said. Todd gave me his phone number and I put it in my cell, then gave him a big hug goodbye and left the dreamboat and dreambag behind me in the store.

When I got outside I called Alison to give her Maddy's request for clothing.

"Now she's asking?" Alison asked. "It's the day before. Sort of last minute."

"According to Maddy," I said, "it should have been done without asking." I held the phone away from my ear while Alison shouted out profanities.

"Okay let me see what I can do," Alison said, once she had calmed down. "I'll have some stuff sent over to your room."

"Grace, I'm really sorry," Maddy said on our way back to the hotel after dropping off Bridget. "You have to understand that I have no control over my mother's spending habits. She probably had to buy something for the home." Right, and if the roles were reversed and the bag had been for Maddy, she would not be so relaxed about it.

"I'm just really disappointed," I said. "I carried out my end of the bargain. You didn't." Maddy looked up.

"What exactly do you want me to do?" she asked. "The card's at its limit."

"You could have gone to the ATM," I said.

"You mean take out cash?" she asked.

"Yes, that's what you get from there," I said.

"Grace, I've already told you that I'm an actress. Actresses don't carry cash around with them," she explained.

"As I keep learning the hard way," I said.

CHAPTER 23

❁

Later that day while Maddy and I were getting massages at the spa (which was supposed to be my consolation prize instead of the bag, even though we'd charge it to the room and Piranha would pay), Alison had clothes delivered to our room for Maddy. Five garment bags from all different stores awaited us when we got back.

"Finally she's doing her job," Maddy said, unzipping the first bag. She pulled a denim jacket out.

"What is this?" she asked. She frantically pulled out more of the clothes, clearly inappropriate for a night where everyone else would be in gowns.

"This must be for someone else," I said. "They must have gotten mixed up."

I stood up and went to get my cell phone so I could call Alison and ask her if there had been some sort of mistake. There was a message from her waiting for me.

"Hi Grace, it's Alison. Wanted to make sure the stuff was delivered. Thought the jean jacket would look cute over the empire waist dress. Let me know how it goes."

"It's not a mistake," I said, hanging up. "Seems as though she picked everything out herself."

"Oh my God," Maddy said, pulling out a white ruffled blouse. We examined the rest of the garment bags together, the whole time I wondered what Alison had been thinking when she picked out such childish and frilly clothes for the up and coming It girl.

"I'm going to a red carpet event, not a fucking bridal shower," Maddy cried, as the last piece of clothing was pulled from the bag.

"I'll call Alison," I said.

"I'll talk to her," Maddy said. "Just get her on the phone for me." I dialed.

"Alison speaking," she said.

"Hi, it's Grace. Here's Maddy." I passed her the phone. At first, Maddy didn't become hysterical like I thought she would. She calmly told Alison that there must be a mistake with the clothes sent to her, and would she please call D&G and Dior and have them send some "grown-up" clothing. She listened as Alison responded. Then came the thunder.

"Call fucking Dior!" she screamed. "Or I will have you off the payroll faster than you can spell it!" Maddy passed me the phone while Alison yelled back.

"It's Grace, Alison," I said.

"Did she hear what I said?" she asked. Maddy sat on the floor playing with Beyonce.

"I don't think so," I replied.

"So she didn't like anything," Alison said. "I had to throw together whatever I could. Some of the stuff is really cute."

"I don't think cute is the look she's going for," I said. "Maddy saw a pink dress in the window at Dior. It's strapless and chiffon, I think."

"Tell her to send the blue one also," Maddy piped in.

"I'll call them now," Alison said. "They're probably taken already. After all, the awards are tomorrow, Grace." Why did I feel like she was pinning this on me? This was by no means my fault.

"I know," I said. "Well no harm in trying." I hung up the phone and collapsed on the couch. Somehow I no longer felt relaxed from the massage I had just gotten.

"Grace, did you want to try anything on?" Maddy asked, getting up from the floor. Beyonce jumped up on the couch next to me. Maddy went over and held up the denim jacket.

"I'm sure there's something that will fit you. Not everything's a size small."

"I'd never want to embarrass you by wearing such horrendous duds," I said.

"No, no," she said. For you this stuff is fine. You don't need to be decked out like I do. No one's going to be looking at you."

"Thanks," I said. "You're great for the ego today."

"You know what I mean," Maddy said, walking on the clothes to get to the TV. "I'm going to order a movie." The phone rang again. It was Alison.

"Okay," she said. "I had to beg, but Dior agreed to send over one of the dresses from the window for Maddy. And a pair of shoes as well. Ask her if I should arrange for her hair and make-up?"

"Duh," Maddy said when I asked. I gave Alison Maddy's response, who in return burst out laughing.

"I'm so happy that I don't have to sit through the awards," Maddy said after I'd hung up the phone.

"Oh?" I asked.

"Yeah, I mean could you imagine how boring it would be?" she asked.

"A total yawn, I'm sure," I said.

"But the after parties," she said. "I mean, that's where it's at. I just hope Mischa doesn't follow me around like she always does."

"What a drag," I said. Reality didn't appear as one of Maddy's stronger suits in the short time I'd had the pleasure of knowing her.

A few moments later there was a knock on my door. Beyonce went running and barking, knocking a glass of water over onto Maddy that was sitting on the floor next to her.

"Ugh!" Maddy yelled. I got up to answer the door. It was a bell boy with a big parcel that had been delivered to the hotel.

"Oh my God!" Maddy squealed. "It's my swag bag for tomorrow night. Awesome." She quickly ripped open the package and discovered the Chanel bag that she was supposed to get for me.

"Oh!" Maddy said. I was equally surprised. I assumed that it would be a big basket of goodies. Maddy rummaged around in the box to see if there was anything else. I looked at the ripped paper that the box had been wrapped in. I pointed to the name.

"It's for me," I said.

"Huh? Let me see," Maddy said. "I thought you said my card declined."

"It did," I said.

"Well looks like they must have made a mistake," Maddy said. "So here you go Grace. Thanks for doing the phone interview. Are you happy now?" She plopped it down in my hands and went into the other room. I opened the bag and discovered that along with the card of authenticity, there was also a note card.

Enjoy the bag. My treat. You deserve it!

Love, Todd

"Yes!" I yelled out after Maddy. "I'm very happy now. Thanks."

CHAPTER 24

The next morning I was awoken by my cell phone ringing. I reached over Beyonce, who was snuggled in beside me, and grabbed the phone off the table.

"I'm calling from Teach Rogers' office," the woman on the other end said. "He wanted me to confirm your meeting for tomorrow night."

"Tomorrow night is still great," I said.

"How's seven-thirty?" she asked. "He can meet you in the bar of your hotel."

"Okay," I said. I made a mental note to look Teach Rogers up online later so I'd know what he looked like for when I met up with him. I lay back down, hoping to get in at least one more hour. The phone rang again. This time it was Jake.

"Hey Hollywood," he said. "Miss us yet?"

"From time to time," I teased.

"Did Dorothy from Teach's office call you to confirm the meeting?" he asked.

"Just moments ago," I said. "I'm getting together with him tomorrow night for a drink at my hotel."

"Perfect," Jake said. "I'm faxing you over some documents today so you can read up on what's going on."

"Okay great," I said. "I'll go over them before I meet with him."

"You still coming back to me? Or have you found a new career amongst the rich and famous?" he asked.

"You can count on my return," I said.

"Nice," Jake said. "Hold on, your sister wants to talk to you." Sheryl came on the phone.

"Hey," she said. "How are you holding up?"

"Good," I said. "Tired, but good."

"How's the brat?" Sheryl asked.

"Not bad," I lied. I figured it would be more fun to have a question and answer night for my friends and family when I returned home.

"Well, we miss you," Sheryl said.

"Thanks," I said. "Same here."

"Good luck with Teach Rogers," she said. "Work your magic."

"I'll try," I said.

My head had not yet touched the pillow when the phone rang again. Sleep was obviously not an option anymore. It was Alison.

"Hey Grace," she said. "I just wanted to tell you that I had a huge basket of goodies sent to Chelsea Tate as a reconciliation gift." Oh brother.

"I'll let Maddy know," I said. Alison went on.

"I mean, I know she sort of wanted something really special and original, but I just thought it would be better to do it before they run into each other tonight." Oh brother, again.

"You know, by the time Maddy came up with her perfect gift it would be next Christmas," Alison laughed.

"True," I said.

"Anyway," Alison continued. "Let Maddy know that I've booked Fifi Moretti to do her hair and make-up. Trust me it wasn't easy to drag him away from the clutches of Scarlett Johannson or Anne Hathaway. He agreed to come by after, since they're actually going to the awards and need to be ready earlier."

"Um, Fifi's a man?" I asked.

"You've never heard of him?" Alison asked.

"No," I said.

"Fifi Moretti," she said, as if saying his name again would jar my memory.

"Still no," I said.

"Wow," said Alison. "Anyway, he'll be there at five-thirty. Don't make him wait."

"I won't," I said. "I mean, Maddy won't." I hung up the phone and willed it not to ring again. Beyonce was now sitting up on the bed wagging her tail.

"You'd like Chicago, Beyonce," I said. "Maddy doesn't live there."

I got washed and dressed and took Beyonce downstairs for a walk, stopping by the restaurant to grab a coffee to take out.

"Grace!" a voice called out to me. I turned and saw Chelsea Tate. She was carrying the huge gift basket from Maddy.

"Don't jump, Beyonce," I said, when Chelsea approached.

"Oh my God, you named your dog Beyonce?" Chelsea asked, laughing.

"I'm a huge fan," I said.

"She's so adorable," said Chelsea. She put the basket on the floor and got down on her knees to play with her. I tried to keep the conversation light.

"Do you have your dress all ready for tonight?" I asked.

"Yeah," she said. "It's nothing major. I don't like to make a big deal about these things. I'd be happy if I could just wear a jean jacket over a dress or something like that." I admired her so much.

"Is Mandy wearing something great?" she asked.

"Who?" I said.

"Mandy," she reiterated. Was I a complete dough head?

"Oh, sorry," I said. "Yes, she has something picked out." I prayed to God that Mandy was actually going to be at the awards and I didn't keep digging myself in deeper.

"I got this basket full of expensive stuff and I don't even know who sent it," Chelsea said, laughing.

"What do you mean?" I asked. "Isn't there a card?"

"Well, yeah," she said. "But all the card says is. 'Thanks for being understanding. I look forward to seeing you tonight.' That's it." How could Alison have forgotten to sign Maddy's name to the card? What an idiot.

"So you have no idea who it's from?" I asked.

"Nah," she said. "Probably, just a fan."

"Yeah," I said. "No doubt."

Once I got outside with Beyonce I called Todd to thank him for buying me the bag.

"I am so touched by what you did," I said.

"It was nothing," he said. "After what you went through, you deserved a little happiness."

"I feel funny accepting such an expensive gift," I said.

"Don't think anything of it," he said. "You're very special, and worth every penny of it."

"Well, I owe you one," I said.

"You owe me nothing," he said. "except to continue gracing me with your presence." I laughed.

"Thanks Todd," I said. "So I'll see you and Hunter tonight?"

"Oh, yeah," he said. "But I'm not going with Hunter. Don't get the wrong idea about me."

"Oh?" I asked. "Of course." Had Hunter and Todd had an argument? More importantly, was it over me? Oh no, maybe Todd told Hunter about buying me the bag and Hunter got jealous. The truth was, now I was free game for either one. So whomever made the first move, I'd take.

"I'll see you later, babe," Todd said.

Miraculously Maddy was back at the room by five-thirty and ready for when Fifi Moretti arrived.

"Snap snap," he said walking through the door. "Where's the little star?"

He had pink, teased hair and was dressed in a black pinstripe suit that was so tight I wondered how he would be able to maneuver his arms to do Maddy's hair. His voice was high and he had no less than three pounds of makeup on his face. Beyonce crept over to him and sniffed his leg, as if she too was unsure of what animal kingdom he had arrived from. Fifi squatted down, and surprisingly without splitting his pants, began to whimper and bark quietly at Beyonce. She barked back once and then went to lie down on the couch.

"Are you the dog whisperer?" Maddy asked.

"I'm fluent in nearly a hundred languages," he said. Maddy and I looked at each other, both of us stifling our laughter.

"Sit your fanny down, pumpkin," Fifi said, patting the chair. Maddy obeyed. We both sat in silence as we watched Fifi work wonders on Maddy's mane.

"Pookie, open my case and hand me a long golden extension," Fifi said. Assuming I was Pookie, I searched through his case for an extension. The case reminded me of the one Mary Poppins carries to the Banks' home, where she pulls out a coat rack and other various items. I found three different colors of extension and passed him the color requested.

"Is it the same color as my hair?" Maddy asked.

"Hush!" Fifi commanded. He pointed to the case with his free hand and with a mouthful of bobby pins mumbled, "Mable and Fred." Some sort of hair product I presumed, and searched the case once more. I found nothing with that label on it.

"Sorry, could you repeat what you said?" I asked. His mouth was now clear of the pins.

"Did I not speak English?" Fifi asked. "Needle and thread, please."

"Sorry," I said. I came across a little sewing kit and handed the whole thing to him.

"Put a motor on it, honey. We're on a time limit," Fifi said.

"Sorry," I answered.

"Grace, can you pass me my T-Mobile?" Maddy asked. I reached over to get it off the coffee table, when Fifi suddenly turned and slapped my hand lightly.

"No electronical devices," he said. "We all need to concentrate."

"But I need to tell my friend what time to—"

"NIEN!" Fifi shouted. Maddy slumped down in her chair.

"I guess it can wait," she said. Had I just been witness to a wondrous miracle—discipline? I wanted to grab Fifi and hug the life out of him—ick, scratch that thought. I decided to just be happy inside.

An hour and a half later Fifi was done.

"And Voila!" he shouted, helping Maddy out of her chair. "C'est magnifique, non?"

"Non," Maddy said.

"Quoi?" Fifi said. "What the hell's wrong with it? It looks great." I thought he might cry.

"I know," Maddy said. "I love it."

"So why'd you say no?" he asked.

"I didn't know what you were asking," she said. "I don't speak Spanish."

"French," Fifi said. He was not amused.

"You look magical," I said. Her hair was in ringlets cascading down her back with the extension woven into a bun on top of her head.

"Do you think you could help out Grace a bit?" Maddy asked. "She's coming with me, and she doesn't know an eyeliner from a lip liner." That was completely untrue. It was an eyeliner and an eyebrow pencil that I had confused the other day. Fifi looked me over.

"Feh," he said. "Okay, we try."

Turns out, I wasn't as hopeless as they thought, because less than an hour later I was transformed into a dazzling megastar. My hair was curled. My eyelashes were curled. I had on three coats of black mascara, and a shiny plum color lip gloss. I couldn't wait to see Hunter and Todd. They would definitely be battling it out. Fifi was so pleased with his work he started shouting out names of movie stars that I resembled.

"Like Lara Flynn," he said "Like Jessica Biel. Like—"

"Roseanne Barr!" Maddy shouted from the bedroom. Fifi gasped. My heart sank.

"Just kidding, Grace," she said, coming into the room. "You look stunning. I didn't think it was possible."

The Golden Globes after parties were being held at The Hilton. We had waited at our hotel for Katie, Nibs and Bridget to show up, as they were all joining us. Then a limo picked us up to take us to the party. When we got to the Hilton, it was packed with celebrities and photographers. The awards show had already ended and the people were filing in. We got stuck in line near the elevators on the ground floor where we waited to go upstairs to The Infinity Ballroom, located on the roof. The fire marshal explained that the room was filled to capacity and we needed to wait about ten minutes for it to clear a little.

Maddy, of course, was not happy.

"Call Alison and tell her they're not letting us in," she said. I dialed. Alison didn't answer her cell. She was at another party in the same hotel chaperoning another client who had won an award.

"I'll just leave her a message," I said.

"Tell her to get over here now," Maddy said. "This is ridiculous."

"It's not personal," said the fire marshal. "It's a fire hazard." I smiled at him empathetically.

"Bullshit," Maddy said to him. "You know who I am, right?"

"Well, I—"

"Exactly," she said. "So maybe you should think twice about making us wait like this." Bridget gave her two thumbs up. That received a less friendly response.

"Listen," said the fire marshal. "I wouldn't care if you were Barbara Streisand. No one is going upstairs right now." Maddy turned to me and grabbed my arm.

"Keep calling Alison until she answers," she said. I dialed. Still no answer. "Okay, now I'm just losing it."

"Don't," I said. I dialed again and Alison finally picked up.

"What's the matter?" she asked.

"We can't get upstairs," I said. "They're at capacity."

"Okay," she said. "So then what's the problem?"

"Well, um, Maddy wants to go upstairs," I explained.

"So do you want me to go upstairs and clear out the room so Maddy can go in?" Alison asked. Surely that was what Maddy was hoping for. I was more realistic about it.

"She'll have to wait, just like everyone else," Alison said. I glanced over at Maddy who appeared to have calmed down and was busy text messaging.

"Okay," I said.

"I have way more important things to deal with right now," Alison said.

"I understand," I said.

"Just tell Maddy I'm on my way so she'll at least stop bothering you."

"Good idea," I said.

"Is she coming?" Bridget asked.

"She's making her way over now," I said.

"Thank God," said Maddy.

"Maddy, look," said Katie. "There's Chelsea." We watched as Chelsea was escorted by a bodyguard past the line up and toward another party.

"Chelsea!" Maddy shouted out. I quickly ducked down, so as not to be seen.

"She can't hear you through all the noise," said Nibs. "Call her again."

"Chelsea!" I stayed crouched down. "Damn."

"It's okay. I'm sure she'll be upstairs later anyway," said Bridget. "You can talk to her then."

"Why are we still standing here," said Maddy. "God, is this embarrassing or what? I really need to get a bodyguard too."

A few minutes later, an elevator opened and a small group surged out. Maddy brushed by the fire marshal on her way in.

"Thanks for nothing," she said.

When the elevator doors opened to The Infinity Ballroom I was speechless. It was the most beautiful room I'd ever seen in my life. Ice sculptures lined the entry way and the whole room was decorated in white lights and red roses. There was a large dance floor in the middle of the room with a live band playing. Tables were decorated with black cloths and a lace overlay. It was perhaps the sexiest and classiest room I'd ever seen.

"Here Grace," said Bridget handing me her and Maddy's purses. I gently pushed them away. It was bad enough that Maddy thought I was her slave, but I certainly wouldn't be doing any favors for Bridget.

"Sorry, but I didn't get a degree in Interior Design to hold your purse," I said.

She glared at me and put them on her shoulder.

"So now I have to hold them?" she asked.

"Hey," I said. "I know people that would kill for that job."

"Oh Maddy, there's Hunter David," said Nibs. "Yummy."

"Wrong side, Nibs," I said. "Sorry." A tuxedo-clad Hunter was walking towards us and as Nibs already mentioned, Yummy.

"Hi kids," he said, giving Maddy an obligatory kiss on the cheek.

"'Sup," she said.

"You look great, Maddy," Hunter said.

"Yeah, I know," she responded.

"Hi," I said, giving him a hug.

"Hello beautiful," Hunter said. Bridget jumped in and obstructed the embrace.

"I'm Bridget," she said. "So nice to finally meet you. Maddy talks about you all the time." She fluffed her hair and batted her eyelashes.

"I do?" Maddy asked. Hunter smiled. "No offense, Hunter."

"None taken," he said.

"Let's go shake this party up," Maddy said. She turned to me. "We'll be back."

"Have fun," I said.

Maddy dragged her friends away, on a quest for cooler people to hang out with.

"You look amazing," Hunter said. "Tho thparkly."

"Thanks," I said, smiling. "You don't look too shabby yourself." I looked to see if there were any photographers looming around wanting to take our picture. None were in sight, as they were all busy snapping shots of the Ashtons and Demis of the room.

"Let's get a drink," Hunter said. He took my hand and escorted me over to the bar, where we ordered lychee martinis. I took a sip of my drink. On the other side of the bar Maddy and her entourage were doing shots. Nibs was holding a pink, frilly drink.

"What do you think that is?" Hunter asked.

"The shooters?" I asked. "Probably lemon drops or something."

"No, I meant what that guy is holding?" Hunter asked.

"Oh," I said laughing. "Looks like a strawberry daiquiri." Hunter smiled.

"Probably," he said.

"Do you want one?" I kidded.

"Maybe," he said, winking at me. "There's my friend Preston." I turned and saw a nice looking blonde guy headed in our direction. I wondered if it was a criteria for Hunter that he only hang out with gorgeous people. I couldn't believe how good looking all his friends were.

"Well hello," Preston said. "You must be Grace." I held out my hand. Preston took it and shook it lightly. He seemed awkward.

"Yes," I said, sucking back the rest of my drink. "The girl who's stolen Hunter David's heart." Hunter smiled.

"Do you want a drink, Preston?" Hunter asked.

"Yes," he said. "What's that guy having?" he pointed to Nibs again.

"A daiquiri or something," I said. "Come on, let's do a shot together."

"None for me," Preston said. "It gives me heartburn." Okay, Preston was too much of a wuss for my tastes. I assumed Hunter and him were not that good of friends, considering how unalike they were.

"Okay. Hunter and I will do an extra one for you," I said, not wanting Preston to feel left out. I ordered four shots and did them with Hunter. Preston looked uneasy.

"You guys have fun," he said. "I'll catch up with you later." He walked away.

"Was it something I said?" I asked.

"No, of course not," said Hunter. "Preston's a bit shy. Let's go out to the terrace and get some air."

"Okay, sure," I said.

It was just as packed outside and it was hard to find an open area to stand and chat. I was glad that I'd brought a jacket, because even under the heat lamps—and even with Hunter's warm charm—it was a bit chilly. I saw Preston in the distance talking to one of the waiters and pointed him out to Hunter.

"Hold on one second," he said. "Let me go make sure there's nothing wrong with him." Hunter rushed off and left me standing by myself. I thought it was nice that he was so concerned for his friend, even if his friend was a little off beat.

"Champagne, Miss?" a waiter asked. He was holding a tray of glasses.

"Sure," I said. "Thanks." A few minutes later, Hunter returned.

"Is that Bridget?" he asked, pointing to a girl making out with a guy under a heat lamp.

"She works fast," I said. I'd have to remember to ask her for some tips. I spotted Maddy on a small bridge having her picture taken while Katie and Nibs looked on.

"Well hello there beautiful lady," Todd said. "Don't you look gorgeous."

"Thanks," I said. "Nice tux." He smiled, his dimples giving me the shivers.

"Are you having a good time?" Todd asked.

"Oh yeah, it's great," I said. "I've mostly been hanging out with Hunter." Todd smiled.

"Where is the dashing Hunter David?" Todd asked. I hadn't noticed Hunter had walked off again. "Oh there he is." Todd pointed over to Preston again.

"I think Preston's not feeling well or something," I said. "Hunter keeps going to check on him."

"Oh, brother," said Todd, looking over at them. I couldn't help but wonder why Todd had that attitude.

"What's wrong?" I asked. Todd looked back to me.

"Oh, nothing. Just that Preston can be a little needy at times," he said.

"Yeah, I can sort of tell," I said. "Poor Hunter's just trying to console him, I guess." Todd laughed.

"Something like that," he said. "Anyway, let's get another drink."

"There you are," Maddy said, catching me downing another drink inside. "You better slow down."

"I'm fine," I said, laughing. "Are you having fun?"

"It's fun," she said. "I just am so excited to see Chelsea. Supposedly she's still at another party." I prayed Chelsea was having such a good time at the other party that she wouldn't show up to this one.

"Bridget is making out with a guy she thinks is Hayden Christensen," Maddy said. "Dude's Chinese. I think he works here." I laughed.

"Oh, do you know Todd?" I asked.

"Nice to finally meet you," Todd said, shaking her hand.

"Have we met before?" Maddy asked.

"No," he said.

"I didn't think so," she said. "You're friends with Hunter?"

"Yeah," he said.

"Oh," Maddy said. "Too bad. Let's go, Katie."

"Sorry," I said. "She's sort of rude."

"That's okay," he said. "I get that all the time about Hunter."

"Really?" I asked. Was Maddy not the only one that didn't like Hunter? This was starting to get depressing. No matter, he was still perfect to me.

"Don't look now, but here comes Chelsea Tate," Todd said. I looked around. Maddy was nowhere in sight. Okay, maybe I'd be able to pull this off.

"Hi Grace," she said. "You look so beautiful."

"Thank you," I said. Talk about being on the verge of an anxiety attack. "You do too." Chelsea gave Todd a hug and then told us who the big award winners were. I was happy to hear it was some of my favorites.

"Isn't this a beautiful party?" Chelsea asked.

"Oh yeah," I said. "I've never seen a room like this before. I wish I'd brought my camera."

"Don't worry," she said. "There will be plenty of pictures in all the magazines and newspapers."

"True," I said. Todd pinched my waist, and motioned to my left with his eyes. I looked over and saw Maddy. I felt a warm sweaty feeling go through my body. I was trapped. At that moment, I would rather have been the guy *in Indiana Jones and The Temple of Doom*, the one hanging from two posts getting his heart pulled out by Mola Ram's bare hands. That would have been a much better situation for me.

"Chelsea," Maddy said, "I've been looking for you." Chelsea was clearly shocked, and tried to get away, but Maddy blocked her.

"I don't get it," Chelsea said. "What's going on?"

"You look so nice," Maddy said.

"Thanks?" Chelsea responded, with hesitance. Maddy stood staring at her. "What?"

"Don't I look great too?" Maddy asked.

"Um, yeah," she said. "You look great too." Maddy smiled.

"Fifi Moretti did my hair and make up," she said.

"Oh yeah? Cool," said Chelsea, looking over Maddy's shoulder, probably for her bodyguard to come and save her. I prayed Maddy wouldn't make some dumb comment like how Fifi had also done my hair. Thankfully she was too self-absorbed to even remember he'd worked on me.

"So, did you get my basket?" Maddy asked.

"Your basket?"

"Yeah, I sent you a gift," Maddy said. "Didn't you get it?"

"That was from you?" asked Chelsea.

"Um, yeah," Maddy said. "Didn't you read the card?"

"The card wasn't signed," said Chelsea.

"Oh?" Maddy asked, turning to me. I shrugged my shoulders, pretending I had no idea what Chelsea was talking about.

"I got it, but you didn't sign the card," Chelsea said again. "So, I didn't know it was from you."

"Well, it was," Maddy said.

"Okay," Chelsea said. "Well thanks, I guess. But why did you send me that?" I watched as Maddy started pulling at her hair in frustration. I'd be irritated to if I had tried to make a peace offering with my biggest enemy and she seemed oblivious. I actually felt badly for Maddy and thought of coming clean. I took a deep breath.

"I just thought it would be the right thing to do after everything that's happened," Maddy said. I knew that it would take more than a gift basket to get over being thrown into the Jaws ride at Universal. I should have told Maddy that in the first place.

"What are you up to?" Chelsea asked. Maddy's mouth dropped open.

"Nothing. I swear," She said. "Just after how likable you've become, I wanted to give you something to show how much I appreciate it." I grabbed another glass of champagne off of a tray a waiter was carrying. I was starting to feel very buzzed. I looked over and saw Hunter still talking to Preston. A photographer came and snapped their photo. Damn, I was definitely in the wrong place at the wrong time. Preston wouldn't even appreciate it the way I would.

Chelsea's bodyguard walked over. She looked relieved to see him.

"Is everything okay?" he asked.

"Yeah, everything's great," Maddy said, hugging Chelsea. Chelsea looked at me with a confused expression. I shrugged my shoulders, pretending I now didn't know what Maddy was talking about.

"Don't worry, Chels," Maddy said, when she'd let her out of her embrace. "I've got your back now. You can count on me."

"Um, well, thanks," Chelsea said. "I better get going. I need to find my publicist."

"Okay," Maddy said. Chelsea said goodbye to us and was walking away when Maddy called out to her.

"Chels!" she yelled. Chelsea turned around. Maddy put her hand to her ear as if holding a telephone. "Call me," she said.

"I think that went really well," Katie said.

"Yeah," Maddy said. "But can you see how she looks at me with envy? I feel so bad for her. I'm glad she knows I'm her friend, it seems like she needs one."

Todd caught his drink as it came spitting out of his mouth. I winked and smiled at him.

"I'm going to go see if I can find Jessica Simpson," Maddy said.

"You know her?" Nibs asked.

"No, but I heard she wants to meet me." She grabbed Katie's hand and the three of them went off in pursuit of Ms. Simpson. Todd turned to me and started cracking up.

"I'm so glad you got to see that firsthand," I said.

"It was the highlight of my night," he said. "Wow."

Hunter came over holding two shots of vodka in his hands.

"Sorry I left you for so long," he said, handing me one. Todd rolled his eyes.

"I don't know if I can drink anything else," I said. "I'm pretty blitzed."

"Aw, come on," Hunter said, "just one more." I sucked the shot back and that *one more* was all I needed to jump start the nausea. Feeling lightheaded, I handed my empty shot glass back to Hunter.

"You okay?" Todd asked.

"She's fine," Hunter said, grabbing my waist. At any other moment I would have loved the contact, but right now it didn't feel so good. "Here," he said, handing me another glass. "It's water." I took a huge gulp. It was vodka and soda.

"Oh!" I said. Hunter started laughing.

"Sorry, I couldn't resist," he said.

"You're an asshole," said Todd. He ran over to the bar and got me a bottle of water.

"Thanks," I said. I took a few sips. It didn't help. The Golden Globes after party had moved to my stomach. I needed to excuse myself to go to the bathroom.

"We'll be here," Todd said. I could hear him scolding Hunter as I left.

When I got to the ladies room, there was a long line up all the way out the door.

"Oh no," I said, covering my mouth.

"Tell me about it," said the girl in front of me. "It's like a twenty minute wait." I didn't have twenty minutes. I was lucky if I had five. I made a bee-line for the elevators to go find a bathroom on another floor, but even the thought of being confined inside made me feel sick and by now I could feel the vomit rising. I found the nearest door and opened it. It led to an outside balcony and thankfully no one was out there. I slammed the door shut and leaned over to throw up into an empty plant pot. Five minutes of violent retching later, I stopped. I stood against the closed door and took in some deep breaths. I recounted how much I had had to drink tonight, and then leaned down to yack again.

"Oh mama," I said, slipping down onto the floor. I felt the tears run down my face, hoping that the mascara that Fifi had applied was waterproof.

Suddenly, out of the corner of my eye, I saw a hand holding up a handkerchief. I turned to find a man hidden behind a chaise lounge. I wanted to die.

"Here, wipe your mouth," he said. I took the handkerchief from him and sat down on the chair.

"I guess you just witnessed all that?" I asked.

"Oh, I didn't watch you, don't worry," he said. I sighed. "But I'd have to be deaf not to have heard it." I laughed, slithering closer to the wall. The man moved into the light and handed me a bottle of water.

"Sip it slowly," he said. I drank very slowly, wiping the remainder of my tears and trying to regain my composure. In the light I could see his extremely handsome looks: dark skin with piercing green eyes. It doubled my embarrassment factor.

"I'm a disgusting pig," I said.

"Nah, just a girl who had too much to drink," he said. "I'll let you in on a secret."

"What?" I asked.

"I came out here because I wasn't feeling so hot myself," he said. "Too much vino." I laughed.

"Guess it's been a successful night for both of us then," I said. I pulled off my shoes and flexed my feet.

"Bad shoes?" he asked. I nodded.

"Why are you wearing shoes that hurt your feet?" he asked.

"Because, I wanted to look good." I said. "Supposedly looking better is more important than feeling better."

"I disagree," he said.

"Yeah, me too," I said.

"Are you an actress?" he asked. I shook my head.

"Definitely not. How about you? Are you an act-?"

"Artist," he said.

"Musician?" I asked.

"Sometimes."

"Painter?"

"Most definitely," he said.

"So, a little of everything?"

"A lot of everything," he said. I smiled. "What's your name?" I didn't want to tell him my real name after that mortifying episode.

"Lucy Ricardo," I said. He chuckled.

"I'm Ricky," he said with an accent. He pulled a pack of cigarettes out of his pocket and offered me one.

"No thanks," I said. "And you shouldn't smoke, Ricky," I said, putting on a Lucille Ball voice.

"You European?" he asked.

"No," I said. "I'm from Chicago." He laughed through his smoke. His cackling was infectious, and if it weren't for my disgusting puke-tasting mouth, I'd have loved to join in.

"So um, other than this little incident," Ricky said. "had you been having a good night?"

"Yeah," I said. "It's been great."

"Glad to hear it," Ricky said. "I've been here since before the doors opened, so I'm a little burnt out."

"Why don't you head home?" I asked.

"What and miss all the fun I just started having?" he asked. "No way, Lucy."

Ricky sure had a way with words and it was putting my vomit spell in the distant past. I pulled a pack of gum from my purse and offered him a piece. He declined and I popped one in my mouth.

"So what brings you to LA LA land anyway?" he asked.

"I'm working for a teen diva," I said. "The next big thing."

"Honey, if I had a nickel for every time I heard that one," he said.

"I know," I said. "I can only imagine how many girls think they're the next big thing."

"Everyone wants to be Chelsea Tate?" Ricky asked.

"You don't know the half of it," I said. "I'm working for Maddy Malone." Ricky perked up.

"Really?" he asked.

"Yeah. I'm her guardian," I said. "Well, slave is more like it."

"I hope you're getting paid well for her beatings," he said.

"Yeah, not bad," I said. "I have other things motivating me to stay."

"Like?"

"Work related things, and well, a boy," I said. Hell, might as well let it all out. Ricky smiled.

"Whoever he is, he's very lucky," he said.

"Thanks," I said. "It's sort of moving at a turtle's pace. I'm not sure if it's really going to happen."

"You seem like a girl who can get what she wants," he said.

"I wish," I said. "I just hope I'm not taking the wrong road."

"You should take the road less traveled," Ricky said, lighting a new cigarette.

"Robert Frost," I said.

"He knows best," Ricky said. "I bet your luck is about to change."

"I hope so," I said.

"Are you feeling better yet?"

"Maybe seventy-five percent," I said.

"Hmm, watch the stars with me. Maybe you'll get yourself up to at least eighty-seven," he said. So while mayhem was no doubt going on inside, I sat looking up at the beautiful evening sky with Ricky Ricardo, and I found myself more relaxed than I had been this entire trip.

My cell phone rang snapping me from my trance. It was Maddy.

"Where are you?" she asked. "I've been looking for you. I even got Hunter to help me." She must have been desperate.

"I'm outside," I said. "I'm not feeling well."

"Well, come back in. We're by the bar," she said. Just hearing the word bar stirred my stomach.

"Okay, I'm coming," I said, closing my phone. I turned to Ricky. "I've gotta go."

"Are you going to be okay?" Ricky asked.

"I'll survive," I said. I was sad to have to leave such a comfortable spot, and to say goodbye to my new friend.

"I bet we'll see each other again," Ricky said.

"You think?" I asked.

"Oh yeah," he said. "You just watch."

"Well then, until we meet again," I said, holding out my hand. He took it in his hand and kissed it with a soft touch.

"Yes, until we meet again," he said. I turned and walked back into the party and by that point, I was feeling entirely better. One hundred percent.

I found Maddy standing with Hunter, Preston, and Todd.

"What's wrong?" I asked.

"We want to leave. We're going to go to another party," Maddy said.

"Oh," I said. "I need to go back to the hotel. I'm sick."

"Fine, fine," said Maddy.

"We'll get you home, Grace," Todd said. "Don't worry."

"Will you just call the limo to come get us?" Maddy asked. "I need to go find Bridget and drag her away from whoever she's smooching now."

"Sure," I said, laughing. I called the limo driver that had brought us to the party and told him Maddy and her friends would be out momentarily to carry on to their next destination. I watched as Maddy fluttered about the room a little longer, saying goodbye to all the movie stars.

"I'm just going to the ladies room before we leave," I said to Todd. "I'll be back in a minute."

"No problem," he said. "Take your time." I looked over at Hunter once again in deep conversation with Preston.

This time there was no lineup outside the door. I walked in and came face to face with Chelsea and immediately wanted to throw-up again.

"Well hello there," she said. This was it. She must have found out by now that I was a fraud.

"Hi," I said. "Listen, I'm really sorry that I li-"

"I'm sorry you had to witness what went on before," Chelsea said.

"Huh?"

"I mean you got stuck standing there when you probably had to be with Mandy," she said.

"Oh?"

"Thanks for not walking away and leaving me alone with that monster," she said. "It meant a lot to me. I owe you one." She leaned over and gave me a hug.

"I'll see you later," she said. "Let Mandy know I was looking for her. I've got to leave now." She left the bathroom and I leaned back against the wall, trying to take in what had just happened.

"You okay?" a woman asked who had come out of a stall.

"Yes," I said. I no longer felt sick. In fact, I felt great.

"Children are such strange creatures aren't they?" I asked, before walking out of the bathroom to go find my ride home.

CHAPTER 25

The next morning, while Maddy was in the shower and I was lounging in bed, the phone rang.

"Hello, Miss Daniels, it's Roz," she said, when I had picked up.

"Good morning," I said.

"I just wanted to let you know that we'll have the two bedroom suite that you had requested by the end of the day."

"Oh perfect," I said. "I'll let Maddy know." I hung up and then the next call came in.

"Grace there's a picture of you and Hunter David in the LA Times," Alison said.

"Really?" I asked. How could that have been possible when he spent most of his night with Preston. I didn't even remember any cameras around us during the little time we were together.

"It's a good picture," she said. "Right under one of Johnny Depp."

"What?" I said. "I didn't see him there." Alison laughed.

"Or you for that matter," I added.

"Well I'm thankful for that," she said. "Chelsea's publicist called this morning to find out what's going on." Okay this was it for sure. The hoax was up.

"Oh?" I asked. "What did she say."

"She said that Chelsea had called her and said the basket was from Maddy. Apparently the company had forgotten to put the card in," she said. "Typical. Anyway, Chelsea thought it was a really nice gesture, and her publicist said that she hopes everything will be put to rest now."

"It seemed to go well," I said. Good, no mention of my name.

"Well let's cross our fingers," said Alison. "She also mentioned that Mandy Moore's assistant happened to be there too."

"Yeah," I said. "About that-"

"It's just such a coincidence," Alison said.

"Coincidence?" I asked.

"Well yeah, it's so funny that Mandy Moore's assistant is also named Grace," she said, laughing. "What are the chances?"

"Oh, yeah," I said, bursting out in fake laughter. "So funny."

"Let me know how the shoot goes today," Alison said, before hanging up. I went out onto the balcony and looked up into the sky. Maybe Ricky was right about my luck changing.

I was still feeling a little hung over, so I ordered some tea and Saltine crackers from room service while Maddy was in the shower. She was scheduled to do a photo shoot today. A photographer was taking celeb pictures for a book for charity.

"Is the car here yet?" Maddy asked, coming out of the room with her hair in a towel.

"No," I said. She grabbed her light pink Balenciaga bag off the desk.

"Do you like this color?" she asked. I nodded. "I'm going to buy it in a few other colors. Maybe blue, red, and gold," she said.

"Aren't they five hundred dollars?" I asked. Maddy laughed.

"Are you kidding? I wish," she said. "They're almost two thousand."

When I received the call that the car had arrived Maddy and I headed downstairs.

"You know what Bridget said about you last night?" Maddy asked.

"What?" I asked.

"She thinks that you might be a bit of a starfucker," Maddy said.

"Excuse me?"

"That you're just using me to get to other stars," Maddy said.

"Like who?" I asked.

"Well, um, I don't know," She said. "I guess she meant Hunter and his friend Todd."

"There's no reason for her to think that," I said. "I'm here for you." Anyway, I clearly didn't need Maddy to get to Hunter and Todd, in fact she was a bit of a hindrance.

"And she said—"

"It's okay," I said. "I don't need to know."

"She thinks you're a virgin," she said. I laughed. And so did the limo driver.

"Sorry, Miss," the driver said.

"Ridiculous," I said.

"Yeah, I guess," Maddy said. "Obviously you've had sex."

"Obviously," I said.

"Not with Hunter of course," she said, laughing.

"Of course," I said. Talk about kicking a horse when it was down.

We arrived at a house in Manhattan Beach right on time, for a change. A man directed Maddy to the hair and make-up room, and I went to sit in a comfy swing on the patio outside. There were a few random people walking around while I sat and watched the scenery of trees and water. I began to doze off. About an hour later, a young woman on the crew woke me gently.

"Hi," she said. "I'm taking lunch orders." Her name was Rosie. She was short and chubby, with long black hair. "Will you ask Maddy what sandwich she would like?" She handed me the menu from Sandwich 54, a specialty restaurant in the area. I stretched and went to ask Maddy.

Maddy was getting ready for the photo shoot. She was telling the make-up artist, how she'd just had the best night of her life.

"Everyone wanted to take my picture," she said. "It was so overwhelming. And Dior practically begged me to wear their dress."

"Do you have any photos?" Guy asked.

"Just wait for the next editions of *In Touch* and *Us*," she said. "I'll be in there for sure."

"Maddy, what kind of sandwich would you like for lunch?" I asked, handing her the menu.

"I want a burger and fries," she said, giving it back to me without even reading it. I left and found Rosie sitting in my swing.

"Maddy will have a burger and fries," I said.

"Did she read the menu?" she asked.

"I don't think she did," I said.

"They don't have that," she said. I went back to Maddy. She was bragging to the hairdresser and makeup artist how she had been the bigger person and made amends with Chelsea Tate.

"I think this whole thing is going to make her a better person," Maddy said. "I mean she's so mean spirited, but being the cool cat that I am, I think I knocked some sense into her."

"Hey, Cool Cat," I said. "You have to order a sandwich. They don't have burgers."

"So tell them to order from somewhere else," she said, without hesitation.

"Well I think the problem is that we're sort of in the middle of nowhere and—"

"Extra ketchup with the order, 'k Grace?"

"Is there um, a McDonalds around here?" I asked Rosie.

"I'm sure we can find one," Rosie said, rolling her eyes. "But, I mean Maddy is doing a photo in a bathing suit." I thought how disastrous it would be if someone reminded her of that.

"Make sure you tell them I can't work past three o'clock," Maddy said when I got back to her.

"Why can't you work past three?" I asked.

"Well because it's um, illegal," she said.

"Huh?"

"Well because I'm supposed to do two hours of school while working," she said. I put my finger in my ear to clean it out.

"Oops, sorry," I said. "I think I heard you incorrectly. I thought you just said something about having to do school," I said.

"Well yes, Grace," she said. "Don't you know I'm supposed to be doing school while working?"

"I mean I assumed you must go to school at some point," I explained. "Though this is the first I've heard about it since I've known you."

"Ugh, I can't believe no one mentioned it to you," she said. Either could I. "I'm going to need you to tutor me."

"But, I'm not a teacher," I said.

"Well I know, but I mean you could just sit with me while I do my work," she said.

"Um, okay," I said. "Did you bring all your books with?" I could hardly imagine she'd fit them into the Balenciaga.

"No," she said. "I forgot them."

"So would you like me to write down some multiplication questions for you to answer?" I asked. That I could do.

"No!" she said. "We're just going to have to end at three o'clock so that we can go back to the hotel and I can do school."

"Okay," I said. "I will tell them that."

"Maybe you can go find the girl who's supposed to do the write-up about me and I could get that done while I'm sitting here," Maddy suggested.

"Good idea," I said. I found a bunch of people basking in the sun outside by the water. A few of them were sitting around a picnic table reading various magazines and newspapers.

"Is our star ready yet?" a man with a thick moustache asked.

"Almost," I said. He went back to reading his paper. A few seconds later he looked back up at me.

"Nice photo," he said, referring to the shot of Hunter and me. I smiled. Soon the rest of them had gathered around him to see. And quite suddenly, I was the one being interviewed.

"Is he your boyfriend?"

"No, just a friend."

"Where did you meet him?"

"On the set of *Daisy Mae* through Maddy."

"Who did your hair and make-up?"

"Fifi Moretti," I said. Two girls gasped.

"You are so lucky," one of them said.

"Is that your natural hair color?" I nodded.

Satisfied with my answers, everyone went back to whatever it was they'd been doing. I took a seat and tried to remember why I'd gone there in the first place before I'd been blindsided with questions. Then I recalled it.

"Will one of you be interviewing Maddy?" I asked.

"Yes, me," a tall woman said. "I'm Brenda Rothstein."

"Great," I said. "Maddy wanted me to check if you would mind doing the interview while she's getting ready."

"No problem," Brenda said. She gathered up her stuff and headed back into the house.

"Sure is sunny out here," I said, moving into the shade.

"I know honey," one of the girls said. "A little odd for January."

"Do you always travel with Maddy?" the mustached man asked.

"No, this is the first time," I said. Definitely the last. "I'm an Interior Designer."

"That's great," he said. The questioning began again, and I ended up giving out some cards.

"This is our office in Chicago," I explained. "Hopefully we'll be out here soon, too. I'm meeting with a business associate tonight."

A few minutes later, our discussion was interrupted by Maddy's shrieks coming from inside.

"I will not wear that! Why would you even suggest this. It's totally not in. Where's Grace? Grace!" she screamed.

Brenda came running outside to get me.

"I think you better go in," she said.

I rushed into the house to see what the commotion was about. Maddy stood in a bikini in the middle of the room pointing to a button-down Ralph Lauren shirt.

"Is it the logo?" I asked.

"Yes," she said, her voice shaking. I turned to the stylist, a short thin man wearing a wife beater tank.

"Could I talk to you in private for a minute?" I asked. He followed me out of the room.

"It's not personal," I said. "She's seventeen and maybe just not into classic couture." I felt a sense of pride for using such snazzy lingo.

"I've never heard anyone scream so loud," he said. "It scared me."

"As it does me, daily," I said.

"The shirt's only a cover-up," he continued. "She's not wearing it for the shoot."

"Did you tell her that?" I asked.

"Well, I tried," he said.

"Do you have a similar shirt in Lacoste, maybe?" I asked. "I think she might prefer an alligator to a polo player. The world is your oyster if you can make that happen." His face brightened.

"No problem," he said. "I have a few." He went back to the room and I waited outside the door, leaning against the wall trying to make out what they were saying.

"Perhaps you'd prefer this?" he said. There was silence for a moment.

"Oh yes!" she squealed. When I knew it was safe to leave, I went back outside to call Maddy's mother.

"Hi," I said. "It's Grace."

"Who?" Mrs. Malone said. It had only been two days since we'd spoken. Had she already forgotten me? I hoped so.

"Um, Maddy's guardian," I said.

"Oh!" she said. "Grace. How are you? How was last night?"

"It was really fun," I said. "We had a great time and Maddy and Chel-"

"No, no," Mrs. Malone said. "I meant, how did Maddy look?" Silly old me to think Mrs. Malone would want to hear how Maddy and her number one enemy were now chums.

"She looked great, of course," I said.

"Who took her pictures?" Mrs. Malone asked.

"Well, everyone, I guess," I said.

"Good," she said. "They better put my baby in those magazines next week."

"Oh, I can't imagine that they wouldn't," I said.

"Right, right," she answered.

"Listen, Mrs. Malone, I wanted to ask you about—"

"Honey, can you tell Maddy that I bought a watch today and used the card," she said.

"Oh, um, sure, no problem," I said. "Anyway, I just wanted to ask you about sc-"

"It's Marc Jacobs," she said. "Stunning."

"Right. Of course," I said. "Now, if you'd just let me ask you about Maddy and her schoo-"

"I'm just looking at today's itinerary," she said, cutting me off again. "Is she in a bikini right now for that photographer's book?"

"Yes," I said, then to avoid the next question. "Her body is fantastic." Mrs. Malone laughed.

"Now come on, Grace," she said. "You know as well as I do, that she eats much too much fried food."

"Well, she is a teenager," I said. "It's only natural."

"Grace!" she exclaimed. "Maddy is not an ordinary teenager. She is on her way to winning an Oscar, and if she wants to get there, she can't have cheeseburger thighs." I thought about her lunch order. I'd make sure not to supersize it.

"So anyway, Mrs. Malone," I said, trying one last time. "About Maddy's schooling."

"Schooling?" she asked. "What about it?" Now I felt at a loss for words. What was my question?

"I was just wondering about the rules for Maddy doing school?" I said.

"Did someone there ask you about that?" she asked.

"Well, no," I said. "But Maddy said she wanted to leave early so that she could get some school work done, and I'm just not familiar with the protocol for school." Mrs. Malone started laughing.

"Don't worry about school, Grace. It's not a priority for us where Maddy's concerned," she said.

"That is so sad," I said out loud. Oops.

"What was that, Grace?" Mrs. Malone asked.

"Oh, nothing," I said. "I was just going to say that Maddy will be glad that she doesn't need to do school today." Mrs. Malone started laughing.

"You really have an excellent sense of humor, Grace," she said. I figured she kept saying my name in fear that she would forget it again.

Maddy slept the whole way back to The Springs. The photo shoot had gone well with no more outbursts because of yesteryear logos and Maddy managed to answer the interview questions all by herself. As we approached the hotel, my phone rang.

"Hi Grace, It's Teach," he said. "We still on for tonight?"

"Of course," I answered. I wonder why he was calling when his secretary had already confirmed it.

"Great," he asked.

"How will I know it's you?" I asked.

"Oh, I'm sure we'll find each other, don't worry," he said.

"Okay. See you later," I said.

"Who was that?" Maddy asked, rubbing her eyes.

"Oh, Teach Rogers. Big wig designer in LA," I said.

"Oh yeah?" she said. "I know him." I found that very hard to believe.

"How?" I asked.

"He's really hot," Maddy said. Well, maybe she did then.

"So do you still want to move to the two bedroom when we get back to The Springs?" I asked.

"Duh," she replied.

We entered the hotel and waited for the elevator. It amazed me that there were four separate elevators in the lobby of The Springs, and yet even when all four are open, everyone always piled into the same one. We crowded into the elevator, classical music playing lightly in the background. I found myself pressed against a cute Latino guy. He wore a baseball hat and a faded orange sweatshirt and looked to be in his late twenties.

"Things good?" he asked Maddy.

"Yes," she said, uninterested.

"Going out tonight?" he asked.

"Probably," she said. If Maddy wasn't going to take him up on his invitation to converse, I would.

"I am," I said. He smiled.

"Oh yeah? Where you off to?" he asked. Maddy looked at me, waiting for me to make a fool out of myself in front of these strangers.

"I'm just meeting a um, business associate," I said, "for a drink."

"She's meeting my agent," Maddy interjected. "I need her to help me out with script decisions." Well that wasn't too rude and demeaning.

When we reached the sixth floor, two women left. More breathing room. The doors opened at the eighth floor and no one got off or on.

"Who's pushing the buttons?" I asked of no one in particular. Cute Latino boy laughed.

"A ghost?" he suggested.

I smiled. The elevator finally arrived at our floor and Maddy and I left.

"Later Enrique," she said.

"See you chiquitas," he said. The doors closed.

"Enrique?" I said to Maddy as she skipped down the hall.

"I couldn't tell you in front of him," she laughed. "Anyway, he probably liked that you didn't recognize him. Stars love that."

"Do you?" I asked.

"Of course not, but that's because I'm young, and fresh," she said, twirling around and leaping in the air.

"We need to pack up the room now," I said, entering our suite. I dropped my purse on the table and headed to the bedroom. Maddy ignored me and plopped down on the floor, pulling out the Lacoste shirt and the bikini that she had begged the stylist to let her keep.

"I don't love the color," she said, holding up a shoe. "But they're fine for casual daytime." Next she held up the Ralph Lauren shirt.

"Why did you take that?" I asked. "I thought you're Polo-phobic."

"I'm over it," she said. "I don't mind it anymore. You can borrow it if you want, Grace."

"No thanks," I said. "When I see Ralph Lauren shirts I scream and cry." Maddy laughed.

"Don't make fun," she said.

"So did you want to start your school work while I pack up?" I asked. Maddy howled with laughter.

"You totally fell for it," she said, through her tears.

"Yes, you sure got me," I said, turning to go into the bedroom and gather my stuff together. I heard her turn the television on in the other room.

"You are going to help pack right?" I called out. She ignored me again.

"My favorite show is on," she said. "*Celebrities Uncensored*, I need to see if I'm on."

There was silence in the other room as Maddy anxiously waited to see if she'd made the cut. She watched as celebrities came out of clubs. They were drunk, usually smoking, and always shouting profanities at the cameras.

"Ahhh!" Maddy screamed. I rushed into the room to see if her dream had in fact come true.

"That's so cheap!" she said, pointing at Justin and Cameron. "I was there that night too. Wait, is that my leg? I think those look like my True Religion jeans." She moved closer to the TV. "Yeah, that's totally me. Oh my God, I have to text Nibs and tell him I was on. He's going to be so excited. He lives for this stuff."

"Okay, well I'm going to continue packing," I said. Maddy looked up. Finally some acknowledgment. "It'll go much quicker if you, um, help me." Maddy yawned.

"I'll do the best I can," she said.

The best Maddy could do before falling asleep on the couch was packing up her makeup trunk in the bathroom.

"Great," I said, when I found her ten minutes later after she'd told me she was going to collect her shoes from the entrance way. "Just great."

Two hours later I had managed to get both of our stuff together and a bellboy came to take it all to the two bedroom suite. I considered leaving Maddy there and letting her wake up in the vacant room without leaving her the new key. It would serve her right. But I didn't. I shook her awake to tell her we were leaving.

1413 was our new room, and what a beautiful room at that.

Two spacious bedrooms, each with a king size bed and its own bathroom. There was a giant living room with a huge balcony attached. There were also two entrances from the hallway to our suite. One came through my bedroom, the other through the living room. Now, when Maddy came in late at night, she wouldn't need to wake me, unless she forgot her key. So really the extra entrance didn't matter. At least I wouldn't have to hear her snoring, and it would be nice to not have to sleep on a cot anymore.

"Do I know how to spend other people's money or what?" she asked.

"You're a champ," I said, before collapsing on the plush sofa beside Beyonce to take a half hour power nap before going to meet Teach.

CHAPTER 26

On my way to meet Teach Rogers I thought maybe I should stop and look him up online, but decided to just wing it. Hopefully, he'd seek me out first. I had left Maddy in the room in a crisis over what to wear to go to Hyde, a trendy club.

"Do you really not have time to go to The Beverly Center to pick up a top for me?" she had asked.

"Really," I answered in my groggy state. "I barely have time to brush my hair."

"Well shouldn't my job come before yours?" she asked.

"Nope," I said. "Good luck. I'm sure you will be able to dig something up. Please don't make too much of a mess of your clothes that I folded ever so nicely for you." Beyonce was snuggled up inside the Polo shirt when I left.

"Hi, I'm meeting Teach Rogers," I said to the hostess of the lounge. "Is he here yet?"

"Hmm, I'm not sure," she said. "Go have a look around." I went in and there were a few men scattered about. At the other end of the bar I saw someone familiar. As I got closer, I realized it was Ricky, the smooth-talker from the Golden Globes after-party.

"I guess you were right about us meeting again," I said, smiling. "I didn't realize it would be so soon." He looked up from his martini and returned the smile.

"What a coincidence," he said, rising to give me a hug. "How are you feeling?"

"I'm much better," I said. "Are you staying at the hotel?"

"No. I'm meeting a friend," he said. I scanned the room to figure out which one might be Teach.

"Me too," I said. "Not a friend, though. I have a business meeting."

"Don't let me disturb you," Ricky said.

"Will you be here for a while?" I asked. "I'd love to have a drink when I'm finished."

"I don't mind waiting," he said.

"Cool," I said. I left him and walked around the bar. I spotted a man who looked to be in his early forties, with salt and pepper hair, dressed in a button-down shirt and jeans. He could be Teach. I approached him and he looked up and smiled.

"Hi," I said. "Sorry I'm late. It's so nice to meet you finally."

"Um, yeah," he said. "It's great." He didn't stand up or ask me to sit down. I pulled a chair out and was about to sit down when I heard a woman clearing her throat. A slim brunette glared at me.

"May I help you?" she asked.

"I'm Grace," I said. "I have a meeting with Teach."

"Who?" she asked. Apparently this man was not Teach Rogers.

"I'm sorry," I laughed. "I thought you were someone else." I took another trip around the bar. After asking a few more well-dressed men if they were 'Teach,' I finally clued in.

"Aren't I the dumbest girl on the planet," I said, going back over to Ricky.

"You're a little slow," he said laughing. "But very cute."

"Did you know who I was when we met at the party?" I asked.

"I had a feeling," he said. "But, what a coincidence right?"

"What are the chances," I said. "So you did the decor for all the parties?"

"I sure did," he said, his green eyes sparkling in the candlelight. "What did you think of the pot you threw up in? It was from Tiffany's."

"Great," I laughed. I sat up on the stool beside him. "I can't believe you're such a fraud. Why didn't you tell me your real name last night?" Teach broke out into laughter.

"If I'm not mistaking," he said. "I do believe that you're the one that referred to yourself as Lucy Ricardo." I couldn't argue against that.

"I'll have a glass of red wine," I said to the bartender.

"You're not going to make me carry you home tonight, are you?" Teach asked.

"No," I said. "It's all under control. I swear."

The meeting was a huge success. Teach said he had intended on signing with JD Designs, whether he had met with me or not. Total House was out of the picture.

"But I still wanted to meet you," he said. "I thought it would be nice to see what you were like sober."

After Teach signed a few documents that Jake had faxed over to me, we celebrated with a bottle of champagne.

"I'm going to surprise Jake tomorrow with the news," he said. "Don't go telling him yet. I like watching him sweat it out."

"It would be my pleasure to allow you the honor," I said. I was so excited, I felt like going upstairs and quitting my job with Maddy on the spot. Teach laughed when I told him.

"Nah, see it through," he said. "You can do it."

"I'm losing steam," I said.

"Think of how much you're learning about young Hollywood," he said.

"It's a lesson I could do without," I said.

"Don't be a quitter, Grace," he said. "Your job awaits you when you get home. You have a bright, shining future ahead of you.

Take this time to enjoy yourself. You may never have this opportunity again."

"You're right," I said, putting the papers back in my Chanel bag.

"Very nice," Teach said.

"It was a gift," I said. I told him the story.

"You mean to tell me she's taking credit for a gift someone else gave you?" he asked, laughing.

"I'm afraid so," I sighed.

"Well whoever this Todd is," he said. "He must really think you're special." I was surprised by what he said. I mean buying that purse for me was the nicest thing anyone had ever done for me.

"He's pretty special himself," I said, thinking about how Todd had gotten me home in one piece last night while Hunter and Preston fought the whole way to their own cab.

"I think we are going to be very good friends, Ms. Cerulean," Teach said as we were about to part ways.

"I look forward to it," I said, giving him a hug goodbye. "Thank you for everything."

CHAPTER 27

❀

The sound of the phone woke me from a deep slumber. I looked at the clock. It was three-thirty in the morning.

"Grace?" Maddy said. She sounded distressed. "I need you to come and get me."

"Where are you?" I asked. I prayed this had been a car accident-free evening.

"I'm in the bushes in front of Chelsea Tate's house," she whispered. Well there's something you don't hear everyday. "My friends took off without me."

"I'm not sure I'm comprehending," I said. "Why are you hiding in the bushes?"

"We egged all their cars," she answered. "Then we saw a light go on inside and we made a mad dash, and those twats left me here."

"What the hell are you talking about?" I asked.

"Just come and get me!" she whisper-yelled. "I'll explain it to you after."

"I don't know where Chelsea Tate lives," I said.

"Just write down these directions," she said. "Hurry up before the police get here."

"Holy shit, Maddy. What have you done?" I asked.

"Grace!" she said. I quickly jotted down how to get to the Tate's home.

"Alright, I'll be there soon," I said.

"I'll meet you at the end of the street, don't turn down the lane," she said.

"You stay there, Beyonce," I said. She was at the door wagging her tail. "It's not safe out there for big stars like you."

While driving there, I realized how much I missed OnStar and couldn't wait to get our Yukon back. I tried to think why Maddy would start up this war again between her and Chelsea, but could come up with nothing. After many turns up and down the hills, I arrived at the top of Chelsea's street. I opened the window but Maddy was nowhere in sight. All of a sudden there was a huge thump at the back door, and Maddy opened the door.

"Let's get the fuck out of here," she said, excitement in her voice. "Hurry!" Maddy screamed at me throughout the whole ride down out of the hills, telling me I was going too slow, and did I want the police after me? When I got to the bottom my nerves were shot.

"Are you going to tell me what this is all about?" I asked. "Why I'm once again rescuing you at this hour?"

"We egged the Tates' cars," Maddy said. She already had her T-Mobile out text messaging. "Bridget's the biggest bitch on earth," she said. "She's so dead when I get a hold of her."

"Put that away!" I shouted. "Tell me what happened." Maddy closed the Sidekick.

"I told you," she said. "We egged the cars. All of them." She began to list them.

"The Porsche, the Ferrari, the Mercedes, and the Toyota," she said.

"The Tates have a Toyota?" I asked. Not that it was an important question, but it sort of was.

"It belongs to the housekeeper," Maddy explained. "I actually feel bad about that one. Katie did it. She shouldn't have. It was wrong."

"It was all wrong!" I yelled, startling her.

"Calm down, Grace. It's no biggie," she said. "It was hilarious actually."

"Did you not just jump start your friendship with her last night?" I asked.

"Well yeah," Maddy said. "But this was just a prank. Nothing malicious."

"Since when is egging hundred thousand dollar cars not malicious?" I asked.

"We punk'd her," Maddy said, going back to texting.

"You don't think the security cameras caught it on tape?" I asked. I watched Maddy's face go pale.

"Do you think they have cameras?" she asked.

"You're kidding me, right?" I said. "Of course they do."

"No, no way," she said.

"None of you thought of that?" I asked, "As you were destroying property?"

"Bridget made me do it," Maddy blurted out.

"Since when do you do what Bridget tells you to do?" I asked.

"I don't know. She thought it would be a fun thing to do after hours," Maddy said," "instead of going to another club. I know how you hate when I come home drunk and late and—" I turned and gave her the dirtiest look I could conjure up.

"Stuff," she finished saying.

"So why do you think they left you like that?" I asked. "I mean not only is it illegal what you did, but it's sort of dangerous to leave a young, beautiful ..."

"Aww, thanks Grace," Maddy gleamed.

"... girl stranded at three in the morning," I continued. "Something awful could have happened to you."

"True," she said. "But I guess they figured I could just call you."

"Right," I said. "Of course." Maddy squirmed in her seat and then rested her head against the window.

"It's just not fair," she said.

"What's not fair?" I asked.

"You don't understand. Your life is perfect," she said. I nearly drove off the cliff.

"I mean, your job is so easy. All you have to do is look after me. You don't have to be me," she said. That was a very fascinating statement. And maybe she had a point. Having to look after Maddy probably was a much easier task than being her. I made a mental note to remember that the next time she drove me insane—which would probably be in ten minutes.

I was exhausted and hoped I could drive the last few blocks back to the hotel without us tumbling off the side of the road.

"Chelsea has so many things and is so popular. She doesn't deserve it. She's not even that pretty."

"So only pretty people deserve nice things?" I asked. "No offense, Maddy, and I don't mean to pour salt into the wound, but calling Chelsea 'not pretty' is like saying that Nicole Richie is fat." Maddy laughed.

"You don't need to envy Chelsea," I said. "You have a lot going for yourself too."

"Oh, I'm not envious. Why would I care? I'm way hotter than her," she said.

"Guys want me more," she continued. "Plus, I'm offered so many better roles than she is. I don't take every part that I read for, Grace. You know that, right?" I nodded.

"I'm sure you read lots of scripts," I said. None that I'd seen since I started this job, of course.

"Do you think I've been raised well?" she asked. Was I being punk'd now?

"Of course," I lied.

"I mean my parents try really hard, but they're busy with, um, stuff," she said.

"Of course," I said, pulling into the hotel. She was still talking as we got out of the car. "My mother's worked very hard helping me build my career," she said.

"Definitely," I said. As we walked into the hotel, Maddy pulled out her phone and dialed.

"Bridget, you're a total bitch," she screamed. "How could you leave me standing there? How could you not come back for me?" No response on the other end.

"Oops, guess I got your machine," Maddy said, laughing. "Call me later, hon." She hung up.

"God, it sucks," she said, as we were getting into the elevator. "I just want to be a normal teenager. Why is everything such a big deal? Why does everyone make such a big deal out of what I do?" I was unsure if these were rhetorical questions or if she actually sought an answer. She continued all the way up.

"I mean, what does everyone want from me?" she asked. "I'm only seventeen, I'm not even legal yet." It wasn't the most opportune time, but I couldn't help burst out laughing.

"Grace, I'm serious," she said.

"Sorry," I said, calming down. We got out at our floor and proceeded to the room.

"Ugh, I can't talk about this anymore," Maddy said, holding her stomach. "I'm feeling sick. I really hope they don't have security cameras." I didn't say another word as I opened the door to our room. I suspected the police would be there to collect Maddy in the morning, and I'd tell them that I don't work for Maddy Malone, I work for Mandy Moore.

CHAPTER 28

When I woke up the next morning, Maddy and Beyonce were both in my bed, practically on top of me. Maddy must have crawled in while I was asleep. Figures, I finally get my own room with a big bed and can't even enjoy it.

Maddy didn't have anything work-related to do today which was perfect since we'd probably need to spend the whole day hiding from the cops. The phone rang. It was the auto shop telling me that the Yukon was fixed and did I want them to deliver it to the hotel.

"Yes, thanks," I said.

I went into the living room and opened the balcony door. I stepped outside to check the weather. It was sunny, and warm. I could easily get used to this climate. I stretched my arms in the air and took a deep breath, then went back to my room to get dressed, stopping to order a pot of coffee from room service.

Maddy was snoring lightly in my bed. I found myself feeling sorry for her in some ways. She created so much unnecessary drama for herself. Unfortunately, Maddy's friends were a bunch of bad seeds wanting to ride her coat tails. Unfortunately she'd come across may more of those throughout her career—or even this week. I put on a pair of cropped jeans and a white tank. My hair looked like a rats' nest, so I pulled it into a clip. While I was putting on my shoes my coffee arrived. I poured myself a cup, added cream and sugar, and went to enjoy it on the balcony. Beyonce followed me outside with her food bowl in her mouth.

"Ah, someone's hungry," I said. I took the bowl from her and went back in to get her food. Maddy had arranged at the front desk to have someone go out and buy Beyonce's food.

"It's like room service for dogs," she had said, with great enthusiasm—one that Roz did not share. I returned outside with Beyonce's bowl of food and set it down beside my chair. A few minutes later Maddy came to the door.

"Can't you hear your phone ringing?" she asked.

"No," I said. I purposely didn't bring it out.

"Well here, it's for you," Maddy said, throwing my phone in my lap. "It's Hunter David."

"Hey," he said. "I'm going to Karaoke tonight with a bunch of friends. Do you guys want to come?"

"Oh, hold on, I'll ask her," I said. She stood in the doorway. "Do you want to go to Kar-"

"Nope," she said, and disappeared inside.

"Hi," I said, coming back to the phone. "Maddy doesn't want to go."

"Thank God," he said. "But you'll come, right?" he asked.

"Well, I better check with her," I said. I went inside. "Do you mind if I go with them? Or is tonight the night we throw pumpkins through Dustin Hoffman's windows?"

"Shut up, Grace," Maddy said. "I don't care if you go, and you should let Hunter know for me that just because I worked with him on a movie, doesn't mean I have to be friends with him." I refrained from passing that message along. I told Hunter I'd be thrilled to join his group.

"Great, we'll come pick you up around eight o'clock," he said. I hung up.

"Please don't tell me you're falling for Hunter David," Maddy said.

"No," I said. "I just think he's really nice."

"Well, I've been to Karaoke with him before," Maddy said.

"When?" I asked.

"In Chicago," she said. "Before I even knew you existed. The cast all went one night."

"Oh," I said.

"Yeah," she said. "I can't wait to hear what you think of Hunter's performance."

"What's that supposed to mean?" I asked.

"He's really something up on stage during Karaoke," she explained.

"I don't understand," I said.

"You'll see," she said. She started laughing like Dr. Evil from *Austin Powers*.

"Wah ha ha ha. Wah ha ha ha."

"Oh brother," I said, still curious. "Oh, by the way the Yukon's ready. They're sending it over."

"Fabulous," she said. "Will ADA come pick up the other rental?"

"Hmm, I'll find out," I said. I picked up the phone to call them and they said they'd be happy to come get the car, if I'd just leave the keys with the front desk.

"Grace, can you order me some breakfast while I hop in the shower?" Maddy asked. "French toast. No pancakes. Wait, maybe I want eggs."

"Decisions, decisions," I said.

"Pancakes," she said, "with a side of bacon." I called down to room service, adding a plate of scrambled eggs for myself to her order. I couldn't stop thinking about what Hunter would be like on stage that would cause Maddy to remember it. I imagined he would be similar to Axl Rose or a rock star of that status.

Maddy's Sidekick was beeping on its charger. I walked over and picked it up. I'd never looked at it before. It amazed me how she was able to maneuver so many different gadgets at once. I opened the cover and looked at the screen. There was an instant message from Bridget. I pressed a button, revealing her message. It said:

> *Hey Mad's, sorry 'bout last night. We totally thought you were in the backseat. We didn't notice till a few minutes later. LOL! Are you taking me to the Playboy Mansion tonight?*
> *xox Bridget*

There was no way Maddy would fall for that excuse for stranding her. I looked down at Beyonce, who was licking my ankle. I wondered why Maddy was going to the Playboy Mansion. Perhaps to egg Hugh Heffner's cars?

My cell phone rang. It was Marty.

"Hi Grace," he said. "Everything going okay?"

"Oh yeah," I answered. "Just fine."

"I'm sending over a few scripts for Maddy to read," he said. "Just wanted to make sure she reads them both carefully. I'm trying to negotiate big time for her next role."

"Oh, okay," I said. "That sounds exciting."

"Yeah, but they both need answers by Thursday," he said. "So tell her I'll meet with her Wednesday afternoon and she can give me her decision."

"I'll pass along the message," I said. "And make sure she has them read."

"Who was that?" Maddy asked, walking into the room in a robe and a towel on her head.

"It was Marty," I said.

"Ugh, what does he want now?" she asked.

"He's sending over two scripts for you to read," I explained. "He needs you to decide which movie you want to do by Wednesday."

"Like I have time to read a script," she said. I paused for a moment.

"It must totally suck when work interferes with your life," I said, with sarcasm.

"Totally," she said. She had taken me seriously.

"Marty said he's working on getting you a big salary," I said, thinking that might excite her. Nothing. "Think of all the Fendi and Gucci you could buy." Maddy yawned.

"Whatever," she said. "Maybe you can just read them for me and tell me what they're about."

"So not happening," I said. Maddy's cell phone rang and she dashed to get it. While she gossiped about her evening plans for the night, I grabbed the remote control off the table and turned the television on.

When she hung up the phone she squealed with delight.

"I'm going to a party at the Playboy mansion tonight," she said. I didn't tell her I already knew that.

"Don't you think you're a little young to go to something like that?" I asked.

Maddy laughed.

"What do you think everyone just walks around naked and drunk there?" she asked. I thought about it for a moment.

"Well, yeah," I said. I didn't know what went on at those kind of parties, but I could use my imagination, and I imagined they were things that seventeen year olds should not be involved in.

"You can't shelter me from the world forever, Grace," she said. "I'm growing up right before your very eyes."

"If you say so," I said. "Still, you probably shouldn't go."

"Oh, please," she said. "This coming from the girl that puked her gutts out at the Golden Globes." Really, that had nothing to do with it, but it was the only thing Maddy had to hold against me.

"You're changing the topic," I said.

"I know," Maddy said, smiling. "Maybe they'll ask me to be next month's centerfold."

"Right," I said. That, I wasn't concerned about. I was more concerned about someone asking her to show them how she would pose if she was asked one day to do it. Maddy's phone rang again.

"It's Katie," she said. "I'm not inviting her, so stay quiet." I continued watching TV, while listening to her conversation.

"Hey, what's up?" she said. "Nothing, just hanging out with Grace. She's not feeling very well. She's still hung over from the other night. That lightweight." I looked over at her and gave her a dirty look. Maddy stuck her tongue out at me.

"Yeah, so we're not going out tonight," she continued. "We're just going to have an early dinner and then maybe watch a movie or something. Besides, I'm still mad at you for last night." I could hear Katie's voice screaming through the phone.

"Well you didn't have to leave me there," she said. "Something horrible could have happened to me. I could have been raped, murdered etcetera." More screaming from Katie.

"Whatever," Maddy said. "If you were both smart, you'd have realized that I wouldn't have been in the backseat. I always sit up front." After more arguing Maddy hung up.

"What an idiot," she said.

"Yeah," I said.

"I need new friends," Maddy said. "I hope Paris Hilton will be there tonight. I'd love to be friends with her." I nearly choked on my own saliva.

"Well I do—"

"Don't say anything bad about her, Grace," Maddy said, cutting me off. "You don't even know her. She's never done anything bad to you."

"I'm sure she's a very nice girl," I said. "I just find it odd that you'd go from egging Chelsea Tate's cars to wanting to hang out with Paris Hilton."

"Why?" Maddy asked. "One thing has nothing to do with the other. Paris is so cool, and she seems to know how to have a good time."

"Well, yeah, I know," I said, praying that Paris wouldn't be at the party.

"Who invited you to this party?" I asked.

"Alison told me about it," she said. "Anyway, I need you to go get me a top from The Beverly Center," she said. "I have to wear D&G tonight."

"Why?" I asked. "Is it a theme party?"

"No, because one of those bustiers would look so hot on me. They're like corsets."

"How would I know if it will fit you?" I asked.

"You should know my body like the back of your hand by now," Maddy said, laughing. "I'd go with you but I'm going for lunch at the Ivy with Bridget."

"You're not mad at her anymore?" I asked.

"I can't hold a grudge forever," she said. Some psychiatrist could make a bloody fortune off this kid.

"My credit card is in my Dior saddle bag," she said indicating it on the end table. "What if it declines again?" I asked. "Maybe you should give me cash instead."

"You think I walk around with six hundred bucks in my wallet?" she asked. "I'm an actress, we—"

"Never carry cash," I said, finishing her sentence.

"Right," she said with pride.

"I just don't want to have to deal with your card again," I said.

"I spoke to my mother about it," she said. "She promised she wouldn't use the card for the rest of the week." How considerate.

"Well what size do I get you?" I asked. "It really is something you would need to try on?"

"Just try them on yourself," Maddy said. "Then whatever fits you, get me one that's three sizes smaller. Sounds about right, right?" Maybe in her dreams, but it was her money.

"Sure," I said. "I'm going to go walk Beyonce first."

"Oh, good idea," she said. I went to get Beyonce's leash. "I think I'll get her a dog walker for the rest of the time we're here."

"Why?" I asked.

"Well, I mean you can't walk her all the time," she said.

"True," I said. "I mean sometimes you could think of walking her too."

"I'm just so busy, though," she said, moving magazines around on the coffee table to look like she's busy. "But if you don't mind, then I guess I'll save a few bucks. Can't really charge a dog walker to the room."

When I returned with Beyonce, Maddy was still in the same position on the couch, smoking.

"I wish you'd do that outside," I said.

"You know I was just thinking," she said, ignoring my request. "If you want you can buy yourself a new outfit at the mall too."

"What's the catch?" I asked. "You have another phone interview to do?" Maddy laughed.

"No, no," she said. "I just thought you'd want to get something nice for Karaoke." I raised my eyebrow.

"What are you up to?" I asked.

"Nothing Miss Paranoia," she said. "You should look nice for when you sing on stage, and for when Hunter serenades you. Ha ha."

"Oh please," I said, though I was dying to know if he was going to belt out 'Sweet Child of Mine' or something.

"Anyway, your clothes are so ho-hum, get something good," she said. After that dig, I decided to take her up on her offer.

"Fine." I said.

"Good. I'm going to give you a list of what I want." I watched her tear a page out of the Los Angeles coffee table book and scribble her list.

I was thrilled when the valet brought up the Yukon from the underground parking garage. It looked brand spanking new, dents and scratches gone.

"I've missed you baby," I said, driving out of the hotel. I ran my hand across the OnStar control panel. "You have no idea."

When I got to the mall, I pulled out Maddy's list to check what stores I needed to visit besides D&G. Diesel, and Bloomingdale's. Perfect, I thought; I could probably find a thing or two for myself at those places, too, and hopefully this whole outing wouldn't take too long.

When I explained what I was looking for in D&G, the saleslady looked at me strangely.

"So, let me get this straight," she said. "She wants you to try it on and then buy the one that's three sizes smaller?"

"Yes, that's right," I said.

"But, I mean, well—" she said looking me up and down. "You're not that big."

"Thank you," I said. I wouldn't have thought so either, had Maddy not kept reminding me how much smaller she is.

"Okay, then," the saleslady said. "I'll show you what we have."

She gave me a few different patterns of the same style to try on. They were all size sixes at my request. I thought they fit very well, and wondered if Maddy would object to me picking one up for myself. I figured she would.

"You could probably even wear a four," the saleslady said, handing it to me. I went back into the fitting room to try it on. It fit perfectly.

"Do you like this pattern the best?" I asked of a black bustier with big colorful flowers.

"Yes, definitely on you," she said. "However, what color hair does Maddy have? I'm not familiar with her."

"She's blonde," I said.

"I'd still go with the same one you have on then," she said. "It's the safest bet."

"You're probably right," I said. "So what would be three sizes smaller?"

"A zero. Is this girl a size zero?" she asked. Of course not.

"No," I said. "I think I'll get her the four and tell her that I fit into the eight. She'll be overjoyed." The saleslady laughed.

"Did you want to try the matching mini?" she asked. "It's a great outfit."

"Sure," I said. The last time I'd worn a micro mini was … well I'd never actually worn one in my life.

"You look great," a second saleslady said when I came out of the room.

"Thanks," I said. "It's not for me."

"It should be," she said. I decided to get her the matching skirt, a couple sizes smaller of course.

"Smart girl. I'll wrap it up for you," said the woman that had been helping me. I quickly changed and handed her the outfit, along with Maddy's credit card. While I waited for her to ring it up, I looked around the rest of the store. I wondered if I would ever have the kind of money to shop at D&G. I pulled out a pair of jeans off the rack that were ripped and bleached all over. They were over five hundred dollars. No, I could definitely find better ways to spend my money if I had it.

Finding the rest of Maddy's items didn't take long: a hat from Diesel and boots at Bloomingdales.

Shopping for myself was more difficult because I couldn't figure out how to put an outfit together. Finally a saleslady at Bloomingdale's helped me and I had chosen a fluttery white top and black jeans accessorized with a great belt and scarf.

"Honey, you are stylin'," said the saleslady.

I made it back to the hotel shortly thereafter. Maddy and Bridget had already returned from their lunch at the Ivy.

"How much was everything?" Maddy asked.

"Thirteen-hundred dollars," I said. "And I was nervous every time a saleslady put the card through."

"I told you I cut my mother off," she said. More like she knew Mrs. Malone wouldn't be shopping since she was in Philadelphia with Maddy's brother, Greg, for his hockey tournament.

Maddy tried her outfit on. The D&G bustier barely fit as she tried to squeeze herself into it.

"Thank God these thing stretch," she said, of the non-stretch material.

"Just breathe and hold it in," Bridget said, trying to do up the zipper. After a few grunts, she managed to get it more than halfway up. "There."

"Okay. This is good," Maddy said, clearly uncomfortable. "Fits like a glove."

"It's perfect for a Playboy party," I said. "That's for sure." I watched her modeling it in the mirror. She took the matching micro-mini out of the bag and put it on.

"Oh my god, you guys," she said, "I am so in love with myself right now. Tell me how hot I look."

I smiled but didn't feel like humoring her request for validation. I hoped Bridget would. She didn't.

"Tell me," Maddy pleaded. Since this was what I was getting paid for, I caved.

"You look totally hot," I said.

"I know," she said. She twirled around. "I just won't be able to sit down the whole night." That pleased me. She'd have to stand the whole time at the party, which meant she wouldn't be able to reveal anything up that micro mini.

"Okay, Bridget," Maddy said. "Now we can deal with what you're going to wear tonight. You can borrow something."

"I don't get a new outfit like Grace did?" she asked. "That's not fair."

"You should have thought of that before leaving me in Booneyville last night," Maddy said. They argued about it more as they walked into Maddy's bedroom. I picked my own parcels off the floor and went into my room.

"I got some new duds, Beyonce," I said. She was curled up in a ball on my bed.

"Hunter won't even know what hit him."

I went back into the living room to get Beyonce a dog treat when Maddy's phone rang again. She came running into the living room half naked.

"Unknown number," she said, looking at the ID. "Maybe it's Paris!" She jumped on the couch and answered.

"Hi! Maddy Malone speaking," she said. "Oh, hi Katie." She was seemed quite disappointed. "I thought you might be Paris. That's right THE Paris Hilton might call me," she said. I heard Katie screaming sounds of joy through the phone.

"Oh my God," Maddy continued. "I look so hot for tonight. Grace went and got me this new D&G bustier, and matching skirt, and I'm—" Bridget came dashing out of the bedroom.

"No! No! Shh," she said, jumping on Maddy who had just ruined her own lie.

"So uh, Katie," Maddy said, doomed to lose a friend, "I've decided to go to the Playboy party after all. Did you want to come with?"

CHAPTER 29

"Got your singing voice ready?" Hunter asked when I got into the cab. "I've been warming up mine for the past hour." I got into the backseat with Todd and Preston. Hunter was in the front.

"Just so you know," Todd said. "I don't sing. I only came with because I wanted to have a good laugh with you over Hunter's performance."

"Oh be quiet, you pansy," Hunter said. "You're so jealous."

It seemed Hunter had quite the Karaoke reputation. I wonder if he really was about to break out as a rock star.

"I'm not a very good singer," I said. "I'll need something a little less rock and roll."

"How about some fancy show tunes?" Hunter asked, kidding.

"For me, maybe," I said. "I'd think something by Aerosmith would suit you." Todd and Preston both broke out in laughter.

"Where's Maddy tonight?" Todd asked.

"She went to a party at the Playboy mansion, in search of Paris Hilton."

"Alison must be doing some major overtime," Hunter said. "to get her into all these parties."

The taxi soon pulled into a place called "Karaoke."

"Great name for a Karaoke place," I said, laughing. "It's like calling a restaurant "Restaurant."

"Well it makes sense," Preston said in a serious tone. I didn't understand how Preston and Hunter were such good friends. They were like polar opposites. Hunter was too easy going to be bogged down by a friend like that.

I watched crowds of people hurrying inside. Hunter paid the driver and we got out. Hunter and Preston dashed to the door in front of Todd and I.

"Hurry up, slowpokes," Hunter said, holding the door open. I was hit by waves of smoke when we entered. On stage, a chunky Asian man was singing 'All Out of Love,' by Air Supply, in Japanese.

Hunter had made a reservation beforehand and a hostess in a red, cleavage revealing dress, seated us.

"Can I take your order?" a waitress asked, once we had all been seated.

"Yes," Hunter said, ordering a round of lemon drop shots and gin and tonic chasers.

The waitress returned with a tray of drinks—I felt drunk just looking at it. I'd seriously have to consider a trip to AA when I got back to Chicago.

"Here's my credit card," said Hunter, giving it to the waitress. "Just keep a tab running for us." I loved how he took charge like that. I felt safe with him, as if he was my protector.

When the Asian man finished singing, his friends went wild with cheering. Hunter put two fingers in his mouth and whistled.

"If you don't cheer people on, they won't cheer you on," Hunter said. I started clapping too.

"So what are you going to sing?" Hunter asked. I grabbed the song book.

"I don't know," I said. "There's so many choices." Preston took the order form for the songs and started writing down songs lickity-split.

"They have their favorites," Todd explained.

"Hey, look who's getting on stage," said Hunter. It was a plus-size woman with long brown hair and huge breasts.

"I'd like to dedicate this song to my date tonight," she said in a husky voice.

"It's Fat Inga," said Hunter. I looked at him oddly.

"No, really, that's what she calls herself," he said. "She sings at karaoke bars all over the city. She's famous in The Valley. She brings a different date every time, these skinny guys and—"

"There he is," Preston said, subtly pointing out Fat Inga's date who was sitting at a table near us with a glass of red wine. He was bald except for wiry black hair around the edges and was wearing horn-rimmed glasses.

"He looks a little like Mr. Slate from *The Flintstones*, I said.

"For sure," Todd said, laughing. We sat patiently waiting to see what song she chose.

"May I have your attention please," she said as music began to play. "May I have your attention please." I sat in shock as Fat Inga belted out a song by Eminem. I had expected something along the lines of "Endless Love", by Lionel Ritchie and Diana Ross. Fat Inga danced around the stage, her big bosoms bouncing in her face. Arnold tapped his fingers to the beat.

"More drinks," Todd said to the waitress. She returned with another full tray. Fat Inga jumped off the stage and approached her date, grabbing his face and shaking her hips around in it. He slapped her ass every time she turned.

We laughed and kept drinking. When Inga had finished the crowd gave her a standing ovation. She blew kisses to the audience and returned to her seat.

"That was fantastic," Hunter laughed.

"I can't top that," I said.

"Oh, I can," Hunter said. Todd rolled his eyes.

"This is going to be embarrassing," he said. "I'm going to the bathroom."

Two songs later, Hunter was called to the stage. I couldn't wait to see what song he'd be singing. He got into his ready position. He reminded me of Bon Jovi.

Todd rejoined the table as the music came on. I looked for the words on the screen. The musical interlude sounded familiar, but I couldn't place it at first. It was light, fluffy—it was "Singing in the Rain". Oh my goodness. Poor Hunter. I leaned into Todd.

"They gave him the wrong song," I whispered.

"Uh, nope," Todd said. "Just watch."

Hunter sang and tap danced to Singing in the Rain, as if he were Gene Kelly. His sex appeal was declining at a rapid speed.

"He's kidding, right?" I asked.

"Why would you say that?" Preston asked. "I think it's wonderful." I was starting to get a little weirded out over how much Preston kissed Hunter's ass. The show tunes didn't stop there. Next up, Hunter sang, "What I did for Love", from *A Chorus Line*, and then "New York New York". His big finale was a duet with Preston singing "Matchmaker" from *Fiddler on the Roof*. I'm not sure how long my mouth stayed open for, but when the performance was finally over and I closed it, it was very sore.

"What did you think?" Hunter asked, sitting down and grabbing my hand from across the table.

"You were great," I said, which wasn't a total lie. He was great, just not what I was hoping for.

"You guys are total fairies," Todd said.

"You're just jealous, Toddy," said Preston. Toddy? After the next person sang, I was called up to sing. I quickly did a shot of vodka.

"Hit it, girl," shouted Hunter. My song began to play—"Jungle Love". I turned the mic on. It made a piercing noise.

"Oops," I said. There were a few boos from the audience, then a bit of laughter. I started singing. The music was a head of my lyrics so I had to speed it up a bit. Thanks to my buzz, I forgot about how self-conscious I had been. I tried to get more into it, dancing around as I sang. I looked down and saw Todd smiling back at me. I loosened up more, doing a few pivot turns, swinging around the pole that was off to the side. I leaned down to Hunter, about to serenade him and saw Preston nearly on top of him. God that kid was so needy.

"Oh-wee-oh-wee-oh," I sang. This was sort of fun. I felt brave and in control and didn't even care that my voice was cracking a bit. I looked back down at my fans. I smiled thinking how maybe I should be a rock star or something.

"Oh-wee-oh-wee-OHHH!" I cried out. I stopped dead in my tracks. Hunter and Preston were making out. KISSING. They were kissing!

Todd looked over to see what had just bolted me from the blue, and quickly joined me on stage, grabbing the mic from me to finish off the song. The same Todd, who never sings at Karaoke, sang while I stood there trying to recover from the trauma I had just experienced.

The lights went on and everyone started clapping. Hunter had released his lips from Preston's and used two fingers to whistle.

I stayed fairly quiet for the rest of the night. I felt like a fool for ever believing that a guy as good looking as Hunter David would be straight and that into me.

"I wasn't sure if you knew," Todd said, when Hunter and Preston had gotten up to sing the *Charles in Charge* theme song.

"I had no clue," I said.

"I'm sorry," Todd said. "He keeps it quiet in fear of not getting roles."

"I understand," I said, even though I didn't. Quiet? I'd hardly call sucking face with your boyfriend in public quiet.

"I'll be right back," I said, when Hunter and Preston returned to the table. "I need to go get some air."

"You okay, babe?" Hunter asked. I nodded, quickly rushing outside.

I leaned up against the brick wall on the side of Karaoke. I felt sick, but not sick enough to throw up again. Just uneasy. I took my phone out of my purse and started to dial Jen, but hung up. I was too embarrassed to even tell my best friend. Instead, I dialed the one person I knew that could relate to feeling both lonely and let down by the people around her.

"Hi Maddy," I said. "I just wanted to check in and see if you're okay."

CHAPTER 30

"Are you feeling better, Grace?" Maddy asked the next day on our way to her video shoot for *Daisy Mae.*

"Sort of," I said. I actually wasn't, but in teenage years, I had wallowed in my sorrows for long enough.

"Good," she said. "You're not mad at me right for not telling you?"

"It would have been helpful to know," I said. Apparently Maddy had found out the night of The Golden Globes party.

"I just couldn't be the one to break your heart," Maddy said.

"I'm sure," I said. "Better to allow myself to make an ass of myself on stage while singing." Maddy looked out the window. She seemed to be in pensive thought as she puffed away on her cigarette.

"Come on, Grace," she finally said. "Do you know how many girls find out the guy they like is gay per day?" I turned to her.

"No," I said. "How many?"

"Yeah, it's very common these days," Bridget said.

"I guess I've been living under a rock," I said.

"Okay," Maddy said. "How about this, think about how many millions of girls around the globe must have been devastated when Lance Bass came out of the closet."

"Oh, please," I said. "That's totally different."

"Why?" she asked. Good question since I really hadn't known Hunter David for long enough to consider myself his confidant. I had only worked up an image of who I thought he was. So I was just another fan. But, I still felt this wasn't the same as the Lance Bass situation.

"It's different," I said. "Because Lance Bass actually made an announcement. So now everyone knows. Hunter David did not announce that he is gay. I found out the hard way."

"So you would be less upset if last night didn't happen, and tomorrow Hunter David made an announcement to the media?" Maddy asked. Damn, why had she chosen to be smart today? I slumped down in my seat.

"You're confusing me," I said.

"Yes!" Maddy said, pleased that she had stumped me.

"Are we almost in Pasadena?" Bridget asked, leaning toward the back of the driver's seat.

"Shouldn't be much longer now," he answered.

"I really hope the other girls in the video don't try to look hotter than me. I'll totally freak," Maddy said, referring to her costars from *Daisy Mae*.

"Why can't they look good?" I asked.

"Well, it's fine if they look good," she said. "They just can't look as good as me."

"I thought they're not going to be there," Bridget said.

"They're not," Maddy said. "I'm just saying."

Alison had mentioned to me earlier that the director thought it would be best for everyone if the other actors filmed their parts in the video at a later date than Maddy, considering all the problems they'd had with Maddy's jealousy problem while filming the movie. She had tried to get Kimberly Thompson's stand-in fired because she thought her hair was smoother than Maddy's. It had been quite disastrous.

We pulled into the driveway of a large building, our driver nearly running over some roosters running rampant. A few children were sitting on the lawn.

"Why are they here?" Maddy asked, indicating the children. "No outsiders are allowed to watch. Plus I'm not signing any autographs today. I've already decided." A little Mexican girl was sitting cross-legged. She had big puppy dog eyes and curly hair with a red bow in it. I doubted that an autograph from Maddy was high on her wish list.

"This is like Taco Bell-Ville," laughed Maddy. I noticed the driver glare in the rear-view mirror.

A production assistant named Moe greeted us as we got out of the car and then led us to Maddy's trailer.

"Gross," Maddy said of the less luxurious trailer than she was used to. The faint odor of old shoes was unpleasant.

"I don't know if I'm going to stay here the whole day," Bridget said, standing on the trailer steps.

"Why not?" Maddy said. "You have something better to do?"

"Well, I thought maybe I'd—" she began. Maddy flashed her a dirty look. "I guess I can stay for a while." Bridget stepped into the trailer and sat down in a chair.

A few moments later there was a knock at the door. I opened it. It was Debra Glyder, the stylist I'd chosen Maddy's clothes with. She was holding Maddy's wardrobe on hangers. We said hello and I helped her get the clothing inside.

"How are you feeling, Maddy?" Debra asked.

"Fine, why?" asked Maddy.

"I mean are you feeling better from last week?" Debra asked.

"I don't know what you're talking about," Maddy said. I inched my way toward her and gave her a light kick in the shin.

"Ouch!" she said. "Oh, from when I was sick. Yes, much better thanks."

"Great," Debra said. She stayed for a few minutes showing Maddy the outfits for the different scenes. Once Debra had left, Maddy and Bridget began to sort through the clothes. Maddy picked up a tank top. It was a pale blue Michael Stars.

"Blech," she said. "Grace, can you ask Debra to come back with other choices? These are terrible."

"I thought you said you would like whatever I chose for you," I said.

"Grace chose all this stuff?" Bridget asked. "No wonder."

"Hey," I said.

"Sorry," Bridget said. "I forgot you're overly sensitive today."

"I just want to see what else is available," Maddy said. I opened the trailer door and called for Moe.

"Could you ask if Debra could bring back a selection of other tops for Maddy to choose from?" I asked.

Moe held up his walkie-talkie:

"Hey Debra, go to two please." He paused and awaited a response. "Maddy would like to see a few other clothing options."

"I'll be right there," Debra said. A few moments later there was a knock. Debra stepped in with some new things. Her hair was messed and she seemed frazzled. She left and Maddy looked through the new tops.

"I guess these are a little better, but I'll need different pants now," she said, holding up a pair of black cargos. "Can you get Moe?" I swung the door open again and called for him. He was standing at the bottom of the stairs.

"Do you need something else?" he asked.

"I hate to bother you again," I said. "Could you ask Debra to also bring some more pants for Maddy?" Moe smiled and nodded. A few moments later there was another knock on the door.

"Can I come in?" Debra asked, poking her head through. She had a line of sweat above her lip.

"Yup," Maddy said. Debra entered and showed Maddy the pants.

"Okay, I'll try these," Maddy said.

"Do you need anything else?" Debra asked. "So I don't have to keep running back and forth. It's sort of far."

"No, I think that this should be okay," Maddy said. Debra left without any gratitude from Maddy for her efforts, though she didn't seem phased by it.

"Hurry up and get dressed," said Bridget. "So we don't have to be in this hell-hole all day." Maddy grabbed her clothes and went to the back of the trailer. Ten minutes later she appeared in her bra.

"Grace, can you ask Moe to tell Debra to bring the first shirt back? I'll wear it," Maddy said.

"The Michael Stars one?" I asked.

"Yes," she said. "Maybe it will look better on."

"Oh brother," said Bridget.

"Shut it!" Maddy said, throwing a shoe at her. I found Moe and let him know. I went back in and sat down feeling the mental exhaustion that Maddy was provoking in me.

"Alison's calling me," Maddy said, tossing her ringing cell in my direction.

"Hi," I said, answering.

"Please tell me that you didn't egg the Tate's cars the other night," Alison said.

"It's Grace," I said.

"Please tell me Maddy didn't egg the Tate's cars the other night," Alison said, repeating herself.

"Why?" I asked. "What happened."

"What happened is that *The Real Scoop Magazine* just called to verify the story," Alison said. "Put Maddy on the phone."

"Alison needs to speak to you," I said, giving Maddy back her phone.

"Um, I'm sort of busy," she said.

"Well, this is sort of important," I said. Maddy took the phone from my hands and put it on mute.

"Okay, Grace," Maddy said. "Pity party is over. It's time for you to get back to work."

"Pardon?" I asked.

"I am in the middle of a work day," she said. "So whatever Alison wants can wait until I'm done doing my job. Please tell her."

"But it's about—"

"I don't care," she said. "You're working for me right now, not Alison. I've tried to be as patient as possible over the Hunter David situation, but I really need you to focus now."

"Alrighty then," I said, taking the phone back. "I will try and focus on my job."

"Thank you," Maddy said. "I appreciate it."

"Hi Alison," I said. "It's Grace again."

"What's going on?" Alison asked. I cleared my throat.

"Unfortunately, you have disturbed Maddy during a work day, and she has requested that I tell you she will call you back later," I explained.

"I see," said Alison. "Well hopefully *The Real Scoop* doesn't run their story before I hear from her."

"Yes," I said. "I could see how that might be disastrous. I'll tell her to call you as soon as possible."

"Whatever," Alison said, hanging up. I gave Maddy back her phone and went and sat down.

"She called to ask if you had—"

"I don't care," Maddy said. "Tell me later."

"Okay," I answered, hoping that *The Real Scoop* would run their story. It would serve her right.

I watched as Maddy took a little plastic bag out of her purse and placed it on the table in front of me.

"What this?" I asked.

"Rhinestones," she said. "I thought it would be fun if we did a little art project. She reached back into her bag and took out a tube of crazy glue.

"What are you going to rhinestone?" I asked.

"My Blackberry," she said.

"Cool," Bridget said, joining us at the table. "What kind of design are you going to do?"

"I don't know," Maddy said. "I thought Grace could design something since she's a designer."

"For houses," I said. "I'm not much of a bedazzler."

"Well, whatever. I was thinking of an argyle pattern," she said, running her finger along her Blackberry. "Or maybe paisley. With my initials right in the middle. What do you think?"

"That will take you forever," Bridget said.

"We're going to be here for hours," Maddy said. "This will help pass the time."

She poured the bag of colorful rhinestones out on the table, some of them falling on the floor. Then she took a notepad and pencil out of her purse and handed it to me.

"You might want to sketch out the design first," Maddy said.

"Well, um, okay," I said. I quickly scribbled my interpretation of what Maddy wanted on the paper.

"Are you going to be able to figure that out?" Maddy asked, giving it back. "'Cuz I sure can't. Is that the best you can do?" I felt like I had just been scolded by a teacher.

"Sorry," I said. "I'll make it more legible." I redid the drawing, making the proper crossings in the argyle design, and neater printing of the MM.

"Yeah that's better," Maddy said. She sat down at the table and Bridget and I stood in awe as Maddy glued the rhinestones onto her BlackBerry one by one.

A few minutes later the hair and make-up people came in to get Maddy ready for the shoot.

"Just a second," Maddy said. "I just want to finish this." I looked at the two women standing with their trunks. There was no way I would allow Maddy to make these people wait while she did the whole device.

"Put the rhinestones away, Monet," I said. "Time to do your hair."

"Okay, okay," she said, sliding it across the table. "Here finish it for me, Grace."

"I can't do this," I said, laughing. "I'll go insane."

"No, no, no," she said. "It'll calm you from your anxiety from last night. Plus you just saw how much fun it is." I saw, and I believed that walking on glass would be way more fun.

"Just do a bit," she said. "I'll be good if you do." An offer that most likely had no merit, but was worth a try.

"Alright," I said. "I'll glue your stinking rhinestones on while you get ready."

"Cool," she said, jumping into the chair. I looked down at the pattern I'd drawn out. Then I took the tube of glue and started squeezing it onto the little rhinestones. After half an hour, not only was I dizzy and almost legally blind, but I had hardly made a dent.

"This is so stupid," I said, looking up. "I'm taking a break."

"No, don't stop," Maddy said from her chair. I need to get it done."

"Why?" I asked.

"Oh my God Grace. What's your problem?" Bridget asked. "Everyone has all their devices rhinestoned. Paris, Nicole, Lindsay. I mean do you really want Maddy to be so out of place at parties?"

"Yeah," Maddy said. "I look like such a fool when they're not all done. Like I'm not complete as a person."

"Can't you just puffy paint them? Or glue sparkles on?" I asked. "It would be so much easier."

"Unlike you, Grace," Maddy said, turning her head away from the girl who was trying to curl it. "I don't like to take the easy way out. I like to be challenged. Puffy painting your phone might be ok in your world, but in my world it means failure." Silence filled the trailer. I tried to make sense of what she had just said, deciphering all the irony, and delusion in those words, but it made my head hurt even more than gluing rhinestones did. Everyone was waiting for me to respond, and I tried to decide if this was a battle I should choose to fight. It wasn't.

"Oh, alright," I said. "Fine."

By the time Maddy was finished getting made up for the video, I was ready to collapse.

"Grace, you can stop now," she said. I looked up, while she continued delegating. "Bridget will take over. You have to come to set with me." I watched the expression on Bridget's face grow dim.

"Don't let us down, slugger," I said, handing her the tube of glue. "We don't want Maddy to be out of place at parties."

Not that I would ever admit it to Bridget, or Maddy for that matter, but once I got to set and watched Maddy shoot the video, I sort of wished I was back in the dingy trailer rhinestoning her BlackBerry. Maddy turned into a complete nutcase. She fought with the choreographer because she thought his dance moves were "stupid," and wanted to add her own hip hop stuff in.

"Do you think I need these people calling the tabloids to say I'm a klutz on stage?" she asked. "Grace, call Marty and tell him to request a closed set while I learn the steps."

"Oh brother," Marty said, when I relayed Maddy's message. "Thanks Grace, I'll give the director a call." I watched the chain reaction as the director's assistant's phone rang and she passed the phone along to him. So everyone on the crew left, and unfortunately I had to stay and watch Maddy try and learn the steps.

"Five, six, seven, eight," the choreographer clapped. "Right foot, left foot, kick ball change. No Maddy, that's wrong." I watched Maddy's face turn red after each mistake. Finally the choreographer walked away.

"I'll be back," he said, walking out the back door. "I need a break."

"Fuck!" Maddy screamed. "Grace, can you go talk to him and ask him to make it easier? I'm not Baryshnikov, you know." I didn't know what Maddy's problem was, considering that even I had the dance down pat by now. I went out to find the choreographer. He was on his cell phone.

"What the fuck do you want me to do?" he said. "She can't even do a fucking pivot turn properly."

"Eh hem," I cleared my throat.

"I'll call you back," he said, hanging up.

"Hi," I said, as friendly as possible. "Listen I know this is frustrating for you."

"Actually," he said. "It's annoying as fuck!"

"Right," I said. "Well that too."

"This dance is easier than fucking "Hands Up" from Club Med," he said, inhaling his cigarette. "For some reason, some idiot told me she knew how to dance."

"Yeah, well maybe they meant at a club," I said. The choreographer half smiled.

"They've called in a body double to do the dancing for her. She should be here soon," he said.

"Oh?" I asked.

"It was her agent's idea," said the choreographer. Good old Marty saving the day.

"Let's go back in," he said, putting out his butt. "I'll make her think she's doing a wonderful job, so the crew can come back in at least and get her on film." He dialed the director's assistant and said to give him five more minutes. We went back inside where we found Maddy lying in the middle of the floor pretending to be asleep.

"Chop chop," the choreographer said, clapping his hands in front of her face. "Back to work. I'm going to change it a little." Maddy rubbed her eyes and stood up. I watched as the choreographer simplified the dance. It was so easy that a two-year-old could have followed along. Maddy seemed happy with the changes.

"Now that's more like it," she said.

The director, producer, and crew returned to the room, busying themselves with getting the set ready to film.

"Rolling," the director said, after the ninth take. "And action." I watched as Maddy side stepped her way through the basic routine and finally got it right.

"And.... cut!" the director yelled. "That's a wrap." Everyone cheered and high-fived each other. Maddy thanked everyone, gave the choreographer a quick hug, and ran over to me.

"Let's go," she said. I gathered up our things and headed back to the trailer with her.

On our way we passed the girl who was Maddy's double. She smiled at us and kept on walking.

"What the fuck?" Maddy asked, turning to check her out from behind. "That's my double?"

"I guess," I said.

"Good God, she looks like a bubby," she said, laughing. She turned and gave me a serious look. "Oh, sorry Grace, that means Grandmother in my new religion."

When we got back to the trailer, Bridget was dead asleep at the table. The leftover rhinestones were sprawled across the table.

"Shh," Maddy motioned to me. She went over to Bridget and began gluing the rhinestones to her face while she slept.

"Maddy," I said. She started laughing and Bridget opened her eyes.

"Wha-" she said, lifting her head. "Oh, you're done?"

"Yup," Maddy said. "Let's go." I picked the BlackBerry up off the table and analyzed it.

"It looks great," I said. "Nice work Bridget." Maddy reached over and grabbed it my hand, scrutinizing each stone.

"They're not that even," she said. Bridget looked like she might cry. "But, good enough." She tossed it in her bag.

"Fuck Maddy, this is crazy glue you know," Bridget said, trying to pull the rhinestones off her face. Maddy broke out into laughter.

"I know," she said. "Okay let's go." Her BlackBerry started ringing in her hands.

It was Alison. I'd already forgotten about her.

"What does she want anyway?" Maddy asked.

"She wanted to ask you if you egged the Tates' cars," I said. "One of the magazines called her to verify the story." Maddy screamed so loud that the rhinestones nearly jumped off her BlackBerry and back into the plastic bag she'd brought them in.

"I swear on my mother's life I didn't do it, Alison," Maddy said, on our way home from the video shoot. She had begged me not to rat her out before she called Alison back.

"I will buy you anything," she said. "I'll buy you a car. Do you want me to buy you your own Yukon? I'll have it sent to Chicago."

"Don't be ridiculous," I said, though the offer was tempting.

"I just don't know if I can fully trust you not tell on me," she said.

"You can trust me," I said. "I'm not going to say a word."

"I'm not going to say a word either," Bridget piped in.

"Of course you're not, fuck-o, you were there too," Maddy said. "You'd be going down with me." Bridget kept her mouth shut after that response.

"I don't know who it was, Alison," Maddy said. "I'd never do such an immature thing, you know that. Fine hold on a second." She handed me the phone. "She wants to speak to you."

"Hi," I said.

"Did she do it or not?" Alison asked.

"No," I said, crossing my fingers. "She really didn't. Honestly."

"The Tates are furious," Alison said. She started chuckling. "Figures it's the one night when Mr. Tate forgot to turn the security system on." I smiled, hardly able to believe Maddy's good fortune.

"Well, okay," Alison said. "I'll lay off, but I really hope you're not covering for her, Grace. I mean because we're supposed to be on the same team."

"No, I'm not covering for her," I lied. "Don't worry. I'm with you." I hung up the phone. Maddy reached over and hugged me tight.

"Thank you, Grace," she said. "I really mean it."

"No problem," I said. The truth is that sometimes even young diva actresses like Maddy Malone, just need to get a break.

CHAPTER 31

That night I had a terrible nightmare. I was in Fred Segal with Hunter David and I was trying to kiss him, but every time I moved closer to him he would squirt crazy glue at me. Then when I cleared the glue from my eyes, I'd see him kissing Preston. I had to get out of there. I finally made it outside the store and when I looked back everything was rhinestoned. The cars on the streets, the trees, the parking meters, everything. There was someone was calling out my name.

"Over here Grace, run," he said. It was Todd in the get-a-way car. I started running towards him, but Maddy's shoes that I was wearing were too tight and made it hard to move. Todd started driving his rhinestoned car away.

"Wait," I screamed. "Wait!" But no sounds came out of my mouth. I looked down and I saw Beyonce. She was wearing a rhinestone collar. I picked her up and tried running with her. Hunter and Preston were outside the store now, yelling at me to leave Beyonce.

"She has rhinestones," Hunter yelled. "You have to leave her." I tried pulling her collar off her, but it was glued onto her neck.

"I won't leave her," I cried. "I won't leave her. I won't—"

"Grace, wake up!" I opened my eyes. Maddy was standing over my bed. "You were crying out in your sleep."

"I can't speak," I mouthed.

"What?" she asked.

"I can't speak," I mouthed again.

"What's wrong with you?" she asked. "You're scaring me."

"Sorry," I said, finding my voice. "Where's Beyonce?"

"She's right there," Maddy said, pointing to my feet where Beyonce was lying.

"Oh, okay. Phew," I said.

"You really like her, don't you?" Maddy asked.

"Yeah," I said. "I really do."

"Interesting," Maddy said. "Well, can I go back to bed now? Or do you need me to stay with you?"

"I'm okay," I said.

"Cool," she said. "See you in the morning."

"Thanks for checking on me, Maddy," I said.

"It's the least I could do," she said.

I had been so charmed by Maddy's display of concern at that moment, that I almost forgot all the horribleness that she was. I remembered in the morning though, when I tried to wake her for her meeting with Marty.

"You have to cancel my meeting Grace, I'm too exhausted to go," she said through the covers. She was exhausted? I'd been up since the crack of dawn and had managed to get Beyonce walked and fed, plus skimmed through both scripts, since she hadn't read them.

"You need to choose a movie," I said. "Marty said that-"

"I know what he said," she snapped. "I planned to wake up early to read them, but I was up all night taking care of you." Oh brother.

"Well I can tell you what they're about," I said. "That might help a little."

"Okay fine," she said. She pulled the covers down so I could see her mascara covered face. Why that girl didn't remove her make-up every night was beyond me.

"So the first one is *Teen Sours*, a comedy about a rich, popular girl who spends much of her time acting on her jealousy of one of her peers, a girl who didn't come from a wealthy family but who was very beautiful and easily attracted the boys," I said.

"Perfect," Maddy said. "I'll take that one. I want to play the rich, popular, beautiful girl."

"No, no," I said. "The beautiful one is the one that doesn't come from money."

"Oh," Maddy said. "Shit, okay what's the other one about?" She closed her eyes while I explained.

"Well it's called *On the Other Side of the Sun*. It's a period piece."

"That's disgusting," she said.

"I meant that it takes place in another century," I said.

"I know," she said, laughing. "Sorry, carry on."

"Well it's about a girl that—"

"Is she pretty?" Maddy asked.

"Well, yeah, I think so. Anyway, her father is murdered by a—"

"Is she popular?" she asked.

"I suppose," I said.

"Okay, sounds great," she said.

"That's it?" I asked. "You don't want to know the rest?"

"Well is there anything else really important that I need to know?" she asked.

"Yes," I said. "The beautiful, popular girl is the mastermind behind her father's murder, so she—"

"It's fine, Grace," Maddy said. "I'll sign on for that one." I couldn't believe that this was how she was making her decision, though at the same time in terms of her maturing acting career it probably was the better choice than a cheesy teen flick.

"Okay," I said. "There you go. Now you can go to your meeting prepared."

"Cool," she said, pulling the covers back up. "Go ahead and let Marty know that I'll be there soon."

"But—"

"Have breakfast with him or something," she said. "I'll be there in half an hour."

"Oh, alright," I said. "But hurry up."

I found Marty in the lobby downstairs. It was the first time I'd be meeting him in person, but he wasn't hard to spot, considering the description Maddy had given.

"He has gray hair and a huge nose," she said. Easy enough.

"Hi, I'm Grace," I said. He stood up and shook my hand.

"Nice to finally meet you in person," he said. "Will Maddy be blessing us with her presence this morning?"

"She'll be down in half an hour," I said. "She suggested we go have breakfast."

"Well then, shall we?" Marty said, linking his arm in mine.

We went to the hotel restaurant and were seated at a table on the patio. It was a sunny day, a refreshing breeze in the air.

"Is it too cold out here for you?" Marty asked.

"I'm from Chicago," I said. "This feels like Mexico." Marty smiled and opened his briefcase. He pulled out copies of the two scripts.

"She read them, right?" he asked.

"Right," I lied.

"Fuck, I knew she wouldn't," he said. "I don't know why the fuck I bother. I really don't." Really, I didn't know why anyone bothered, but it wasn't my place to say because for some strange reason I was still here too.

"If it helps," I said. "I read them and told her what they were about, and she liked *On the Other Side of The Sun*." Marty burst out laughing.

"I don't believe you," he said. "She would choose a possible Oscar nomination over a fantastic wardrobe?"

"Right," I said laughing. "She said she's willing to take a wardrobe cut to play the pretty popular girl in the period piece."

"Is that what she said?" he asked.

"Well yes, basically." I said. A waiter came by to take our breakfast order and pour us coffee.

"Why would she think that the poor girl in the teen comedy is prettier than her character?" he asked.

"Um, because that's what I told her," I said. "Am I wrong?" I guess I could have gotten the wrong impression of the characters considering how early in the morning I had read it.

"Well, yeah," Marty said. "Her character is rich, popular, and beautiful. The character descriptions are on the first page."

"I definitely missed that," I said. "Well I guess we'll have to see what she wants then when she comes down."

"IF she comes down," Marty said.

"Oh ye of little faith," I said.

"I'll bet you breakfast she doesn't show," he said.

"So if I win, Piranha pays," I said. "If you win Piranha pays?"

"That's right," he said.

"You're on."

So there I sat with Maddy's agent, enjoying a leisurely breakfast, and after the half hour there was still no sign of her. She didn't answer the phone in the room when I called so I tried her cell.

"It's her machine," I said, covering the phone. I left a message telling her to get her butt down to the hotel cafe immediately.

"Sorry about this," I said.

"Oh, I'm used to it," he said. "Here, let me leave her a message." He dialed Maddy's cell on his phone.

"Maddy, it's Marty," he said. "I just wanted to let you know that I need your decision within the next hour. We're looking at a three million dollar paycheck for you, but if you're too busy to talk to me about it, I'm sure there's another teen star around who'd jump at the chance. Talk to you later, bye."

"Three million dollars?" I asked. "Are you serious?"

"Hopefully," Marty said. "She really deserves it at this point in her career." At that instant, I wanted to reach over with my fist and knock some sense into him. Maddy Malone deserved to make three million dollars? My ass deserved it more. Within two minutes my cell phone rang.

"I guess she understands the language of money," I said.

"They always do," Marty said, smirking.

"Hi Maddy," I said. "We're waiting for you down here."

"Right," she said. "And please tell Marty that I'm so sorry but something came up and I couldn't make it."

"Pardon me?"

"I can't come," she said. "However, I got his message and three mil sounds fab."

"I know," I said. "But see I made a mistake when I described the movies to you. The girl in the teen comedy is actually really—"

"Grace, I don't care," she said. "Tell him I want to do the one we decided on."

"I know, Maddy but just listen for a second because—"

"Tell him!" she ordered.

"Alright, I will," I said. No reason to be yelled at, she'd get her money whether she was pretty in skinny jeans, or pretty in a petticoat.

"Where are you?" I asked.

"I'm at the mall with Katie and Nibs," she said. "The most wonderful thing has happened."

"What?" I asked.

"I'll tell you later," she said. "Just tell Marty that I'm really sorry but I put all my trust in you. Thanks Grace." She hung up.

"So?" Marty asked.

"*On the Other Side of the Sun* it is," I said.

"Okay then," he said, lifting his water glass. "Nice work, Grace. Cheers." I raised my glass to his.

Hunter called me three times during the day, leaving messages how he really needed to talk to me. I was positive he wanted to apologize for not telling me he was gay, and for leading me on making me think that he was really interested in me. I kept thinking back to our trip down the red carpet and how he had told the paparazzi that we were an item and we'd been dating for a few months. It's not that I was mad at him for being gay, I was more mad at myself for behaving like a teenager with a silly crush on someone so unattainable anyway. Finally at four o'clock I decided to answer the phone and take the plunge. I'd listen to what he had to say, probably accept his apology and just go on being friends.

"Oh there you are," Hunter said, when he answered. "I've been calling you all day."

"I know," I said. "Sorry about that."

"It's okay," he said. "I need to tell you something." I sat down on the edge of the bed, and braced myself for the apology.

"Okay," I said. "What is it?"

"A friend of mine has a small boutique store on Robinson," he said, "near the Ivy."

"Okay," I said. What did that have to do with Hunter being gay?

"Well he just called me and told me he kicked Maddy and her friends out of his store for defaming property," said Hunter.

"Uh huh," I said. I listened as Hunter went on to tell me that Maddy and her friends were sitting on the couches ripping up all the new magazines Hunter's friend had displayed in his store. Then proceeded to explain how Maddy tried on more than a dozen pairs of jeans and at least twenty different tops, and left everything scattered over the floor. Finally Hunter's friend said that if Maddy and her friends didn't leave the store instantly, he would call security and have them removed.

"Can you believe it?" he asked, with great excitement in his voice.

"Well, yeah sort of," I said. "It's Maddy. So was there something else you wanted to tell me?" I figured he was just leading into the story by telling me the silly Maddy story, of which at this moment, she could have blown up The Ivy with dynamite, and I'd still rather here Hunter's apology.

"Yeah," he said. "There was something else."

"Okay," I said.

"The director of *Daisy Mae* called to ask me to go to that charity function Maddy's going to on Friday night as well," he said. "He wants me to be there. So I guess I'll get to see you there."

"Oh, right," I said. "Yeah. I'll be there with her."

"Cool," he said. "I'm so glad. I love hanging out with you Grace. You are so awesome."

"Mm, yeah, you too," I said.

"Okay, I'll call you later. Just wanted to let you know what our darling is up to today." I hung up the phone and lay back on the bed. So much for our heart to heart talk.

Maddy returned at five-thirty, lugging in five giant shopping bags and dumping them on the floor.

"You've been out shopping this whole time?" I asked.

"Well we stopped for lunch," she said., "but yeah."

"What's the occasion?" I asked.

"You'll never believe the fortune I just spent," she said, pulling out designer tops and jeans from the bags.

"I'm sure," I said. "So what was the wonderful thing that happened?" She continued ignoring my question, reaching into a brown bag and pulling out a large beige Marc Jacobs bag. She stood up and modeled it for me.

"Nice," I said.

"What?" she asked. "That's your reaction to the most beautiful thing you've ever laid eyes on?" I started laughing.

"Would you say the bag enhances my beauty?" she asked, holding it up to her face.

"It brings out the speckles of green in your eyes," I said. She smiled. "Oh, I have something for you too," she said. Had she decided to buy me a new bag afterall?

"Here," she said, dropping a bunch of perfume samples into my hands. "They gave them to me when I bought the bag. It's a new scent."

"Gee thanks," I said. Then something occurred to me.

"So how did you pay for everything? I'm assuming this went over your daily credit card limit."

"Aha!" Maddy said. "You are so smart, Grace."

"Thanks," I answered.

"That's what I was celebrating," she said. "My credit card company raised my daily limit to three thousand dollars."

"Excuse me?" I said.

"After you left to go meet Marty my mother called me and told me the good news," she said. "Isn't that wonderful?"

"You mean to tell me that you did not show up for the meeting because of this?" I asked, running my hands over her various shopping bags.

"I knew I was in good hands with you there, Grace," she said. I sat down on the couch beside Beyonce shaking my head.

"I just don't get it," I said.

"Get what?" Maddy asked.

"Why you would blow off a meeting that in the end will bring you three million dollars," I explained. "To run off and go shopping for the day."

"I didn't blow off my meeting," she said. "He just wanted to know what movie I wanted to sign on to. It's not like I sent you to replace me in the film."

"But it's your responsibility to talk things over with your agent, not mine," I said. I could see I was starting to hit a nerve, because the expression on Maddy's face was growing angry.

"What are you saying?" she asked. "You think that I don't take my career seriously?"

"I'm just trying to tell you, as a friend."

"Let me tell you something, Grace," Maddy yelled. "We are not friends. You work for me. Got it?"

"I know, but—"

"So don't ever refer to me as your friend. I know who my friends are," she said. I realized that there was no rationalizing with her, and we were completely off topic now anyway.

"Okay then," I said. "My mistake, we are not friends. I'm sorry to have even suggested it." Maddy got up and grabbed a few of her parcels and stormed off into her room.

"I'm taking a nap," she said, "You just put me in the worst mood." She slammed the door behind her. Nice treatment considering I was probably the only real friend Maddy has ever had.

CHAPTER 32

"Can you believe he called to personally invite me?" Maddy asked. We were in the car driving to Fred Segal in Santa Monica to buy Billy Welder a Birthday present.

"I mean I don't even think Ashlee Simpson got a call," she said. How would she know that anyway?

"I guess you're very special," I said.

"Well, duh, of course," she said. "Obviously he wants me."

"Obviously." Billy Welder was the lead singer of Global Warning, a rock group. He had dashing looks and a strong, sexy, voice similar to Eddy Vedder of Pearl Jam.

"You'll need to get him something too, Grace," Maddy said. "Maybe a tie or something?" Maddy had informed me that we'd be going straight from The Panda Bear Charity Ball to Billy Welder's party.

"Are you sure you don't need to stick around for longer than an hour, considering you're the main attraction at the event?" I asked.

"Nope," Maddy said. "Just say my speech and leave. I don't even need to sign autographs, Alison said."

"But maybe you should," I said. "I mean these are terminally ill children."

"Whatevs, Grace," she said. She pulled out her T-Mobile and the text messaging began. "Bridget is going to die that I got invited to his birthday. She is so not coming with me."

"Why?" I asked.

"Cuz I don't want any of my friends there," Maddy said. It was the one time I wished I was her friend so I wouldn't have to go either.

"I'm not spending a hundred dollars on a tie for someone I don't know," I said, while we walked around Fred Segal.

"Why?" Maddy asked. "Is that a lot?"

I nodded. Maddy's concept of money was slightly different than mine.

"I'm thinking more like twenty-five dollars," I said.

"Oh my God, Grace," she wailed. "You're going to make me look like the biggest fool if you buy him something so cheap."

"Thirty dollars," I said. I was firm. Maddy squinted at me. She was in deep thought. As deep as she could be.

"Okay, you put in thirty," she said. "I'll pay the rest. I know how money's tight for you and all."

"Fine," I said. If Maddy wanted to put in some extra money to make herself look good, I didn't mind.

"Get him this one," she said. She held up a black tie with white stripes.

"Fine," I said, assuming that Billy Welder would toss it to the side with the rest of his cheap gifts anyway. Maddy had the tie gift-wrapped, then moved on to find something special for her to get Billy.

"What size shoes do you think he wears?" she asked, stopping to look at a few styles.

"You can't get him shoes," I said. "It's too personal."

"I happen to know him very well," she said. "I mean he did invite me personally."

"You said that his assistant left a message," I said.

"She left a message saying that Billy wanted me to come. Hello, I'd take it as a hint that we're close."

"Right," I said. "Let's look at the shoes."

"I guess he's about a size ten-and-a-half," Maddy said, holding up a trendy sneaker.

"What makes you say that?" I asked.

"It seems like a good number," she said.

"So you're just going to guess his shoe size and hope they fit?" I asked. She nodded. "What if Ashlee Simpson really does know his shoe size and gets him a pair that fits, and yours don't." She looked at me in horror.

"You're right," she said, putting them down. "I can't get him shoes. Let's look at the jeans."

Maddy decided on a pair of sterling silver cuff links—little dice. I had to convince her that since she was unsure of his religion, buying him the pair shaped in the Star of David might be inappropriate.

"I think he'll love them," I said, holding the two parcels as we left the store.

"Yeah, well he likes to gamble, so dice are perfect," she said. "He goes to Vegas all the time."

"Oh, yeah?" I asked. "Did he tell you that?"

"Of course not," she said. "We're not at that level yet. I read it in *Star* magazine."

"Oh," I said, laughing.

"You have no idea how much of a challenge this is for me," Maddy said on our way to the car.

"What do you mean?" I asked.

"Well Billy doesn't drink or do drugs," she said.

"Isn't that a good thing?" I asked. She stopped dead in her tracks.

"Are you kidding me," she said. "How is he going to fall for me if he's always sober?"

"Oh, come on," I said. "That means he's truly into you if he's not looking at you with beer goggles on." Maddy started walking again.

"Honestly, Grace. Sometimes I think you're living in a different era. You are so 1950," she said.

"Think of how accomplished you'll feel if you can land him," I said.

"I just wish he did coke or something," she said, ignoring me. "Maybe I could slip something into his water."

"Maddy!" I shrieked.

"Just kidding, Grace," she said, laughing and running ahead.

From a block away, we could see a policeman slapping a parking ticket down on to the car windshield.

"No!" Maddy screamed, taking off after him. "We didn't go that much over. Wait." It was slightly embarrassing watching her make such a spectacle of herself, but then it got worse.

"Grace, Grace!" she was yelling steps away from finally catching up to him. "It's hot cop! It's hot cop." I felt the excitement run through my body as I picked up my speed to catch up. What were the chances that we'd run into him again. I didn't even care that he'd just given me a ticket. I was steps away from Maddy and she grabbed onto his shoulder, which was a bold thing to do to a man carrying a gun. He turned around. Except it wasn't Hot Cop. It was a lady cop. Maddy gasped.

"What do you think you're doing?" asked the policewoman.

"Oh," Maddy said. "Um, you gave us a parking ticket."

"And?"

"And, well, um, we didn't deserve it," said Maddy.

"Which car?" she asked looking back down the street.

"The Yukon," Maddy said.

"You were parked over your time limit," the policewoman said, turning and walking away.

"No, wait!" Maddy shouted. She turned around again. "I'm Maddy Malone."

"So?"

"So, um, didn't you get my autograph I sent down to the police station for um, everyone?" she asked. The policewoman turned and walked away.

"I swear, Maddy," I said, "Sometimes I think if it weren't for bad luck, I'd have no luck at all."

"Huh?" she said.

"Oh nothing. Let's go."

When I returned from walking Beyonce, I found Maddy sprawled across the living room with pens and paper everywhere.

"Thank God you're back, Grace," she said. "I'm so stuck. I don't know what to write."

"Oh," I said, taking off Beyonce's leash. "You need help with your speech for tomorrow night?"

"My speech?" she asked. "Of course not. I need help writing Billy Welder's Birthday card."

"Oh," I said. Foolish of me to think she was actually working on something important.

"Well what do you want to say to him?" I asked, sitting down beside her.

"I want to tell him that he's so amazing and that I'm so happy we've become so close," she said. "But I don't want to sound desperate."

"Right," I said. "Well, I'd keep it simple."

"This is what I have so far," she said. "Dear William—is it dumb to call him by his given name?"

"Do you call him William when you're talking to him?" I asked.

"Well, no," she said. "But I want to start."

"Won't he think it's strange if suddenly you're calling him William in his card and you've never addressed him as that to his face?" I asked. She sat thinking about it for a minute.

"Good point," she said. "Hold on a second." She stood up and ran over to her cell phone and started dialing.

"I got his machine," she whispered. "Oh hi William, it's Maddy. I just wanted to tell you that I'm so excited for your Birthday party tomorrow night. Thanks so much for inviting me. See you tomorrow. Bye William." She hung up, then came and sat back down.

"Okay," she said. "Dear William." She stopped reading.

"Now what?" I asked.

"That's all I have so far," she said, laughing. "I swear this is so stressful."

"Did you already write your speech for the Panda Bear Charity Ball?" I asked. "Because you should probably get that done as well." Maddy grabbed a thick green marker and a piece of blank paper and handed it to me.

"Here," she said. "Can you start it while I write the card?"

"I don't know what to write," I said. "I know nothing about this event."

"Oh brother," Maddy said. She stood up and went over to a big manila envelope sitting on the desk.

"Here," she said. "All the information is in here. Just skim through it."

I opened up the envelope and took out the pamphlets. The Panda Bear Charity Ball raised money for terminally ill children. It provided programs, such as art and music classes as well as sending them on vacations with their families. There was a letter from a ten-year-old girl named Beth that was addressed to Maddy. She wrote how she couldn't wait to meet her favorite star and how *The Window Pain* was her favorite movie.

"This is really sweet," I said, showing her the letter.

"Yeah, yeah," Maddy said.

"Did you read it?" I asked.

"Mm-mm," she said.

"Do you want me to read it to you?" I asked.

"No," she said. "I won't be able to concentrate. Just start writing the speech."

"Okay," I said. I put the green marker down and chose a pencil instead. Then I set up my writing area at the coffee table rather than on the floor.

An hour later, I had composed a lovely, heartwarming speech for Maddy while she still worked her way through the card for Billy "William" Welder.

"I'm done," I said. She looked up.

"Already?" she asked.

"Yeah," I said. "I mean I wrote out a first draft. You can add your own personal touches.

"Let me see it," she said. I handed her the speech and she glanced at it at rapid speed.

"It's perfect," she said. "Thanks Grace."

"What do you mean?" I asked. "It's far from perfect. It's just sort of a rough—"

"Really, I mean it," she said. "It's great. Now listen to my card." I sat back on the couch amazed and sickened over where Maddy's priorities lay.

CHAPTER 33

❀

The next morning there were a frenzy of phone calls regarding The Panda Bear Charity Ball.

"It starts at seven o'clock sharp," Alison said. "And Maddy will be called up right at the beginning, so tell her it starts at six-thirty so that she'll be there on time."

"I will, don't worry," I said. "She will not be late for this one, I promise you."

"Thanks," Alison said. "We're all counting on you." The pressure made me queasy.

"What will she be wearing?" Mrs. Malone asked.

"I'm not sure," I said. Bad answer.

"What do you mean?" she shrieked.

"She hasn't mentioned it," I said. I know that she had tried on a dozen outfits for Billy's party, before deciding she needed to go buy something new.

"A gown," Mrs. Malone said. "She needs a gown. Drag her out of bed and get her to Saks at once."

"Okay," I said.

"Make sure she gets her nails done," Mrs. Malone said.

"She had them done the other day," I said.

"She needs them done again. The polish has surely chipped by now."

"Okay, Mrs. Malone," I said.

"Grace, I'm really counting on you," she said. "This is a huge event for Maddy. She needs to look phenomenal."

"She will," I said.

At eleven o'clock, I got Maddy out of bed to go to Saks. I figured she probably wouldn't want to wear the Dior dress that she'd worn to The Golden Globes, that was now scrunched in a ball in her cupboard, even though she had told Alison that she'd already returned it to the store.

"I don't see why I need such a fancy dress," Maddy said, browsing through the racks in the store.

"I guess because it's a fancy party," I said.

"What are you wearing?" Maddy asked.

"Your mother told me to wear a pantsuit," I said.

"Ugh, she's such a bitch," she said. "Okay fine, I guess. If you want you can borrow one of my tops to wear underneath it."

"Thanks," I said. An offer I would take her up on.

Maddy reluctantly tried on a few different gowns and in the end decided on a cherry red jersey, one shoulder, beaded dress, by Nicole Miller.

"You look beautiful," I said. It was the truth.

"Thanks Grace," she said. We went down to the shoe department where she chose a pair of Stuart Weitzman black satin strappy shoes.

"Guess Hunter's my date at this shin-dig," she said. "Jealous?"

"I'm over it," I said.

"Yeah whatever," Maddy said. She was only half right. I was mostly over it. Hunter didn't need to explain himself to me. I had created this fantasy image of him, and I had been wrong, however, I still thought very highly of him as a friend as he'd been a savior for me during this trip.

"Shut up, and let's go," I said, as the saleslady gave Maddy back her card.

We walked out of Saks and onto the street when Maddy's phone started ringing.

"Oh hello, William," she said. "Okay sorry. Hi Billy." I couldn't help but laugh. Now Maddy would have to change her card.

"Okay," she said. "I'll be there. See you later." She hung up.

"What did William—oops, I mean Billy want?" I asked. Maddy gave me the finger.

"He invited me to his pre-party at his house," she said. "At six o'clock."

"Well you won't be able to go to that," I said.

"Why not?" she asked.

"Because, you need to be at the charity event for six-thirty," I said.

"Don't worry, Grace," she said, putting her arm on my shoulder. "We'll get to the church on time."

"I don't have to go the pre-party, do I?" I asked.

"Of course," she said. "You need to give him your gift." I could already feel my anxiety level rising.

"Oh yeah," I said. That damn tie.

"We'll stop by the pre-party and then be on our way," she said. "I promise I'll be quick. Besides, his house is on the way to the event."

"Okay," I said, feeling somewhat relieved.

At six-twenty when we were still inside Billy Welder's house, I was no longer feeling that relief. Maddy had followed Billy to the back of the house and not yet emerged. I was sitting in the family room with a few of his other friends.

"You wanna drag?" one of them asked, passing me a joint.

"No thanks," I said. "I'm not staying that long." I looked over at Maddy's dress hanging on a hook in the hallway. She was supposed to have changed into it by now.

"Does anyone know where Billy and Maddy went?" I asked. They all looked up. "It's just that Maddy needs to be at an event soon, and we really need to leave."

"Probably in the back," one of the girls said. "I don't know why she's here anyway. I mean she's sort of young." I shrugged my shoulders. "Go through the long corridor to the left. It leads to the patio out back. I'm sure she's there fawning all over him."

"Thanks," I said. It was now six-twenty-seven and I was starting to get the cold sweats.

I found Maddy outside, sitting on the ground at Billy's feet, smoking. Billy was drinking a can of Red Bull.

"Maddy, sorry, but we need to leave now," I said. She jumped up when she saw me.

"Oh hi Grace," she said. "Yeah, about that little event. Just call Alison and tell her I've decided not to go."

"What?"

"Yeah, I'm having too much fun here," she said. "See if they can reschedule." I assumed she was kidding.

"Very funny, Maddy," I said. "Okay, let's go. You need to change and we need to leave right away." Maddy grabbed my arm and led me toward the steps that led down to the swimming pool.

"Don't embarrass me, Grace," she said. "I'm not a baby. I can make my own decisions."

"Honestly," I said. "We don't have time for this game, Maddy. We really need to go." She sat down on a bench at the bottom of the stairs.

"I'm not going," she said.

"But you're the guest of honor," I said. "They're all waiting for you there. You have to go."

"No I don't," she said, picking at her split ends. "Just call Alison and see if they can postpone it."

"They can't postpone it!" I shouted.

"Relax," she said. "Of course they can. I'm the highlight of the evening."

"Maddy, they're all at the party right now," I said. "The Panda Bear Charity event is right now. The children want to see you. That's why they're there."

"Well, if they want to see me that bad, they can wait until next week, or next month or—"

"They might not live until next month!" I screamed.

"Why not?" she asked.

"Because they're terminally ill! You know what that means? That means they're going to die!" I said.

"Honestly Grace," Maddy said. "You are such a pessimist," I couldn't take it anymore. New heights of selfishness had been masterfully achieved.

"Everything okay down there?" Billy asked, from the top of the steps.

"Yeah, just one second, Billy," Maddy said.

"Okay, Grace," she said. "You go on ahead, and explain to them that I won't be coming tonight. Just make something up. Trust me, it's not a big deal. A lot of celebs don't show up to events they're invited to."

"I can't," I said. "I can't face them. They all expected me to get you there on time."

"You'll have to go without me. You have my speech. Just say it, adding in your own personal touch," she said, with sarcasm. I stood in shock. I couldn't even move.

"Well go," she said. "You're going to be late." I turned and started running up the steps before I said all the horrible things I was thinking, out loud. When I got to the top, I decided that it was about time I said all the horrible things I was thinking, out loud. Maddy came up the steps and went to sit back at Billy's feet.

"I am so disappointed in you," I said, as I walked back to them.

"What?" she said.

"You are letting down a hundred kids whose dream was to meet they're favorite movie star, you. Instead you are so heartless you can't even have any compassion towards them" I said. I could feel the tears in my eyes, but I wouldn't let them fall.

"Grace, you really need to go," Maddy said.

"Yeah, I do need to go," I said. "I need to go and stand in your place and explain to everyone that you are nothing but a mean spoiled bitch, and one day you will live to regret how much you're going to hurt these kids tonight."

"Goodbye Grace," she said, turning her back to me. There was nothing left for me say. I turned and ran back through the house.

"Thanks for the tie," Billy yelled from behind.

I ran over to where Billy's friends were sitting and quickly grabbed the joint from their hands. I took two puffs and handed it back.

On my way out the front door, I knocked Maddy's dress off the hook and kicked it, leaving my foot print on the back.

Once I started the car, I realized that I had no idea how to get to the event. Maddy had the directions in her purse. I started the car and pulled out of the driveway, pushing the OnStar button.

"You are connecting to OnStar," the computerized voice said.

"Welcome to OnStar," a live voice said over a speaker. "This is Janice, How can I help you Miss. Malone?"

"I need to get to the Four Seasons really fast," I said. I waited for her reply, and instead got a dial tone. I'd lost the connection.

"Fuck!" I said. I pushed the button again.

"Welcome to OnStar. This is De-"

"I need to get to The Four Seasons," I said, cutting her off.

"Okay, I'd be happy to help you," she said. "Right now you are driving on—" The line went dead again. This couldn't be happening.

"Fucking OnStar!" I shouted, pushing the button again.

"Welcome to OnSta-"

"Help me! I need to get to The Four Seasons!"

"Okay, Miss Malone," she said. "Right now you are driving on—"

"I know! I know! I know what street I'm on," I screamed, like a psycho "Please help me get there, please."

"Okay, Miss Malone Are you in trouble? Do you need me to call 9-1-1?"

"NO! I need you to get me to the Four Seasons as fast as possible," I said, feeling a tear run down my cheek. My cell phone was ringing in my bag. I saw it was Alison. It was six-forty. Ten minutes after the time I promised I'd have Maddy there by. I tried to calm down as OnStar directed me out of the hills and back onto the streets.

"Now make a right onto Doheny, and you should see it at the end," she said. I saw the sign up ahead. In five minutes Maddy would be called up to the podium and Maddy wasn't going to be there.

"Okay," I said. "Okay, I see it. Thank you."

"No problem, Miss Malone," she said. It would thrill me if after hanging up the phone with me, the OnStar staff called the tabloids to reveal to them what a bitch Maddy Malone was.

I pulled into the Four Seasons and barely had it in park before I jumped out.

"Thank you!" I yelled back to the valet as I snatched the ticket out of his hands and went running inside. My cell phone was still ringing. It was seven o'clock.

I was huffing and puffing by the time I made it into the main ballroom. There was a choir at the front just finishing up the song "What the World Needs Now is Love, Sweet Love. Next a woman got on stage and started praising Maddy Malone, and how exciting it was for the children that she was here tonight.

"Grace!" I heard a voice say. I looked around and saw Alison.

"And now we'd like to call onto the stage our guest of honor, Maddy Malone." Applause and cheers commenced and I watched as people searched the room looking for Maddy.

"Where is she?" Alison asked, when she able to make it over to me.

"She's not coming," I whimpered.

"What do you mean? Where is she?"

"She's not com-"

"Eh hem," said the woman at the front. "Once again, Maddy Malone."

"Grace, do something!" Alison said, grabbing my arm, nearly pulling me to the ground.

"Okay," I said. "Okay, I will."

I walked up to the front of the room, past Hunter's table, and past all the other various celebrities that were sitting nearby. Through my foggy vision, I was sure I saw Denzel. There were six rows of chairs set up in front of the stage filled with the children. Hundreds of eyes stared at me as I took a stance up at the microphone.

"Hi, I'm Grace Daniels," I said. The microphone was too loud and it made a loud squeaking noise. All the kids screamed and covered their ears. A few adults came over to quiet them down. I looked over at Hunter, and by the expression on his face could tell he felt horrible for me. Once it was quiet, I spoke again.

"I know that you were all expecting Maddy to be up here on stage tonight and not me but—" I looked down into the eyes of a little girl, who had lost her hair from chemotherapy. She was holding a disposable camera. I felt a huge lump in my throat. I swallowed.

"I mean, Maddy wanted to be here," I continued. "She really did; however due to a, um, well she wasn't feeling—" I looked back down at all the dying children and realized I could not stand there and make the usual excuse that Maddy was sick, when these kids were all sick and had no trouble getting there. I took the scrunched up speech I'd written out of my purse and unfolded it. I couldn't read it through my tears. So I cleared my throat and decided to wing it.

"She wanted me to tell you how much it means to her that you would honor her at such a—" I looked around at the colorful room. "Beautiful event."

Suddenly all the children started cheering and clapping. Wow, I guess I was really on a roll. How? I don't know, considering it was evident that I was making this up as I went along, but then again, I guess children don't notice that sort of thing. I looked over at Alison, whose face had regained its natural color. She was motioning me to turn around. I did, and right behind me was Maddy in the Nicole Miller dress, that had my footprint on the back. I smiled as she came closer to me, mouthing the words, "Thank you." I handed her the speech and stepped aside as she took the mic from me.

"Hi everyone," Maddy said, once the crowd had gone quiet again. "I want to start off by apologizing for being late."

"That's okay, Maddy!" one of the kids yelled out.

"It's not okay," Maddy said. "You see there was somewhere else that I thought I had to be." She paused and looked over at me and winked. "But I didn't. I appreciate that all of you took the time to attend this event tonight. I know that for some of you it was probably not easy to get here." She held up the speech in her hand. "I had someone help me prepare a speech but—" she looked back at me again. "I thought it would be best if I said some things with my own personal touches." I felt that lump in my throat coming back. She looked down at the children and addressed them.

"I've never seen so many beautiful children in one room," she said. "And so well behaved, I might add. Your parents must be very proud of you. I know I am." I watched as all the children smiled and giggled with great delight.

"It is so great to be in a room where there's so much love," Maddy continued. "And speaking of love, did you all happen to catch my dashingly handsome co-star from my upcoming movie *Daisy Mae*, sitting up front? Hunter David, everyone." There were more cheers as Hunter stood up and waved.

"The Panda Bear Charity means so much to me, and I'm thrilled that you would choose me to help represent it and I'd like to thank everyone who continuously donates their time and money. Everyday, you help to make dreams come true for thousands of children across North America." She paused while there was applause from the audience.

"I believe that it is so important to live our lives to the fullest, no matter how long or how short of a time we may be here for. Every day should be a lesson. Every day we should try something new, and always do what we love to do. I love to dance so I dance everyday." She broke out into some hip hop dance moves, which in turn made the children squeal with laughter. She stopped and continued.

"During the past few weeks while I've been working hard in LA—well sometimes maybe not that hard," she said, laughing. "I've come to realize that there are important parts of life that sometimes we take advantage of and forget that they're there. For instance, flowers. Has everyone noticed the beautiful arrangements that are dispersed around the room? Aren't they the best flowers you've ever seen?" she asked. Everyone was looking around the room, including myself, as they had gone unnoticed by me as well.

"Yes," all the children answered as well as most of the adults.

"Whoever did the flowers, you did a wonderful job," Maddy said. "Thank you."

"Thank you!" the children shouted. They were in awe of her. It was simply amazing. Maddy continued.

"I've learned something else during this trip to LA, and that is sometimes all we really need is one friend who cares. I want everyone in this room to stand up and hug someone they care about," she said. "I'm going to start it off, and I want everyone to follow." Maddy put the mic down and came over to me and hugged me.

"I'm so sorry, Grace. You were right," she whispered. "About everything." I hugged her back and looked out into the audience where I observed the most amazing thing happening. Everyone was hugging. Just a room full of people hugging. I saw one of the little girls go over to Hunter and hand him a large sunflower. She wrapped her arms around his neck. I saw a tear run down his face, and then felt one running down my own.

"Alison," I said afterward, while Maddy was signing autographs and taking pictures with her fans. "I wanted to tell you something, and I thought you should be the first to know."

"What's that, Grace?" she asked.

"Maddy Malone made me cry," I said. Alison smiled and put her arm around me.

"Welcome to the club, kiddo," she said.

AFTERWORD

"Passengers, this is your captain. We will be landing at Chicago O'Hare Airport in twenty minutes. The time is now four-fifteen. Please take your seats and fasten your seatbelts. Flight attendants, please prepare for arrival. Check and cross check."

I gazed out the window and saw my city below. It looked snowy and cold, yet I felt a warm excitement to be arriving there. I was excited to sleep in my own bed, even if it wasn't king size with a chocolate placed on the pillow, nightly. I couldn't wait to go to work on Monday and celebrate the new merger with Teach Rogers. I had faxed a picture of the exact Chloe bag that I wanted Jake to get me, as a thank-you gift for solidifying the deal.

I felt a little like Dorothy must have felt as she returned home from Oz. Though I could have left Los Angeles whenever I'd wanted, simply by clicking my heels three times or just catching a return flight, I now knew that I'd needed this trip to know how strong I am inside.

I smiled remembering my last night spent with Hunter and Todd. They had joined me for dinner in the fancy restaurant at The Springs. I had asked Maddy to come, but she had plans to spend her last night with her friends. Or to be more precise, Billy Welder was going to be at The Spider Room and Maddy felt like she owed it to him to go, considering how nice he had been to drive her to The Four Season for the Panda Bear Charity event, and then not even showing up for his party after. She felt that buying bottles of champagne for his table all night (even if he wasn't going to drink them) would make up for it.

Maddy had suggested that I charge the dinner to the room for one last hurrah, or the last "ha ha," as Hunter called it. I was just happy I'd be long gone when Piranha got the bill for the hotel.

Saying goodbye to Hunter and Todd was more emotional for me than I had thought it would be. Though life had taken an interesting turn, and perhaps at the time a devastating one where Hunter was concerned, I knew that my friendship with both of them would stand the test of time. There was a bond between us, impossible to explain with words, but it existed, and that's what was important.

"I wish you weren't leaving," Hunter said, as his car was brought up by the valet. "It was almost too much fun."

"I know," I said, barely able to speak.

"You are always welcome here, babe," Todd said. "So come back soon, because I'm going to be missing you round the clock." I hugged them both so tight, not knowing how I was going to let them go.

The plane landed smoothly and slowly moved along the runway to the gate. Now I could see the snow lightly falling against the window. The airplane taxied to a stop; the seatbelt light turned off; and as I gathered my things, I thought of Maddy.

I wasn't sure what our goodbye was going to be like, or how I would feel during it. She'd been so awful most of the time that it had become a dream for me to never have to see her again. But when she finally redeemed herself at the charity event, I felt different towards her. I had witnessed an incredible shift in Maddy, and it was something that no one but myself would ever know. Maddy Malone was an *It girl* and I could only hope that Hollywood wasn't setting her up to fall. Maddy's star qualities now shone through brighter than the padlock on a new Chloe bag.

"You be good," I said. "And take care of yourself." We were standing in JFK, and about to part ways.

"I will," she said. "You too." Her eyes began to water and she looked away. I knew she wasn't acting.

"Grace, I don't want to say goodbye. I mean, it's too final," she said.

"I know," I said. Suddenly her face brightened.

"I learned this new Kabbalah word the other day," she said. "It means until we meet again."

"What's the word?" I asked.

"L'hitraot," she said.

"Okay," I said. "L'hitraot, Maddy."

"L'hitraot, Grace." She wrapped her arms around me and a tear rolled down my face because I knew it would be a very long time before we met again.

On my way to exit the plane, I passed a stewardess standing in the aisle collecting earphones.

"Excuse me?" I asked.

"Yes?" she answered.

"I feel sort of silly asking you this, but do you have an extra pack of Clodhoppers I could take with me?" She smiled and walked over to one of the shelves and returned with two packs.

"Thanks," I said, smiling. I placed them in the pocket on the side of my Prada dog carrier that held a sleeping Beyonce, my new dog. Then I zipped it up, and headed for home.

978-0-595-43007-9
0-595-43007-4

W I T H D R A W N
FROM THE COLLECTION OF
FONTAINEBLEAU LIBRARY

Printed in the United States
78663LV00001B/22